To Dinah Wiener

Face to Face

Alison Brodie

CORONET BOOKS
Hodder and Stoughton

First published in Great Britain in 1998 by Hodder and Stoughton
A division of Hodder Headline PLC
First published in paperback in 1999 by Hodder and Stoughton
A Coronet Paperback

10 9 8 7 6 5 4 3

Printed and bound in Great Britain by
Mackays of Chatham PLC, Chatham, Kent

Hodder and Stoughton
A division of Hodder Headline PLC
338 Euston Road
London NW1 3BH

Face to Face

'Hello.' It was Douglas, coming to stand beside her. 'You look fantastic!'

'Do you think so?' she asked innocently. 'Do you like the dress?'

His eyes roamed her body, his head nodding enthusiastically. 'Aye – that I do. It's very bonny.'

She felt powerful and sexy and beautiful – at ease with this vestige of normality. Now Douglas was seeing her as she truly was: beautiful, sophisticated . . . untouchable. As she sipped her champagne, she closed her eyes in ecstasy, taking on her role of glamorous supermodel. 'Mmm . . . civilisation,' she murmured. 'I couldn't survive without champagne, you know,' she told Douglas. 'Champagne and caviar.'

He chuckled. 'Me neither.'

Peri stopped in mid sip and looked at him. He thinks I'm joking, she thought incredulously . . .

About the author

Born to a Glaswegian father and a Geordie mother, Alison Brodie grew up in the Scottish Highlands, Cyprus and Arabia. A hippy traveller at eighteen, she lived in Athens as an artist before heading overland to India. On her return to Britain, she was talent-scouted by a London modelling agency, soon appearing on magazine covers and TV commercials throughout Europe. She was adopted by a Scottish regiment as their mascot.

Alison has finally settled down, happily living and writing in Surrey. *Face to Face* is her first novel.

ACKNOWLEDGEMENTS

My thanks go to the following for their help and advice: the RAF Search and Rescue, ARCC Kinloss; the Casualty Department at Raigmore Hospital, Inverness; and the Scottish Natural Heritage in Edinburgh.

Chapter One

Silence. The poolside chairs stood empty, the perfect pile of fluffy white towels lay undisturbed. From the marble walls tiny spotlights radiated their soft glow across the still blue water, whilst all around, the delicate bouquet of bergamot and lavender perfumed the warm steamy air.

Suddenly, a long red fingernail hit the spa button, churning the water into life, breaking the silence with the sound of bubbling. In the same instant, the owner of the red fingernail stiffened, staring at it with mounting suspicion. *'Shit!'* The word was like a whiplash as a pair of green, cat-like eyes peered closely at the crack in the red varnish. *'I don't believe it!'* The woman's long thin body sank deeper into the water as her turbanned head fell back against the edge of the spa.

'What's happening to me?' she whispered. 'Why is everything going wrong?' She could feel the pimple, tight and hot on her chin, and she so much wanted to touch it; but that was strictly forbidden. It would be her beauty therapist who would deal with it, not her. No longer was she the little girl who could appease her anxieties by squeezing a pimple or biting her nails or nibbling her hair. No. Not any more. Responsibility came with owning the most expensive body in the business; it deserved respect and, accordingly, it could only be cared for by the most highly skilled professionals.

Nervously, she hooked out a strand of long black hair from

under her turban and held it up to her eyes for close inspection. No split ends – thank goodness for *that*. She could always depend on Eduardo and his liposebum almond oil therapy. Satisfied, she tucked her hair back into place, paused for a moment and listened, straining to hear the sound of voices. *Jesus*. It was so eerie. She peered through the hanging mass of artificial foliage which blocked her view of the poolside. Still empty. It made her feel uneasy, isolated. She knew that most people would relish the chance of being alone in this place, but not her; she had to have people around – not necessarily to talk to – but as a diversion, a safeguard against having to be left alone with herself and her thoughts. It wouldn't be so bad if there was a television in here to keep her company.

With a long sigh, she arched her neck and gazed up at the domed ceiling, feeling the bubbles pummelling her buttocks and considering the new girl on reception. She had sounded Spanish. A foreigner. Was that the reason why she hadn't shown any sign of recognition? Probably. After all, how could a foreigner be expected to know that Peri Lomax had once been the Velvet Girl? That her name had been linked with Matt Bruce? That she had opened the Fendi show in Paris wearing nothing but a diamond-studded g-string and a cape of Arctic fox? She closed her eyes tightly against the feeling of overwhelming despair. Who was she kidding? No one recognised her any more, not even taxi drivers.

Miserably, she opened her eyes and let her gaze follow the curve of the wall, down the line of a marble column, along the tiled floor to where her mobile lay on top of a fluffy white towel. It was silent. Its very silence seemed to scream the awful truth: *nobody wants Peri Lomax.* And yet, up until a couple of months ago, it had rung constantly, trilling out to her that once again she had been chosen, chosen from the thousands of other beautiful girls in the world. It had been her friend then, but now, now it lay there cold and silent . . . and she *hated* it.

What had she done wrong? She was still as beautiful as ever, still courting the tabloid press at every given opportunity, still appearing at the right places with the right people. She remained as charming and talented as ever, naturally outshining everyone else in her acting classes; and still she waited . . . waited for the one lucky break that would catapult her into the outer-stratosphere of celebrity status. She had come so close, so very close, but now she knew it wasn't going to happen. Not now. It was too late. She was on her way down . . . down to making TV commercials for oven chips and baby wipes while steadily sinking into oblivion . . . *No!* That must never happen. She needed to be in front of a camera, to be the focus of attention, to be pampered, wanted, admired: if it was all taken away from her, then there would be nothing left to live for.

So? What was happening? Was she out of fashion? Had she offended someone of importance? She bit her lip thoughtfully. The last job had not gone too well. It had been a nightmare of delayed flights, bad weather, a clumsy hotel porter and a photographer with shingles. From day one she had complained vociferously; by day four, she had been irritated to sense the sullen hostility from those around her. She had ignored them; the photographer was young and unestablished, not in a position to alter the course of her career.

She stared hard at the ceiling. Last year her diary had been overflowing with her tiny scribbled handwriting, but this year it still looked brand-new, page after page blank. The only entry for March read: *Saturday 27th. International Film Awards. 6pm backstage.* Backstage! She was only there as an understudy to Caroline Morris in case she suddenly broke her neck or something. No such luck. There would be no alternative but to sit and watch someone else wearing Igor de Vere's ballgown; watch someone else sashaying onto the stage, waving to the cheering crowd and eager cameras, knowing that twelve million viewers were tuned in at that moment. *Christ!* It wasn't fair!

Mags wasn't helping, either. She was still sweet and motherly but nowadays she always sounded in a rush. 'Look, Peri,' she had said with hurried kindness, 'there's no need for you to keep phoning. I'll call you as soon as a job comes in. Just wait. *Ciao.* Love you.' So Peri had waited, but the call had never come.

Miserably she closed her eyes, slowly rolling her head from side to side, trying to ease the tension in her neck and wondering whether she should pray. But what was the point of that? She'd had a childhood of praying and what had it done for her? Absolutely nothing! Unbidden, a memory floated into her consciousness, as if drifting towards her through a veil of mist . . .

. . . she is standing by a white wooden gate, holding Aunty Doris's hand as they watch her mother walk away. How she prays and prays that her beautiful black-haired mother will turn and wave. Just once. But no – she just keeps on walking, her red pointed shoes clicking sharply on the pavement, the sound growing fainter and fainter, until there is silence. 'Well, that's that then,' says Aunty Doris, speaking to the empty street. Something in her Aunty's voice makes her look up with a quiver of fear. 'But she's coming back, isn't she?' Aunty Doris gazes down sadly for a moment and then slowly she shakes her head . . .

Peri squeezed her eyes tight against the tears and pain. Why? Why did she leave me? Why? For God's sake, Peri, stop thinking about it! But the memories would not leave her in peace . . .

. . . a stiff lady with a briefcase is sitting at the dining table filling out pink forms. Aunty Doris is telling the lady things about her, private things. Then Aunty Doris turns to her, saying over and over, 'I'm so sorry, Peri, so sorry, so sorry.' There is sadness in her eyes. And pity.

This was too much! Peri sat bolt upright, blanking out the image. 'Great!' she muttered furiously. 'Haven't I got enough problems without having to think about *that.*' She was going for swim, she decided, jumping to her feet; she wasn't going to hang around here and wallow in misery. Suddenly, the sound of voices caught her attention. Through the hanging foliage she could make out two figures walking along the far end of the pool; as she leant forward to get a better look, one of the figures spotted her. *Shit!* It was

Saffron, perfectly tanned from her assignment in Sri Lanka. Peri could only acknowledge her with a brief nod before drawing back behind the screen of plastic flowers and sitting down, acutely conscious of her own white limbs. 'Don't come over here, *please*,' she murmured, squinting to get a better look. *Hell.* Saffron and the other girl were heading this way!

'Having a day off?' came a silky voice echoing within the marbled walls, followed by the sound of giggling.

Peri drew back, wanting to run, wanting to hide her white body, but knowing she was trapped. In the next instant the curtain of plastic flowers was pulled aside and Saffron stood there, smiling contemptuously down at her. 'Peri! Darling!' The hazel-brown eyes swept over her. 'I was beginning to think you'd crawled into a hole to hibernate. I haven't seen you in *months*.' The other girl came up and stood beside her, staring down at Peri with open curiosity.

Affecting nonchalance, Peri stretched her arms out along the rim of the spa, gut-wrenchingly jealous that the long legs that stood before her were tanned to a dark golden brown. 'I've just taken some time off – that's all.'

'Really?' Saffron's pencilled eyebrows arched slightly in mild disbelief as her hands smoothed back her long dark hair from her glossy brown forehead. She flashed a nasty smile. 'I hope you can forgive me for stealing the Pernot job, but, as Mags always says, we look so alike. But I guess, this time, they were going for the *fun* angle.'

As Peri's gaze flickered over the smug complacent face above her, she was overwhelmed with an urge to leap out of the water, grip her fingers around that thin brown neck and squeeze tight; to take revenge for all the malicious gossip, snide remarks and stolen jobs.

Saffron looked down at the water below. 'Is it broken?'

'What?'

'The spa. Is it broken?'

Peri suddenly realised that the water lay still. How long had it been like that? Hastily she pressed the black button and, once again, the water bubbled around her.

Saffron yawned. 'Are you going to the Decleor audition this afternoon? Simply everybody's going.'

'Probably.' Peri shrugged again, but her mind raced. Decleor audition? What Decleor audition? Mags hadn't told her about any Decleor audition!

Saffron adjusted the strap of her bikini top. 'I've just got back from Sri Lanka. Yet *another* commercial for American Express, but it was such fun.' Her eyes swept over Peri once more. 'Why on earth haven't you got a tan like everybody else? The white malnourished look is out of fashion – didn't you know?'

Peri looked up at her steadily, showing no sign of the hatred that boiled inside. 'That doesn't bother me. Everybody else can follow fashion like mindless *sheep* but I refuse to allow my skin to shrivel up like an Indian's scrotum.'

Saffron's eyebrows lifted in mock alarm, her hard eyes glinting. 'Oh dear, oh dear, how grisly. If I didn't know you better, I would think that you were jealous of me.'

'Huh!' Peri sneered, rolling her eyes to heaven.

Saffron threw her friend a knowing look as she began to move off. 'I mustn't waste my time, otherwise I'll be late for my seaweed wrap. It's just so difficult finding time to come here with all the work I'm getting. See you at the Decleor audition.' Turning, she whispered something to her friend which prompted the girl to giggle and look back over her shoulder at Peri.

As soon as the curtain of flowers swung shut, Peri sat bolt upright, fists clenched, heart pounding. The bitch! Why couldn't she just tell the cow to sod off? After all, she would have no hesitation in saying it to practically anyone else, so why didn't she say it to Saffron? Why did she continue to play this game of veiled malice? Why should she feel inferior? But she couldn't help it. It was the way that Saffron looked at her, as if somehow she knew the truth, knew that Peri Lomax was just a common fraud, a nobody. Peri gazed down into the bubbling water. That bitch was watching her career disintegrate, gloating in triumph, confident that Peri Lomax was finally finished.

'Jesus,' she breathed, 'I've got to do something. I've *got* to. It can't end like this!' She was going to go straight to the agency and confront Mags face to face whether she liked it or not, and find out what was going on.

Suddenly there was the sound of beeping. She swung round. *Her mobile phone!* It was calling to her. Her immediate reaction was to leap out of the water and throw herself across the marble floor and grab it, but she stopped herself in time, aware that Saffron would be watching. Instead, she sighed loudly as if annoyed as being bothered by the noise, and slowly got to her feet, slipping into her towelling robe and bending forward to pick it up. 'Hello,' she said in a slow, bored voice. 'Peri here.'

'Peri! Darling!' It was Mags, speaking excitedly. 'Do you want the good news or the good news?'

Peri caught her breath, electrified by the excitement in her agent's voice. Something wonderful was about to happen. She knew it. She just knew it!

'You're not going to believe this.' Mags spoke eagerly, as if bursting with news. 'I got a call from Helmut Reuther's studio yesterday afternoon. You remember the audition – last October – Munich? The—'

'Yes, yes, I remember,' Peri interrupted swiftly, desperate to know more.

'Apparently, he loved your portfolio and loved the polaroids and loved –' she paused tantalisingly '– *you!*'

'No!'

'Yes!' Mags squealed.

'I got it?'

'Of course! Do you realise what this will mean? You are going to be *the* woman to spearhead the fashion world into the millennium.'

Peri's heart began to thump. 'Oh, my God! Oh, my God!'

'And there's more,' declared Mags triumphantly. 'You probably haven't heard about Caroline Morris yet?'

'No. What?'

'Big bust-ups all round. I won't go into it now. You'll read all about it in tomorrow's headlines. Enough to say that she won't be co-hosting anything for a very long time!'

Peri could hardly believe her luck. 'So that means I'm going to take her place at the Film Awards?'

'It's not that simple,' Mags insisted. 'Don't forget, you were only going to be there in case of a last-minute emergency. You can't expect to take her place just like that. Who are you to these people? Your recent track record isn't going to let you walk into her shoes.' Mags took a deep breath. 'So? What have I done? I've phoned the organisers. Told them you're Helmut Reuther's new girl, budding star and all that stuff, let them believe you're on next month's cover of *Hi!*. While they're thinking it over, I phone *Hi!* and tell them you're Helmut Reuther's new girl and that you're hosting the Film Awards and that you're a budding new star, blah, blah, blah. Finally, I get it all in the bag. First you do the Helmut Reuther job, then you do the Film Awards and then you do *Hi!*. The only snag is, the editor at *Hi!* can't promise to put you on the front cover. But I'm still working on it. So? What do you think?'

Peri could hardly breathe. 'I'm . . . I'm speechless.'

'It was a Catch-22 situation. But we've done it. These three jobs will put you in the big league. You're going to be on the cover of every glossy around the globe – an overnight sensation – a celebrity. Not only will you have a face and a body but you're also going to have a *name!*'

Peri squeezed her eyes shut in silent gratitude. At last! After all the years of dedication, of back-stabbing, of bitter disappointments and brief glories, her dream was about to come true. Stardom! Beautiful stardom! It now lay before her, waiting. She was going to be worshipped by the masses and craved by the media; film scripts would flood in and she would pick out the juiciest roles with the biggest budgets . . . maybe an action romance with a tragic ending . . . Audiences all around the world would weep into sodden handkerchiefs . . . and Peri Lomax would finally become a *star!* At the thought of it, she could feel her joy and excitement welling up, making her want to fly around the room, to run out into the street and hug people, to . . .

'. . . and I'm glad for your sake, Peri.' The excitement in Mags's voice had drained away, leaving a sober wistful tone. 'You deserve it.'

Peri felt a delayed rush of gratitude. 'Oh, Mags!' she exclaimed. 'I owe it all to you. Really.' Now, buoyed up on her wave of good fortune, she simply forgot the months of desperation and depression, simply forgot that her agent had been too busy for her.

'That's so sweet of you,' Mags replied, 'but enough of this back-slapping.' She had switched back to her tough business voice. 'First things first: Helmut Reuther hasn't given us much notice. You'll be leaving next Friday and—'

'Next Friday? Gosh, that's a bit sudden!'

'Absolutely. But the sooner you do it, the sooner you get to be *famous*.' Mags trilled the word 'famous', making it sound like an advertising jingle.

Peri could feel her heart pounding with excitement. 'Yeah, you're right. What's my destination?' She had a fleeting image of sparkling blue sea lapping silver sand under a hot sun.

'Well, you'll be flying from Luton,' Mags said cheerfully, 'which will make a change! And I'll arrange for the limo to pick you up at your place.'

Peri thought fast. Hot sun. She would pack her new silver bikini, the pink Armani beach robe, her gold sandals, and of course her new Ricardo sunglasses.

'Unfortunately, you won't be flying Concorde this trip,' Mags explained. 'But it doesn't matter since you'll only be on the plane for an hour. It's an internal flight. To Inverness.'

Peri's thoughts tumbled to a halt. 'Inverness?' she asked, bewildered.

'That's right,' Mags said brightly.

'But that's in Scotland—'

'That's right. It's an unusual location, I must admit, but

Helmut says you're going to look perfect among the gorse and heather of the Scottish Highlands.'

'Scottish Highlands?' Peri echoed, trying to work out in her brain what this would mean. 'But, surely—' Questions and images spun around in her brain preventing her from constructing a sentence.

'The countryside is meant to be very beautiful,' Mags assured her. 'Lots of mountains and stuff.'

'But surely I won't have to work outside?'

'You will – some of the time – yes.'

'But it's still March,' Peri protested. 'I'll freeze!'

Mags laughed gaily. 'Helmut won't let you freeze, and anyway, it's only for six days. You will be there and back before you know it.'

Six days! Peri grew silent, picturing in her mind's eye a bleak hilltop with storm clouds swirling overhead and an icy wind drying her skin to the texture of crêpe. The thought of it made her feel sick. Why, why had it got to be like this? She wanted the job, of course – but why did it have to be in *Scotland*? Why couldn't she have gone to Bali or Mauritius? Somewhere civilised.

'There's something else I should mention,' Mags continued cautiously. 'In some of the shots, Helmut might want to use an Irish wolfhound.'

'What?'

'I know, I know,' Mags said hurriedly. 'I told him you don't like dogs.'

'Don't like dogs!' Peri said in amazement. 'I *hate* dogs, I *loathe* dogs – *you* know that. I'm sorry, Mags, but I can't possibly work with a . . .' She stopped, suddenly conscious of the shrill note in her voice and hastily slipped into the nearest tanning cubicle and closed the door, shutting out the risk of Saffron overhearing.

'It's not definite,' Mags explained. 'Helmut said he *might* use a dog. But, anyway, darling, it doesn't matter if he wants to use a rhinoceros – this is your chance to make it *big!*'

'Jeeesus!' Peri exclaimed, stretching the word out on a long, low breath. 'Why has it got to be like *this?* It's not fair!'

'Listen, darling, I think you will have to be brave about this.' Although Mags had spoken softly, there had been an unmistakable note of warning in her voice. 'I am going to have to tell you something . . .' She paused for a moment, as if reluctant to continue, then she began again. 'In the last six months I've been watching your career heading nowhere. It's become stagnant. You've become stagnant. True?'

Peri felt as if she had been punched in the stomach. 'I . . . I . . .'

Mags continued briskly, 'To be brutally frank, darling, you were either heading for an exhibition stand at Earls Court, or I was going to have to tell you to re-invent yourself. You know – create a scandal: give Richard Taylor a blow job in the back of a car, or shoot someone. Remember what I always say? Bad publicity is better than no publicity. But now you don't have to do *any* of that. It's all falling into your lap, Peri, so just be *grateful.*'

'But I . . .' Peri stammered, confused. What had Mags just called her? Stagnant?

'Hang on,' Mags interrupted. 'Tula's handing me a fax.' There was the sound of rustling paper and then silence.

Stagnant? Peri tried to think through her jumbled thoughts. I've become stagnant? Exhibition stand at Earls Court? What the hell is she talking about?

Abruptly, Mags was back on line. 'It's okay,' she announced cheerfully. 'I've just got a fax from Helmut's assistant: he's definitely decided *not* to use a dog.'

Peri wasn't listening. Having digested the awful things that Mags had just told her, she was consumed with a raging fury. How *dare* she! How cruel! So all this time Mags had been sitting complacently in her plush office thinking: *Peri's stagnant. Her career is stagnant. She'll have to be the next one out with the garbage.*

Mags broke the silence. 'Peri? Are you still there?'

Peri refused to speak. She could feel her cheeks burning with shame and fury. What would have happened if she hadn't got the Helmut Reuther job? Eh? Her photograph would have been ripped off the wall, torn up and dumped in the wastepaper bin – that's what would have happened.

'Come on, Peri,' Mags said wearily. 'There's no reason to sulk.'

'I have every reason to sulk when my agent – my dearest *friend* – tells me that I'm *stagnant*. How could you?'

'Where do you think I've been for the past six months?' Mags said patiently. 'On Planet Mars? . . . No – I've been here in Wardour Street, painfully aware that the demand for you has slowly dried up. You know it. I know it. But things are about to change. It's not going to be easy, but if you want to get to the top, you're going to have to start toeing the line. You're going to have to stop making waves every time something goes wrong. Okay, maybe this job will be a little uncomfortable, but you're not in a position to call the shots. Maybe one day you will, but not now.' She hesitated for a moment. 'And I think you're going to have to work on your personality.'

'My personality?' Peri retorted, scowling at the wall. 'There's nothing wrong with my personality!'

There was a pause. 'Let's discuss it face to face, eh? Come over to my place tonight. I'll order Thai – you like that, don't you?' The voice was soft now, sugar-sweet.

Peri tutted sharply but made no reply. A moment ago she had been deliriously happy knowing that she had got the Helmut Reuther job – but now! Now she felt as if she'd been shot down in flames.

'This job may be a little uncomfortable,' Mags repeated firmly. 'And I would rather you were going somewhere warm, but you're not. Just keep reminding yourself that as soon as you're finished in Scotland, you'll be straight back here, getting ready for the Film Awards and—'

'The Film Awards!' Peri cried. How could she have forgotten! 'And the dress! That's the twenty-seventh! I'm not going to have enough time to get ready for it.'

'Calm down. Calm down. You'll be flying back from Scotland on the twenty-fourth which means that you're going to have three clear days before you've got to be on stage. That's plenty of time and I'll have your itinerary waiting as soon as you land at Luton: rehearsal times, final dress fitting, hairstylist, everything. Don't worry.'

'Gosh, it's all happening at once!' Peri exclaimed. Now, with images of the Film Awards flashing through her brain, she was consumed by a mounting almost-unbearable excitement, making it impossible to concentrate on her agent's words.

'. . . and get plenty of sleep and don't get stressed out,' Mags continued. 'You know how you worry.'

'Okay.'

'Protect your skin at all times, don't forget to take your magnesium and Starflower supplements, and go easy on the sleeping pills.'

'Yeah. Okay.'

'The Film Awards will be your first blast of media coverage, so you've got to look your best!'

'I know – I know!' Peri agreed breathlessly. She didn't need to be told. As co-host to the International Film Awards, she was going to be televised – live – to the whole world! The paparazzi would be there in swarms, pushing and shoving, buzzing with the excitement of a new face. *Who is this beautiful creature?* they would ask themselves. *Why isn't she a star?* Of course, Mags would feed them little titbits of information beforehand, just to get them excited. They would be told that Peri had become Helmut Reuther's favourite model, his muse, and that the dress she would be wearing was the final creation of the legendary Igor de Vere.

Mags suddenly spoke in a rush: 'Look, Peri, I've got to go, but I'll see you at my place tonight. Eight o'clock. Okay?'

'Okay.'

'And remember, Peri, everything hinges on the Helmut Reuther job. If it goes wrong, you lose the Film Awards and you lose *Hi!* magazine. You'll be back to square one. Remember that. Okay – see you later. *Ciao*.'

Abruptly the line went dead. In a daze, Peri lowered the phone from her ear and switched it off, gazing into blankness. This was incredible. Incredible! She'd done it! At last – she'd done it! Feeling herself tremble, she sank slowly onto the sunbed behind her and gazed at the floor, overwhelmed by the enormity of what had just happened.

Saffron! Peri snapped out of her trance. Why was she still sitting there when she should be out there gloating to Saffron and seeing her slimy smile frozen to her slimy face! Peri lunged for the door and, immediately, she was out on the poolside, searching the heads in the swimming pool, searching the faces in the spa. Saffron had gone. Then she remembered: Saffron would be having her seaweed body wrap. Right! Peri stuck the mobile in her robe pocket and picked up her towel and hurried towards the changing rooms. She would get dressed and wait in reception, ready to casually bump into Saffron when she came through. Ha! She wanted to hug herself with glee. This was going to be a moment she would savour for the rest of her life!

On the edge of her happiness lurked the echo of her agent's words: *You have become stagnant, Peri. Your career has become stagnant.* She tried to push them away but they kept on coming back until she had to face them squarely. How could Mags have said such things? How could she have been so cruel? Peri felt a strange, unsettling distrust towards the woman, knowing that it would be impossible to forget those words, and, for a moment, she had an overwhelming urge to phone her back and tell her what a stupid old cow she was. But – no! That was one thing she couldn't do. Not yet . . .

'Well, I'm on my way to the *top*,' Peri muttered, throwing open her locker door and pulling out her clothes. 'And when I get there, *no one* 's going to dare speak to me like that. I will never again be pitied. No way. I'm going to be invincible, untouchable. I'm going to be a *star!*'

'You didn't tell her, did you?'

Mags shrugged and shuffled the papers on her desk, avoiding Tula's gaze.

'You didn't, did you?' Tula repeated.

This was too much! Who the hell was the boss round here? Mags slapped her hands down on the desk and glared up at Tula. 'I know what I'm doing! I'm the one who's handled her for the last eight years. If I had told her, she would have refused the assignment. Correct?'

Tula shrugged her shoulders in silent disagreement before turning to the coffee percolator.

Mags watched Tula pour coffee into her cup, irritated that this woman could be so annoying. 'I *know* Peri,' Mags insisted angrily. 'She would have exploded – thrown a godalmighty tantrum. But this way, she's going to be stuck out in the middle of . . . of . . . I don't know exactly where, before she discovers the truth. And then she'll have no choice but to do as she's told.'

'I don't think you're being fair to her,' Tula answered, carrying her coffee and a croissant over to her desk.

'Fair?' Mags exclaimed. 'Who do you think I'm dealing with here? A Teletubby?' She sighed and continued in a patient voice. 'No – I am not dealing with a Teletubby. I am dealing with a highly charged prima donna, someone who can be devastatingly unreasonable and downright hostile.'

'Sure. But something like this could send her over to Models Five.'

'She won't leave. She needs me. I've been like a mother to her, sending her flowers on her birthday, listening to her problems, giving her a shoulder to cry on. Who else would have done all that?'

Tula nodded thoughtfully.

'And I'm sick of getting complaints about her temper

tantrums. She's going to have to sort out her personality – big time! Only then will I start to go easy on her.'

'Mmm.' Tula turned and picked up her telephone receiver, punching the numbers with a long pink fingernail before slipping off her pearl-encrusted earring and putting the receiver to her ear, effectively cutting off further conversation.

Irritably, Mags tapped her pen against her coffee cup, swinging her gaze from Tula to the photographs pinned up on the opposite wall. Photographs of perfect happy faces with dazzling carefree smiles, and there in the middle, the sullen face of Peri, her long green eyes ever-watchful, like the eyes of a street cat. That was her appeal, that look. Of course, she couldn't be used to advertise a fun family holiday but she was good for expensive liqueurs and fur coats. Well, that look is certainly coming into fashion now, Mags thought triumphantly. And it's taken eight years. Swiftly, her mind swept back across the years to the morning when Peri had first walked into the agency, wearing a cheap, black plastic mac and clutching her second-rate photos in a big, brown envelope.

She had been nervous, which was natural, but – unlike any other model Mags had interviewed – Peri had shown no signs of friendliness. In fact, she had seemed strangely hostile, staring suspiciously across the desk with those beautiful green eyes, her long black hair framing a thin pale face. Mags couldn't explain it to herself, but she had immediately signed her up, and then she had spent the rest of the day wondering if she'd made the right decision. But the girl had survived, eventually getting regular work, and for a couple of years she had been really successful. Mags took a sip of coffee. Maybe Peri would have had greater success if she had been more amenable, more co-operative, more friendly – but that wasn't in her nature.

Well, it was going to have to be in her nature now, Mags thought decisively, now that she was heading for celebrity status. There would be chat shows, one-on-ones for the American press, face-time with shrewd and cunning journalists, charity functions, visiting sick kids, script meetings – the lot. And only she, Mags, would be able to tell her what to say and what to think. Briskly, she picked up her telephone and punched in the code numbers for the Madison Agency and waited, listening to the ringing tone connecting her with the States. No – Peri would not leave the agency, even though, on Friday afternoon at about one o'clock, she would be screaming abuse down the telephone and threatening to. But she wouldn't go through with it. Not now. Now, she had too much to lose.

Her call was anwered abruptly. 'Hi! Madison. Mary-Eloise speaking.'

'Mary-Eloise. Hi. It's Mags. I thought you should be the first to know: Peri Lomax got the Helmut Reuther job.'

'No!'

'Yep. *And* she's replacing Caroline Morris at the Film Awards.'

'Wow!'

Mags could guess that the American woman was running this information rapidly through her brain, calculating the outcome and deciding how best she could use Peri. 'And I've got *Hi!* wanting her for next month's cover,' Mags added complacently.

'Bring her to breakfast,' Mary-Eloise said quickly. 'How about Mezzo's – it's on your block. Next Friday?'

'No can do. She'll be on her way to Scotland then.'

'Scotland? Why Scotland?'

'The Helmut Reuther job.'

'Oh.' Mary-Eloise seemed to think about this for a moment before continuing. 'So – you tell me when's a good time.'

'It will have to be within the next five days.'

'That's difficult.'

'It's up to you. But I'm telling you as a friend, that as soon as Peri Lomax goes live on the twenty-seventh, she's going to be taking off like a rocket!'

Chapter Two

Low black clouds filled the morning sky, moving steadily northwards over the barren hills, while down in deep hollows an icy wind stirred the crisp winter leaves, sending them spiralling up into the air, rasping harshly in the vast and empty silence.

On the brow of a hill stood a man and a dog. Perfectly still. Through narrowed eyes, the man gazed up at something deep within the clouds, and in his hand he held a long leather strap which fell to the ground, snaking through the grass towards the lump of mangled flesh and tiny bones tied at its end. Beside him, the dog sat patiently, staring down at the lump of flesh with bright inquisitive eyes, his wet nose quivering gently with the scent of it.

Slowly, the man raised his arm and began to swing the leather strap above his head, around and around, emitting a strange shrill cry – the sound instantly whipped away on the wind and smothered. But the cry had been heard; with a sudden break in the cloud-cover, a large bird could be seen high overhead, flapping swiftly as it gazed down on its circling prey. Then it dived, dropping down through the sky on long pointed wings . . . down . . . down . . . closing in fast now . . . wings spreading as talons arched forward, thudding into the soft flesh and carrying it onwards, low above the ground. On a flat rock the bird came to rest and, here, the razor-sharp beak began to rip and pull, smearing the rock with blood.

Blood . . . Impassively, the man watched and remembered; images of war, like slides in a projector, slotted into place, one after another. The neat red circle in Sam's skull where the bullet had entered. The splash of red – like a can of red paint tossed in the air – as the anti-personnel mine leapt from the earth and exploded into Andy's stomach. The little girl slumped over the shattered wall as if in sleep. The man closed his eyes tight, his face crumpled with the pain of his memories. So many people dead. All for no reason. They had simply become casualties of a dictator's whim. Casualties of yet another never-ending war that the world would simply forget by next week's edition of the Sunday papers.

Slowly, he opened his eyes and looked down at the dog at his heels, remembering the terrified puppy cowering in the bombed-out shelter. As a professional, he should have left it there or shot it out of pity, but – no – he had taken it and brought it back in the Hercules, tucked inside a canvas bag strapped across his chest. A pathetic gesture in the face of all that death and destruction, but a gesture that he was never to regret. Now he knelt down on one knee and smoothed the hair back from the dog's head, looking down into a pair of brown, adoring eyes. 'You've been my wee pal, haven't you?' The man stared at the dog thoughtfully. 'Life certainly took a turn for both of us, didn't it, eh? But we're finally at peace now.' He rested his hand on the dog's back and looked out over the hills. This was his land now – MacLeod land. Inherited on his father's death. When he had been young, he had devised grand schemes for this land, schemes that would make him rich: leasing it to the Ministry of Defence as a training ground for elite forces; or, better still, turning the place into a centre for the training of bodyguards, high-class bodyguards who would one day protect presidents. But the years of army service were destined to change him forever. When at last he had returned home, he had been sad and disillusioned, tired of guns, tired of fighting, wanting peace, wanting a way out. And so he had climbed this hill to this very same spot and had looked out across his land and he had asked himself, 'What am I going to do with my life?'

The question had floated off into the vast emptiness, unanswered. He had been trained for war; there was nothing else he could do. Nothing. Miserably, he had begun to retrace his steps back down the hillside and it was then that he had seen, away in the distance, a magnificent bird wheeling on up-thermals. Was it a honey buzzard? No. Honey buzzards were now extinct in the Scottish Highlands. His heart began to beat faster – could this be a rare sighting of a goshawk? He strained his eyes to identify it but it was too far away. 'You won't last long,' he had muttered, knowing that it would end up trapped in a wall of netting or shot by a rich landowner's gamekeeper whose job it was to protect the game-chicks for the autumn shoot. 'The stupidity of men,' he had muttered, going on his way. Then, an idea had flashed across his brain, making him stop and think hard. Yes! Why not? A wildlife sanctuary. He could create a wildlife sanctuary. He would have to get some sort of grant . . . and there could be a visitors' centre and there could be salmon fishing . . . and he could lease some of the land for sheep rearing . . . and . . . And there was so much he could do.

His question had been answered!

Within the week he had begun his apprenticeship with the bemused but willing vet down in Mairloch. Within one month he had fenced his land, opening up large areas of the forest canopy and erecting nest boxes, all the while amassing books and reports on nature conservation. Within three months he had a management grant from Scottish Natural Heritage and full support from the RSPB. Within four months he had converted the outhouse into an animal surgery, enabling him to deal promptly with the casualties of man: a goshawk wounded by a shotgun, or a hare with its leg ripped by a steel trap.

Now, four years on, he had witnessed two successive broods of snowy owls, and had taken part in establishing the sparrowhawk in the skies above his Highland hills once more; and, tomorrow morning, he would write his yearly report to

Scottish Natural Heritage stating that, with constant surveillance against poachers, the population of wildcats and badgers on his land had doubled.

He would never be rich, but – finally – he was happy.

'Och, well,' he said, giving the dog a final pat before standing up. 'We'd better get back tae the house before that woman starts climbing that ladder.' He was reluctant to return, knowing that the place would be thick with the smell of air-freshener and disinfectant, smells that would put him off his supper.

But Mrs Craig had been adamant. 'These folk will be paying good money tae stay here,' she had said, pouring bleach into the kitchen sink. 'So the least you can do – for once – is tae let me give the house a decent cleaning.' He had frowned at her then, but she was a tough old bird. 'Dinna look at me like that, Douglas MacLeod. They're fancy folk who will expect the best, not your usual shabby lot with binoculars glued tae their eyesockets. And there'll be a lassie with them, too.' She had turned away from the sink, pulling on pink rubber gloves while surveying the kitchen with slow, anxious eyes. She glanced first at the piles of old newspapers on the floor by the door, then at the empty jam jars along the shelves, then across to the threadbare armchair with its broken leg propped up on two books, and over to the dog basket in the corner with its red tartan rug matted with hair.

Watching her gaze drifting up to the peeling patch on the wall, he had sensed that she was viewing the room as if through the eyes of their 'fancy' visitors and it made him suspect that perhaps – this time – his jam jars would not be safe from her busy hands.

She had looked up at him then, speaking gravely. 'You *did* tell them what they were coming tae, didn't you?'

'Of course I did,' he had said, beginning to feel irritated.

'And there's just the three of them?'

'Aye. There's Otto, who's been organising it all, and his boss who's some big photographer in Germany; and then there's the lassie.'

'And they'll be arriving next Wednesday?'

'Well, the two men will be, but the lassie will be arriving on Friday.'

'And is she German, too?'

'I dinna ken.'

'Did you ask her name?'

'No. Otto didna say. He just called her "the model".'

Mrs Craig had stared at him then. 'The model?' she repeated.

'Aye – that's what he said.' He had turned to the coat stand and had taken down his jacket.

'Are you telling me that there's a model coming *here?*'

He had turned to her, putting on his jacket, puzzled by the look on her face. 'Aye.'

'But I thought they were coming tae take photographs of the scenery.'

'Aye. That they will.'

'But they're going tae have a model with them, too?'

'Aye.' He saw her face set hard.

'Right!' she had burst out, furiously jabbing a finger towards the newspapers on the floor. 'They're out of here – now! Get shot o' them!' Then the finger had targeted his jam jars. 'Get them out of my sight or they'll be in the bin.'

'But . . .' he had begun to protest, but there was no stopping her; it was as if something had suddenly enraged her.

'That dog blanket goes on the compost and the basket is away oot in the hall and then you can put your hand in your pocket – for once – and buy a duvet.'

This had thrown him. 'A duvet?'

'Aye. Wi' flowers on it. And a pink towel.'

He had tried to reason with her but her strange fury had trampled him underfoot.

'And you'll have tae take me over tae Janet's tae borrow her fan heater and some china cups.' She had turned back to the sink and had slammed her pink gloved hands on the rim of it. 'What a disaster,' she had muttered, shaking her head. 'A complete disaster.'

This had been too much for him. 'This is no' a hotel,' he had retorted angrily. 'And I'm no' pretending that it is. I'm no' away out to buy a duvet! These folk took it upon themselves tae come here. I never invited them. And I'll remind you, Mrs Craig, that when I took over this house, the roof here –' he pointed to the ceiling – 'was rotten and leaking. And who fixed it? Me. There was no electricity and no plumbing, there wasnae rugs on the floor nor curtains at the windows – but look at the place now, eh?' He had taken his black woollen hat off the coat stand and jammed it on his head. 'Now there's hot water when it is needed, and if a body feels the cold they only need to come in here to get warm. Perhaps it's no' the Ritz but I'm sure these fancy folk will survive to tell the tale!' He had marched to the door then, thrusting his feet into wellington boots. 'I'm away off to sort out the silage tank and fly Kirsty. Don't go climbing that ladder before I get back.' And with these words he was out of the door.

That had been two hours ago. Now it was time to head back. Time to dust the cobwebs off the ceiling and turn the mattresses.

'What a lot of fuss,' he muttered, straightening up. 'I'm going tae be glad when these fancy folk are away home and we're left in peace.'

Chapter Three

Shafts of warm, apricot light shone in through the windows along one side of the cabin, offering a deceptive warmth on such a cold morning, stimulating the tired-looking businessmen to chatter, their voices an indistinct murmur against the drone of the engine.

Sitting at the rear of the plane, Peri Lomax watched the backs of their heads, her mouth full of hairgrips as she nimbly secured the short black hairpiece on top of her head. When she had finished, she picked up a pair of false eyelashes and placed them on the lid of her vanity case, carefully spreading glue along each rim. It had been such a dash to get to the airport that morning that she hadn't even had time to put on lipstick. Six o'clock departure. How ridiculous! When she had first found out about it, she had 'mentioned' it to Mags, but that had only brought forth excuses about availability. Well, there was no excuse for the choice of airline, Peri thought, studying the miniature-sized cabin with its limp, urine-coloured curtains and threadbare carpet. Scotair? She had never heard of it! It sounded like something from a Noddy book. She angled her mirror on the seat in front and began to settle a false eyelash along the curve of her left eye.

Thankfully, there were only a few passengers and, as they were all grouped down at the front, she'd had complete privacy to make herself look stunning. Helmut Reuther is not going to be disappointed with me, she thought grimly, drawing a beauty spot onto her right cheek with a brown kohl pencil. Over the years she had become an expert in applying her own make-up, often refusing the help of make-up artists; after all, didn't she know her own face better than anyone else? From the age of twelve, she had begun to experiment with it, scanning the pages of beauty magazines for guidance; and when the other girls had started wearing white lipstick, she had begun to wear pink lip-liner and gloss. Of course, make-up had been forbidden to them, so Peri had kept it secret, realising its importance and knowing that it would be her face alone that would give her the chance to escape her dreary existence. And she had been right. While all the other girls with their white lipstick were packing at Tesco's, she was jetting off to exotic locations to be treated like royalty.

Except for today, she thought irritably, smoothing anti-ageing gloss over her full shapely lips and studying her sullen face in the mirror. Normally a mere glance at her beautiful face would fill her with joy, but not now. Why Scotland? she thought bitterly. Anushka was going to Zanzibar, Vikki was going to Morocco and Saffron had just returned from Sri Lanka. While she, Peri, was going to *Scotland*. Why couldn't she go somewhere civilised like everybody else?

But she wasn't about to make a fuss. No. Not any more. She was going to adhere to everything that Mags had told her that evening in her apartment. 'You have to change your personality,' her agent had said, pouring rice wine into tiny glasses. 'Be a little more sensitive to other people's feelings. And smile. Be pleasant and co-operative, even if you don't feel like it.' Suddenly she had changed tack. 'You know *Mary Poppins*, don't you?'

Mystified, Peri had nodded.

'Well, if you don't know how to behave, think: *Mary Poppins!*'

Peri had given her a dubious look, causing Mags to bang the bottle down on the table in exasperation.

'Listen, Peri. Helmut Reuther can make or break you. So think about it! And, remember, as a celebrity, you cannot afford to become unpopular.'

Obediently, Peri had listened but made no comment, determined not to show the woman that she was going to heed her advice – let her sweat! But, in that moment, Peri had vowed to herself that she *would* change; she *would* become sensitive to other people's feelings. She *would* smile. It couldn't be that difficult. And, of course, the effort would be worth it, if it was going to increase her popularity. Once again, she began to imagine how she would flaunt her success before the other models and see the glint of jealousy flash across their eyes, see their smiles stiffen. It would serve them right, too, because *they* were the sort who'd had everything in life: mothers, fathers, pets, possessions . . . and love. They were girls who belonged, who would always belong, and, sure, *they* had known the love of a mother but, in the end, it would be *Peri Lomax* who would know the love of the *world!* And that was a million times better, wasn't it?

Absent-mindedly she studied her fingernails, feeling a glow of triumph wash over her, as she recalled that morning in reception when she had 'bumped' into Saffron and had casually mentioned her news. Ha! Saffron's smile had slid off her face like a lump of cold cream.

This was just the start. If being pleasant was going to help her career, then Peri Lomax was about to have a character change. Complacently, she began to visualise the next ten days spread out like a sequence of film clips . . .

. . . greeting Helmut Reuther with a big smile and thanking him for giving her this opportunity of visiting such a wild and beautiful country . . . wearing ancestral Scottish jewellery and plum-coloured velvet, her hair coiled up onto the top of her head, transformed into a Scottish countess, posing alongside a roaring log fire, one arm on the edge of a vast marble mantelpiece with its stuffed eagle and glass-domed clock. Then a brief shoot among the topiary, laughing at the cold and feeling the wind blowing through her hair . . . dashing back into the warmth

of the hotel, flushed and excited, ordering smoked salmon sandwiches and camomile tea, surrounded by coffee tables piled high with copies of Country Life *and the staff – stiff-backed but deferential – treating her like a queen . . . sitting beneath an ancient chandelier, eating venison and drinking ruby-red wine from a crystal glass, radiating charm, laughing uproariously at Helmut Reuther's anecdotes . . . everyone – even the staff – thinking how sweet and funny she is. Then Helmut Reuther kissing her farewell at the airport and telling her how wonderful she has been. London. The Film Awards. Putting on that very special ballgown and witnessing the look of sheer delight on Igor de Vere's face. Standing on stage with the lights sparkling on her diamonds and listening to the roar of applause, the bank of cameras directed straight at her . . . twelve million people watching . . .*

'Please fasten your safety belts.' It was the voice of the captain. 'We will shortly be landing at Inverness Airport.'

'About time!' Peri murmured, unjamming her knees from the seat in front and rubbing them back to life. She couldn't wait to get off this heap of junk. How could anyone expect her to travel in this way when she was accustomed to flying on Concorde, drinking champagne for breakfast and being pampered by fawning staff? Thank goodness Saffron couldn't see her like this.

There was one dried apricot left, so she peeled it from the cellophane wrapping and popped it in her mouth, thankful that she had thought to bring them with her, otherwise she would have starved. The breakfast had been utterly disgusting – a plate of greasy bacon and rubbery scrambled eggs – and when she had told the stewardess to take it away, the woman had simply picked up her plate without a word of apology and had actually just taken it away! Stupid creature. She watched as the woman bustled up and down the aisle, her upholstered breasts practically bursting the buttons on her blouse, and smiling ingratiatingly at the tatty-looking businessmen; and yet she had failed to show a glimmer of recognition or deference towards Peri. For goodness' sake, Peri thought irritably, I used to be plastered on every billboard across the country with my face twenty feet high! And it wasn't *that* long ago that I appeared in every prime-time commercial slot across the world – so she can't pretend she's never seen me!

The woman was coming back up the plane now, checking seat belts, and, as she leant across the aisle passengers, her breasts were almost touching their faces. 'Thank God I'm not in an aisle seat,' Peri muttered sourly, turning to look out of the window, 'or I'd be smothered to death.'

They were leaving behind the pearly pink stratosphere and were now beginning to cut down through thick heavy cloud, moving fast, the grey darkness seeming to swallow up the bright apricot light. Suddenly, unexpectedly, they burst out of the cloud and into a clear blue sky; the cabin once again flooded with light. Down below, the mountains rose up to meet them, clear in every detail. At first she felt a sense of awe, but that was rapidly followed by a sickening dread. There was nothing but mountains, vast lonely mountains, hump-backed and timeless, stretching away into a veil of pink mist; and twisting through the mountains lay a ribbon of grey water, its stillness broken only by a silvery cloud reflection floating across its surface. Up on the high ground the snow sparkled white in the early morning sun but in the shaded folds of the hills it lay in deep purple shadows, like old bruises. There was nothing else to see. No cars, no lorries, no roads, no houses, no people, nothing.

'Great,' Peri muttered angrily. 'This is just *great.*' She began to pack her make-up back into her vanity case. Well, it was only for six days, she hastily reminded herself, and the time would positively whizz by. She put on her sunglasses and snapped her case shut. She must keep reminding herself that these six days would be the most important days of her career: working with the great Helmut Reuther. Now, she was going to be *the* woman to spearhead the fashion world into the next millennium! So, considering all she would gain, being stuck in Scotland for a few days would be a small price to pay.

Packed and ready to go, she looked out of the window once more. Big purple clouds rolled across the mountains, coming nearer, blocking out the sunlight. The plane was losing height and now she could see the tops of the fir trees, a grey river with a boat on it, a road and a car. They were nearly there. Suddenly, she felt a tingling sensation in the pit of her tummy, a feeling of dread, excitement and fear all mixed up together. What would happen in the next six days? Why did she have such a strange feeling? A small airstrip was coming into view; a square, concrete building stood to one side of it, which, she presumed, would be the arrivals building. Helmut's assistant Otto would be in there waiting for her. Of course, Helmut Reuther himself wouldn't be there – oh no, he was too great a photographer to pick up his models from the airport.

As the plane taxied to a halt, Peri wrapped her red tartan shawl around her neck, shrugged into her suede fleece-lined coat and picked up her vanity case and joined the queue for the exit, ignoring the stares from the businessmen. Of course she was accustomed to being stared at; in fact, she accepted it as her due and couldn't help but be amused at the way people tried to stare without seeming to be obvious, surreptitiously glancing around as if suddenly interested in their surroundings but all the while eager to feast their eyes on her. In Rome and Madrid it was different; there they just stared openly, appreciatively, smiling to her as if she herself had been the creator of such beauty.

'I do hope you enjoyed your flight.' It was the stewardess again, smiling her ingratiating smile as she bade farewell to the passengers. 'And we look forward to seeing you again very soon.'

'Yeah,' Peri murmured heavily as she walked past. In six days she would be going home, probably on the same plane. Six days. Would the days go quickly or unbearably slowly? Well, whatever happened, she would be glad to see this heap of junk again, knowing that it would take her back to London and civilisation and the start of a wonderful new life.

Absorbed in these thoughts, she stepped out of the door and straight into the freezing blast of a bitter wind. She gasped with the shock of it, feeling the icy sleet stinging her cheeks, the force of it tearing through her long hair and whipping it about her face. Swiftly, she put the collar of her coat up around her ears and stumbled down the steps, head bent against the wind as she followed the other passengers towards the small concrete building at the edge of the tarmac. This is not a fashion shoot, she thought grimly, this is a polar expedition! Why, why, why has it got to be like this?

She longed for the comfort of her hotel bedroom, warm and luxurious. Would she have her own Jacuzzi? No, of course not. That was a silly idea. But it would have everything that a five-star hotel could provide. There could even be an old-fashioned bath with big brass taps and standing on lions' paws. And beyond the tall sash windows would be the view of manicured lawns sweeping down to an elegant fountain. She didn't know the name of the hotel nor where it was – but that didn't matter because Otto would be waiting for her in the arrivals lounge to whisk her away.

On reaching the terminal entrance, the automatic door slid open before her, and, with the wind pushing from behind, she was blown inside and there she stood for a moment, ruffled up and dazed, her ears throbbing with the cold.

Oh, but the warmth in the building was bliss, sheer and heavenly bliss, and, as she stood by the window waiting for her luggage, she stared out on the grey and stormy landscape with a deep and growing conviction that she was destined to loathe every minute in this godforsaken country.

As expected, Otto was waiting in the arrivals hall, waving when he saw her; which she thought was a bit silly since he was the only one waiting there, so she could hardly miss him. Somehow he seemed different from when she had met him in Munich; then he had looked happier, healthier, but now he looked anxious. In fact, he looked like a sick and worried rabbit, with his long white face, his pale hair and his light-coloured eyes.

'I'm sorry about the flight,' he said at once. 'There was nothing else available. Was it okay?'

Peri wanted to tell him that it had *not* been okay, but she remembered her agent's words: *Be pleasant and co-operate.* So instead she answered Otto in a quiet voice, 'It was a little uncomfortable,' and waited for his response to her brave stoicism.

But Otto hadn't seemed to notice. 'I must apologise in advance,' he continued, taking her trolley from her and steering it towards the doors. 'I did not want to come here but *he* insisted.' The man seemed agitated, as if talking more to himself than to her.

Peri hurried to keep up with him. 'Well, it's not too late,' she said eagerly, 'we could catch another flight this afternoon. To . . . um . . . to . . . I don't know where, but somewhere.'

'No, no,' Otto shook his head vigorously. 'Once Helmut has got an idea in his head, there is nothing I can do to change it.'

They went through the automatic doors and into the icy blast, all conversation cut off now as they hurried across to the car. 'Bloody hell!' Peri exclaimed, throwing herself into the car and banging the door shut.

Otto stowed the luggage in the boot and got in beside her. 'I couldn't possibly work in this cold,' she told him. 'Look at my nose.' She took out a hand mirror and studied her reflection. 'It's bright red.'

'I know, I know,' Otto muttered, without looking at her. He started the engine and steered the car out into the road. 'But there is nothing I can do.'

Peri was glad to have an ally, someone else who didn't want to be here. If he was going to complain, so was she. 'But why couldn't we have gone somewhere warm, somewhere civilised? Like Mauritius or the Seychelles?'

Otto shook his head. 'That is not what he wants. He needs to have harsh light and untamed wilderness . . . a hard-looking woman in a hard land.'

Peri was silent, mulling over his words. 'Hard-looking?' she queried after a moment. 'But I'm not hard-looking!'

'No, of course you are not,' he said quickly, as if realising his mistake. 'But he will want you to *pretend* to be. No make-up, no jewellery, no—'

'No make-up!' She sat bolt upright and twisted round to stare at him. 'You can't be serious?'

He lifted his shoulders helplessly but kept his eyes on the road.

'I look hideous without make-up. I *have* to wear it.' Words from the lecture Mags had given her flashed across her brain but she pushed them aside. How could she be pleasant and co-operative *now?*

'It's his idea, not mine,' Otto said quickly, defending himself.

'This is ridiculous!' She stopped and thought about it. Maybe Otto had got it wrong. He was a foreigner and had probably misunderstood what he had been told. Suddenly she felt a dart of fear. Had Helmut changed his mind about using the Irish wolfhound? 'He's not using a dog, is he?'

'No.' Otto shook his head. 'He decided against it.'

Peri breathed with relief. 'Thank goodness for *that!*'

'But, I presume you know . . . um . . .' He hesitated.

Peri glanced at him. 'Know? Know what?'

'Were you not informed?' He kept his eyes firmly on the road. 'Helmut has decided to use a raptor in some of the shots.'

Peri frowned at the road ahead. It sounded like some sort of dinosaur. 'A raptor?' she queried, turning back to him.

'Yes.'

'What's a raptor?'

'Well, it's a . . . um . . . a . . .'

'Otto!' Peri said in a cold, steady voice. 'What the hell is a raptor?'

He spoke quickly. 'It is a bird of prey.'

She gazed at him in astonishment, absorbing the words, searching for a simple explanation. Of course, she thought, he obviously means that a bird will be tied to a post or just flapping about on the horizon. 'I presume this bird will be part of the background?'

'Yes, yes,' he nodded firmly. 'Indeed so.'

She studied him through narrowed eyes, judging his sincerity, then, satisfied, she sat back in her seat, knowing that Mags would strictly forbid her to go anywhere near a vicious bird. She was far too valuable. And, anyway, she wasn't insured for anything like that.

'Don't worry,' he assured her. 'Helmut always treats his models with the greatest of delicacy and he will want you to be happy.' He changed gear as he took a steep bend in the road. 'He's chosen some wonderful designs for you: Pietra Miele, Boco, San Lorenzo, but the finale will be a full-length leopard-skin coat. Fake, I'm afraid, but it looks real. Helmut will want you to look beautiful in it, like a Russian princess, with make-up and tiara, standing on the edge of a magnificent waterfall.'

Now, *this* sounded more like it!

'You are very lucky to be chosen for this assignment,' he reminded her gently. 'We have seen hundreds of girls but Helmut preferred you above the rest. Do you realise that you will be captured on celluloid by the greatest photographer of all time?'

Peri glowed with his compliments, and, taking off her sunglasses, she held up her mirror once more, admiring the slant of her green eyes and the arched curve of her fine black eyebrows. 'I do realise how lucky I am,' she agreed, shaping an eyebrow with the tips of two fingers, 'and I shall work harder than I have ever done before.' And, of course, there was no reason to worry about this make-up thing. After all, why would Helmut want to pay an exorbitant fee for a top-class model and then tell her not to look beautiful; he might as well save his money and pick out a girl from the street. No. Maybe Helmut would want her to look 'natural' in some of the shots, but he would certainly not suggest that she should work without make-up. No photographer would ever suggest that.

'I am pleased that you are so understanding,' Otto told her. 'And when we are sitting on the plane heading back to London we shall pat ourselves on the back and say: *well done.*'

Peri smiled complacently and gazed out of the window. They were driving higher and higher up through the mountains. She would certainly have a story to tell at the Film Awards, she realised, beginning to rehearse in her head what she would say to the paparazzi: 'I worked in sub zero temperatures,' she would tell them, 'in hard, dangerous conditions . . . but I survived'. Then she would smile bravely. 'And it was worth it – for the honour of working with Helmut Reuther.' She yawned. Up to her left was a waterfall, cascading silver out of the mist and down the mountainside, and on her right was a sheer drop to a deep purple valley. Suddenly she realised that she hadn't seen another car since they'd left the airport. It was slightly unnerving to think that there were just the two of them out here in the middle of nowhere, driving higher and higher, further and further from any civilisation. 'Are we nearly there?'

'No. The journey will take almost two hours.'

'Two hours!' she wailed, but immediately silenced herself as she remembered the vow she had made to herself. 'Lovely scenery,' she murmured. How was she going to spend the next two hours stuck in this smelly old car with a boring, pasty-faced German and nothing to look at but mountains? She studied him from the corner of her eyes. The guy had no personality. He was the type who would disappear in a crowd at a cocktail party. She felt no curiosity towards him – in fact, she had no curiosity towards anyone, unless that person wore hand-made shoes and drove a Ferrari – and she abhorred the colour of his jumper. What shade was it? Muddy peach or rotten apricot? And his jacket! Ergh! It was like one of those anoraks worn by weirdos – the sort of weirdos who spent all their time train-spotting or bird-watching. Thoroughly bored with her German companion, she turned, and, as she did so, her eyes alighted on a huge hairy beast standing in the middle of the road in front of them, malevolent and unflinching. *'Oh, my*

God!' she cried, clutching the dashboard, staring with horrified fascination at its long pointed horns, horns that were the length of a man's arm.

'There is no need to be afraid,' Otto assured her, bringing the car to a slow halt.

'With horns like *that?* You must be joking!' As she looked, she saw more and more of the monstrous creatures dotted about the hillside. 'They look positively prehistoric. What are they?'

'Highland cattle.' There was a 'toot' sound as he pressed his thumb briefly on the horn, but the animal did not move.

'I can't believe that they're allowed to roam free like this. Why aren't they locked up in a zoo or something?'

'They are not dangerous, please believe me.'

But Peri did not believe him. She was trying to gauge the ferocity of the animal but – as its eyes were completely hidden behind a thick shaggy fringe – it was impossible to judge. 'Why doesn't he cross the road?' Impatient with Otto's gentle tooting, she leant over and pressed the heel of her hand down hard on the horn, filling the air with one long raucous blast. The animal did not move but continued to gaze at them as if in thoughtful contemplation, its massive jaws chomping from side to side. Then, in the silence that followed, it lifted its massive head and walked slowly across the road and onto the grass verge.

'Thank God for that!' she exclaimed, peering at it as they drove passed. 'Phew! That was a narrow escape.'

'It is completely harmless,' Otto insisted. 'It is just like a normal cow.'

'Mmm,' Peri murmured heavily, sinking back in her seat.

They drove on in silence, the road taking them up and over, and around and down, up and over . . . Although Peri was on the alert for more hairy beasts, she soon began to feel sleepy. 'Would you mind if I had a nap?' she asked, reclining her seat.

'No, of course not,' came his reply. 'I shall wake you when we arrive.'

* * *

The sound of tyres on gravel woke her. They had stopped in some sort of yard in front of a big old crumbling house. There was a rusty broken-down car in a corner and a huge mountain of logs piled up against the wall. The place was obviously derelict. 'What's happened?'

'We have arrived,' Otto explained.

She sat up and looked around, peering suspiciously from over the rim of her sunglasses. A chicken strutted across the yard, stopping to peck at a rotten apple lying in the mud. Against the wall of the house sagged a makeshift bench and from the broken gutter above it, water dripped down into a barrel. This was no five-star Highland hotel. This was some sort of bolt-hole for terrorists. Obviously this must be the location for their first shoot. 'Can't we go to the hotel first?'

Otto glanced at her as he switched off the engine. 'What do you mean?'

Peri sighed while rolling her eyes to heaven: the pain of having to work with foreigners! 'Hotel,' she said slowly, enunciating the word; but she could tell from the man's expression that he still didn't understand. At that moment her door opened and she looked up to see Helmut's suntanned face grinning down at her. He was bundled up in a thick cream-coloured jumper and scarf, his thin blond hair sticking out from underneath a green tartan cap.

'Peri!' he exclaimed, throwing the door wide. 'Thank you for coming.' He took her hand and helped her out of the car. 'I cannot apologise for the cold, nor the howling wind, nor this . . .' he put his hands out, palms up, and gestured to their surroundings '. . . because it is perfect.' He smiled at her. 'Your agent has told me that you will be hosting the International Film Awards on Saturday. That is impressive. So I must look after you carefully until then, eh?' He had now taken her elbow and began steering her towards the door of the house, while Otto followed behind with her bags.

'Otto,' Helmut said over his shoulder, 'can you please take Peri's luggage up to her room.'

Peri's gaze travelled across the decaying brickwork to the dark sightless windows, waiting to see, at any moment, evil eyes peering down from behind the curtains. Otto was taking her bags up to her room? She had a room? *Here?*

'You will look magnificent,' Helmut continued. 'An Eco-warrior. From now on, I want you to think: Mother Earth, hunger, survival.'

Peri couldn't think anything. It was as if her brain was unable to connect words to her mouth. Now she was inside a warm and spacious kitchen, with a low-beamed ceiling and flagstone floor and the smell of school cabbage. Slowly, she removed her sunglasses and looked around. In the corner, by the stove, stood a shabby moth-eaten armchair covered in an old woollen patchwork blanket, looking as if it were home to a million fleas, and over by the stone sink stood a grey-haired woman pouring boiling water into a teapot. At that moment, Peri felt something soft brush against her leg and she looked down to see that a striped cat with a big bushy tail had followed them in.

'Hello, dear,' the old woman said in a Scottish accent. 'I'm just making a pot o' tea. Would you like a cup?'

Slowly, Peri nodded. She could feel the cat winding its soft purring body around her leg, and as it did so, it seemed to soothe away the sense of evil foreboding; but still she remained cautious. As the door closed behind her she spotted an axe leaning against the wall and alongside it a pair of enormous black boots – army boots – encrusted in mud. Who did they belong to? She dragged her eyes away and looked at Helmut, trying to concentrate on what he was telling her.

'—and this is Mrs Craig,' Helmut was saying. 'She will be looking after us.'

Peri gazed suspiciously at the woman. *Looking after us.* She didn't like the sound of that. 'That will be nice,' she lied, trying to smile but wanting to demand: looking after us? In this place? For how long? Two hours? One night? Six days?

'Well, I will certainly do ma best.' The old woman smiled

at Peri and came forward holding out a plate. 'Here's a plate for you. Now you just sit doon and help yerself.'

Peri took the plate and sat down, staring blankly at the food before her. She would have to ask what was going on; but how would she phrase it? She began to listen carefully to the chatter around her, waiting for clues, but nothing was revealed. Maybe they would be here for the afternoon and then drive on to the hotel later? Probably. After all, why should someone like Helmut Reuther want to stay in a place like this? Plus, Mags would have warned her about it. No. There was nothing to worry about; she was just being neurotic. This was obviously a location shoot. This set-up had been done countless of times: a beautiful model wearing an expensive fur coat or designer evening dress, posing within the confines of a slum or backstreet. No problem. She would be sleeping in a four-poster bed before the day was through. Having brushed off her fears, she began to relax, turning her attention to the food on the table, aware of her hunger. But there was nothing there but sugar and stodge – cakes, scones, shortbread and jam tarts – all poison to her system. 'Could I possibly have a smoked salmon sandwich?' she asked quietly, 'on wholemeal bread? No cucumber, just a slice of lemon?'

'Och.' The woman became flustered. 'I don't have smoked salmon, I'm afraid, nor wholemeal bread. But I've some cheese and white bread – will that do you?'

This is a joke! Peri thought scornfully. Smoked salmon is the only decent thing about this bloody country and she hasn't got any!

'I suppose so,' she answered sulkily and watched as the woman began to cut thick slices of cheese and put them between two wedges of buttered bread on a plate, finally adding two enormous pickled onions. Peri accepted it politely but all the time she wanted to wail: 'I don't want to be here! I don't want to be here! I want to be at the hotel!' . . . *The hotel?* Her thoughts ground to a halt. Slowly, she tried to recall the last few days. No one had actually mentioned 'hotel' to her when she was being given her instructions; in fact, no one had told her anything, apart from the flight times. Mags had kept saying that the assignment would be a little unusual – that was all. But? . . . She was being neurotic, she reminded herself; and she would simply have to ignore her fears.

Through mouthfuls of cream and strawberry jam, Helmut was explaining that he and Otto had been searching the area for the right locations. 'I want you to embrace nature – abandon all those pretty images that are contrived and false. You shall be a woman of the earth, Peri – wild and strong, in harmony with the forces of nature around you. A role model for the coming millennium. Except for one or two shots, you will be completely natural: no make-up, no lipstick, no nail varnish. Nothing. Together we shall create a timeless image.' He paused, and, as if sensing her feelings, he cocked his head and spoke softly: 'Trust me.'

Peri's brain was racing. *No make-up*. So Otto hadn't got it wrong. She began to speak but a crumb caught in her throat and made her cough. When she was able to speak, she found that she had difficulty constructing a sentence in her head. 'I am . . . um . . . very honoured that you have chosen me for this assignment,' she began hesitantly, 'but I do not feel very comfortable with the idea of . . . um . . . not wearing make-up.' She stopped and waited for his reply.

'I completely understand,' he told her kindly. 'It will seem strange at first but then you will not even be aware of it. You have a perfect face, Peri. A face that does not need paints and falsities.'

Peri knew she should be pleased, complimented, but instead she felt overwhelming panic. She had to wear make-up. She had to. It was her armour against the world. To be utterly beautiful was to set oneself apart from others, to feel superior, confident, strong. She *always* wore it. And now? Now she was going to look hideous! Now her face was going to appear on the cover of *Vogue – without make-up!* At the the thought of it, she just wanted to crumple down on the floor and weep.

'Okay,' Helmut continued, 'we have three hours of daylight left. We must not waste them.' He turned to the housekeeper. 'Mrs Craig, will you please show Peri to her room.'

He turned back to Peri. 'Take your sandwich with you. Otto will come up in a moment and show you what to wear. And don't forget to remove all traces of make-up and nail varnish, and it will not be necessary for you to brush your hair.'

'Here's your tea,' the woman said, handing Peri a cup of treacle-brown liquid.

Abstractedly, Peri looked down at it and shook her head. 'I can't drink this.'

'Oh dear. Is there something wrong wi' it?'

Wearily, Peri gazed at the woman. Did it matter? Did anything matter any more?

'Shall I make you a fresh cup?' the woman suggested.

Peri shook her head. 'I only drink camomile tea.'

'Oh, dear, I don't have any of that either,' said the woman, obviously distressed.

The flustered, helpless look on the woman's face was beginning to annoy Peri. 'I've brought some with me,' she murmured, slowly getting to her feet and taking the cheese sandwich off her plate. What could she say to Helmut? Should she plead with him? No. It would be useless. There was no choice, now, but to do as he asked. But she would not be able to work without make-up; she would not have the confidence. This was too terrible!

'Shall I take you up to your room first?' the woman asked kindly.

Peri nodded. Dispiritedly, she followed the woman out of the kitchen. Maybe, she thought desperately, when he sees how ugly I am without make-up, he'll change his mind. He will see how my eyes disappear to tiny slits when I remove my mascara and eyeliner and eyeshadow and eyelashes. He will discover how pale I am without foundation and blusher and contour cream.

As she followed the woman out into the hallway, she noticed

that the cat was coming too, his big, bushy tail waving in the air. The woman was saying something as they mounted the stairs, pointing back at the cat and frowning, but Peri was too preoccupied to listen. Jesus! She hadn't had a chance to ask how long they were staying. Of course – this woman would know! Now they were heading down some sort of corridor, cold and bleak, towards a large picture hanging on the wall at the far end. Approaching it, she saw that it was an old-fashioned painting of a harem girl in a cap of gold coins, gazing into a bowl of yellow fish. Then the woman opened a door to the right of it and went in. 'I'm afraid we don't have central heating,' she explained, leading the way into a small bedroom, 'but this little heater will keep you warm. Now if there is anything at all you want, you just have tae ask. Okay?'

Peri's gaze swept over the drab little room. There was a strange musty smell, a smell that seemed almost familiar. 'Am I . . . ?' She paused and rearranged her words. 'How long will you be looking after us?'

'Why, for the rest of your stay.'

Peri hazarded a guess. 'Six days?'

'Aye, that's right. Until you leave for your aeroplane on Wednesday morning.'

Peri studied the toe of her boot. *Six days!* Six fucking days! This had to be a nightmare. Did Mags have any idea what—?

'Is that all right wi' you?'

'What?' Peri looked at the woman.

'Is there a problem wi' that?'

Peri frowned. What was the woman talking about? 'Problem with what?'

'With me looking after you.'

Peri's frown deepened. Then, suddenly, she realised what the woman meant. 'Of course not,' she snapped irritably. Why was she wasting time talking to this woman? She had to *think*, for God's sake!

'That's fine then.' The woman plumped up a pillow. 'Can I get you anything before I go?'

Yes! Peri wanted to scream. You can get me a fucking five-star hotel! But, instead, she silently stared at the rusty fan heater as it whirred and clacked, throwing out wave upon wave of dusty heat. She knew she should say something polite, but it was impossible.

'I've also put an electric blanket on your bed.' The woman hovered in the silence. 'Well . . . um . . . I'll go and start making the dinner,' she said after a moment and turned for the door.

Peri opened her mouth to speak but then closed it again. She wanted to know if she would have to share a bathroom but she knew it would be a waste of time to ask.

When the woman had gone, Peri remained standing in the middle of the room, her gaze moving slowly over the ugly Victorian dressing table and the worn carpet to the faded lilac-coloured eiderdown tucked under the sagging mattress. 'They can't expect me to stay here,' she muttered furiously. 'I'm Peri Lomax, or have they forgotten that?' She felt so humiliated but so thankful that Saffron could not see her at this moment.

Taking two steps into the centre of the room, she came in line with the tall mottled mirror above the dressing table, and there she stood and gazed at herself, drawing comfort from her presence in the mirror, desperate to salvage some hope and pleasure by merely looking at her own beauty. She looked different, though. She was as beautiful as ever, of course, but in a way she had never seen before. There, in the dim light, her skin looked ghostly white against the backdrop of deep shadows; and her hair, which was normally kept in order, tumbled about her face and down over her red tartan shawl. But it was more than this. It was the way her reflection appeared through the old and mottled glass, faded and colourless, as if looking out from the shadows of another time, a time long gone. It was as if she were looking at a ghost of herself . . .

It would make a great photograph, she realised suddenly. She would tell Helmut about this angle, this light – he would be pleased. But, maybe, she wouldn't tell him; not if he still insisted that she couldn't wear make-up. How could he be so stupid in not wanting her to wear it? Why pay so much money for her and then want her to look like an ordinary person?

With a feeling of utter helplessness, Peri wandered over to the window. How much of all this was Mags aware of? She felt tempted to take out her mobile and phone her to complain; but she knew that she wouldn't get any sympathy from that quarter. Mags would only repeat what she had said before: *Don't make waves . . . co-operate . . . this assignment will make you an overnight celebrity . . . it doesn't matter if he wants to use a rhinoceros*. But if Mags was told about this place, she would relent, wouldn't she? She would insist that Peri be treated properly . . . or would she? Peri shivered.

She sank down on the edge of the bed, and, realising that she was still holding her sandwich, she took a bite of it and chewed slowly, gazing out of the window at the tin roof of a lean-to shed below, to the gnarled blackened tree behind it and the bleak windswept hills beyond; then away to the horizon, to the hulking black mountains shrouded in heavy rolling cloud. From down below came the clanging sound of a metal bucket rolling across concrete. This was like coming to the end of the road, she thought, with nothing beyond but a vast grey emptiness, a no-man's land. She would remember every detail of this place so that she could tell Mags everything about it. Glancing at the lilac-coloured eiderdown, she wished with all her heart that she could curl up beneath it and sleep through the next six days.

A heavy knock at the door startled her and she jumped to her feet and spun round. 'Who's there?'

'It is me. Otto. I've brought your change of clothes.'

'Come in,' she said wearily, dropping the remainder of her sandwich onto the dressing table.

Otto pushed the door open and came in, his arms cradling a mound of clothes and plastic bags. 'Ah, you have a warm room. You are fortunate. My room is cold.' He dropped his load onto the bed, and peered at her, his brows furrowing into his worried-rabbit look. 'Quickly, please, remove your make-up. We do not have much time.'

Peri set her mouth in a mutinous line and walked over to her vanity case, throwing open the lid and taking out a bottle of cleansing cream and cotton wool. 'I would have thought it only polite if either you or Helmut had informed my agent about all this.'

'All this?'

'The state of my accommodation,' Peri explained, squeezing cream onto a ball of cotton wool. 'And the fact that I am being ordered for the first time in my career to go in front of a camera without the slightest bit of make-up.'

Otto was staring at her. 'She didn't tell you?'

Peri froze and stared at him, feeling a sick, sliding sensation in the pit of her stomach. *Mags had known!*

'Your agent didn't tell you?' Otto repeated. He looked shocked.

Peri didn't like the way he was staring at her. She turned back to the mirror. 'Well, she did mention something,' she lied. 'But I've been so busy that I haven't had time to talk to her.' Fury coursed through her blood. The bitch! She dragged the cotton wool across her skin and stared at herself in the mirror with narrow glinting eyes. As soon as Otto was out of the room she was going to get the mobile out and phone. Tell her what a horrid, sneaky bitch she was . . .

'Are you on good terms with your agent?' Otto asked slowly, watching her closely in the mirror. 'There seems—'

'We're fine,' Peri interrupted cheerfully. 'Great. Just a lack of communication now and again. That's all.'

Appearing satisfied with her answer, he carried on laying her clothes across the bed, giving her instructions as he did so. 'That is all,' he said at last. 'We will wait in the kitchen for you.'

As soon as he was out of the door, Peri dived for her mobile and switched it on. So Mags had known what sort of place this would be, known that she would be forbidden to wear make-up. Angrily, she punched the numbers and held it to her ear. She waited. What other horrors had Mags kept from her, eh? The bitch! Thank God she had remembered to charge up the batteries to her mobile. What was that noise? All she could hear was crackling and whining. Must be a wrong number. She punched the numbers again and waited . . . *still* the same crackling and whining! Why? The answer suddenly struck her. Slowly, she switched off the mobile and stared out of the window at the vast range of mountains along the horizon. She wasn't getting a signal, was she? It was those bloody mountains – she was surrounded by them!

Exasperated, she tossed the mobile back into her vanity case and began to get changed. She would use the telephone in the kitchen, she decided; when everyone had gone to bed. Or . . . she stopped and stared out of the window once more . . . if she could get to the top of that mountain over there, and . . . no! That was a stupid idea. She wasn't going to start climbing up mountains. She would wait until tonight and use the phone in the kitchen. Anyway, there was no time to think about it now. Quickly she got undressed and put on the green woollen dress, thrusting her arms into the brown cardigan, buckling a belt, smoothing black woolly tights over her legs, throwing the hessian cape over her shoulders and pulling on a pair of big brown boots. Then she looked at herself in the mirror. She looked drab and impoverished. Well, if Helmut didn't send her rushing back upstairs to get prettied up, there must be something wrong with him. She was tempted to put on a little mascara, a hint of gloss perhaps – but no. He was *really* going to see how ugly she could look!

At the door, she stopped and then turned back into the room, going over to her vanity case and taking out a box of camomile teabags. 'I'm going to need a cup of this by the time I get back,' she muttered. With a sudden rush of anxiety, her hand was back in the case, rummaging frantically, searching. Where was it? What if she had left it behind? Suddenly her hand touched the metal box and she brought it out and opened it, checking the contents: six sleeping tablets, six Prozac, six Temazepam. Thank God! Should she take a Temazepam now? No. She would have to pace herself. Things were going to get worse, she could sense it; and she was going to need as much help as she could get.

Patches of bright sunshine chased cloud shadows swiftly across the purple hills while, overhead, a big brown bird fluttered helplessly, tossed up in the wind. With the back of her hand, Peri wiped the drip from the end of her nose and continued to gaze down across the valley, feeling the cold wind on her bare face and visualising her skin, delicate and exposed, shrivelling up like a prune.

The afternoon seemed interminable. She had been standing on top of the hill for an hour – maybe more – it was difficult to judge. The cold had long since numbed her toes and fingers and the icy wind had made her ears ache. Thankfully, she had discovered a refuge during a break in shooting. It stood behind her on the other side of the hill, a derelict one-room cottage, overhung with the gnarled and twisted trunk of a dead tree and surrounded by fallen rock. Admittedly, it could not provide warmth but it offered a brief respite from the merciless wind.

Helmut had given her a long wooden staff to hold, with instructions to look proud and fierce. She was an Eco-warrior, he had told her, a woman of courage, a woman who fought to save the planet from destruction and greed. But it was difficult to look proud and fierce, Peri thought miserably, when all the time she just wanted to creep into a corner and weep. She could tell that he was not pleased with her. It was so frustrating; she wanted him to be pleased with her, to praise her. Tomorrow she would try harder but for now she was just too cold. Abstractedly, her gaze travelled the length of the river which snaked along the valley floor far below; one minute it gleamed silver, the next it dulled to a flat grey. There was nothing else to see, no cars, no lorries, no people, no buildings, just a lonely river and a vast mountain range stretching away as far as the eye could see. Desolate. Cold. Impatiently, she glanced down at Helmut who stood below, almost at the foot of the hill, and for a moment she considered the angle of the camera, knowing that she would appear to be high up with only the swirling clouds as a backdrop. She hoped that he would keep at that distance and not do a close-up. What would people think when they saw the photographs of her like this? They probably wouldn't be able to recognise her. And yet Helmut had had the audacity to compliment her when she had first appeared at the kitchen door, saying, 'Perfect, Peri, perfect.' If he had been anybody other than Helmut Reuther, she would have had no hesitation in throwing a godalmighty tantrum. Thank goodness Saffron couldn't see her like this!

Jesus! She was so cold, so very, very cold and, oh, how she yearned to be back at the house, snuggled up by the stove in the kitchen. She no longer cared that it was shabby and neglected – it was warm, and that was all that mattered now. She watched Helmut intently. Surely it was time for another break? But apparently not; he was slotting in yet another film cartridge. Her gaze travelled over to Otto. He was busy stamping his feet and clapping his mittened hands to keep warm and from his mouth came puffs of white steam. He was obviously as unhappy as she was, and that gave her some small comfort.

Oh, why didn't I bring my mobile with me? she berated herself; this would have been an ideal opportunity to phone Mags. Once again, she began to play over in her mind their recent conversations, trying to work out what had gone on behind her back. So Mags had known all along, she thought bitterly, and that was why she gave me that lecture, preparing me for what was to come. The sneaky bitch – why hadn't she told me? And what about all those horrid things she had said back in London – telling me I'm stagnant, that my career's stagnant, that I was going to end up on an exhibition stand at Earls Court? Apart from her anger, Peri was heartbroken. Over the years, Mags had become like a mother to her, and so she had come to trust her, to feel fond of her, but now *this* had happened! Well, it just proved to her that Mags was just like everybody else. She had trusted so many people in her life and yet all of them had dumped on her, all of them . . .

. . . the lady is smiling at her. She's wearing a pretty yellow dress and daisy earrings and her face comes down close and she is saying magical things, things like: 'I have come to take you home with me. Would you like that? You can bring your teddy too. I'm going to be your mummy now and you can have your very own bedroom.' The other girls are watching as they walk to the door. They are jealous because Peri Lomax is lovable and they are not. Now she is sitting in the car beside the lady and the lady is talking again. 'Shall we go and buy a goldfish? Then we can go to Woolworths to buy you your favourite sweeties . . .'

Peri turned her face sharply into the wind, feeling icy fingers brushing back her hair, desperate to freeze out the memories but aware that they were inexorably seeping back . . .

. . . it is raining. The pretty lady doesn't smile any more. She is crying and saying that she will be too ill to look after a little girl . . .

'Peri!'

The shout startled Peri, bringing her sharply back to the present.

'Okay,' Helmut shouted from below. 'You can take a rest.'

Folding her cape across her chest, she turned and stumbled down into the shelter of the derelict cottage, immediately pulling the blanket around her shoulders and sinking down in a corner with her knees bent to her chin. A heavy sadness lay like a lump in her chest. Why had she allowed herself to think of her childhood? Her policy had always been to forget it, to blank it out, so why was she thinking about it now? But she knew why: this always happened when she felt weak or depressed or lay in bed with flu. Then she would have to tell herself firmly that it was all in the past. It couldn't hurt her any more. It was finished.

She stared at the ground, knowing that her memories would never have got to her if she had been on some exotic beach sipping a dry martini and feeling the sun on her face, a cool silk evening dress fluttering gently against the warm glow of her suntanned legs. Now her gaze travelled over her boots and skirt, glad that these 'designer' clothes lay in the dirt. She loathed them. Who in their right mind would wear something like this? The colours were dowdy and faded, there was a snag in the hem of the cape and the dress was over-long and shapeless. Helmut had even smeared mud on her cheek 'for effect'. She was angry at him, and she was angry at herself; why had she left her mobile back at the house? This was the ideal opportunity to make the call – she was up high enough! In fact, she would probably be able to phone Hong Kong! This was the best time to get Mags, too, because she would be alone in her apartment and not busy at the office. What was she doing now? Lying back in her Jacuzzi, troubled by her deception and feeling horribly guilty? Or worrying about what to wear for dinner?

Resting her chin on her knees, Peri idly picked up a stone to put on a pile by her foot and imagined what she herself would have been doing in London at that moment. She could always dream herself out of an unpleasant situation; it was a skill that she had perfected in childhood. And now, as she sat in the fading light with the sound of howling wind around her, she could see herself taking tea at the Savoy, warm and cosy, with bags and bags of shopping around her feet and a cup of steaming camomile tea on a starched white tablecloth in front of her. As the image began to fade, she sighed and picked up another stone, her thoughts swirling, seeking out another image to give her comfort. The Film Awards night! Giant banks of paparazzi ranged on either side of the entrance, their voices calling out to her, 'Peri! Peri! Over here!' She would be wearing the ballgown – Igor de Vere's creation. Layers and layers of silver chiffon. Diamonds! Diamonds around her throat, her hair, her arms, everywhere! Now she could see herself coming onto the stage at the International Film Awards ceremony, smiling at the flashing cameras and smiling graciously. Floating across the ballroom. Hollywood producers and casting agents staring . . . staring . . . staring . . .

Suddenly, she snapped to attention. From the corner of her eye, she had caught a movement. In the shadows – a creature!

She spun round. It was a dog! A vicious dog! Coming straight at her, its long slavering tongue hanging from between its teeth, its eyes staring. With her heart pounding, she jumped to her feet, raising the stone above her shoulder, ready to strike.

'What do you think yer doing?' It was a man's voice, a very loud Scottish voice, but she didn't dare take her eyes off the dog to see who it was.

The man lowered his voice. 'Bruce – come here.'

As soon as the dog had turned its back, she felt safe enough to dart a look in the direction of the voice. It was a man, peering in through the narrow gap in the far wall, his lower face swaddled with scarves, a black woollen hat tight against his head.

'He . . . he . . . he was going to attack me,' she stammered.

'Och! For goodness' sake, woman – don't talk sae daft.'

Although his voice was loud, she instinctively sensed from its tone that he would do her no harm.

He looked her up and down before he spoke again, sounding suddenly weary. 'Where are the others?'

Peri glanced over her shoulder. 'Outside.'

He nodded gravely. 'Now listen tae me,' he said patiently. 'You can stay tonight but tomorrow I want you off my land. I'm sick of having to clear up your beer cans and all yer filth and muck.'

Peri scowled. 'I beg your pard—?'

He cut her short. 'Do you realise how much damage you do to the wildlife? Eh?'

Now Peri was angry, ready to do battle, but thoroughly confused and not quite sure what the battle was to be about.

'Animals cut their mouths on empty cans,' the man continued. 'Did you know that?'

This was getting too much. He was obviously the village idiot. Well, she'd had too much fucking shit thrown at her today to have to listen to *him*. 'Yes, yes,' she said patiently, as if placating a child. 'Now why don't you go away and play with the fairies, like a good little boy.'

That silenced him. Ha! He just stared at her with round,

astonished eyes. Then suddenly he ducked his head and began squeezing sideways through the gap in the wall, his big boots scraping and sliding on the rubble beneath his feet, bricks bursting from their mortar and tumbling onto the floor.

Jesus! Peri thought in alarm. What's he doing? He was coming into the cottage! As he straightened up before her, he seemed to get bigger and bigger, practically filling the room. The guy was enormous!

'Right!' he snarled, pulling the scarf down from his mouth and staring at her with cold blue eyes. 'I am now going to throw you and your friends off my land.'

As he took a step towards her, she hastily stepped back, coming up hard against a wall of stone. 'Don't you dare touch me,' she cried, feeling panic grip her chest as she watched him get nearer. 'All I have to do is shout. I've got friends out there – lots of them – men with *knives!*'

'I'm sure you have. And I'll deal with them after I've dealt with you!' Suddenly he dropped to one knee in front of her, an arm came around the back of her legs and she was hoisted up and over his shoulder.

It had happened so quickly. 'Help!' she screamed, hanging upside-down and hammering her fists against his back. *'Help!'*

The man was heading towards the door. He was walking off with her! Now the others would see him – come to her rescue – but no! They were down the other side of the mountain! They wouldn't see him. Desperately, she wriggled and kicked, but couldn't break free from his powerful grip. 'Put me down! You can't do this!'

'Yes, I can.'

'My friends are killers – and they're going to *get* you for this!'

Then she heard Otto's voice. 'Peri! Peri!' It was barely audible at that distance but it was getting closer.

Frantically, she pushed her hands against the man's back, levering herself up so that she could swivel her head towards the doorway. 'I'm in here! Quick! Help!'

Otto tripped as he came through the door, his pink mittened hand grabbing the wall to stop himself falling forward. 'Oh!' he exclaimed mildly and stopped and stared, cocking his head at right angles to peer at Peri's face. 'What is happening?'

'*What is happening?*' Peri screamed in disbelief. 'What the fuck do you think is happening?'

The man stopped abruptly. 'Do you know this woman?' he asked, sounding incredulous.

Otto coughed. 'Yes, Douglas . . . um . . . I think you had better put her down.'

Promptly, she was put on her feet. *'Douglas?'* she hissed, spinning round to glare at Otto, but pointing a stiff finger at the man. 'You *know* this man?'

'Yes, of course,' Otto replied. 'Douglas is our host. He has been kind enough to let us stay in his house and use his land.'

'What?' Peri could only stare at Otto in disbelief.

'Wait a minute,' the man began slowly. 'You're not the . . . the . . . ?'

She turned slowly and looked at him.

The anger had gone from his face and now he looked amazed. 'But surely . . . you're not the . . . the . . . model?'

If she had been a man, she would have punched him in the face.

'Of course,' Otto answered enthusiastically. 'Peri is the one of the most beautiful women in the world.'

Peri saw by the expression on the man's face that he was having difficulty in believing it. *She was getting out of here.*

'Now that your Neanderthal friend has quite finished playing cavemen – can we get back to work?' she muttered coldly, brushing past Otto and out of the doorway. She did not even glance at the man. She hated him.

'I'm sorry,' the man shouted. 'I didn't realise. I thought you were someone else.'

'Piss off,' she muttered, and carried on walking.

As she again took up position on the brow of the hill, she could hear Helmut issuing instructions from below. Further along she spotted the man and his dog staring at her. Then, when she looked again, they were gone. 'I hope they don't expect me to converse with that . . . that . . . moron,' she muttered, and frowned heavily towards the camera, her lips set in a hard line, her cheeks ablaze with shame and fury.

'*Wunderbar*! *Wunderbar*!' Helmut shouted. 'That is what I want!' Then he grinned and turned to Otto and she heard him chattering excitedly in German.

'This can't be happening!' she muttered, staring into the clouds. 'This can't be happening!'

The bathwater came up to her chin and it was hot, gloriously hot, warming her very bones. She had been lying there for an hour or more, topping it up, but now there was no more hot water. Within a few minutes the bath would be cold. But she didn't want to get out, she didn't want to feel the icy air on her warm wet body. She would remain for a couple of minutes more, she decided, sticking her big toe up the warm tap and thinking back over the events of that afternoon. The man had hardly been apologetic, had he? And Otto! After a bit of flapping about and looking worried, he had simply let the matter drop as if nothing had happened! That's *another* thing I'm going to tell Mags! she thought angrily. I'm going to make bloody sure that by the time this is all over, she's going to be riddled with guilt.

She scooped up a handful of foam and squashed it between her palms, remembering the look of pure astonishment on that man's face when he had realised who she was. God, he was repulsive! Was it any wonder that someone like *him* lived in a place like *this!* She looked around the bathroom with narrowed, hostile eyes. Over the towel-rail hung threadbare towels, limp and grey, looking more abrasive than absorbent, and above her head hung a cloud of steam, blotting out the ceiling and misting over the mirror above the basin. On the wall below the basin was a patch of tiles, criss-crossed with veins of black mould, and on the floor there was a sheet of linoleum, its pink and yellow flower-pattern faded and cracked by the years. This reality was a bitter gut-wrenching disappointment after her glowing fantasies of that morning; instead of a five-star country-house hotel with staff who treated her like a queen, she had ended up in a freezing hovel with some ape-man who'd treated her like a sack of potatoes. It was sickening to realise that everything she had encountered that day was completely the opposite of how she had imagined it would be, apart from this old-fashioned bathtub, that is, which indeed stood on lions' paws. How ironic! Wistfully she thought of her own bathroom with its deep soft creamy-coloured carpet, its under-floor heating, its mirrored walls, the piles of soft creamy-coloured fluffy towels that appeared by magic every morning, all spotlessly clean. She longed with all her heart to go back, to be warm again, to feel rich, to feel cocooned.

'I hate this place,' she muttered. 'I hate this place more than anywhere else on earth.' Why the hell did we have to stay *here?* she thought bitterly. And how did Helmut find this place? How did *anyone* find this place? Had he stuck a pin in a map, or what?

The bathwater was begining to lose its heat and now she had no choice. She had to get out. Quickly she shot up, jumped out onto the mat and scrubbed her limbs frantically with a handful of grey towelling and threw on her dressing gown. 'What is this?' she muttered through chattering teeth. 'Endurance training?' She dashed across the corridor to her room, banged the door shut and stood in front of her whirring, clacketing fan heater, feeling the hot air tickling her legs. Her little friend. She didn't mind the noise of it now; it made her warm, and for that she was grateful.

Dropping the towel to the floor, she hurriedly pulled a sea-green cashmere dress over her head, smoothing it down over her thin body before slipping into a pair of silk knickers and tights. Next she sat down at the dressing table and began carefully to apply her make-up, grimly determined to look her very, very best. She wanted to see the shock on that man's face when he walked into dinner, see him stare, open-mouthed as he realised that – yes, indeed – here was one of the most beautiful women in the world. Ha! That would show *him!*

The big fluffy-tailed cat which had been sleeping in the folds of her coat on the bed jumped down and padded across to her. 'Hallo, Hamish,' she said gently. 'Have you come to see me?' She scooped his soft, purring body onto her knee and began to stroke him. He was the only good thing about this place. From the moment she had arrived, he had followed her, wanting to be stroked and cuddled, purring and looking up at her with big dreamy eyes, and she had felt sorry for him, imagining the awful existence that he must have to lead. Now he sat quietly on her knee watching her reflection in the mirror as she continued to apply her make-up. With a steady hand, she drew a line of kohl along her upper eyelid and out past the corner of her eye, and all the while her thoughts ranged backwards and forwards across the day, ending with a jolt at the ruined cottage on the hill. It was unbelievable, what that man had done to her! It made her skin crawl just thinking about it. How dare he? If she'd had a gun, she would have shot him. *Christ.* Someone should tell him that this was the twentieth century and that he couldn't go around behaving like some . . . some . . . Viking! And the look of disbelief on his face! Anger boiled in her chest. Well – *she* would show *him!* The moment she walked into dinner, he was going to feel foolish, embarrassed, clumsily apologising for his behaviour, falling over himself to be nice to her, but she would simply look at him as if he had crawled from under a stone. And as the dinner progressed, she would discuss the art of photography with Helmut and emphasise how important it was that she was able to relinquish her make-up and finery for the sake of that art. Yeah – that sounded good.

She applied the final coat of mascara and sat back, admiring herself in the mirror. 'Right, pussy,' she said, pressing the cat against her chest and standing up. 'Let's go and show him what the most beautiful woman in the world looks like, eh?' As a final act, she sprayed Elysium into the centre of the room, and, with Hamish safely cradled in her arms, she walked through the cloud of perfume and out of the door.

Halfway down the stairs, she stopped and sniffed the air. It was difficult to distinguish any smell apart from her perfume but she was sure she could smell the aroma of boeuf bourguignon wafting towards her. Saliva oozed onto her tongue. She was starving! Swiftly, she got to the foot of the stairs and headed for the kitchen. When she reached the door, she glanced down and saw that Hamish's little nose was up in the air too, sniffing just like her, and for a moment she smiled indulgently down at him. Then she gave him a little squeeze and carried on into the kitchen.

The smell came from the stove and she headed straight to it, coming to stand beside Mrs Craig, who stood stirring a big pot full of bubbling gravy and carrots and meat, and bits of green stuff, and onions and little sausages.

'Hogman's Stovies,' Mrs Caig explained. 'And I'm just putting the dumplings in now.' She glanced at Peri and her eyes widened. 'Why – you look lovely!' she exclaimed.

'Thank you.' Peri continued to stare into the pot, feeling a gnawing hunger in her stomach. When Hamish began wriggling to be free, she put him on the floor, where he started to miaow and circle Mrs Craig's legs.

'Are you hungry, Hamish?' the woman asked him kindly. 'Here ye go.' She spooned meat and gravy into a bowl and set it down on a sheet of newspaper by the front door. 'Mind, it's hot.'

Peri watched the cat as it paced backwards and forwards in front of the steaming food, and she knew that, if she could, she would have taken it from him.

'I cannae understand why your boss wants you to look like some peasant,' said Mrs Craig, 'when you're such a bonnie lass.' She prodded the dumplings, one at a time, submerging them for a moment before they bounced back up. She glanced briefly up at Peri before speaking again. 'Douglas told me what happened,' she said softly.

'Douglas?' Peri repeated absent-mindedly watching a dumpling soaking up the thick gravy.

'You met him this afternoon on Briar's Fell.'

The man and the name suddenly connected. *'Him!'*

'Aye.' Mrs Craig nodded. 'He is mortified. He's wanting a chance tae explain tae . . .' At the sound of footsteps, the woman stopped and glanced over her shoulder.

Helmut and Otto were coming into the kitchen, chattering. Helmut smiled when he saw Peri. 'Good evening, Peri. You are looking particularly beautiful tonight.'

'Thank you.' She kept her voice pleasant but yearned to be able to snap at him: *Now you know what I could look like, if it wasn't for you and your stupid ideas!*

The two men scraped back their chairs and sat down, Helmut reaching forward to a bottle of wine and a corkscrew. 'A glass of wine, Peri?' He sounded cheerful.

Peri sat down at the table. 'Yes, please.' This was her chance to charm and amuse, just as she had planned, but she was far too hungry to string a sentence together, let alone think of something witty to say.

'And you, Mrs Craig?' Helmut asked. 'Would you like a glass of wine?'

'Och, no, no, no.' The woman giggled and shook her head. 'It'll go straight tae ma head.'

Helmut cocked an eyebrow. 'Well – that is the best place for it to go, *ja?*' He beamed a smile at Otto and then at Peri, as if enfolding them with his good humour.

'Here ye go.' Mrs Craig set down two plates of steaming food, one for Otto and one for Helmut, and then turned to Peri. 'Otto instructed me on your diet,' she said, and went over to the fridge and opened the door, taking out a plate. 'I hope you'll like it.' She came back to the table and set the plate in front of Peri. It was a hard-boiled egg salad. 'And that's my very own beetroot relish,' she added proudly.

Peri stared down at the lettuce leaves in front of her and then she looked across at the dumplings in Helmut's stew.

Hunger made her feel quite desperate. 'The salad looks nice,' she said sweetly, 'but I want what they've got.'

'Surely.' Mrs Craig smiled delightedly. 'It's much better for a body tae have a big hot meal inside it. Especially when it's cold.'

Peri had her knife and fork ready as the woman put the steaming food in front of her. Hamish jumped up onto her knee and settled himself down, stretching his neck towards her plate, his quivering nose only inches from her food, so she put her fork down, scooped him up under his tummy and dropped him onto the floor. Then she pulled her chair closer to the table and began to eat.

'It was an unfortunate meeting you had with Douglas this afternoon,' said Helmut, shaking pepper over his food. 'I was talking to him while you were upstairs getting ready. He wants a chance to apologise.'

'Hmm.' Peri mumbled through a mouthful of hot, tasty lamb and mashed potato. She didn't want the thought of that man to spoil her meal.

'He thought you were someone else,' Mrs Craig added. 'And he hoped that he didn't frighten you.'

Peri released her knife and fork and they clattered down onto her plate. 'Of course he frightened me! He threw me over his shoulder like a sack of potatoes and tried to abduct me.'

'Oh, dear, oh dear,' Mrs Craig said anxiously, shaking her head. 'That's just terrible . . . terrible!'

'Wait one moment.' It was Helmut holding up a hand to stop the conversation. 'Are you sure, Peri, that you did not antagonise him in any way?'

Peri pointed to her chest. 'Me? Of course not! He came along and peered at me through a hole in the wall and then started blabbering about me leaving my filth around and animals cutting their lips and naturally, of course, I thought he was the village idiot and I told him to go away and play with the fairies.'

There was a loud gasp from Mrs Craig, which promptly

encouraged Peri to elaborate. 'Then he went berserk and rushed in, threatening me, and then he threw me over his shoulder and tried to run away with me but luckily Otto got to me just in time and stopped him.'

Now there was silence. All eyes fixed on her. To her left was Otto, looking unhappy, as if wanting to say something but not daring to. Helmut sat studying her quizzically, his eyes bright with amusement. Over by the stove stood Mrs Craig, with the stamp of sheer and utter horror on her face. Peri much preferred the look on Mrs Craig's face – it gave her an immediate and heart-warming glow of malicious triumph. That man was going to be in trouble now! Hopefully, the woman was a gossip and she would go out and tell everyone, and then the man's reputation would be totally destroyed.

Otto coughed nervously. 'We must not forget that Douglas believed you to be a . . . a . . .'

'A what?' Peri swung round to meet his gaze.

'. . . a trespasser,' he finished lamely.

'That's right,' Mrs Craig hurriedly agreed. 'He thought you were another one o' those New Age travellers – you ken? They're a clatty lot, always leaving their rubbish behind and—' She stopped and bit her lip, her eyes widening in apprehension as she realised what she had said.

Peri frowned at her. 'Pardon?'

'Well . . .' Mrs Craig made a show of brushing down her apron. 'I . . .'

'Do I honestly *look* like a New Age traveller?'

The woman gazed at her miserably. 'Not *now*, no, but . . .'

'One minute.' Helmut held up his hand once more. 'Douglas can be forgiven for thinking you were a New Age traveller, Peri, because you looked like one. Do not be offended by his mistake, because this is the image we are trying to portray. And, it seems, we have succeeded.' He smiled. 'You are one of a new breed of people; people who will live in trees in order to save them from destruction; a breed of people who are surfacing and making their voices heard, telling the world that the earth is being destroyed by greed. So – let us forgive Douglas for this mistake, shall we?' He looked around the table for confirmation, and immediately Otto and Mrs Craig answered him with nods of agreement. All except Peri, who bowed her head over the table with grim stubborness and began pushing a carrot around her plate with a fork. 'Peri?' Helmut coaxed gently. 'Do you agree with me?'

She glanced up at him and nodded reluctantly. What else could she do? He was, after all, the most important person in her life at that moment. Suddenly she realised that the man who had caused all this trouble still hadn't appeared. 'Where is he, anyway?'

'Douglas?' Mrs Craig ventured.

'Yes.'

'He won't be back until late,' Mrs Craig explained, putting a bottle of brown sauce on the table. 'Someone in the village has found an injured owl and he's gone tae help. He's so kind and gentle with animals, you know.' The woman spoke warmly as if encouraging Peri to like him. 'Even the vet in Mairloch asks for his help.' She turned back to the stove and began pouring milk into a pan and stirring it. 'If you ask him nicely, he's sure to take you round and show you his animals.'

'Animals?'

'Aye. This is a wildlife reserve,' Mrs Craig explained. 'Douglas built it up all by himself and he takes in injured animals and mends them and puts them back into the wild.'

Peri loaded her fork with a piece of meat and dumpling. Why didn't this silly old woman stop wittering on about that man?

'It's all very quiet up there right now,' Mrs Craig continued, stirring the pan. 'But come the spring, those sheds are full of animals, and it makes me wonder sometimes how Douglas can cope. But he's a kind soul and I've never known him to turn away an animal yet.'

'Oh, really?' Peri tried to sound interested. She was sure she could smell rhubarb crumble.

'You wouldn't think, to look at him, that he could be so gentle – but he is.' With gloved hands, Mrs Craig opened the oven door and took out a steaming fruit pudding and put it on the hob. 'He was in the army, you know.' Turning slightly, she leant forward and whispered conspiratorially. 'Don't say anything, but . . . he used to be in the SAS.' She straightened up and nodded importantly. 'But don't tell him I told you,' she added quickly. 'And don't ask him questions.'

'Okay,' Peri promised. 'I won't.' Ask him questions? she thought contemptuously. What a joke! I've got as much interest in him as I have in a . . . a slug. But now I know why he acts the way he does: he still thinks he's fighting a war. Well, I'll have to make sure I'm never left alone with him – he's probably unhinged.

Helmut had begun to ask the woman questions about the man, which she was evidently keen to answer, leaving Peri to sigh with resignation as she continued to eat, concentrating solely on her food and trying to ignore the conversation. Soon she could eat no more, and after mopping up the last of her gravy with a dumpling, she sat back in her chair, feeling as if her stomach was about to explode. She hadn't felt like this in years! And it had been very naughty of her, but she hadn't been able to resist it. She would have to leave the room before any more food was put in front of her. 'Will you excuse me?' she said, standing up. 'I can't possibly eat another thing.'

'But surely you'll be wanting a wee bit of clootie dumpling and custard?'

It sounded like calorific suicide. Peri shook her head vehemently. 'No, thanks.'

'You've done well,' Mrs Craig said, picking up the empty plate. 'And I'll bring you a cup of coffee through in just a moment.'

'Do you have decaff?' Peri asked.

'Decaff?' Mrs Craig repeated.

'Decaffeinated coffee,' Peri explained.

'Och, no. I'm sorry. But shall I make you a cup of your camomile tea?'

'No. Don't bother.' Peri picked up her glass of wine and headed for the door. 'I've got my wine.'

'I switched on your electric blanket earlier,' Mrs Craig told her. 'So it will be nice and warm for ye.'

Peri paused at the door and turned to look at the housekeeper. Perhaps the woman wasn't too bad after all. 'Thanks,' she said. The woman smiled and, to Peri, it seemed almost like a smile of encouragement, as if in some way the woman was trying to convey sympathy and understanding. And pity. But Peri Lomax didn't need *anybody's* pity. Slightly irritated now, she turned and carried on through to the sitting room.

With a yawn, she sank into a deep battered sofa in front of a log fire and stared into the flames for a moment. Then she glanced along the mantelpiece at the row of framed photographs, but they didn't interest her, and neither did the paintings on the wall, nor the shelves of books and knick-knacks in the corner. Now her eyes scanned the room for a television, but there wasn't one. There was a magazine lying open on the sofa beside her and she picked it up and desultorily began to flick through the pages. There were no fashion spreads, no media gossip, just page after page of animals. She stopped at a picture of playful badgers and read the caption: *Badgers living on top of a proposed development are being lured to new setts with peanut butter sandwiches. They usually eat earthworms, but are partial to peanuts. 'Badgers have very fixed ideas and you have to encourage them to move,' says a spokeswoman from the National Federation of Badger Groups.* Peri rifled through the pages to find out what she was reading. On the front cover there was a picture of a deer and the words *Wildlife Conservation.* In disgust, she threw the magazine onto the floor and gazed into the fire.

When Hamish jumped up onto her lap, she began to stroke him, feeling his purring chest against her knee, and still she could hear Mrs Craig in the kitchen chattering on about that man. What a bore! She got up, holding Hamish under one arm, and went over and closed the door, shutting out the noise. Then she sat back down again and yawned widely, gazing, as if in a dream, into the crackling flames and feeling her eyelids grow heavy with sleep. There was no way she was going to be able to stay awake long enough to telephone Mags, and anyway she had no idea what time the others would be going to bed. No, she would have to wait until tomorrow. Maybe it was for the best, she decided, because, with a tummy full of hot food, and with the warmth from the crackling fire and the purring cat against her knee and her utter, utter tiredness, she couldn't muster any fury now even if she tried.

'Well, sweetie,' she whispered to Hamish. 'I've managed to survive the first day.' She yawned. 'Only five more to go.'

Chapter Four

Peri awoke to a knock at the door. At first she was confused, disorientated, rubbing a hand across her face and feeling the tip of her nose icy cold. There was the sound of crockery rattling on a tray. Someone was coming into the room.

'Good morning.' It was a woman's voice. A cheerful Scottish voice.

With her eyes becoming accustomed to the gloom, Peri could see that it was the woman – the woman from the previous day. Struggling to sit up, she looked around, feeling a sickening dread settling upon her chest. She was still here! And there was that musty smell again. Unbidden, a distant memory flashed across her brain . . .

. . . eyes opening, seeing the row of lampshades along the ceiling, seeing the row of beds along the wall, seeing the row of sleeping heads . . . And then that feeling of sick dread as she realised that she was back where she had started. And always that musty smell.

'Did you sleep well?' The woman was putting a tray on the bedside table.

'Yeah,' Peri murmured listlessly, pulling the eiderdown up around her shoulders and knowing that another dreary day lay ahead. She tried to whip up enthusiasm by casting her thoughts forward to Saturday, to the Awards ceremony, but this time it didn't work. Nothing could penetrate this fog of depression.

The woman was smiling brightly. 'Here's a cup of camomile

tea and a bite of toast. I'll have porridge and sausages ready for you when you come doon the stairs.'

'No thanks,' Peri said quietly. 'I'm not hungry.'

'Are you sure?' The woman looked shocked. 'You're going to be out in that cold all day – you've got tae eat something.'

Peri stared at the daylight filtering through the flower-patterned curtains. 'I'll be okay.'

The woman clicked her tongue. 'It's too cold for you to be standing about all day, anyway. I don't know what your boss is thinking of.' She switched on the fan heater and opened the curtains. 'Have you brought some thermals with you?'

'No.' Peri wasn't interested in thermals, she just wanted to curl up under the eiderdown and pretend the world had gone away.

'Well, I've a spare vest and long-johns you can borrow,' the woman said briskly, turning to the dressing table and opening a drawer. 'They'll fit you if you tighten the draw-strings.' She came towards Peri carrying something woolly and soft-looking, smelling of lavender. 'Here ye go.' She must have noticed Peri's expression, because she added, 'They might not look very glamorous but they will keep you warm. I wear mine right through tae April.'

Peri lifted her hand and took them from her. What did it matter, anyway? she thought miserably, staring down at them.

Mrs Craig slowly sat down on the edge of the bed. 'Och, lassie, you're no' very happy tae be here, are you?' she asked gently.

This sudden and unexpected kindness made Peri want to fall into her arms and weep, but instead she shook her head, keeping her eyes downcast.

'It's only for a few more days and the time will go soon enough.'

Peri nodded.

Mrs Craig tutted. 'I cannae understand why your boss wants to come here at this time of year, anyway. It's bitter, bitter cold – and that wind! Especially on high ground.'

She shuddered. 'I can imagine you're not best pleased with him.'

With her lips pressed tightly shut, Peri looked up and shook her head. The woman was studying her with kind, thoughtful eyes and then, suddenly, she smiled, creasing up all the lines around her eyes. 'What an idiot he is, eh?'

To Peri's surprise, she found herself smiling too.

This seemed to satisfy the woman. 'Good girl.' She patted Peri's hand and stood up. 'I want you to know that I gave Douglas a good talking-to last night. There was no excuse for him throwing you over his shoulder like that. The great ox! I told him that it's bad enough you having tae bide in a place like this, without him behaving the way he did.'

Peri's sadness was promptly swept away. At the mention of the man's name, she was filled with furious indignation but this was quickly replaced by a surge of triumph. So, he'd got into trouble – *good!* That would teach him! Aware of the long-johns in her hands, she held them up at arm's length to study them. They looked ridiculous! The woman couldn't be serious.

Mrs Craig began to walk to the door. 'I'll be down in the kitchen if you need me.' She turned in the doorway and spoke with mock severity, pointing a stern finger at the long-johns. 'Mind you wear those breeks!'

Peri smiled again. 'Okay. Okay.' She was beginning to like Mrs Craig and the way she fussed – just like a mother would. When the door had closed, Peri sipped her tea and gazed out of the window, once more feeling the dread of the coming day. It was windy outside. She could see the cloud shadows racing swiftly across the purple hills, chasing one another before disappearing over the tops of the mountains. As if mesmerised, she watched the clouds in the sky, billowing and swirling, spreading and folding, and with them went her thoughts . . .

. . . she is looking down the empty street, straining to hear once more the sound of clicking heels but there is only silence. 'Come on,' Aunty Doris says to her, squeezing her hand. 'Let's go and put a pie in the oven.' But she shakes her head, slipping her hand free so that

she can stay and wait. She waits and waits but the street lies desolate and bare, refusing to give her what she wants. Then she realises what she has to do. She looks down at the little teddy bear in her hand and understands why her mother has given it to her; it's because she's got to look after him now, and cuddle him when he is scared and wipe away his tears . . .

Quickly, Peri swung out of bed, pushing away the memory, angry at herself for allowing it to intrude. She couldn't afford to think about the past – ever – because it weakened her confidence, making her feel grey and ugly inside, dragging her down, down, into suffocating depression. She had to keep her mind on the future and never look back. That was her policy and she *had* to stick to it. With her teeth chattering, she threw on her dressing gown and tied it tightly, rubbing her arms to keep herself warm.

'Peri?' It was Otto, tapping on the door.

'Come in,' she answered quickly, grateful for the intrusion. Now she was anxious for work. Anything, anything, so long as it kept her one step ahead of the memories.

'Did you sleep well?' he asked with his arms full of clothes.

'Yeah, great,' she answered, forcing a cheerful note into her voice. She noticed that his eyes looked puffy as if from lack of sleep, but she didn't care. Why should she be the only one to suffer?

'Good.' He spread the clothes across the bed. 'Helmut would like to start work as soon as you are ready. And he would ask you not to brush your hair for this shot.'

Oh, no! She'd forgotten about all that. This was going to be one awful bloody day – she just knew it. She would take a Prozac. No! she decided firmly. She would *not* take a Prozac. This wasn't going to beat her! She would simply close off her mind to everything and simply go through the motions, forcing herself to think ahead, to the Film Awards, to Igor de Vere's dress, to sparkling diamonds and satin shoes. And when the Awards ceremony is over, she thought grimly, I will hold up my glass of champagne and toast myself, remembering this moment and knowing that it is all far, far behind me. Another bad memory to add to the rest.

'—and wear both belts.' Fussing and frowning, Otto was explaining in which order to put on the clothes and which accessories to wear. 'It's going to be a long day today,' he added. 'We shall be working outside for most of the morning and tonight we shall be going to a local bar to shoot a San Lorenzo evening dress. Then you will be required to wear full make-up.'

Peri raised her eyebrows questioningly.

'It's just a one-off,' Otto explained. 'Helmut is doing it as a favour for San Lorenzo. They are good friends.'

Peri sighed. 'Which means that I'm still expected to spend the rest of the time looking like a New Age traveller?'

'I am afraid so – but put your trust in Helmut – he has vision. His ideas disturb and evolve what is fashionable. By the start of next season, every woman will want to be you.' He walked to the door. 'We will be down in the yard when you are ready.'

'Okay.' Peri felt a glimmer of excitement as she imagined what it would be like, knowing that every woman would want to be *her*. And what would Saffron think about it? Ha! With a surge of enthusiasm, Peri went to pick up the first article of clothing from the bed, but stopped, realising that she still held Mrs Craig's vest and long-johns in her hand. She shrugged her shoulders. 'Why not?' she muttered and took off her dressing gown and silk pyjamas, before slipping the vest over her head. It would be a shame, she thought wryly, for me to catch pneumonia seven days before the Awards. The long-johns were too loose, so she gathered up the waistline with the drawstrings, avoiding the temptation to look at herself in the mirror. 'I must look pitiful.' Next she put on the long chain-mail dress, a leather tunic and a hooded cloak, putting her feet into the ugly brown boots which she had been wearing the previous afternoon. 'I presume I'm allowed to brush my teeth,' she murmured, clumping into the bathroom with her toothbrush and paste, and making a determined effort not to catch sight of herself in the mirror.

When she came out into the yard, Helmut was setting up the camera in front of the rusty old car she had noticed the day before. He clapped his hands as she approached him. 'Good. Peri. Good. You look perfect.'

Perfect! she thought wryly. Perfect for what? Squatting in a flat in Brixton? It was humiliating to have to look like this. Horrid. And, without make-up, she felt somehow naked and vulnerable. It was hard to imagine that *any* woman would want to look the way she did at that moment.

'The natural look suits you,' Helmut assured her. 'You do not need make-up.'

'Thank you.' She tried to smile, and then looked away, not wanting him to see the anger in her eyes. Why should this one man dictate fashion? And why did silly women follow him like sheep?

'Now,' Helmut said. 'I want you to get up on the bonnet of the car.'

Otto had a stool ready, holding out a hand to help her. She took his hand and clambered up, feeling the icy cold metal against her fingers, and as she settled into position, Otto handed her a little cushion to sit on. Helmut arranged her skirts, then, satisfied, he stepped back and took a polaroid photograph, studying it thoughtfully.

Meanwhile, Peri studied the camera. It was too close for her liking. She watched as Helmut put the photograph into his pocket and moved the tripod a few feet back, towards the house. That's better, Peri thought, satisfied, but a few more feet would be even better.

'One more polaroid,' Helmut called out.

She set her face towards the camera for yet another test photograph. Then she waited. Like any other shoot, there was always this long drawn-out start while the photographer hummed and hawed, rubbed his chin, moved the tripod one inch to the right, then moved the tripod two inches to the left.

Peri yawned and looked up at the house. Above the rooftop, the sun shone brightly and she closed her eyes and lifted her face to it, savouring its tepid warmth and feeling some of her anger and resentment melt away. With every breath, she could feel the cold air in her nostrils, pure and fresh, invigorating. Impulsively, she took a mighty breath, filling her lungs, but all at once the oxygen hit her brain and sent her reeling and just in time she put out a hand and stopped herself from falling off the car.

'*Gut, näher bringen,*' Helmut called out as Otto shifted the reflector towards the car.

Feeling slightly giddy, Peri watched them for a moment, steadying her eyes, and then she looked away. The far corner of the yard still lay in deep shadow, the cobblestones frosted over where the sun had not yet reached. From the great chimney a thread of smoke curled up into the still blue sky and, from close at hand, came the harsh caw-caw screech of a bird, the sound of it cutting through the silence. Turning slightly, she could see clouds of mist clinging to the row of evergreen bushes against the wall, and, up on the topmost branches, hung droplets of water, quivering and sparkling in the sunshine. Over on the other side of the wall, the sun bathed the meadow, casting a veil of shimmering silk across the dewy grass. Clouds of vapour rose up from the ground as if the earth were steaming, making her think of the exhaust fumes floating low above the traffic crawling through Fulham on a bright and frosty morning. London. There was nothing quite like that sharp, acrid smell of carbon dioxide to remind her that she was right in the centre of life, caught up in the excitement of the hustle and bustle and missing none of the action. She tried to think what she would be doing at that moment. Saturday morning . . . ? Well, she would certainly be in bed at this time, probably drinking fresh orange juice, eating sliced kiwi fruit and watching something on cable. Then, she would get . . .

Suddenly, she heard the sound of scraping metal, and with mild curiosity she turned to see what it was.

A man had come into the yard, and, with his back to her, was shutting the gate behind him. Then she saw the black and white dog. It was the same dog from the previous day, which meant . . . ! She stiffened, ready for battle.

The man was turning and now he smiled at her. 'Good morning, Peri.' His teeth looked white against his weatherbeaten skin and his thick curly hair shone a reddish-brown in the sunshine.

She glared at him. Why was he grinning at her like that? As if she were his friend! She turned away and stared out across the meadow, listening to Helmut and Otto greeting him warmly. From the corner of her eye, she could see him coming towards her.

'Are we making you comfortable?' he asked, standing before her.

Slowly, she turned to him, and found herself looking into a pair of sparkling blue eyes. A part of her brain registered that he was handsome, but she pushed this traitorous thought aside. 'Where?' she snapped. 'Here?' She jerked her chin at the roof of the car and then towards the house. 'Or in *there?*'

He barked out a laugh, throwing his head back and she saw again the flash of strong white teeth. The stupid man thinks I'm being amusing, she thought acidly.

'No, no,' he said. 'I mean, in the house.'

'I think I might survive,' she answered coldly, smarting at the humiliation of what he had done to her the previous day. Why didn't he just piss off? She didn't like the way he was staring at her. God! how she wished that she didn't look so ugly. How could she act superior looking like *this?*

'If there is anything you need, please don't hesitate to ask me.' He held up towards her a tiny bunch of snowdrops. 'This is to apologise for my behaviour yesterday. I thought you were . . . um . . . someone else. I hope you can forgive me.'

She stared at the snowdrops, resisting the urge to snatch them from his hand, throw them on the ground and grind them into the dirt with her heel; she didn't have that luxury because

Helmut was watching. 'Thank you,' she murmured, taking them from him and putting them on her lap. Snowdrops! she thought incredulously. What is this? Some fucking fairytale?

'I'm going in to make myself a hot drink. Would you like one?'

'No, thank you, Donald.' This forced politeness was giving her a headache.

'My name's not Donald. It's Douglas.'

She stared at him blankly. 'Oh.' Over his shoulder she saw Helmut and Otto moving back towards the gate, discussing something beyond it. Now was her chance. 'I'm surprised you're not called Attila,' she said scornfully, keeping her voice low and curling her lip as she eyed him from his boots up to his face. 'Attila the Hun.'

'Hey!' he said, looking at her closely. 'I've said I'm sorry. Can't we forget about yesterday?'

'No!' she hissed. 'I will never forget about *yesterday!*' Alerted to the sight of Helmut and Otto returning to within earshot as they resumed their positions by the camera, she abruptly smiled and continued in a loud and cheerful voice: 'It's been lovely chatting to you, Donald, but if you will excuse me, I think it's time I got back to work. Perhaps you have a field to dig, or something.'

There was nothing more that the man could say, now that Helmut had begun to issue instructions, so, with an undecided look, he moved away. But the black and white mongrel remained sitting, staring up at her with his long pink tongue lolling down from between two pointed teeth, his tail swishing the ground as if he, too, presumed she was a friend. What a joke! She could just imagine that mangy, matted fur crawing with lice. Ugh! She flicked a hand at him. 'Shoo. Shoo.' The dog didn't move but continued to wag his tail, looking up at her as if he had found a new playmate. 'My God,' Peri muttered under her breath. 'He's as stupid as his master.'

'Come on, Bruce,' the man called, and, immediately the dog was up and following him. 'I'll be back out in about an hour,' the man said to Helmut and made towards the house, the dog close at his heels.

Peri groaned. She didn't want that Neanderthal and his dog hanging about her. She turned to Helmut. 'Is he going to be working with us?'

'Douglas?'

She nodded.

'Oh, yes. He will be indispensable.'

Peri tried not to frown. Obviously, she wouldn't be able to get rid of the man. But the dog? 'Um . . . Helmut?' she asked sweetly. 'As you know, I don't like dogs, so, when Douglas returns can you tell him to keep his dog away from me? Shut it up in a kennel or something?'

'Yes, sure.' Helmut moved the tripod a few inches. 'But I can assure you that the dog is completely harmless.'

'Maybe so, but I would be grateful if you would tell him.'

'Sure,' Helmut said absent-mindedly, seeming more preoccupied with his camera than with her request. 'I would like you to move closer to the edge. Yes. Good.'

For an hour they worked smoothly. One minute she was posing by the car, and in the next she was in the car, then finally she was back up on the roof and thankful for the little pillow under her bottom. All the while Helmut gave precise instructions while Peri listened carefully, concentrating on the effect he was trying to achieve. But, gradually her hands became colder and colder until all she could think about was the pain in her fingertips and the drip from her nose.

Then Douglas appeared. 'Mrs Craig has put a snack out on the table when you're ready,' he informed them, coming across the yard to join them. The dog padded along beside him, happily wagging its tail and licking Helmut's hand as he stopped to stroke it.

'We are nearly finished here,' Helmut told him, going down on one knee to ruffle the dog's ears. 'And Peri has asked me to tell you that she doesn't like dogs and would be grateful if you would keep Bruce away from her.'

'Yes, fine,' Douglas said pleasantly, nodding to Peri. 'No problem.'

Peri scowled. That was not what she wanted. 'Actually,' she said, 'I feel rather uncomfortable with it being so near. Could you please take it away?'

'You don't have to worry about Bruce,' Douglas said pleasantly. 'He's a real softie – wouldn't harm a fly.'

Was this stupid man deliberately trying to antagonise her? 'I'm sure he is,' she replied coldly. 'But I don't want to have to look at him, so could you please get rid of him?' She rolled her hand in the air. 'Lock him in a cupboard or something.'

Douglas had stopped smiling. Now he was looking at her through narrowed eyes, his face grim. 'I will tell Bruce to keep away from you but I will not lock him in a cupboard.'

'Why not?' she demanded. 'It's only a dog and if it's making me unhappy you should do as I say!'

'Bruce is not just any dog,' Douglas said coldly. 'He is my friend, my helper. This is his home and you have no right to come here and order me to lock him away.'

She couldn't believe what she was hearing! Didn't he realise who he was talking to? 'How dare you . . . ?' Incredulity prevented her from saying more. She looked to Helmut for support but he just shrugged helplessly. It was unbelievable that they were not doing what she wanted. Right! she thought indignantly, let's see if my extortionately expensive acting classes have been worth it. Concentrating hard and remembering all that she had been taught, she relaxed her face muscles and pressed her lips together, furrowing her brow as if on the edge of tears. 'I'm sorry, Helmut,' she burst out. 'It's just that I'm terrified of dogs – ever since I was attacked by an Alsatian when I was a little girl.' Pressing a hand over her eyes, she hung her head, allowing a tiny almost-imperceptible sob to escape.

The lie worked instantly. The three men rushed straight over. 'I'm sorry,' Douglas said, sounding mortified. 'I didn't realise. Why didn't you say? I'll go and shut Bruce in the back room immediately.'

'Oh, Helmut, I'm sorry to be such a nuisance,' she wailed softly.

'You're not being a nuisance,' Douglas insisted. 'We just didn't realise.'

As Otto patted her hand, Helmut gave her his handkerchief and said, 'I didn't know you were frightened by dogs.'

Peering through her fingers, she could see Douglas leading the dog into the house. 'It's the look in that dog's eyes,' she whimpered, taking the handkerchief and blowing her nose. She felt wonderfully clever. 'I just knew I couldn't trust it.'

'I know, I know,' Otto said soothingly. 'The dog has gone now, so you do not need to worry.'

She could have stopped acting, now that the dog was gone, but she continued to sniff, enjoying all the attention and wanting to making the most of it.

'We will take a rest now,' Helmut said after a moment. 'There's something I need to discuss with you – an idea I have. And I would like to have your opinion.' As he put out a hand to help her down from the car roof, Douglas was already striding back across the yard towards them. 'Let me help you,' Douglas offered, and in the next minute he had put his hands around her waist and had swung her effortlessly down in front of him.

Briefly, she had caught the smell of woodsmoke from his jacket. 'You didn't have to do that,' she said icily, furious that he had had the audacity to touch her yet again. Without looking at him, she straightened her cloak then brushed it with her hand as if brushing off all traces of him. Then she followed Otto across the yard and into the house. Who the hell did that man think he was? How dare he lay his hands on her?

All thoughts of him swiftly evaporated as she entered the kitchen. It was so warm, deliriously warm, making her cold cheeks and fingers tingle, and the air was filled with the smells of baking bread and cinnamon. She didn't want to go back out into the cold. She wanted to stay *here!*

'There's a hot drink fer you,' Mrs Craig said, handing her a cup of camomile tea. 'Would you like some fruit cake?'

Peri pressed her hands around her cup, grateful for the soothing warmth penetrating her flesh, and glancing at the fruit cake and sandwiches laid out on the table. 'No, thanks,' she replied. In the corner by the stove stood the battered armchair covered in the woollen patchwork blanket, looking so warm, so cosy, that she longed to curl up in it and order everyone to go away. Instead, she sat on a hard wooden chair at the kitchen table, waiting for Helmut's instructions.

Mrs Craig offered her a banana, an egg sandwich, a bag of crisps, but Peri refused them all. It was as if the woman was trying to fatten her up. After the gigantic meal the previous night, Peri had discovered that her stomach was positively bulging, so she had vowed not to eat anything until that evening.

'I am very pleased with this morning's work,' Helmut told her, sitting down at the opposite end of the table. 'And I have a wonderful idea for the next shot, but –' he put his head to one side – 'I will need your co-operation. Now Otto has informed me that your agent – for some reason – has withheld information from you . . .' He paused, slightly embarrassed, and waited for her response.

'Oh, no, no,' she lied quickly. 'It's simply a breakdown in communications. I've just been so busy, dashing here and there.' She rolled her hands in the air and made a wry face, but at the same time she was beginning to feel slightly uneasy. Why was Helmut looking so stern?

He nodded solemnly. 'I see.'

Peri couldn't tell if he believed her or not. 'Well, it doesn't matter now,' she said gaily. 'We're here and everything's fine.' She smiled at him, coaxing him to smile again, wanting to dissolve this sudden tension in the air.

But he didn't smile. 'Maybe,' he said, spooning sugar into his coffee and stirring it. 'I have had great difficulty in searching for a location such as this, but it is not only the location that is necessary for what I want.' He put the spoon on the table and looked at her. 'I wanted to find a special kind of bird, something unusual, something that would strike the imagination, and I have found it here.' He picked up his mug of coffee and took a sip.

A bird? Peri's brain raced. Otto had told her something about a bird. When they were in the car. On the way here. What was it? What did he call it? – a ranter? – a rapet? – raptor! That was it! 'Do you mean the raptor?' she said nonchalantly, picking up her mug of tea and blowing across its surface.

Helmut beamed. 'Ah, you know! Good!' He sounded relieved. 'So, what do you think?'

She shrugged. 'Fine.' What was there to think? She would hardly see the thing if it was going to be flapping about above her head.

'Good. Good.' The tension which had hovered above the kitchen table suddenly cleared. 'It will be a magnificent photograph. My trademark for future generations. Imagine it . . .' He spread out his fingers in front of his face, his eyes glazed and far-seeing. 'You are standing alone, high on a mountain with a backdrop of storm clouds, your cape blowing back in the wind, a falconer's glove on your hand and a falcon – wild and savage – gripping onto that glove.' His words trailed away into the silence and then, snapping out of his reverie, he smiled triumphantly at Peri.

Peri stared at him. In the silence, she heard a clock ticking – tick-tock, tick-tock, tick-tock, tick-tock – and from outside the window came the sound of a twig scratching across the glass. She tried to absorb what Helmut had told her, to make a picture of it in her mind, but she couldn't. He was telling her that a wild and savage bird was going to sit on her. That was impossible. A mistake. But as she stared at him, she had a dreadful feeling that this was not a mistake. But he couldn't force her – could he? And if she refused, would he get angry? Would he cancel the job? Get someone else? Oh, God, no! But she couldn't do what he was asking of her. Her heart thudded and her throat was tight, as if at any moment she would suffocate. But she didn't have to do it. She could get out of it. How bad would it be if she lost the job? She just had to stop this buzzing in her brain . . . to think clearly . . . work it all out.

Helmut was smiling up at the housekeeper. 'May I please have a piece of your delicious fruit cake, Mrs Craig?' he asked.

Peri cleared her throat. 'Did Mags – my agent – did she, er, think this was a good idea?'

'Oh, yes,' Helmut said, reaching forward to take a slice of fruit cake from a plate.

She felt her heart thud. 'That's good,' she murmured, looking down at her tea so that no one could see the anger in her eyes. The bitch! *She had known all along!* On rapid reflection, the enormity of Mags's betrayal hit her, overwhelming her with fury. Her immediate impulse was to jump up and smash the plates and cups against the wall, to pick up the axe that was lying by the door and hurl it into the sideboard; but instead she could only sit calmly and stare into her tea.

Mrs Craig began to chat to Douglas as she sliced a carving knife through a loaf of bread, while on the other side of the table Helmut and Otto were chatting easily, knowing that the crisis was over and that everything would now go according to plan. They're all too stupid and ignorant to have any idea how I feel, Peri thought angrily. She picked up a teaspoon and began to turn it around and around in her hand, thinking hard. In her mind's eye she could see Mags, leaning forward, her face earnest and concerned, warning her to be co-operative, to be pleasant. 'It doesn't matter if he wants to use a rhinoceros,' Mags had said. 'This is your chance to make the big league.' So – Peri thought with calm resignation – *this* is what it was all about.

'Are you sure you don't want a piece of fruit cake?' Mrs Craig asked her again. 'It's full of fruit and nuts.'

Without looking up from her teaspoon, Peri shook her head. She wanted time, time to think about Mags and all the horrible vindictive things that she would say to her, but she didn't have that time – not yet. She must concentrate on the present, find out what lay in store, prepare herself. Maybe it wasn't as bad as it seemed. First there were questions to be asked, but she didn't know where to begin. 'How . . . um . . . big is it?'

'What?' Helmut asked. 'The falcon?'

She nodded.

'Well . . .' He brushed a cake crumb from his lips and held out his hands, as if measuring an invisible object in front of him. Douglas was now doing the same, but the distance between his hands was less than the distance between Helmut's.

'About sixty centimetres,' Helmut decided reasonably.

Douglas eyed the distance between Helmut's hands. 'No, no,' he said. 'More like fifty.'

Peri nodded calmly but her brain spun. The bird was gigantic! She could feel fear uncurling, like a snake, in the pit of her stomach. 'I'm not quite sure what you want me to do with this . . . this bird,' she said quietly.

'You need only to hold it – that is all,' Helmut assured her. 'But first, Douglas will take you up to the aviary and introduce you. He is the expert and he will show you what to do.'

She transferred her gaze to Douglas and saw him cheerfully nodding, as if he was in fact about to take her on a jolly spree. Could he sense her fear? And if he did, was he looking forward to the prospect of seeing her suffer? Maybe he was some psycho who hated women. Looking at him, he seemed quite normal, so she couldn't tell . . .

'Now, Peri,' Helmut was saying as he began to spread butter over his cake. 'Are you eating anything?'

She shook her head. 'No.'

'There's no time to lose. Douglas can take you up now.' He put his knife on the side of his plate and looked at her with a smile. 'You will be in good hands, I assure you.'

She stood up and walked to the door. There was nothing else she could do.

'Have you done anything like this before?' Douglas asked pleasantly, opening the gate to let her pass through.

'Of course not!' she snapped. He was such a moron. 'Do

I look the type to walk around with a *buzzard* perched on my arm?'

He chuckled and it made her want to spit at him. She hated him. She hated Helmut. She hated Mags. She hated everyone. Why was this happening to her? She could feel herself wound up tight, ready to snap.

'Tell me if I'm wrong,' he began gently. 'But I got the impression back there that you're not too happy about this.'

'Happy?' she cried wildly, staring in amazement. 'Happy? Of course I'm not *happy!*'

'There's nothing to be afraid of, you know.'

Peri suddenly stopped in her tracks and glared up at him. 'This bird is wild, right?'

Douglas nodded, seeming bewildered by her attack. 'That's right.'

'This bird eats live animals – *right?*'

Douglas nodded. 'Yes.'

'And in a couple of minutes I am going to be eyeball to eyeball with this fucking . . . *eagle* . . . and you're telling me not to be afraid!' She snorted with contempt at his stupidity and walked on, shaking her head in disbelief.

Douglas chuckled again and fell into step beside her. 'Well, I must say, I've never heard such colourful language coming from a lassie before.'

'Oh, *really*? I'm surprised.' Now that she was alone with this man, there was no reason for her to pretend to be nice.

'Everything will be fine, just fine,' Douglas assured her.

'Everything will be just fine,' Peri mimicked. 'That's what my agent told me and now look what's happened!' She stopped and swung out her arms to the world. 'I'm stuck out here in . . . in . . . in God knows where, frozen to the bone and waiting to have my eyeballs plucked out by some vicious bird!'

Douglas grinned down at her. 'Och, don't be so dramatic.' He began to walk on. 'You'll survive, don't worry.'

He had spoken impatiently, which made it quite clear to her that he was belittling her fears and trying to make her seem like some neurotic female. In retaliation, she screwed up her face into an ugly grimace and sneered at his back. 'I hate you!' she muttered softly, so softly that he couldn't hear, but loud enough for her to get the satisfaction of hearing the words herself.

'I want to apologise again for yesterday,' Douglas told her, pausing to wait for her to catch up. 'I thought you were . . . a . . . trespasser. We usually get them about this time of year.'

'I would have thought it blatantly obvious, to anyone with a brain in their head, who I was.'

'Are you kidding?' he exclaimed. 'I don't know where you got those clothes from but I wouldn't have thought a model from London would be wearing them.'

'Well – for your information – they're designer clothes that Helmut chose to bring, and that outfit I was wearing would cost at least five thousand pounds.'

'No!'

'Yes!'

'I've got better-looking clothes in the bottom of the hall cupboard.'

'It's not the same!'

'Oh, really? Well, tell me,' he said, gesturing to her clothes. 'Would you go out on the town wearing that lot?'

She looked down at herself. She wanted to say 'yes' to prove a point, but at the same time she had a clear and vivid image of herself walking into Annabel's looking like this, and it was not difficult to imagine the horrified expressions on those snooty-nosed faces! She nearly smiled at the thought of it. 'Actually . . . um . . . no, I suppose I wouldn't. But it doesn't mean to say they're not fashionable.'

Douglas shook his head sternly. 'If I went tae pick up a lassie and she came to the door looking the way you do, I would tell her not to be so daft and go away in and get changed!'

His pompous indigation was so silly that it seemed to tickle something inside her, and suddenly she found herself smiling.

'You should smile more often,' Douglas said earnestly. 'It suits you.'

She immediately stopped. 'Thanks,' she replied sarcastically. Why had she let herself smile? It would only make him think that he could amuse her.

'Do you see down there?' he said, pointing away to the distance. 'There's a . . .'

He had begun to tell her something but she wasn't listening. She had come to a halt and now looked around. They were halfway up the hillside. High enough, she decided, swiftly putting a hand into her pocket and taking out her mobile. This was it! 'Could you leave me alone,' she told Douglas. 'I need to make a private call.'

'Sure.'

She watched him walk over to a fallen tree and sit down. Satisfied that he was far enough away, she began to jab her finger down on the buttons, her anger growing with each number as she focused, once more, on Mags and her deceitful betrayal. As soon as she finished dialling, she slammed the phone against her ear and waited, conscious now of her rapid breathing and flushed cheeks. 'Come on! Come on!' she muttered impatiently.

Margaret-Anne 'Mags' Stanwick smiled benignly at the row of beautiful girls sitting against the wall with their brand-new portfolios clutched to their flat chests, their eyes wide and uncertain. God, they're getting younger by the minute, she thought, walking past with a bag of croissants cradled in her arms. She had started the agency at thirty and, now, at fifty-something, this daily parade of youth was beginning to make her feel old, as if somehow she were being left behind. But she wasn't jealous of their youth. No. Youth was a burden of insecurities, uncertainties, vulnerability. No, she was happy the way she was: the Queen Bee, elegant and rich, manipulator of destinies, ruler of a small but powerful empire.

With a nudge of her shoulder, she pushed open the door and entered into the inner sanctum of that empire. Now she could hear the ringing of telephones, the voices of her bookers – perfectly modulated and efficient – the hum of the fax, the pop-pop of the percolator, the smell of Cabochard perfume and Puerto Rican coffee beans. She smiled complacently. This was her creation: a sophisticated machine, well-oiled in the hands of hard-nosed professionals, nurturing and bringing to flower the shy and lanky girls who came through the door.

She went into the kitchenette and dumped the carrier bag on the table, taking out a croissant. Then she took a cup and saucer from the cupboard and went out to the percolator, waving her croissant in greeting at Tula who sat at her desk with the telephone to her ear. Humming softly, Mags poured coffee into her cup. Now that she was in the office, her brain was set in work mode, listing out the calls she had to make, the invoices she had to sign, the girls she had to intervew, lunch dates she had to fix, worldwide buyouts, time limitations, usages and billboard deals.

'Did you get me a pain au chocolat?' It was Tula, brushing past her and into the kitchenette.

'They sold out.'

'Typical!' Tula re-emerged, eating a croissant. 'Peri still hasn't phoned.'

'I didn't think she would,' Mags said, picking up her cup of coffee and leading the way over to her desk. 'Okay, she would have got a shock – sure – but then she would have realised that there was no alternative but to bite the bullet.'

'Mmm,' Tula murmured doubtfully. 'I hope so.'

'It will be fine.' Mags put her cup and saucer on her desk, unbuttoned her silk jacket and draped it over the back of her chair. 'Don't forget, she's had a taste of what it's like to hit rock bottom, so now she's going to be only too desperate to claw herself back up.'

'I suppose you're right. But if she's going to be as big as we think she is, we're going to have to handle her a lot more carefully.'

'I will,' Mags insisted. '*After* she's completed this job.'

'Well, I'm glad I'm not the one who has to talk to her when she *does* phone.'

Mags laughed at Tula's emphatic declaration. 'She won't phone. After all, if she was going to call, she would have done it by now.' She drew a hard-backed folder towards her across the desk and opened it, scanning the sheets of paper within. 'But I might give her a call tomorrow.' As she spoke, her private telephone shrilled and she casually picked it up and put it to her ear. 'Hello. Mags speaking.' There was silence. 'Hello?' she repeated, slightly impatiently now. She could hear rapid breathing and then a cold, measured voice said: 'Hello.' It sounded like a threat. 'Who *is* this?' Mags demanded.

'Fucking Boadicea!'

'Oh, Peri! It's *you!*' Although taken off balance, Mags was quick to put a note of delight in her voice. 'How nice. I was just about to call you. Everything going okay?'

Peri gave a nasty laugh. '*You* are asking *me* if everything's going okay?' Each word was measured, weighted with incredulity.

'Well – yes.' Mags glanced up to see Tula sitting on the edge of the desk, sliding a perfectly manicured fingernail sharply across her throat and grimacing.

'Yeah,' Peri said, switching to a friendly voice. 'Everything's going okay, apart from one or two minor upsets – you know, the usual thing: sleeping in a freezing hovel miles from civilisation, being attacked by a vicious dog, living under the same roof as the village idiot, who – by the way – has a nasty habit of abducting females . . .'

Mags gasped. 'No!' Was this true? What the hell was happening up there?

'. . . that I'm not allowed to wear make-up and, therefore, I look like the Kensington bag-lady on a bad day, and in fact things are *so* okay that I'm just about to get my face ripped apart by some eagle.'

'Eagle?' Mags froze. Helmut Reuther didn't say anything about an eagle! 'He didn't say anything about an eagle,' she said hurriedly. 'He said it was a falcon . . . a small raptor.'

'So you *knew!*'

'Well . . . yes . . . but he didn't say anything about an eagle. He said it would be a falcon.'

'What's the difference!' Peri screamed. 'It's still going to rip my face apart.'

'There's a big difference. A *very* big difference. Just tell me,' she said slowly but firmly, 'is it an eagle or a falcon?' She held her breath and waited.

After a moment's silence, Peri answered sulkily, 'A falcon.'

Mags released her breath. Evidently Peri was exaggerating everything that was happening to her. 'Thank goodness for that!'

'What?'

'Listen, Peri, there's nothing to worry about. Some people even keep them as pets.'

'*Pets?* Maybe Rambo keeps them as pets but I'm not going to go anywhere near one in this lifetime.'

'Have you seen it?'

'No – but I don't have to.'

'Let me speak to the handler.'

'The what?'

'The handler. Helmut told me there would be someone qualified to look after you. Is there?'

'Well, I don't know.' Peri sounded unsure. 'There's this man with me . . .'

'Is he looking after you?'

'Um . . . I suppose he's meant to . . . yes.'

'Can I speak to this man?'

'But he's the village idiot.'

'Peri, can I *please* speak to him?' This girl could be *so* annoying!

Peri tutted rudely. 'All right.'

There was brief silence and then Mags heard Peri calling out to someone. 'Will you come here,' Peri shouted, 'My agent has to speak to you.'

The reply was muffled but Mags could hear every word of it. 'If you say please,' shouted a man's voice.

Immediately, Peri was back on the line, speaking furiously. 'He's not coming.'

Mags pressed her fingertips against her forehead, trying to ease the tension in her skull. 'Peri,' she said quietly. 'Just say "please" to the man.'

Peri tutted again. Silence. '*Please!*' Peri shouted out to the man, stretching the word with sarcasm.

Silence again. Mags looked up at Tula to see her raising her eyebrows in mock alarm and munching her croissant, evidently enjoying herself. Behind Tula, on the wall, was the photograph of Peri, green eyes seeming to stare right at her. Why hadn't Saffron got this job? she thought wearily. And why hadn't she got the Film Awards too? It would have been so much easier, . . . for everyone.

'Hello. Douglas MacLeod speaking.'

Mags was startled to hear such a clear and articulate voice, expecting from Peri's description to hear an incoherent mumble. 'Oh, hello. This is Margaret-Anne Stanwick – Peri's agent. Would you kindly tell me, in all honesty, if Peri will be in any danger with this bird?'

'No. None whatsoever. I can assure you that the bird has been well handled and poses no risk.'

Clearly this was not a village idiot. 'I am relieved to hear it,' she answered. 'You may be aware by now that Peri is not too happy with this assignment . . .' She broke off, listening to the deep chuckle on the other end of the line.

'Yes,' said the man. 'Peri has made her feelings known.'

Mags just adored the sound of this man's voice. It was so deep, so sexy, so Scottish. Mmmm. But did his appearance match his voice? Was he tall and strong, or thin and weedy? She just had to know. 'I am sure Peri will be perfectly safe in your hands,' she said, dropping her voice an octave.

'Aye. Don't you worry. I'm sure Peri will telephone you later tae tell you how she gets on and . . .'

'Mags!' It was Peri again. Evidently she had snatched the phone from the man's hand. 'So that's it – is it?'

'Listen, darling, the man says there's no danger and I believe him, so . . .'

'But he's the village—'

'Listen!' Mags cut her short, speaking sternly now because the sweet mummy voice was obviously not working. 'You want to be famous, don't you? You want to be a star? You want to be stinking rich, don't you?' She waited for Peri's reply.

'Yeah,' came a mumbled assent.

'Well, work with this bloody bird! You've got to do this for Helmut, especially as I told him you had agreed to do it. You can't back out of it now. Only this morning I was on the phone to the editor of *Hi!* and she says that if you can get even *one* transparency from Helmut, she'll use it on next month's cover. Think of it! This is make-or-break time, Peri. It's *your* decision. It's not just a question of *whether* you will do this shot, but how nice and agreeable you are in *doing* it.'

'But I don't want to get my face ripped apart.'

'You won't. Trust me.'

'But I want you to know that I'm not happy about any of this.'

'I know. I know,' Mags said soothingly. 'I have been deceitful but it's been necessary, hasn't it? Mm? I have only been thinking what is best for you.'

Silence.

'You wouldn't have accepted the job if you had known, would you?' Mags coaxed. 'Then you would have lost an opportunity of a lifetime. Darling, you need someone like Helmut, someone who will project you in a way that will catch and hold the world's attention.' Suddenly, she had a flash of inspiration. 'Of course, you don't have to do this, you know. You could come home and Saffron could take your place.'

'No!' Peri burst out, and then, as if realising that she had responded too violently, she continued in a calm voice. 'I'm not saying I'm not going to *do* the job – I'm just saying that I'm not *happy* about it.'

'I know. I know. I completely understand.'

'But I am not going to take any risks!'

Evidently Peri was taking her final chance to assert herself, but Mags had won. 'Of course not, darling,' she agreed. 'And if there's anything that might harm you, get on the phone to me immediately. I'm not having my favourite girl getting hurt. Okay?'

'Okay.'

'Look, Peri, I've got to go. I've got someone waiting on the other line. But call me later and tell me how you get on. Promise?'

'Yeah.'

She could hear the resentment in Peri's voice. 'Love you lots. *Ciao.*' She dropped the receiver into its cradle and slumped across her desk, putting her head in her arms. 'Give me a Prozac,' she groaned, and then on hearing Tula's giggle, she looked up.

'Ding ding,' Tula exclaimed in a deep, gruff voice. 'And at the end of Round One, Mags the Brute has beaten Peri the Prima Donna into the corner.' Tula smiled, standing up and brushing the crumbs from her skirt and into the wastepaper basket. 'The firm but gentle touch,' she said in her normal voice. 'You were good.'

'Was I?' Mags was pleased, suddenly feeling puffed up with cleverness. She had always prided herself on her powers of manipulation, and although she had never had children she knew she had a mother's natural instincts.

'I've been thinking,' Tula said, sauntering over to the wall of photographs, 'that Peri has got the right sort of personality to be a star. She's tough, self-centred and has the ego of a Hollywood star. She's going to shoot right to the top.'

'Let's hope so.' Mags watched as Tula thumbtacked a photograph of Saffron onto the green felt. It showed her outside La Scala in Milan holding a glass of champagne; it was a great photo, perfect for her next model card.

'Wouldn't you just love to be a fly on the wall?' Tula remarked.

'What do you mean?'

'Up there.' Tula jerked her head up to the ceiling. 'In Scotland. Seeing how Peri is handling the situation.'

'Well, actually, I would. But not for Peri's sake. I have just spoken to a man with the sexiest voice in the whole world and I would *love* to see what he looks like.'

Tula was taking down a photograph of Monica. 'He's probably got ginger whiskers sprouting from his ears,' she said, ripping the photograph in half and putting the pieces into a wastepaper bin. 'With bandy legs and a squint.'

Mags laughed. 'You're wrong. I just know it. But I can't help feeling sorry for him because Peri has obviously taken a dislike to him.'

'So – what's new?' Tula covered the empty space on the wall with a photograph of Avril, the new red-headed girl, pinning it securely with a thumbtack.

Mags watched in silence, an idea forming in her head. 'Listen, Tula, there's something I want you to do. Leave it for a couple of days and then phone Peri and tell her how much I care for her, remind her of everything I have done for her and say something along the lines of: "Mags has done so much for you and you just don't care. She worries about you and wants you to be happy but you don't seem to be grateful . . . blah, blah, blah." How does that sound?'

'Fine.' Tula agreed, heading over to the fax machine. 'Good idea.'

Mags idly shifted her gaze from Tula, and looked back at the wall of photographs, singling out the face of Peri and staring hard at it. 'You could have the world,' she murmured, 'if you would only do as I tell you.'

'She's actually meant to look after me! Can you *believe* it!' Peri thrust the mobile phone into her pocket and glared at Douglas. 'Yet all she cares about is her big fat commission! If I hadn't got this job, she would've dropped me like hot potato. It would be, *So sorry, Peri, but I have to let you go*.' Douglas didn't seem to be paying attention; with his arms folded across his chest, he was thoughtfully scuffing a rock with the toe of his boot. Well, she didn't care if he was listening or not; it was simply convenient to have someone to complain to.

Now he was studying her thoughtfully. 'Are you happy with what you do?'

'Of course I'm happy!' she snapped. She began to march on and then stopped and looked around, realising that she didn't know where she was marching to. 'Where's this bird?' she demanded.

'Over the brow of the hill,' he said, pointing. Then he put his hand behind her elbow to steer her in the right direction but she jerked her arm away. 'Jesus!' he exclaimed. 'You're like a bloody wild cat. Why are you being so hostile? I've apologised to you about yesterday, and you've told me what you think of me, so let's forget what happened and be friends.'

'Why?' Peri asked, walking in the direction he had pointed. 'Why should we be friends?'

Douglas hesitated and then quickened his pace to catch up with her. 'Well . . . er . . . well, if you don't want to be friends, it doesn't mean to say we've got to be enemies.'

Peri thought about it. 'Why do we have to be *anything* to each other? I don't know you. You don't know me. So let's leave it at that.' She was aware that he was looking at her now, but she refused to meet his eyes.

Douglas perservered: 'If we're going to be working together for the next week, we might as well be friendly towards each other, surely?'

Peri sighed loudly. 'I don't see why.'

Douglas said no more, and in silence they walked on. Why doesn't he say something? she thought irritably. His silence was making her feel uncomfortable. 'Okay,' she conceded, sighing heavily. 'Okay, okay, okay. You be nice to me, and I will *try* and be nice to you.'

He laughed harshly. 'Don't do me any favours!'

She stopped rigid and slowly turned her head to look up

at him. 'Why am I having this conversation? I've got enough crap in my life at this moment without having to *think* about being friends with *you!*' She was amazed to see a big grin spreading across his face. His teeth were startling white against the ruddiness of his skin and his eyes sparkled blue in the sunshine. Suddenly she felt his hands grabbing her by her arms, and at the touch of them she immediately struggled to break free but his grip tightened, pinning her arms against her sides.

'Hey, hey!' he exclaimed, laughing at her furious struggle. 'Calm down! I just want to say that I am offering you my friendship, whatever happens. I understand how grim this place must seem to you, and since I cannot offer you luxury, the least I can do is to offer you my friendship.'

She stopped struggling and looked at him steadily for a moment. The mischievous twinkle in his eyes had gone now, replaced with an expression of resolute sincerity. He almost looked genuine. 'Good,' she said briskly. 'Now that we've got *that* sorted out, maybe you would be kind enough to release me.'

With a weary sigh, he dropped his hands to his sides. 'Sure,' he murmured in a low defeated voice. 'Sure.'

'Thank you.' She straightened her cloak with calm dignity and carried on walking.

'Do you know,' he said matter-of-factly, 'that if you keep wearing that expression, it's going to be etched onto your face by the time you're sixty.'

It was now obvious to Peri that she was dealing with a woman-hater. The guy had a problem! She didn't allow herself to get angry, she just sneered, throwing him a cursory glance. 'Yeah?' she answered, 'Well, *that's* not going to bother me – Scottie! – because when I'm sixty, I'm not going to give a damn what I look like! I'm going to be spending the rest of my life lazing under a tropical sun, surrounded by servants and untold wealth while you are going to be crippled by arthritis, hobbling from one dreary room to another, a lonely miserable old man with nothing but a mangy old dog to keep you company!' She was pleased to see that this had wiped that self-satisfied look off his face, and now he walked along with a sombre, thoughtful expression, gazing at the ground in silence. Ha! she thought triumphantly; I've hit a nerve!

'I may live alone,' he said quietly. 'But I will never be lonely, not with the friends that I have and the animals I will care for.' He gave her a sidelong glance. 'And I will not feel miserable because I will always have a purpose to my life.'

He had spoken with such dignity that she was taken aback, having expected him to respond with anger. His words echoed in her brain, and in that moment something stirred inside her, a feeling of emptiness stretching away, away . . . but she quickly pushed it aside and turned her thoughts back to him, determined to think of a nasty rejoinder.

'There she is,' he said, pointing a finger.

'What?' She looked in the direction in which he was pointing and saw a group of huts and a big wire-mesh cage over the brow of the hill.

'Kirsty,' he said simply.

'Kirsty?' she queried, peering in the direction of his pointed finger.

'Yep. She's the lady we've come tae visit.'

In her anger, the bird had slipped her mind, but now she felt the muscles in her stomach tighten as she strained her eyes to get a better look. From that distance, it looked like a sparrow but with each step that she took, it got bigger and bigger, until, at last, pressing her nose against the wire-meshing, she could feel her heart palpitating. Even though she had never seen an eagle, she could guess that this bird was probably the same size. It was enormous! And its beak! Its claws! Oh, God!

'Meet Kirsty,' Douglas said, standing beside her. 'A peregrine falcon, very rare. Less than a thousand pairs left in the wild. Don't be alarmed if she suddenly screeches – that's her way of communicating.'

Without taking her eyes from the bird, Peri nodded, feeling a strange tingling in her spine as she realised that this was the first time in her life that she had come face to face with a truly wild creature. It looked so proud, so sure of itself, staring at her with a steady haughty glare, its big golden eyes unblinking, deadly. A predator. A magnificent predator. The brownish grey markings on the white breast feathers looked as if they could have been painted with a very fine brush, the slanted eyes outlined in bright yellow, and the beak a perfect curve in a perfectly shaped head.

'What do you think?' Douglas asked.

'She's beautiful,' Peri whispered, immediately startled by her words. 'But I don't want to go near her,' she added quickly.

'Och, don't be daft. Kirsty's harmless. She's had a very rough time of it, too. I found her about two months ago. Someone had shot a bullet through her tail feathers.'

'No!'

'Aye, I'm afraid so.'

'But *why*?'

'Och, because the world is full of stupid folk.'

Peri had heard the anger in his voice and she could understand it. She turned back to gaze at the falcon. 'Who would want to destroy something so beautiful?' she said. 'Okay, maybe it's vicious – but it can't help that because that's the way it was made.'

'I wish the rest of the world thought like that.' Douglas pushed open the wire-mesh door and went in. 'Come on in and say hello.'

Peri hesitated. 'Are you sure she's not going to bite? She looks awfully fierce.'

Douglas laughed. 'That's how she's meant to look.'

Despite her nervousness, Peri felt vaguely irritated by the way Douglas seemed to laugh at practically everything she said. But this was not the time to make an issue of it, though. She followed him in and stopped a little way back and watched as he stroked the bird's head and spoke gently to it.

'Hello, Kirsty,' he said. 'I've brought someone to meet you.'

He turned to Peri. 'Come over here and stroke her. She won't hurt you.'

Peri shook her head, folded her arms across her chest and stayed put.

The man laughed again. 'Och, come on!'

'Why do you laugh at *everything* I say?' she snapped, irritated beyond belief. 'You'd think that—'

'Let's argue about it later, eh?' he suggested. 'But for now, let's concentrate on the matter at hand. First off, you just need tae stroke Kirsty's head, and, as you can see, she enjoys a bit of fussing.'

Peri waited until Douglas's back was turned, before sidling up to him and slowly putting a hand out towards the bird. 'Good girl, Kirsty,' she whispered, stroking one finger back across the silky head. 'Good girl.' She was ready to jerk her arm away, anticipating that vicious beak turning and slashing at her wrist, but instead the bird sat completely still, its eyes half-closed as if enjoying the touch of her finger. For a moment she couldn't believe that she was really doing this!

'You are very lucky to have this opportunity,' Douglas assured her.

Immediately she was ready with a sarcastic retort but she stopped herself short, realising that it did not seem right . . . in the circumstances.

'What I'm going to do now is give her some dinner,' Douglas chatted. 'And then she'll be ready to pose for the camera.' As he turned to take a glove from the shelf, the falcon suddenly gave a piercing shriek, throwing out its wings and violently beating the air.

Peri was only inches away. She screamed with terror and swung away, dashing for the door – she could almost feel those vicious talons ripping into the back of her neck.

Douglas grabbed her wrist. 'Hey – steady on!'

'Let me go!' She was panting so hard that she could hardly speak. 'I'm out of here! I'm phoning Mags.'

He swung her round to face him. 'Listen, Kirsty was only

stretching her wings. Imagine if you were tied to a chair all day and couldn't walk about. Well, that's how she feels. She just got a bit excited. She wants tae be up there . . .' Douglas jerked his head towards the sky. 'She wants tae fly.' He looked steadily into Peri's eyes. 'There is *nothing* to be afraid of. I promise.'

As she looked up into his eyes, she could almost believe him.

'Listen,' he said gently, releasing her wrist. 'Let's take it a step at a time. Just watch me – nothing else. Okay?' He slipped his hand into a big leather glove and returned to Kirsty, holding his gloved hand parallel with the perch. Immediately, Kirsty beat the air with her wings and hopped onto his glove, ruffling her wings for a moment before settling them against her sides. 'Kirsty hasn't had anything to eat since yesterday, so I've got to feed her. You just come along and watch.' He took a plastic bag down off the wall and carried the bird towards the wire-mesh door. Immediately Peri stepped out of the way, keeping her eyes fixed firmly on the falcon.

'Honestly, there's nothing to be afraid of,' Douglas said over his shoulder as he walked out onto the hillside.

'I didn't know I'd have to do this,' she muttered peevishly, trailing behind. 'Nobody told me.'

'Well, they should have,' Douglas said, leading the way across the hill. 'And if you feel that you can't go through with this – it's *their* problem, not yours.'

'No, it's not,' Peri murmured, speaking almost to herself.

'Of course it is – they can't force you!'

Peri didn't bother to explain; he wouldn't understand how crucial it was to please Helmut Reuther and not to risk being replaced by someone else . . . someone like Saffron! She wanted to do it – she *really* did! But at the thought of that falcon sitting on her arm with its razor-sharp beak only inches away from her beautiful eyes, she suddenly went weak with fear, knowing that she would probably end up peeing in her pants. Suddenly she felt depressed, defeated, knowing deep in her heart that she would not be able to do what was asked of her. This is all such a waste of time, she thought bitterly. I might as well go back to the house and start packing my bags.

'I've got Kirsty's dinner tied to the end of this rope,' Douglas explained. 'But she has to work for it – otherwise she'd end up looking as fat as a partridge.'

She could tell that he was trying to relax her but she was too depressed to respond, foreseeing her glittering future slowly disintegrating. She was going to be sent back to London so that Saffron could replace her and then everyone would know that Peri Lomax had been replaced. And the Film Awards? They would not want a nonentity co-hosting something so important, so they would have to replace her. Then Mags would call her into the office. 'Peri,' she would say, pretending to be sad. 'I think the time has come when we both know that you have outgrown this agency and that another agency would serve you better.' And all the while, the other girls would be gleefully whispering behind her back.

'. . . Kirsty is about two years old,' Douglas was saying. 'And she can fly at speeds of up to ninety miles per hour.'

Peri was looking at the bird with growing resentment. 'Really?' she answered, beginning to wish that whoever it was who had taken a shot at Kirsty had done a better job. A sudden icy wind sprang up, whipping her hair across her face and she combed it back with her fingertips and held it against the nape of her neck. They were cresting the hill now; she could see a bank of dark grey clouds moved steadily towards them, blotting out the wintry sun and taking away what little warmth it had given.

'This is us,' Douglas said, stopping in front of a T-shaped pole embedded deep into the barren ground. 'You stay here and watch. It will only take a few minutes.' Smoothly, he transferred the bird onto the perch and then turned and strode off down the hill.

Left alone with the falcon, she eyed it nervously and shuffled further away, but it seemed totally unconcerned by her presence, gazing instead at Douglas's receding back.

Douglas was about halfway down the hill now. Beyond him the vast mountains rolled away to the horizon, and here and there she could see glints of silver, making her wonder if they could be waterfalls. Douglas had come to a halt and now pulled a long leather strap from the plastic bag he was carrying. He looked towards Kirsty before lifting the strap and swinging it above his head, around and around, making a loud, high-pitched *kee kee* sound.

There was the sound of beating wings, and Peri turned just in time to see Kirsty shoot past her, diving like a missile towards the lump at the end of the rope. Talons out, the falcon was only inches away from snatching it, but at the last second Douglas jerked the rope leaving the falcon to soar on, talons empty. Flapping rapidly, it rose high, high in the sky, circling slowly before gliding down and gently settling itself onto the perch once more.

Peri watched in awe. This was *real* nature, not some documentary on Sky TV. She could see the golden eyes now, staring fiercely, intent only on the leather rope in Douglas's hand, and she could imagine that very few little furry animals would escape those vicious talons.

Again and again, Douglas repeated the swings, until finally the bird caught the end of the strap and brought it down to earth, stooping over its prey and ripping it apart with its beak.

With his job done, Douglas came back up the hill towards Peri. 'What do you think?'

'Cool. Really cool.'

Douglas raised his eyebrows in bewilderment. 'Cool?'

'Yeah. Cool.' She tried to think of another word to explain it.

'Spectacular,' she said at last. 'It was spectacular.'

He smiled, well-satisfied. 'A wonderful sight, eh?'

'Yeah. But why doesn't she fly away?'

'Well, she could if she wanted to, but falcons are lazy creatures so if food comes easily to them, they will stick around; and that's fine by me because I've been waiting for her to get a little stronger before releasing her back into the wild.'

'Will she go?'

'Aye,' he said firmly. 'Because I will simply stop feeding her and then she'll have no choice.'

'Will she come back to see you?'

Douglas shook his head. 'No. Never. When she's gone – she's gone for good.'

'Oh!' Peri returned her gaze to the falcon. His words had made her feel strangely melancholic.

'I'll be sorry to see her go but it's best that she returns to the wild and finds a mate.' He made the same *kee kee* noise again and the bird flew across and gently landed on his glove.

Instinctively, Peri stepped back.

Douglas stroked the bird's chest. 'It's vitally important that Kirsty has chicks because the more peregrine falcons there are, the less chance of their extinction. So it was lucky that Helmut chose to come here because the money he's paying me will help towards my conservation work; and these birds need as much help as they can get, what with farmers shooting them and men from the cities coming to steal their eggs.'

'Steal their eggs?' Peri exclaimed.

'Aye. You can sell a clutch of peregrine eggs abroad for about five thousand pounds. The same amount as you would get for that gear you're wearing.'

'Oh.' Peri looked down at her clothes. His words seemed suddenly to have turned her thoughts upside-down, and for a moment she didn't know what to think.

As Douglas was speaking, the bird was gently pecking him on the fingers. 'Now you've seen that Kirsty is totally harmless – why don't you try holding her?'

Peri shook her head. 'I can't. I'm not used to this sort of thing. I've lived in a city all my life.'

Douglas was silent for a moment before continuing, 'Every year we have groups of school children come up from the cities to visit. Well, last year, I was nursing a sparrowhawk – a bit similar to a peregrine – and we had a group over from Aberdeen. When it came to stroking it, all the children were too nervous, except for one wee girl – Megan was her name. Unfortunately she had cerebral palsy, so we had to carry her and her wheelchair up the hill. When she saw the hawk, she immediately asked to touch it, and then, after only a few minutes, she had put on this falconer's glove.' Douglas pulled a small leather glove from his jacket pocket to show Peri. 'And, with no fuss at all, she ended up holding the sparrowhawk, with me supporting her arm. You should have seen her eyes sparkle when she watched that hawk soar into the sky. I could almost imagine that her heart was up there too, soaring with it.'

In her mind's eye, Peri could clearly picture the scene, and for a moment she felt a tear prick her eye, but almost immediately she got a grip on herself, realising that he was making it up to boost her confidence, to make her go through with it; because, of course, he would lose money if this job didn't go ahead. 'You're lying,' she announced. 'You're just saying it to make me do it!'

Eyes wide in astonishment, he went as if to speak but no words came forth. 'Phew!' he said at last. 'You can certainly use your words like Kirsty can use her talons! Haven't you heard of common civility? You can't just call someone a liar.'

'Yes, I can – if they're feeding me a load of crap.'

He was thoughtful now, his eyes searching her face. 'I'm beginning tae think that you have as little trust in humans as you do in this falcon here.'

Peri looked away, biting back the words she wanted to say: *Yes, you're absolutely right! I don't have trust in humans and neither would you if you'd gone through what I had.* 'If I want to be psychoanalysed,' she told him coolly, glancing up at him, 'I will go to a shrink, thank you.'

He was silent for a moment. 'Aye – you're right. It's no' my place to cast judgement. Anyway, we're starting tae sound like a couple of bickering weans.'

'I think we need an interpreter,' she said irritably. 'I have no idea what you're saying.'

'We sound like squabbling children,' he explained. Suddenly, a smile crossed his face. 'Well, there's something I think we can both agree on: there doesn't look much chance of us becoming friends.'

'Good,' she replied stiffly.

'Well, that aside, we're here to do a job, whether we like it or not. So let's get on wi' it.' He put his hand in his pocket and took something out.

Suspiciously, Peri looked at what he was holding. It appeared to be some kind of egg cosy made from leather.

'I've got something here that will help you,' he said, holding it up. 'It's a hood for covering a falcon's head; you'll probably feel more at ease knowing that Kirsty can't see you. It's been a couple of months since she's had to wear it, so I'll just see if she's still okay wi' it.' As he spoke, he slipped the hood over bird's head. 'There – she's immobilised.' He handed Peri the small leather glove. 'Put that on and see if it fits.'

Peri shook her head at the glove. 'I'm not going to.'

'Och, come on! If a wee lassie with cerebral palsy can do it, so can you!'

'How do I know you're telling the truth?'

'You know I'm telling the truth,' he ordered. 'Now put on the glove.'

'I've enjoyed our little adventure,' she said, turning away, 'but I'm going to phone my agent and tell her the bird is too vicious.'

'Coward!'

She swung back to him. 'I beg your pardon?!'

'I said you're a coward!'

'How dare you!' She felt her cheeks flush with anger. In that instant, she was almost compelled to hold the bloody thing – to show him! But commonsense prevailed and she answered in a cold voice, 'You've got an attitude problem, *buster*.'

'And you're a weak-bellied Sassenach!'

She gasped. She didn't know the meaning of 'Sassenach' but she didn't have to. He had thrown some disgusting insult at her. 'No wonder you're stuck out here with a withered old woman!' she hissed. 'Nobody else will have you, that's why.'

'There's plenty of ladies who would have me,' he retorted.

'Oh, yeah?' She looked around the barren hillside. 'So? Where are they? Eh? Still living in caves? With hairy armpits!'

Douglas stiffened. 'There's nothing wrong with hairy armpits.'

'Aha! So they *do* have hairy armpits!'

Now he was on the defensive. 'There's nothing wrong with that. It's natural.'

Peri shuddered delicately. 'Erghh! They must be *so* gross!'

'The women of the Highlands are some of the most beautiful in the world,' he retorted icily. 'And *they* have the manners of a *lady!*'

'Yeah! Well, they've got more sense than to come round here and have to deal with your ego problem and your rudeness and . . .'

'Ha!' he exclaimed. '*That's* the pot calling the kettle black.'

Peri stopped, confused; not understanding his meaning. 'What?' she snapped.

'You're the pot calling the kettle black,' he repeated. 'You're describing yourself but you don't know it.'

'Yeah?' she snarled.

'Yeah!'

She arched an eyebrow. 'Well, I sure haven't got a personality problem like *you!*'

'Personality!' He laughed harshly. 'You've got the personality of a viper.'

She stared at him steadily, silently, and in that moment she became aware that Kirsty was ruffling her feathers and jerking her head, as if agitated by their shouting. Douglas, too, must have noticed because he immediately took off Kirsty's hood and transferred her onto the perch behind them.

She waited for him to turn back to her, before folding her

arms across her chest, ready to continue their battle. 'You have no idea who you are talking to, do you?'

He eyed her cautiously. 'What do you mean?'

'I mean, you are talking to the next *Madonna.* I'm going to be a megastar and have bodyguards as big as tanks, big enough to pick up people like you and grind them into the dirt.'

'Och, aye,' he retorted, looking around the hillside. 'So? Where are *they?*'

'I'm not a megastar – yet – but I will be soon. Because when I've finished this job, every director in Hollywood will . . .' She stopped abruptly. *When I've finished this job,* she thought, repeating the words over and over in her brain. But she wouldn't be finishing this job, would she? She shivered, suddenly feeling strangely lost, as if some invisible anchor had come loose, sending her adrift into empty space.

'What's the matter?' Douglas asked, seeming puzzled.

'Nothing.' All the fight had gone out of her and depression settled like a grey blanket. She stared at the falcon. Maybe she could share the assignment with Saffron? Saffron could do this bird bit and she could do the rest? No! That would be impossible. Whatever happened, Saffron must not become part of the equation.

'This job's important to you, isn't it?' Douglas asked quietly.

She nodded and hung her head. He was speaking kindly, but his kindness could not touch her or give her comfort.

'Listen to me,' he coaxed. 'Let's forget our animosity for the moment. Let's work together on this. It will be of benefit for both of us. We are going to do this one step at a time. Don't think about anything but my instructions. Okay?'

He had spoken in a firm, authoratitive voice, a voice that somehow seemed to propel her forward, and she responded with a nod, raising her head and fixing her gaze on the horizon and taking a deep breath to steady herself. 'Okay,' she replied.

'Take the glove,' he said.

She took the glove.

'Now put your hand into it.'

She put her hand inside it.

'Does it fit?'

She nodded. 'Yes.' She waited, studying her glove and knowing exactly what he was about to do.

'Hold out your arm.'

Again, she fixed her eyes on the horizon and held out her arm, rigid. There was a gentle fluttering breeze and then the pressure of two talons gripping into the leather at her wrist. There was surprisingly little weight. Peri looked from the corner of her eye. Fuck! It was sitting on her! And it wasn't wearing that hood! It began to ruffle its feathers gently, casually removing a stray feather with its beak before staring about, its big golden eyes glancing to and fro across the landscape, seeming totally disinterested in Peri.

'Jesus Christ!' she murmured and then added in a firm but encouraging voice, 'Good girl, Kirsty, good girl.' She wanted Kirsty to know – right from the start – that she was a friend and not her next meal.

Douglas smiled. 'How does that feel?'

With wide eyes, she exhaled on a long breath. 'Phew!' she exclaimed. It was amazing! This bird wasn't going to hurt her; in fact, it was just using her as a convenient perch. Why had she been so scared? This was easy!

'The two of you look great together,' Douglas said. 'Helmut certainly seems to know what he's doing.'

'Do we really look good together?' she asked.

'Fantastic! Kirsty truly complements your beauty.'

As she gazed at the falcon, she was suddenly overwhelmed with a sense of awe – awe that this wild and noble creature had accepted her like this. It made her feel strangely humble. Close up, she could see every tiny detail of its body, the fine downy feathers where the wing joined the body, a thin streak of blood along the hard grey beak, and the specks of amber in the big luminous eyes. Now she would *really* have something to tell the paparazzi! *I handled a vicious raptor*, she would say, *and, yes, I was terrified. But I was working with the great and wonderful Helmut Reuther, so I simply had to ignore my fear.*

'You've done well,' Douglas said, taking off his leather glove. 'And tomorrow I will teach you how to fly her. But for now, I'd better go down and tell the others that we're ready.' He put the leather glove in his pocket. 'You'd better put Kirsty back on her perch – she can get heavy after a while.'

Peri had watched Douglas earlier, and now knew what to do. She lifted the falcon up towards the perch, parallel with the bar, and held her arm steady, watching the falcon as it pushed off from her glove and hopped onto the perch. It was so easy! She felt wonderfully clever, and for a second, she was almost tempted to skip with delight.

Douglas had begun to tie the thin leather straps on Kirsty's legs. 'These are called jesses,' he explained, 'and they will stop her from flying off. Right. Will you be okay here by yourself?'

Peri nodded and stroked a finger down over Kirsty's chest. 'I'll be fine and . . . thanks.' She looked up at him and smiled wryly. 'I've been a pain. I'm sorry.'

'Nae bother. I understand that it must be hard on you being in such a strange environment and having to do something that frightens you. You're probably as sweet as an angel when you're at home.'

She turned back to the falcon. 'Yeah,' she agreed softly, not wanting to dispel his theory by telling him that she was always a pain, wherever she went. He had turned to walk away and silently she watched him go. 'Well, *he*'s not a goody-two-shoes either!' she muttered sourly. 'After all, he called me a coward, and a weak-bellied something or other!' She could just imagine what they must have looked like standing there on the top of the hill; two complete strangers waving their arms about and hurling abuse at one another – for what? She felt a smile touch her lips.

Douglas had made rapid progress down the hillside and now only his head and torso remained in view. 'I suppose you're not *that* horrid,' she murmured. 'And I certainly gave *you* as good as I got!' A big grin spread across her face. 'Hairy armpits! Ha! That one scored a bull's-eye.' She was aware that Douglas was moving nimbly, swiftly, which seemed unusual for a man of such bulk; and in a few seconds he would be out of sight. Suddenly she felt a surge of gratitude. If it hadn't been for him she would never have had the courage to handle the falcon. Mags would have been furious. Then Saffron would have replaced her, taking all the glory for herself. Peri Lomax would have been destroyed. But Douglas had saved her career, and yet she had been so nasty to him, and had said such horrible things and had made him lock his dog away. 'Douglas,' she shouted out.

He turned swiftly. 'Yep?'

'I don't mind having your dog around if you want to let it out of the house.'

'Are you sure?'

She nodded. 'As long as it doesn't come too close.'

'Okay, Peri.' He grinned and waved and walked on down the hill. Then suddenly he stopped and swung around, heading back towards her. 'What am I doing?' he told her as he approached. 'Let's phone the house on your mobile and save me the trek, eh?'

'Oh, right, of course.' She took it out of her pocket and gave it to him. 'Press that button, there,' she told him. 'And then you can speak into that bit.'

He did as she instructed. 'It's been a few years since I've used something like this,' he said, carefully pressing a big calloused finger down on the buttons. 'Mrs Craig is going to get a surprise to hear my voice on the telephone.'

'Tell her you've really abducted me this time,' Peri suggested, feeling suddenly mischievous. 'Tell her that you're going to have your wicked way with me!'

Douglas grinned as he pressed the final number. 'Don't you give me ideas,' he said and held the phone to his ear and waited. 'The thing is: she *will* believe me! I don't know what you've been telling her but I'm definitely the bad guy.'

'Good.' Peri chuckled and smiled cheekily as she listened to him talking to Mrs Craig.

'Will you tell Helmut and Otto that we are ready for them?' he said into the mobile. 'And point them in the right direction? And you can tell them to bring Bruce along too.' But it was evident that Mrs Craig had a lot to say. 'Okay,' Douglas said at last. 'Okay. Aye. Okay. Dinna fash yerself. I'll look after her. Aye. Cheerio. Aye. Right. Goodbye.' He took the mobile from his ear and studied it. 'How do I turn it off?'

Peri took it from him. 'You just press this button here,' she said, demonstrating. 'What did Mrs Craig have to say?'

'She says she's glad tae let Bruce out of the house because he's been howling like a banshee and she says she's been worrying about you. She thinks it's too cold for you tae be out here and for me tae bring you in if you get chilly. And she's sending up a flask of soup and mind I make sure you have some.'

'A real boy scout!' she said cheekily, looking up at him from the corner of her eyes.

'Och, aye,' he muttered bashfully. 'Let's walk around a bit to keep warm. If we'd had more time, I would've taken you over to see my rabbits and a wee pine marten.'

'Wow!' she exclaimed. 'You really know how to show a girl a good time!' She watched him chuckle self-consciously and it made her wonder, for a moment, how she could have hated him so. He seemed a totally different person from the one she had met the previous afternoon. 'But, seriously, I wouldn't mind seeing your rabbits and things.' She brushed her hair back from her face. 'You really care for animals, don't you?' she asked.

'Aye. I do. I sometimes care more for animals than I do for humans. Humans do so much damage to each other and to the world around them. I see my job as picking up the pieces, trying to make good the damage they do.' He stopped and pointed over towards the distant horizon. 'Out there is the Caledonian pine forest, once the home to beavers and wolves and wild boar. But now – now they've all been hunted into extinction and the forest reduced to one per cent of its former glory.'

'Oh. That's a shame.' She didn't know what else to say, but she could tell by the growing enthusiasm in his voice that she was in for a wildlife lecture.

'But the tide is turning,' he said fervently. 'Conservation is beginning to think big, aiming to restore on such a grand scale that it could almost match people's old capacity for destruction. Scottish Natural Heritage has just announced that it will be reintroducing beavers within the next two years. Isn't that marvellous! And just to think, beavers have been extinct in the Highlands for over three hundred years!'

Looking at his bright and eager face, Peri could tell that he was expecting some delighted response from her. 'Gosh!' she replied.

He seemed to give her a minute to absorb this information before continuing, 'And once we have established our primary forests, we can reintroduce the grey wolf.'

'Wolf?'

'Aye. But that won't be for another fifty years or so, depending on the feasibility studies.'

'Wolf?' Peri repeated, perplexed. 'You want to . . .' She hesitated and then swept out her hand, gesturing to the surrounding hills '. . . You want to have wolves walking around here?'

'Aye. Of course.' He stopped and looked at her intently. 'Wolves are not dangerous, you know.'

She responded by arching an eyebrow, signifying her disbelief.

'There's no evidence of a healthy wolf killing a human,' he said. 'And if they have, it's because they've been rabid or their cubs have been threatened.'

'Well, I think you should give it a bit more thought before bringing in a whole lot of wolves. What does Mrs Craig think about it?'

Douglas grinned. 'It's no' me on my own going to reintroduce them. It's no' my idea! And anyway, in fifty years' time, I'll be in no fit state to do the job.'

'Well, I think it's a silly idea.'

'No, it's not. You know nothing about them. And because of stories like Little Red Riding Hood, everyone assumes that they are man-eaters – well, they're not.'

'Mmm,' she said doubtfully.

Douglas picked up a twig. 'Can you imagine what it would be like to replace fields with forests and to have wild animals roaming free once more?' He poked the twig down inside the back of his jacket and started to scratch his back with it. 'Lynx, wild boar, golden eagle. They live on the European mainland, so why can't they live here?'

Peri shrugged. She couldn't understand why he could be bothered by it all. Did it matter?

'If we just sit back and allow our animals to become extinct, how are we going to explain it to our children?'

Well, *she* wasn't going to have children, so that didn't concern her. But, watching his enthusiasm, she thought it was probably wise not to mention it. He had taken the twig from the back of his neck and held it loosely in his hand, swinging it, when suddenly, from nowhere, up bounded his dog, snatching the twig from his hand.

'Hiya, Bruce,' Douglas exclaimed, bending forward to play tug-of-war with the stick. 'So you've been howling, eh?' As the dog jerked the stick, it growled, and although Peri knew it was being playful, she couldn't help but tense up. For some unknown reason, she had always been wary of dogs, especially mongrels like this one.

Glancing back down the hill, she saw Helmut and Otto trudging upwards, carrying a tripod and camera and cases. Douglas had seen them too. 'They look as if they need some help,' he said, releasing the stick and starting down the hill with the dog bounding along beside him. Peri watched as Douglas met up with them, chatting as if he'd known them for years, totally at ease as if in fact *he* was the one who was in charge.

'Well done, Peri!' Helmut exclaimed as he got closer. 'Douglas has just informed me that you have been a joy to work with.'

Peri smiled hesitantly. Was he being sarcastic? No. He was being serious.

Smiling broadly, Helmut began to wriggle out of his back-pack. 'You are a very brave lady, Peri, and I thank you for doing this for me. It will be worth the effort. You will see.'

Peri nodded demurely, secretly proud of herself and grateful that he would never know how close she had been to taking the next flight home.

He now stood beside her, studying the landscape. 'Right – shall we get started? We will move further along the hill – I don't want the cage in the shot.' As the camera was set up, Peri got into position with the falcon on her glove. 'Wonderful, wonderful,' Helmut said, coming up to her and clicking the light meter. 'This is exactly how I had imagined it would be.' For the next hour he worked swiftly and silently, frowning heavily in concentration.

Meanwhile Douglas stood out of range watching them, the dog sitting patiently at his heels, clearly just as interested as his master. In between takes, Douglas came forward and held the falcon, relieving Peri of its weight. 'I'm no photographer,' he said to her, 'but I reckon these photographs are going to look fantastic.'

'Do you think so?' she asked innocently, knowing without a doubt that they would be spectacular.

'Aye, I do.' He stroked the falcon's head. 'I hope you don't mind me asking – it's just that I've been wondering – were either of your parents foreign?'

'No.' She answered more sharply than she intended, but she hated this sort of question. It made her feel uncomfortable . . . ashamed. Now she wanted him to go away.

'It's just that you've got very exotic eyes,' he continued. 'The way they slant up and . . .'

'I'm English, if that's what you want to know,' she said coolly. Why was he prying? Why couldn't he shut up?

'Aye. I know. I'm just asking about your forebears and if—'

'There is nothing in my past of any interest. It's gone. Forgotten.' She saw the puzzled look on his face and sighed. 'Look, Douglas,' she said firmly. 'I like you. You're nice. And I'm grateful for everything you have done for me, but, at three o'clock on Wednesday morning I shall be leaving and we shall never see each other again, so there's no point in exchanging life stories, is there?'

Douglas seemed taken aback but shrugged his shoulders. 'Sure,' he said quietly, 'okay.'

She could sense his hurt bewilderment and it made her feel strangely sad. Now they stood side by side in awkward silence. Should she explain? After all, she would never see him again after Wednesday so what harm would it do if he were to know the truth about her?

'We will take a break,' Helmut shouted, and Douglas promptly turned away, carrying Kirsty towards her perch.

The moment for explanation had gone. As she watched him walk off, she reminded herself that he was a nobody, so why bother with explanations? She swung away and went over to Otto, and stood and watched him busily opening up parcels of sandwiches and pouring soup from a tartan flask into mugs. 'Cold, isn't it?' she murmured by way of conversation.

He answered with a slow shake of his head, handing her a mug of soup and muttering under his breath, 'I will be thankful to go home.'

'Me too.' It was obvious that Otto was in no mood for conversation, so she carried her soup over to a fallen tree and sat down, cupping the warm mug in her hands and staring out at the vast and rolling land. It was windy up here on the top of the hill, the clouds swirled above her head and the pine trees down on the ridge swayed and creaked. In the far distance the mountains were blue and along the skyline there were streaks of purple and pink. There were no houses, no roads, nothing. It was eerie. How could someone choose to *live* here? And people actually came here for their holidays! She would go to the Seychelles, she decided, immediately after the Film Awards, just for a couple of weeks, take some magazines for company and soak up the sun. It would probably be her last break for a long time.

'Here you go.' It was Douglas, holding out a sandwich as he walked towards her.

After the way she had just spoken to him, she was surprised that he was still being nice. But why? She shook her head at the sandwich. 'No, thanks, Douglas.' The dog had padded alongside his master and now sat wagging his tail as if happy to see her. It was apparent that the man and the dog were not going to be rebuffed.

'Aren't you hungry?' Douglas asked.

'Yes, I am, but I don't eat during the day.'

He looked surprised. 'Why not?'

'Because I can't afford to put on weight.'

'What?'

The look of sheer amazement on his face made her want to smile. He was such an idiot. 'You think I'm too thin, don't you?'

He reddened and looked away. 'Well . . .'

'It's the fashion, Douglas – didn't you know?'

He was frowning at her now. 'But surely folk don't want to see a bonnie lass like you looking so, so . . .'

'Emaciated?' she said, completing his sentence. 'What you mean is: you would prefer to see someone like me with big boobs and a big bum.'

'Well, I don't know.' Douglas narrowed his eyes and took a bite of his sandwich, munching slowly, as if pretending to consider very carefully what she had said. Then he nodded solemnly. 'Yes – I think I would.'

By the jaunty angle of his eyebrows, she knew he was trying to amuse her. Suddenly she felt devilish. She would shock him and wipe that expression off his face. 'There are some models who are much thinner than me,' she said innocently, watching his eyebrows converge into a frown of disbelief.

'But that's just *terrible!*'

'They're so thin, their ribs stick out,' she carried on. 'And to stay like that, they make themselvs vomit after every meal.' Now he was looking aghast. 'But I don't do that,' she said. 'I'm just careful about what I eat and most days all I have is three litres of Evian water, to cleanse my system.'

Douglas looked at her sternly. 'Well, that's just stupid. A body needs nourishment, vitamins; how's it going to get all that with a barrel of water? You're going to end up with osteoporosis.'

She shrugged. 'But I'm fit, and you can't say my skin doesn't glow.' She tilted her face up so he could get a better look at her skin.

But he was obviously not impressed. 'You might be fit now but you'll suffer when you get older.'

It was fun getting him all riled up. 'And what about Mrs Craig? She thinks I'm too thin, too, doesn't she?'

He laughed suddenly. 'Och, you should hear her! *That lassie needs a few decent meals inside her,*' he mimicked, wobbling his head. '*Just let her stay with me for a week or two and I would soon put some meat on her. Poor lassie – she's just a rickle of banes.*'

Peri had to smile at the way he was trying to mimic Mrs Craig – he was totally useless at it. 'You'll have to translate,' she said.

He shook his head. 'No. You don't want tae know the meaning of that.'

Suddenly there was a shout. It was Helmut, waving to them. 'Okay, everbody, back to work. No more smiles, Peri. Remember to think hardship . . . poverty. Be fierce!'

Douglas had taken her empty mug from her hand, and as he started to walk away with it he suddenly looked back, glowering dramatically from beneath his bushy eyebrows and baring his teeth.

Peri guffawed. She couldn't help herself. The stupid man looked so silly!

'Peri!' Helmut thundered, 'no smiling.'

She jerked to attention, wiping the smile off her face and quickly slipping on the leather glove, Douglas forgotten as she awaited further instructions.

'We will work for one more hour,' Helmut told her, 'and then you can relax for the rest of the afternoon.' He began to load the camera. 'I want you to look especially glamorous for this evening's shoot and I will explain in more detail when we return to the house; but you will be pleased to know that you are permitted to wear full make-up, false nails, false hair, false eyelashes, false anything!'

She wondered if he was mocking her, but she didn't care; she was too relieved by the prospect of being herself once more.

'Here you go.' Douglas came towards her holding Kirsty and swiftly the falcon went from his glove on to hers, seeming content to return to Peri once again.

'I feel as if I've doing this for *years*,' she whispered.

Douglas whispered back. 'Well – you certainly *look* as if you've been doing it for years.'

Overwhelmed with sudden gratitude for all that he had done for her, she gazed steadily into his eyes and spoke sincerely. 'Thank you, Douglas. I really mean it.'

He seemed taken aback for a moment and then smiled bashfully. 'Och, don't be daft. All you needed was a bit of a shove. And if you're wanting to learn more about raptors, I'm off to keep watch on an eagle's nest this afternoon, if you want to put on your wellies and come wi' me.'

That's how he sees me, Peri thought: in wellies and long shapeless clothes and tatty hair. He's never seen me in my natural state. 'I would've loved to,' she lied pleasantly. 'But I will have to get ready for tonight.'

He nodded. 'Sure, okay.'

'Are you coming with us tonight?' she asked casually.

'Aye.'

She was glad but she didn't show it. At last he would see her as she was meant to be seen – breathtakingly beautiful! And as he was so used to Scottish cavewomen with hairy armpits, he would be all the more astounded! Ha!

There was a shout from Helmut. 'Please – I am waiting to begin.'

Swiftly, Douglas stepped backwards, as Peri turned quickly to face the camera, obediently arranging her features into a sullen but haughty expression, gleefully thinking of the coming night. She would be elegant but a little flirtatious, glamorous but sophisticated, and . . . untouchable. 'Then, maybe,' she muttered waspishly, 'he might stop thinking of me as the girl-next-door and start treating me with the deference that I deserve!'

Peri added the second coat of icecream-pink lipstick and blotted her lips with tissue paper. Next, she added another coat of lipstick and painted it over with shiny gloss. Now she was ready to go, but instead she sat and stared at herself in the mirror. She didn't feel at all glamorous or elegant, and the thought of flirting all night had lost its appeal. She was full of chicken casserole and apple pie and she just wanted to curl up in front of the fire and stroke the cat. She looked with jealousy at Hamish stretched out across the eiderdown, too bloated to jump down from the bed and come over and sit on her knee. Through the gap in the curtain, she could see the blackness beyond. In London there would be street lights shining outside her window all through the night and there would people and cars and noise. But here? It was so silent, she might as well be on the moon. People moaned about the noise of London, but she rather liked the sound of traffic and late-night laughter drifting up from the street. Somehow, it made her feel less alone. The only noise she hated was the sound of high-heels clicking harshly in the silence of the night . . .

With a sigh she stood up, collected her coat and vanity case, and made her way down to the kitchen where Otto was waiting for her, sitting snugly in the battered armchair by the stove and chatting to Mrs Craig who stood at the sink washing a pan. It sounded as if they were discussing apple strudel. Otto promptly stood up when he saw her. 'Ready?'

Mrs Craig turned from the sink. 'You look like a film star!' she exclaimed. 'The lads up at the Osprey are going to get the surprise of their lives.' She dried her hands in a teatowel. 'Och, I nearly forgot. A lady telephoned to you. Mags, I think she called herself, and she wants you tae telephone her as soon as possible.'

'I'll phone her when I get back,' Peri lied, determined that Mags should stew in her guilt and worry for as long as possible.

'Are you going tae be warm enough?' As usual Mrs Craig began to fuss, insisting that Peri wear a pair of woollen gloves and giving her a rug to put over her legs for the journey.

Peri loved the attention and made no effort to protest.

Meanwhile, Otto stood impatiently by the door. 'We have to go now,' he said at last. 'Helmut and Douglas will be waiting for us.'

'See you later, Mrs Craig,' Peri said, following Otto out of the door.

The woman came out into the yard with them. 'Mind, if any of the lads get drunk or unruly, you just mention my name,' she said sternly.

'I should be okay,' Peri called over her shoulder as she headed for the car, 'with three bodyguards to look after me!' The night was pitch black, the yard illuminated only by the yellow glow from the kitchen windows, and she had to tread carefully across the cobblestones to avoid snapping off a stiletto heel. Everything was silent except for the clacking of her heels and the sudden yelp of some wild animal far off in the distance. As she settled herself in the car, she looked towards the house and saw that Mrs Craig's small plump body had become a dark silhouette, framed in the doorway against the soft glow of the kitchen lights. Suddenly she looked so tiny. Should they be leaving this old woman here by herself, out here in the middle of nowhere, miles from any other house? But before she could voice her concern, Otto was speaking.

'The bar that we will be using is in a hotel,' he said, turning the key in the ignition, 'but it is not as grand as it sounds. It is a rough sort of place, totally in keeping with the theme of Helmut's work.' He accelerated slowly as he manoeuvred the car out through the gate. 'But it should be warm and I have secured a room upstairs where you can get changed.'

All concern for the woman was swept aside as Peri turned her attention towards the evening. 'As long as I'm warm, that's all I care about.' She wrapped the warm blanket around her legs and put her mittened hands up her coat sleeves. 'Will Douglas be working with us this evening?' She spoke lightly, off-handedly, not wanting Otto to suspect her interest.

'Yes, he should be. He's been with Helmut this afternoon, checking out tomorrow's locations but they should be at the hotel by now.' Otto's voice dropped to a mutter. 'I hope that he hasn't been drinking whisky. Then he becomes a monster to work with!'

She was shocked. 'Douglas?'

'No! No!' Otto retorted impatiently. 'Helmut. He will either complain about every little detail or he will be extremely jolly. Either way, it is so exhausting for me.'

'Yeah.' She gazed out of the window into the blackness. Well, Helmut would have no complaints with her because she looked absolutely stunning, especially her eyes – she had drawn grey kohl along the inner edges which made them look greener, more intense. Now she was impatient to get to the hotel, to see the expression on Douglas's face. She turned to Otto. 'How long before we get there?'

'In daylight it takes only twenty minutes but at night . . .' His voice petered out.

Peri gazed out into the black night. Except for the glow of the headlamps on the narrow road ahead, there was no other light. Just utter blackness. Goodness knew what sort of animals lurked out there! 'It's spooky, isn't it?' she muttered.

'Spooky?' Otto queried.

'It means scary . . . frightening,' Peri explained.

'That is true,' he agreed. 'I would not want to have an accident in this place.' He drove cautiously, concentrating on the narrow winding road, his eyes straining to see into the blackness beyond the beam of headlights.

Peri didn't want to think of that eerie blackness outside the window. She wanted to think about herself. 'Have you spoken to my agent today?' she asked, trying to sound casual.

'No, but Helmut did.'

She kept the casual note in her voice. 'Oh? What did he say?'

'He told her that everything is going to schedule.'

Peri didn't want to know about any schedule, she wanted to know what had been said about *her*. 'Did Helmut mention anything about me?'

'Yes, he did.'

'Well, what?'

Otto slowed as they reached a steep, sharp bend. 'He said he was pleased with you.'

Pleased! she thought irritably. After everything I have had to do for him today, he is *pleased*. He should be indebted to me, overjoyed, amazed . . . not *pleased*.

'Did he say anything else?'

Otto pressed his foot on the brake as they came down over a hill. 'Yes.'

She was beginning to get exasperated. She knew that he had to concentrate on the road but he could still *talk* to her, couldn't he? 'So, what else did he say?'

'Your agent asked him if one of his photographs could be used for a magazine cover, and he said—' Otto swung the steering wheel sharply, avoiding a fallen tree at the side of the road.

Peri now sat erect, eagerly waiting to hear more. 'And? And

what?' This was like getting blood out of a stone, she thought, exasperated.

At last, he continued, 'He said that he would think about it before making a decision.'

'Did my agent say which magazine it would be used for?'

'Yes. She said it would be for *Hi!*.'

'Mmm.' Peri sank back in her seat. So Mags was pushing for the photo, was she? But, what if Helmut said no? It would be a dreadful pity. With her face on the cover of *Hi!*, it would give her immediate world-wide coverage. But Helmut was undecided, was he? Well, she would have to help him decide! Although she had never slept with a man to further her career, she could understand – at a time like this – why some of the girls resorted to it. Anyway, that was a waste of time because Helmut was obviously gay. 'You must have some influence over Helmut,' she said sweetly. 'Couldn't you persuade him to release the negative?'

'Sometimes he listens to me, sometimes not. But I will try.'

'Thank you. I would be so grateful. I *really* would, Otto.' So, this guy had some influence; now she wished that she had been nicer to him from the start.

He had lapsed into silence, concentrating on the road ahead, which left Peri to pleasantly imagine how she would look on the front cover of *Hi!* and mentally skimming through a list of questions that would be asked of her, and the answers she would give. And what could she wear? De Vere's dress, of course! Saffron would be so, so jealous! It made Peri feel as if she could burst with happiness. At last, after all those miserable months, her future now beckoned brightly, full of hope and excitement and riches.

Cocooned in her dreams, the journey passed quickly, and as they began to wind their way down the mountainside she could see the twinkling lights of a distant town shining way down in the blackness, welcoming them. 'We are nearly there,' Otto said, sounding relieved.

She gazed at the twinkling lights. Douglas was down there, somewhere, waiting. What would he think when he saw her? He would be stunned, speechless, feeling inferior in the presence of such beauty and probably showing signs of nervousness; men were normally like that, except, of course, for those multi-millionaires with their Ferraris and ocean-going yachts, who were too confident in themselves to feel inferior to anyone.

'As I said, Helmut was very pleased with your work today.' Otto pressed his foot on the accelerator as they came to a straight stretch of road. 'It was exactly how he wanted it.'

Alert to his compliments, her attention swung back to him. 'I'm so glad,' she replied, 'although it has been difficult for me.'

'It has been difficult for *all* of us,' he corrected her.

Peri made no comment but thought: it has been a hell of a lot more difficult for *me* than it has for *you!*

They were approaching the town. The main street cut through the small grey buildings in a straight line, illuminated on both sides by an inordinate number of streetlamps, their hard glare shining mercilessly down on the empty pavements. And it seemed to Peri that all these lights had been put there as if to compensate for the total lack of them everywhere else.

'Here we are.' Otto stopped the car in front of a small shabby hotel and got out. From above the door hung a rusty sign with the picture of a bird in flight and the words *The Osprey Hotel* in white chipped paint. Otto took a couple of bags from the boot of the car and turned towards the building.

'Aren't you going to lock the car?' she asked, standing by her door.

He shook his head. 'It will be okay.'

She shrugged and followed him into the hotel. There, she stopped and looked about for a moment. This was exactly how she imagined it would be. The entrance hall was lit with a single lightbulb and the air was thick with the smell of mildew and neglect. The walls were covered in a maroon-coloured flock wallpaper and up above the staircase hung moth-eaten stags' heads and grinning weasels in glass cases. On the first floor Otto unlocked a door into a cheap-looking bedroom. 'Unfortunately, this is not the Ritz.'

'Evidently!' Peri glanced around, imagining bed-bugs in the mattress and mice behind the skirting boards. 'I'm surprised that they're allowed to call this place a hotel,' Peri remarked sourly, beginning to get undressed. She wondered if, after this experience, she would be so ready to complain if there were no fresh flowers in her suite at the George V, or that the obscure brand of bottled water in her bathroom at the Dorchester was not her usual Evian.

Otto had turned to the ironing board which stood in front of the wardrobe. 'Take a look at this,' he said, holding up a shimmering silver evening dress with a hemline of frothing silver organza. 'San Lorenzo.'

'It's beautiful,' Peri breathed, taking it from him and holding it at arm's length to admire it. She put it back over the ironing board and slipped off her vest, noticing that Otto had politely turned away. This was unnecessary because she was accustomed to being naked in crowded backstage rooms wearing only a g-string and surrounded by paparazzi; but it was a nice gesture. She slipped the dress over her head, smoothing the soft clinging material down over her hips, twirling from one side to another, watching the organza float around her ankles. It was then that she saw the bulge. She gasped, staring down in horror. She looked positively *pregnant*! 'Otto,' she wailed, pointing to her stomach. *'Look!'*

He spun round, immediately clamping his hand over his mouth in horror. 'You have eaten too much,' he accused her. 'This is terrible. Terrible. Breathe in. More. *More!*'

She breathed in until she was red in the face, but still the bulge would not go away. 'Oh, God!'

'It was the apple pie!' he said angrily. '*Why* did you eat apple pie before a shoot? What is Helmut going to say?' He looked around in agitation and spotted a silver purse lying on the bed. 'Hold this against your stomach,' he said, thrusting it at her. 'And keep it there!'

She took the bag. 'I was just so hungry,' she wailed.

With pursed lips, he fastened a diamante necklace around her throat. 'You are a supermodel – supermodels do not gobble up apple pie before a shoot!' He handed her a pair of diamante earrings and waited while she put them on, and then said, 'Let's go.'

After a hasty glance in the mirror, she followed him out of the room and into the icy corridor. 'I'm sorry – really,' she said, treading carefully down the stairs, clutching the purse against her stomach. How could she have been so stupid? But she had been *so* hungry!

Now they were entering the bar and swiftly her eyes searched for Helmut, but she couldn't see him, just a group of big beefy men in tartan kilts sitting under a huge shield at the far end of the room. Where was Helmut?

What would he say if he saw her bulge? God – it would be so embarrassing! And Otto had said that if Helmut had been drinking whisky he would turn into a monster. How she prayed that he hadn't been drinking whisky.

The heat radiating from the vast log fire enveloped her like a cosy blanket and she was grateful for it. At least she would be warm. As she continued her search for Helmut, she noticed that the walls were covered in red tartan and from the ceiling above the mantelpiece hung two great axes.

Gradually, the babble of Scottish voices died away and a hush rippled through the room as, one by one, the men in kilts turned to stare at her, their eyes round with astonishment. Of course she was accustomed to people staring, but she had never before experienced such a deathly silence. She could almost see herself walking into the room, her glossy black hair coiled on top of her head, her long slender throat sweeping down to a diamante necklace, her fine silky dress outlining the shape of her nipples. At any moment now, Douglas would see her like this, and, at the thought of it, she suddenly felt a tingling sensation in the pit of her stomach.

Through the archway she spotted Helmut and immediately she gripped the purse closer to her stomach. Otto was making straight for him and she followed behind, avoiding the stares of the people around her. As they came under the arch and into a larger room, she caught sight of Douglas. He was standing in the far corner with his back to her, laughing with his friends. As if sensing the hush in the air, his friends casually looked across and when they saw her their eyes widened in astonishment. This caused Douglas to pause mid-speech and to turn around, curious to know what they had seen.

Peri thrilled with his reaction; his eyes looked as if they would pop out of his head and the glass of beer that he had been lifting stopped, poised halfway to his lips. She flashed him a sexy smile, knowing that it would make him flustered and embarrassed, and create a stir among his friends.

'Don't forget to keep the bag across your stomach,' Otto hissed. They were approaching Helmut who was kneeling on the floor in front of a metal case.

'Has he been drinking whisky?' Peri whispered to Otto.

'I do not know.'

Helmut stood up when he saw Peri and smiled. '*Wunderbar*,' he said, spreading out his arms in greeting. 'I have a surprise for you.' He turned to the table and took a bottle out of an ice bucket, holding it up. 'Bollinger '75.'

'Oh, thank you!' Peri exclaimed, surprised and delighted. How did he know? It was her favourite! But her surprise did not prevent her from searching for his glass. There were four glasses, she discovered, all empty.

As he poured champagne into all of them, she heaved a sigh of relief. He wasn't drinking whisky, after all; he was drinking champagne.

Helmut beamed, clinking his glass against hers. '*Prost!* I am delighted with this morning's work. Let us hope it continues.'

Peri gave him her most charming smile. Was this the best

time to ask him if he would release a photograph for publication? Maybe not. Maybe at the end of the evening, when he had drunk more champagne, when he was more relaxed, when the job was finished. Suddenly, she heard a cough behind her.

'Hello.' It was Douglas, coming to stand beside her. 'You look fantastic!'

'Do you think so?' she asked innocently. 'Do you like the dress?'

His eyes roamed her body, his head nodding enthusiastically. 'Aye – that I do. It's very bonny.'

She felt powerful and sexy and beautiful, at ease with this vestige of normality. Now Douglas was seeing her as she truly was: beautiful, sophisticated . . . untouchable. As she sipped her champagne, she closed her eyes in ecstasy, taking on her role of glamorous supermodel. 'Mmm . . . civilisation,' she murmured. 'I couldn't survive without champagne, you know,' she told Douglas. 'Champagne and caviare.'

He chuckled. 'Me neither.'

Peri stopped in mid sip and looked at him. He thinks I'm joking, she thought incredulously, faintly aggravated by his stupidity.

He had accepted a glass of champagne from Helmut and now held it to his lips. 'I havnae had many of these,' he declared, grinning down at her, and threw the contents down his throat. Immediately he spluttered as his face crumpling in agony. 'The bubbles have gone up my nose!' he whined, rubbing his nose vigorously with the back of his hand. Helmut laughed before turning away to reply to something that Otto was showing him.

Peri was furious. 'Good!' she snapped, angry at the way he was destroying the glamourous mystique that she was trying to achieve.

'It tastes like Irn-Bru,' Douglas continued. 'Only fizzier.'

Peri frowned. 'Iron Brew?' It sounded like some sort of medicine.

Douglas nodded. 'It's a fizzy lemonade drunk by the Glasgow steel workers!'

She narrowed her eyes menacingly. He was trying to wind her up! One of his eyebrows was cocked and the other was down and he had a cheeky, jaunty attitude as if trying to goad her. 'Champagne needs a delicate palate,' she told him coolly. 'And anyone with the palate of an *ape* would . . .'

'Okay, okay,' Helmut interrupted. 'Enough chatter. We have work to do. Peri, would you please go and stand by the bar? You may take your drink with you.'

Ruffled up with irritation, she moved across to the bar, angry that she was unable to retaliate against Douglas. Just in time, she remembered to hold the purse across her stomach. She was so grateful for it. She waited while Helmut studied the polaroid photograph, determined not to let her gaze drift across to Douglas. He was a country yokel, she decided, too uncouth to know how to converse with a lady. Helmut approached her with the light meter, clicking it in concentration and muttering. Then he was back behind the camera, and they started work. But after only a few minutes, he stopped, obviously dissatisfied. He turned to Douglas. 'I would like you to stand beside Peri. Would you do that for me?'

Douglas had been lounging back in an armchair, watching the proceedings; now he sat up in alarm. *'Me?'*

Helmut nodded. 'Only for a short time, and you can take your drink with you.'

Douglas's face was fiery red as he walked across to Peri. 'You'll have to tell me what to do,' he whispered fiercely.

Buoyed up with vicious glee, she watched his discomfort. 'Well, it's a pity about your hair,' she said grimly.

He brushed his hand down over his thick wiry hair. 'Does that look better?'

'No – not really.' She felt wicked. 'Your hair's too flat. Comb your fingers back through your scalp.'

He did as she suggested and then looked at her for judgement. From the other end of the bar, one of his friends gave a wolf whistle, causing a wave of uproarious laughter, but Douglas only grinned good-naturedly, his cheeks still crimson.

Peri put her head to one side as she considered him, maliciously pleased that his hair was now looking like the end of a loo brush. 'Mmm,' she murmured, frowning. 'No. That's worse. Try brushing it down over your forehead.'

As he began to brush his hair forward, one of his friends shouted out, 'Hey, Douglas, de yer want tae borrow ma curlers?' There followed uproarious laughter, but all the while Helmut seemed oblivious to it as he peered into his viewfinder. 'Good,' he muttered to himself. 'That's good. Move closer to each other,' he told them. 'Douglas – don't look at the camera. Talk to each other. Closer. Closer.' Helmut's head popped up from behind the camera. 'Peri – can you *please* move closer to Douglas? I'm sure he's not going to *eat* you!'

'Yes, he will!' shouted a jovial voice from amongst Douglas's friends.

Helmut straightened up and glared stiffly towards the direction of the voice. There was immediate silence. Peri glanced over to see what was happening. Douglas's friends had stopped grinning; one of them made a wry smile of apology while the other three had turned back to the bar and begun studying their beers with immense concentration.

'Thank you,' Helmut announced, and resumed his place behind the camera. 'Peri – please move closer to Douglas.'

Peri blushed and shuffled an inch closer. She didn't want to move closer to Douglas. It made her feel uneasy.

'Right,' Douglas whispered to her. 'What are we going to talk about?'

His eyes were only inches away and as she looked up into them she noticed how blue they were, making her think of sunshine sparkling on a tropical sea. For a moment, she wondered whether he was wearing tinted lenses, but of course he wouldn't be. He would be reasonably photogenic, she decided, and wondered if he realised that his face would appear in magazines all over the world. 'Do you realise,' she said gravely, 'that your face is going to appear on the cover of millions of magazines all over the world?'

'No!'

'Oh, yes,' she assured him, before heaving a sigh of regret. 'It's such a pity about your hair.'

The silly grin had gone from his face and now he looked uncomfortable and tense. As he went to brush his fingers through his hair once again, he suddenly stopped and grinned. 'What the heck! I'm no model. If they don't like how I look – tough!' He took a sip of beer and rested his elbow on the bar, relaxed and confident once again.

She was determined to wipe that smug look off his face. 'Have you arranged your fee for this?' she asked pleasantly.

'What do you mean?'

'Well, surely Helmut has discussed it with you. You don't want to be thought of as free labour, do you?'

Douglas looked bemused. 'No.'

'You should demand five hundred pounds at the very least!'

He stared at her. 'Is that what you get?'

'No.' She shook her head. 'I get more. Much, much more.'

He continued to stare at her, obviously thinking about what she had said. 'No, I couldnae ask for a penny more than I'm already getting. But – *five hundred pounds!* That would be enough to pay for six months' supply of animal feed.'

Animal feed! she thought incredulously. Why doesn't he get central heating put in and buy some decent soap! She took a sip of champagne, watching his friends from over the rim of her glass as they chatted quietly amongst themselves, throwing surreptitious glances at her, obviously fascinated by her. They would remember her for a very long time. So, too, would Douglas. In fact, he would probably never forget her. She drained her glass and put it on the bar. How long would it take for her to forget him? A week? A day? An hour? What would be his reaction when he finally discovered that, all this time, she had been destined to become a megastar? He would curl up with embarrassment, recalling how he had treated her, as if she had been just . . . just . . . *a pal!*

'You've certainly made an impact tonight,' Douglas whispered. 'They've never seen anyone like you before.'

Now she was suspicious of his compliments, wary of what he would say next.

'I was wondering: would you like to come to our ceilidh in June?'

'Kaylee?'

'It's a party. The ladies bring along haggis and clapshot – that's potatoes mashed with parsnips. Delicious! We have our own fiddler and the band comes up from the valley to play Scottish reels. It's probably not what you're used to but you'd enjoy it.'

She had never heard of anything so unappealing in all her life. 'That sounds fun,' she lied. 'Let me think about it.' In June she would be attending the Berkeley Square Ball to mingle with the elite of society, to drink Kir Royale from ice sculptures and eat delectable pieces of dim sum. She would certainly not come all the way up here to eat haggis and dance a jig!

'It would be great if you could come.'

'I can't promise,' she said, sounding suitably earnest. 'But I will try.' For a second, she was tempted to inform him that she normally charged for appearances at parties, but she decided against it, not knowing what stupid remark he would make.

Helmut had straightened up and ripped out the cartridge from the back of the camera. 'You may take a rest,' he told them, turning to say something to Otto.

'Would you like some more champagne?' Douglas asked, picking up her glass.

'Yes, please.' She watched him walk across to the table and take the bottle of champagne out of the ice bucket. Sometimes he can seem like a thug, she thought, and at other times he can act like a real gentleman, soft and caring, protective . . . someone who wouldn't stand by and watch some poor girl on the tube being sexually hassled by a weirdo. How would he react? Would he be polite and tell the guy to move away or would he punch him in the face? Recalling her first meeting with him, she knew exactly what he would do.

He was coming towards her now, holding out her glass. 'Here you go.'

'Thanks.'

'Shall we continue?' Helmut said, tilting the angle of the reflector before returning to the camera. 'I want smiles! Laughter! Look as if you're having fun.'

'Oh, God!' Peri groaned under her breath. 'I don't feel like laughing. Say something amusing.'

Douglas shrugged his shoulders helplessly. 'Err . . .' Suddenly he grinned and bent sideways to whisper in her ear. 'I gather that you've taken a fancy to wearing Mrs Craig's underwear!'

'Oh, *no!*' Peri groaned, putting a hand over her face to cover her embarrassment.

'Please, Peri,' Helmut said impatiently. 'Could I possibly see your face?'

She removed her hand at once and whispered fiercely under her breath. 'You *beast!*' Even though her cheeks were burning, there had been something comical in the way he had spoken and she found that she couldn't be angry.

Douglas continued in an earnest voice: 'I think you would look gorgeous in anything – even Mrs Craig's long-johns!'

Peri snorted and swung her head away, biting her lip to prevent herself from laughing. This was all too absurd! If he would only keep quiet, she would be able to stay in control. Thankfully, he remained silent.

She faced the camera once more, poised and composed, but aware that her eyes danced and that the bubbly feeling inside her chest was still there. Douglas was also facing the camera. She glanced up at him and saw his solemn expression. Good. He was going to behave himself.

Then, without taking his eyes from the camera, he began to whisper from the corner of his mouth. 'You'd look good in her girdle, too.'

The bubbly feeling exploded into laughter. She couldn't stop herself. The sound of it burst from her lips, convulsing her body forward helplessly. It was a strange and wonderful sound, a sound she had never heard before. Through watering eyes she could see everyone staring, some looking surprised, some looking amused. Helmut wasn't looking amused. 'I'm sorry,' she gasped. But she couldn't stop herself. Everything suddenly seemed so funny. Helmut was peering suspiciously at her from under beetled eyebrows. This was too much. She burst into fresh laughter. 'I'm . . . s-sorry!' she gurgled, 'I don't mean to.' Tears poured down her cheeks and she had to press a hand against the pain in her side.

She took the handful of tissues that Otto offered and began to dab the corners of her eyes. The laughter was draining away and the bubbly feeling was gone, but she felt amazingly refreshed. 'Sorry about that,' she said, handing the ball of tissues back to Otto.

'I think you will need to repair the damage,' Helmut said wearily.

'Damage?'

He jerked his chin towards her. 'Your face.'

'Oh. Right.'

Otto briskly came forward with her vanity case and put it on the bar. 'I believe you will need this.'

'Thanks.' She took out a mirror and looked at herself. *Jesus Christ*. Her face was ravaged! Her nose was red, her eyes were bloodshot, and there were streaks of black mascara down her cheeks. So that's what laughter does, she thought, tilting her head to one side to squeeze eyedrops into her eyes. Not a pretty sight. But, at that moment, she really didn't care!

Within minutes she had repaired the damage, and with a disapproving look Otto removed her vanity case and took it back to the table.

'I'm sorry,' Douglas whispered.

'That's okay,' she whispered back. What a pity, she thought; here is Douglas looking mortified while Helmut and Otto are viewing me with extreme disapproval. Why? They should be rejoicing with me; this is the first time that I have every laughed genuinely, uncontrollably, and it is *wonderful!*

Helmut was speaking to Otto now. Then he turned to Peri. 'Would you please get rid of your bag,' he said in mild exasperation. 'I think we have seen enough of it.'

'Oh, shit,' Peri murmured, turning her back on Helmut and placing the purse on the counter.

'What's the problem?' Douglas asked.

'Look – just do as I say. When I turn to face you, immediately put your left hand on my right hip. Okay?'

'Yes, sure.' He sounded puzzled.

As she turned, she felt his big wide hand come down on her hip. 'Thanks.'

'I hope you're not trying to seduce me,' he whispered in mock severity.

She blushed. 'Don't be stupid.' His hand seemed to encompass her whole hip and she could feel the heat of it through the material of her dress. 'I don't want Helmut to see my tummy,' she explained. 'I ate too much dinner and my tummy is . . . um . . . well . . . I've got a . . .'

His eyes had travelled downwards as she spoke and now he was looking at her with a smile. 'Pot belly?' he suggested.

'Shh!' she hissed angrily. 'Don't fucking tell everyone!'

He stared at her in amazement. 'I didn't,' he protested. 'I whispered. No one could have heard me.'

She studied the buttons on his shirt, annoyed at herself for speaking so horribly. 'This is not a game,' she said, trying to explain her angry outburst. 'This is my career.'

'I know that,' he whispered harshly. 'I'm not a bloody idiot!'

She glanced up to see him frowning at her. 'Yeah, I know,' she persisted. 'But it's just that Helmut is the one person on planet Earth who can make me famous and—'

'There was no reason for you to be so rude.'

'I know, I know. I'm . . . sorry.' She was surprised to find that it wasn't so difficult to apologise, and immediately she could sense his whole body relax.

Now he was looking down at her with a wry grin. 'That's okay.'

She gave him her sweetest smile, knowing that it would instantly make amends for her rudeness and that he would, once again, be nice to her. She turned her head towards the camera and saw that Helmut was standing straight, studying one corner of the room. 'Okay, Peri,' he said, 'I would like you to sit in that armchair. Alone,' he added.

She remembered to pick up the purse from the bar, using it to cover her stomach as she crossed over to the armchair. As she sat down, she dropped the purse on the floor and draped her arm across her stomach. Thankfully, Helmut had still not noticed. He had picked up the tripod and was moving it into position as Otto scurried about adjusting the reflectors. She wanted desperately to look at herself in the mirror but that would mean crossing over to her vanity case and she couldn't risk Helmut seeing her stomach. She glanced around the walls but there were no mirrors. It was a pity, she thought, that with all the beauty she possessed, she was unable to see it, except by looking in a mirror. That was the reason why she preferred to go to the Savoy for dinner; there, she could sit all evening and admire herself in the vast mirrors along the wall.

Helmut had slotted in a cartridge and was now looking at her through the camera; then he peered at her from over the top of the camera, his eyes narrowing as he studied her from head to toe. She went cold. Had he noticed? His eyes were everywhere, so alert, so watchful. 'Please move the lamp,' he said at last, and immediately Otto came across and lifted the lamp out of the shot. 'That's better,' Helmut said to himself and looked once again through the lens of the camera. 'I want you to look at the far wall, Peri.'

She lifted her chin and gazed at the shield against the wall.

'Good,' Helmut said and the camera flashed.

She was back at work, concentrating solely on the camera

and listening to Helmut's instructions. Briefly, she thought of Douglas, and that was when she glanced over to the bar and saw him staring at her thoughtfully. He's probably thinking how beautiful I am, she mused, and marvelling at how someone like me could end up in a place like this.

She was glad that she was sitting. She was beginning to feel so tired now; the evening seemed to be going on and on and on. Suddenly she longed for her bed, not caring that it had a sagging mattress and that the pillows were flat and there was a draught from the window. She just wanted to sleep.

When at last Helmut was finished, he held up his hand. 'Okay, Peri. That's it. Finished. You can get changed.'

Exhausted, she pushed herself out of the armchair, knowing that if she stayed a minute longer she wouldn't be able to move. Otto brought her vanity case across and together they went back under the archway, smiling in response to the waves from the men at the tables, passing by the great log fire, out into the cold corridor. It was like a dream.

'It was fortunate that Helmut did not see your fat stomach,' Otto said, unlocking the door to the room.

Peri followed him in. 'Yeah,' she murmured, gazing longingly at the bed and wondering whether she could ask to stay for the night. Wearily, she dragged the dress over her head and dropped it on the floor before slipping into Mrs Craig's long warm cosy vest. It was only with an overwhelming effort that she was able to put her clothes on. Otto was moaning on about something but she couldn't quite grasp what he was saying because his words kept floating in and out of her brain and she couldn't hold on to them.

Then they were ready to go. 'Helmut would like us to join him in the bar for a nightcap,' Otto announced, opening the door to let her pass by.

Oh no! she thought desperately, I just want to *sleep*. She held on tight to the banister as she descended the stairs, wanting to wail, 'I just want to sleep! I just want to sleep!' Douglas was standing down below and when he looked up at her, he frowned and came swiftly up the stairs and took her vanity case out of her hand. 'Let's get you home,' he said, supporting her under her elbow.

'Helmut wants us to join him for drinks,' Otto informed him, 'and we . . .'

'You'll have to give Helmut our apologies,' Douglas interrupted. 'Peri's dead on her feet.'

'But—'

'But nothing!' Douglas stopped and Peri could feel his hand tighten on her elbow. 'Peri has been standing out in the freezing cold all day with nothing to eat, she's worked under stress and fear, and then you bring her here and fill her with champagne! *For Christ's sake!*' He nudged her gently, steering her down the stairs and across the hallway to the front door, and it was obvious from his attitude and Otto's silence that the matter was closed.

'Thanks,' she whispered as they came out into the freezing night. A puff of cloud came from her mouth as she spoke.

'Nae bother.'

At the kerbside stood a battered old Land Rover with its engine chugging, a plume of exhaust smoke trailing into the cold night air. He guided her towards it and opened the door, helping her in. 'I've had the heater on. Here. I'll just put this sleeping bag over you.' He tucked her in, closed the door and came round to the driver's side and got in. 'Put this jumper by your head.'

She took it from him, and wedged it between her head and the window, knowing that it was his jumper. It had his smell, carbolic soap and woodsmoke. Hot air blasted up from her feet and over her ankles, deliciously warm. She yawned, feeling her eyelids so heavy that she could hardly keep them open. Now the Land Rover was moving off.

'You okay?' Douglas asked.

'Mmm.' It was such an effort to speak. 'Thank you for making me laugh . . .' Her words trailed away as exhaustion crept over her, numbing her brain as she felt herself helplessly sinking into a deep, deep sleep.

* * *

An icy wind touched her cheek. She opened her eyes. She was being carried in someone's arms. Was it Douglas? A yellow glow in the blackness. She didn't want to be carried. She should be walking, but she was so, so tired. Mrs Craig's voice coming softly from the yellow glow. 'Oh, the poor wee lassie! Take her straight on up.'

Bright light. Smell of warm flour. Dim light. Creaking stairs. That musty smell. Douglas was placing her gently down and she was sinking, sinking into the soft mattress. Bed at last. Now she just wanted everyone to go away. Leave her to sleep. Douglas started to pull off her gloves. 'No, no.' It was Mrs Craig, protesting softly, 'Away ye go. I'll do that.'

Helplessly, Peri could feel herself drifting away, gliding effortlessly into sweet unconsciousness.

Chapter Five

Peri opened her eyes and listened. It was raining. Up on the roof water splashed and gurgled in the guttering, and from the window came the sound of rain hitting the glass, as if handfuls of grit were being hurled against it. She lay still for a moment, waiting for the gloom of a new day to settle, but, to her surprise, it didn't. In fact, she felt remarkably lighthearted. Why? What had happened to make her feel like this? She stretched luxuriously, pointing her toes to the foot of the bed. It could be her biorhythms, she considered, and began to analyse her mood.

At that moment, the sound of rattling crockery heralded Mrs Craig's arrival. 'Did you sleep well?' she asked, carrying in the teatray.

'Like a *log!*'

Mrs Craig chuckled, putting the tray on the bedside cabinet. 'Well, that doesnae surprise me. You were jiggered.'

'It was kind of Douglas to carry me in.'

'Aye.' Mrs Craig went over to the fan heater and switched it on. 'He's a good man. And do you know what I believe? I believe that it will be a very lucky woman indeed who gets tae marry him.'

'Yes, I'm sure you're right,' Peri murmured, not wanting to dispel the woman's illusions. Okay, maybe the guy was kind, but he had nothing to offer a woman apart from this moth-eaten barn and some rabbits. 'It sounds a bit wet outside,' she remarked, wriggling up into a sitting position and reaching for her cup.

'Aye. That it is.' Mrs Craig drew back the curtains, and for a moment gazed out into the rain. 'It's at this time of year when I think the spring will never come; and, oh! how I long for the sun on my face. Tae see the bluebells and wild pansies bobbing their heads in the sunshine. Och, and the smell coming o'er the mountains! 'Tis sweeter than any of yer fancy perfume.' She turned from the window. 'Och, well. It will be worth waiting for.' Then she spied Hamish lying on the eiderdown and frowned. 'I hope that cat's not making a nuisance of himself.'

'No, no. Not at all.' Peri stroked Hamish's head protectively. At her touch, the cat uncurled himself and yawned widely, showing two tiny pointed teeth, and then he gazed up at her with big watery eyes. Peri smiled fondly at him. 'Can I give him a saucer of milk when I come downstairs?'

Mrs Craig threw the cat a disapproving look. 'Aye. Just a wee drop, mind. And don't forget to telephone Mags.'

At the sound of her agent's name, Peri felt a flicker of anger. 'Oh, right, yeah.' She still wasn't going to speak to her. Not yet! Let her stew!

'She sounded truly worried,' Mrs Craig said, bending to pick up Peri's jumper from the floor. 'And she told me to tell you to give her a buzz – *pronto*.'

Peri smiled at this, amused to hear this old Scottish woman repeating her agent's jargon.

Mrs Craig turned for the door, folding the jumper and putting it on the dressing table. 'I'm away doon,' she said, 'and if you're wanting anything, I'll be in the kitchen.'

Moments after the housekeeper had gone, Otto came in, looking tired and miserable. 'Good morning,' he muttered.

'Morning,' she said brightly, sipping her tea. 'Oh, dear, you do look tired.'

Otto groaned and sat, slumped, on the end of the bed. 'This house is so silent! I cannot become accustomed to it.'

He dragged his hands down over his face. 'I live on the corner of the Marienplatz. You know it?' He looked up to see if she did, but she shook her head. 'It's in the centre of Munich,' he explained. 'There is noise twenty-four hours a day. But here . . . !' He sighed helplessly.

'I know what you mean,' Peri agreed. 'If I had to live here, I would have to have cable TV on in every room – full volume – just to remind myself that I wasn't the only person left on planet Earth!'

'I would also.' He yawned. 'Anyway, I came to inform you that we cannot work in this rain. But the weather forecast predicts that the afternoon will be dry. If that is the case, Helmut plans for us to go to a small church – about twelve kilometres from here. It will not be a fashion shoot. Helmut is compiling a series of photographs for his next book which will highlight the romanticism of death.'

'Death?'

'Yes.'

Peri frowned. 'Is there anything you need to tell me?' she asked suspiciously.

Despite his weariness, Otto smiled. 'Do not look alarmed! All you will have to do is look a little sad and stand among the gravestones!'

Peri made a wry face. 'Great,' she said heavily.

But Otto seemed unaware of her sarcasm. 'When we have finished at the church,' he continued, 'we will return to the Osprey Hotel and have dinner. We saw some of the food last night and it looked very good. They serve grilled salmon straight from the river and venison pie with creamed potatoes and leeks. So – this evening – you may eat as much as you like, *after* the shoot!' Although these last words were spoken in a grave censorial voice, his eyes were kind.

Peri bit her lip. 'Sorry about that.'

'Well, it was fortunate that Helmut didn't notice, otherwise he would have gone ape-shit.'

Peri laughed. '*Ape-shit!* How did you learn such a horrid word!'

Otto looked pleased with himself. 'We had builders come over from London for a few months and they taught me their swear words. But it is the first time I've used that particular word.'

'It's a good one,' she praised, nodding her head. 'The perfect word to describe what would have happened if Helmut had seen my tummy!'

Otto laughed. 'That is true.'

Peri continued in a subdued voice. 'Was he annoyed that I didn't join him for drinks?'

'A little – yes – until I explained the situation.' Otto paused and looked at her closely. 'I told him that your friend Douglas had *insisted* on taking you back.'

Peri blushed. 'He's not my *friend*. He would have done the same for anybody.'

Otto judged her words for a moment and then nodded. 'Yes – I think you are right.' He stood up, and headed for the door. 'Now, I am going back to bed; and hopefully I will sleep. See you later.'

'Can I get you anything? Do you want a sleeping tablet?'

He shook his head. 'No. I must be ready to work, in case the weather changes.'

'Okay. Good luck.' As Peri watched the door close behind him, she pondered on what he had said. Would Douglas *really* have done the same for anybody else? Yes – he would. Definitely. At the thought of it, she felt strangely disappointed. She turned her gaze to the window and stared at the rivulets of rain wiggling down the glass, recalling Mrs Craig's words: *it will be a very lucky woman who gets to marry him*. What sort of woman would that be? She would probably be short and plump, jolly and kind, good at cooking bread and cakes; but she wouldn't know how to handle a kohl pencil, or pluck her eyebrows or shape her nails. *And* she would have hairy armpits! Peri grinned to herself, remembering how she and Douglas had squabbled the day before.

Happily, she swung out of bed and put on her dressing gown, tying the cord around her waist. Then, for a moment she stood at the window gazing out at the rain. It looked like a silvery sheet across the landscape, blocking out the view of the mountains and forests. What would she do, now the day lay empty before her? There was no television. No magazines. No shops to visit. No gym. Well, she could sit in front of the log fire and stroke the cat. Or spend a few hours on her beauty routine. She would do both, she decided; but she would do her beauty routine first. She turned purposefully from the window and thought hard. Would she give herself a seaweed bath? No. It would be too cold for that. A body scrub and facial? Yes. Then afterwards she would coat her hair in Eduardo's liposebum almond oil for at least an hour, finishing off with a simple pedicure and manicure, concentrating on her cuticles and applying nail strengthener. 'Right,' she declared. 'I'd better get my stuff together.' She slipped her feet into her pink ballet slippers and carried her vanity case into the bathroom.

Taking her bottles and lotions from the case, she looked around to see where she could put them, but there was no table – no work surface of any sort – only a tiny shelf above the sink which held Douglas's shaving brush and razor and a chipped mug with a toothbrush in it; all of these she put on the floor, replacing them with her own possessions, cramming as much as she could onto the stupidly tiny shelf. Next, she went over to the toilet and had a wee. When she had finished, she stood up, anticipating with dread the thunderous explosion which would reverberate around the silent house as soon as she pulled the chain. But she had to do it. Grasping the old metal handle, she pulled down hard and immediately the bathroom erupted in a thundering roar, shattering the morning's silence. It was deafening! And, although she had become accustomed to it, she couldn't help being embarrassed, knowing that everyone in the house was aware of what she had been doing. That was something else that Douglas should buy – a decent toilet.

Right. Now she would need to get the rest of her things from the fridge. Out on the landing, she paused and listened. It was so silent! Where was everybody? Heading for the stairs, she remembered Hamish and went back to her room and scooped him off the bed. 'Come on, sweetie,' she said. 'I'll get you some milk.' As she came down the stairs, she anticipated the middle stair creaking under her foot, and sure enough it did. That was something else in this house to which she had become accustomed.

Douglas was sitting having his breakfast when she came into the kitchen. He was just lifting a forkful of black pudding to his mouth when he saw her. 'Good morning,' he smiled, lowering his fork. 'Did you sleep well?'

She smiled. 'Yeah. Great.' She looked at the greasy food on his plate and inwardly shuddered. 'Don't you know how much damage that stuff is doing to your system?' He glanced down at his plate and then looked back at her. His blank, questioning face made her think of his dog whenever she shooed it away.

'I dinna care,' he replied. 'I'm only eating like this because you folk are here. The rest o' the time it's porridge fer me.'

'I'm glad to hear it.' She turned to the fridge and opened the door. 'I want to thank you for last night,' she said. 'I appreciate you sticking up for me – although you didn't have to carry me into the house.'

'Aye.' He put the forkful of food in his mouth and began to chew seriously. 'What a struggle. I thought I was going tae do my back in!'

Playfully, she poked her tongue out at him and turned back to the fridge, taking out a bottle of milk and kicking the door shut with her foot. It gave her a cosy feeling having him there, as if he were a big brother, casual, friendly, helpful, someone she was becoming accustomed to, just like the creaking stair and the noisy toilet.

'And how about you?' she asked, placing Hamish gently on the floor. 'Did you get your beauty sleep?'

He guffawed in reply.

'No, honestly,' she said, pretending to be serious. 'Now that you're a male model, you've got to make sure you get plenty of beauty sleep.'

He grinned. 'Well, I guess I'll be having tae do a lot of sleeping.'

She laughed. 'That's true.' She took a large bowl from the dresser and put it on the floor in front of Hamish and began to fill it with milk.

'So you've got yerself a friend,' Douglas commented, nodding towards the cat.

'Yes. Isn't he just adorable?' She filled the bowl to the top, gave Hamish a stroke and straightened up, putting the empty milk bottle on the table. At that moment, a gust of wind hurled the rain against the window and she glanced towards it. 'It's meant to be dry this afternoon, but I can't see that happening. Can you?'

Douglas shrugged. 'The weather up here can change in a blink of an eye – so I cannae say.'

'I don't know whether I want it to rain or not. Helmut has plans for me to hang around some graveyard as soon as the weather clears.'

'Oh, aye. That'll be Duggan Kirk Chapel. I took him there the other day. It's a pretty spot . . . when the sun's shining.'

'Mmm,' Peri murmured doubtfully. She opened the fridge door once again and began filling her pockets with a bottle of witch-hazel eyedrops, half a cucumber, an avocado, a bottle of skin toner, a tube of apricot face scrub and a jar of honey.

'I was wondering what that lot was doing in there,' Douglas said. 'What does "exfoliate" mean?'

'What?' She banged the door shut and turned to him. 'You've got nothing better to do than to stand at the fridge door and read the labels on my bottles?'

Douglas chuckled. 'Well, it's lucky that I can read – otherwise I would've had that lot for ma dinner!'

Peri laughed. It was a lovely sound, frothy and light, and it made her feel happy. 'I refuse to talk to you,' she said airily and folded her arms across her chest, focusing her attention on Hamish, whose little pink tongue was busily lapping up the milk.

'That animal's no' meant to stay in the house,' Douglas said, pouring brown sauce onto the side of his plate. 'He's no' some tabby cat. But I've let him be, because Mrs Craig said that you were taken wi' him.'

'But why can't he stay in the house?' Peri exclaimed, unfolding her arms and bunching her fists. 'You can't possibly force him to live out *there!*'

'Well, normally, I don't need tae, but for some reason he's taken a liking to you.'

Seeing that Hamish had finished, she scooped him up under his tummy and held him in her arms protectively. 'He's taken a liking to me because I care for him. Not like *you*, who forces him to live out in the freezing cold!'

Douglas pointed a fork at the cat. 'He's no' going to stay like that, you know. He might be hand-tame now, because he's young, but in a couple o' months, he's no' going to be letting anyone cuddle him like that.'

'You make him sound like a wild animal!'

Douglas stopped in mid-chew and stared at her. 'You know he's a wildcat, don't you?'

'That is *such* a sick joke!'

Now he was looking worried. 'I'm no' joking. Truly. Didn't Mrs Craig tell you?'

She stiffened and glanced cautiously down at the ball of fluff in her arms before frowning at Douglas. 'You're lying!'

'No, I'm not. Take a look at the tail. You wouldnae see a big bushy tail like that on a domestic cat, nae those big paws and the stripes in his fur. I thought you knew.'

Peri's thoughts darted backwards and forwards. This could

be another one of his wind-ups. Or he could be telling the truth. Or he was lying. She had never been *near* a cat in her life, so how could she know if he was telling the truth?

'It's a *Felis sylvestris grampia*,' Douglas said, getting up from the table and walking to the door. 'Wait a minute – I'll show you.'

Peri waited, determined to ignore the urge to put the cat on the floor, determined not to be taken in – yet again – by one of Douglas's stupid jokes. And yet she felt uncomfortable, suspiciously studying the bushy striped tail and the wide padded feet. How was she to know? Especially as it looked more like a kiddy's pyjama-case than anything else.

Douglas came back carrying a thick book, his index finger pointing to a photograph of a big snarling cat. 'Here: it says *"Wildcat"*.'

'Fuck!' she cried, releasing Hamish and stepping back. 'Why the hell didn't you tell me? My God! he's been sleeping on my bed!' Hamish had fallen on all paws and now stood there, looking stunned.

Douglas burst into a roar of laughter. 'Oh, Peri,' he chortled. 'I'm s-s-sorry.' Now there were tears rolling down his cheeks. 'I d-don't mean tae laugh.'

Peri threw him a disgusted look and turned for the door.

'No, no,' he said, holding her wrist while trying to control his laughter. 'I don't mean to laugh – but your face! It's the funniest . . . sight I've ever . . . seen!'

She jerked her arm to try and free herself but his hand remained clamped around her wrist. 'Let me go!' she shouted.

Suddenly, Mrs Craig appeared in the doorway. 'Whisht! Whisht! – the two of you!' she whispered fiercely. 'Otto is trying tae have his sleep.' Then she caught sight of Douglas's hand clamped around Peri's wrist and her voice rose in anger. 'Douglas MacLeod! What do you think yer doin'? Release Peri at once!'

As soon as her wrist had been released, Peri held it up to her chest and rubbed it, throwing Douglas a reproachful look while pretending that he had hurt her. Now he was going to be in trouble!

'What's got into you, Douglas MacLeod?' Mrs Craig stormed. 'You're behaving like a heathen. First, you throw the lassie over yer shoulder and now you're holding her against her will. Is this fer the same reason why you and Mary McEwan fell out?'

It was obvious that Douglas was trying to make it appear that he was taking the situation seriously, but Peri could see the merriment in his eyes as he gently confronted Mrs Craig, who stood ruffled up with indignation. 'Mary and I did not fall out,' he assured her. 'We simply went our separate ways. And I promise you: I have never manhandled a lassie in my life – not until I met Peri, that is. For some reason, she's got the knack of bringing it out o' me.'

Peri gasped with furious indignation. *'Bullshit!'*

Douglas looked at her, his face bright with amusement. Then he was looking back at Mrs Craig. 'This particular dispute is to do with Hamish. I had thought that you'd mentioned tae Peri that Hamish is wild.'

'But I did!' Mrs Craig turned to Peri. 'I did tell you. Remember? After you had just arrived, when I was taking you up the stairs?'

Peri stared at her, thinking. Yes, Mrs Craig had been telling her something about the cat, but she hadn't been listening, had she? She had been too much in shock. Mrs Craig and Douglas were now looking at her, as if waiting for an answer. 'Yeah, I remember you saying something but I wasn't listening properly.'

'Anyway,' Douglas continued, 'when I explained it to Peri, she was so shocked, it made me laugh. Of course, I didnae mean to laugh and I wanted to reassure her; that's why I grabbed her arm, to stop her from marching off.' He was now looking at Peri. 'I'm sorry.'

Peri didn't know what to say. She could feel Hamish's fluffy body circling her legs as he miaowed to be picked up; but she didn't move.

Mrs Craig picked him up instead. 'Don't be frightened of him, lassie. Besides, he's still a kitten.'

Peri stared at the cat, undecided.

'He was new-born when Douglas found him. The mother had been shot and the litter had died of hunger, except Hamish here. So, Douglas brought him back to the house and nursed him until he was strong enough tae fend for himself. But he's still no' ready to go back into the wild just yet.'

Peri watched as Hamish rubbed the side of his nose with his paw. He was only a kitten, after all, she thought; and he, too, had lost his mother. 'All right then,' she relented and held out her hands, gently taking him into her arms.

'There now!' Mrs Craig announced. 'We're all friends again. I'll put the kettle on.'

As the woman bustled away, Peri gave the cat a stroke and looked up sheepishly at Douglas from under her eyelashes. 'I must have looked like an idiot,' she murmured, realising how she had reacted.

Douglas nodded, grinning. 'T'was magic! I've never seen anything sae funny.' He started to chuckle and soon he was laughing again.

Suddenly, Peri was caught up in his laughter, and each time she pictured how she had screamed and dropped the cat, she laughed even more. Soon, they were falling against each other, laughing helplessly, friends once more.

Peri lay perfectly still on the bed, her hair coated in Eduardo's liposebum almond oil and turbanned in a large towel, her face and neck covered in a thick layer of honey and mashed avocado, and, upon her closed eyelids, two slices of cold cucumber, effectively glued on by the honey and avocado mix. Wedged between each toe were balls of pink fluffy cotton wool which allowed the strawberry-scented nail strengthener to harden without smudging. As usual, the cucumber slices were beginning to make her skin itch and she desperately wanted to claw them off, but she had to suffer them.

'Go, baby, go,' she mimed softly as the music beat into her head. Her Walkman lay on her chest with the wires leading up to the earphones which had been securely lodged inside each ear. She could always time herself by the music; when the second side of the tape ended, she would be ready to clean herself off. But she was still on the first side. The third song was just drifting into silence when she realised that someone was banging on her door.

'Peri?' It was Douglas. Shouting. 'Can I . . . ?'

'Go away!' she yelled. The next song started, effectively wiping out his voice. Why was he bothering her *now?* She would ignore him. Jesus! But what if he came in and saw her like this? With a yank of the wires, her earphones popped out, suddenly exposing her to his angry voice.

'. . . let the cat in,' he was shouting. 'So why are you being so bloody rude?'

She was silent. Suddenly he was silent. Maybe he would just go away, she thought, carefully removing a slice of cucumber from her right eye and peering at the door.

Silence. Then a plaintive miaowing came from outside the door. Hamish!

'Right!' Douglas shouted. 'I'm throwing him in!' The door opened, an arm curved around the door with Hamish at the end of it and then Hamish was flying through the air. Crash! There was the sound of all her bottles on the floor, smashing like skittles against each other.

'Fuck!' she exclaimed, unable to move. 'Get in here, Douglas! Quick!' The door flew open and Douglas leapt in, poised for action, his eyes darting around the room. 'On the *floor!* My bottles. Pick them up.' From the corners of her eyes she could see him kneeling, hurriedly picking up shards of broken glass and putting them on her bedside cabinet.

'How was I tae know you had this lot on the floor?' he muttered furiously.

As she looked, she saw that the plastic bottle of Fleurise cleansing milk had remained intact but that most of it had gone. But worse was to come; all the glass bottles had been broken. She had lost her Clarins Skin Refresher, her Decleor Face Tonic, her witch-hazel eyedrops, her deep nourishing oil which had been made up especially for her in New York and had cost a hundred and twenty dollars. All gone! 'Why the hell did you have to throw Hamish across the room?'

'Hey! Wait a minute!' he exclaimed, throwing her a brief glance. 'If you'd just been civil enough to answer me in the first place, I wouldn't have had to throw him in. You cannae expect me to have to listen to that wailing!'

'What wailing?'

He placed a broken bottle top on the cabinet. 'The cat. What else!'

'Well, I didn't hear him.'

'Ye gan deef, then!' he muttered angrily, bending over to pick up some more glass.

'Pardon?'

'Don't tell me you didnae hear him!'

'But I didn't. I had my music on. *Look.*' She picked up the earphones to show him.

With a pile of broken glass cupped in his palm, he straightened up and studied the wires, frowning, obviously weighing up the meaning in her words. Then his gaze travelled up the wires to her face. As she watched, she saw a big grin spreading across his face like the sun moving across the front of a building, and his eyes twinkled devilishly. 'Christ, Peri! Do you know what you look like?'

He was laughing at her! How dare he! In the excitement, she had completely forgotten how she must look and now she cringed with humiliation, unable to move. She could only lie there, exposed to his scrutiny. 'Would you kindly leave the room?' she said stiffly, peeling the cucumber slice off her left eyebrow. 'I am not lying here for your amusement.'

His smile vanished instantly. 'Och, of course. I'm sorry, Peri. I didn't mean to laugh at you.' He looked about the carpet, suddenly flustered and embarrassed. 'Well . . . um . . . I'll go and get Mrs Craig to clean up the mess.' He turned swiftly and was out of the door.

Peri listened to his footsteps receding down the corridor. What an idiot! Now all her vital beauty products lay shattered on the carpet. She wouldn't be able to get any more now, not until she got back to London. She sighed and stared hard at the ceiling, the picture of her shattered bottles beginning to be replaced by the picture of his flustered face. What must he have thought, seeing her like this? Well, she certainly sent him away with a flea in his ear. It was amusing to see such a big tough man reduced to a flustered wimp. And his expression! She felt the bubbling feeling deep in her tummy, and now it was rising up, up, up; and suddenly she was laughing. 'Poor guy,' she murmured, chuckling to herself. 'He can probably cope with dragging a tractor out of a ditch but he can't cope with an angry female in an avocado face mask!'

There was a movement by her ankle. It felt like Hamish. She lifted her neck slightly and saw Hamish licking his back legs. 'Oh, no,' she cried, hastily sitting up. 'Don't lick that stuff. You'll be poisoned.' Without a moment's hesitation, she swept him up and carried him through to the bathroom, all the while feeling her honey and avocado mask dripping off her face and onto her dressing gown, and knowing, too, that the balls of cotton wool between her toes would be sticking to the nail varnish on her toenails. Her whole beauty routine had been destroyed. 'That Douglas is so *stupid* sometimes,' she muttered angrily, turning on the tap and gently putting Hamish's paw into the stream of running water. 'And *he's* the one who's meant to care for animals!'

Fifteen minutes later, after helping Mrs Craig clear up the mess from the bedroom carpet, Peri changed into jeans and a jumper and finished drying her hair. Now, with nothing more to do, she wandered downstairs and looked around for something or somebody to amuse her. In the sitting room, Douglas and Helmut sat by the window, silently playing a game of chess. When Douglas saw her, he straightened up. 'Everything okay?'

She nodded. 'Yeah.'

'I'm really sorry about the accident. I'll pay for the damage.'

'Don't worry about it.' How could he possibly afford to pay for the damage? she thought impatiently, although it had been very effective in wiping out that musty smell. 'I'm going to get a cup of tea,' she told him and turned away, padding off down the corridor. She guessed that Otto would still be sleeping; well, he had wanted noise and he had certainly got it, with that idiot Douglas banging and screaming at her door! What would she do now? There were no magazines, no television, nothing. There was only Mrs Craig. In the kitchen.

Mrs Craig sat alone at the kitchen table peeling boiled beetroots with inky-red fingers. 'Hello, dear,' she said as Peri came in. 'Make yerself a cup of tea – the water's just boiled.'

'Thanks.'

'I'm famous for my beetroot relish, you know,' Mrs Craig chatted. 'I got the recipe for it handed down to me by my grandmother.'

'Really?' Peri dropped a camomile teabag into a cup and poured boiling water over it, resigned to having to listen to the woman but knowing that it would be far better to be bored by this woman than to be left by herself.

'Do you like beetroot?' the woman continued.

'Yeah. Sure.' Peri carried her cup to the table and sat down.

'Well, you make sure to take some back to London with you.'

'Thanks.' Peri put her elbow on the table and rested her chin in her hand and stared out at the rain. God! she had never been so bored in all her life. She felt she wanted to do something active, to get her body moving. If she were in London right now, she would be at the gym, jogging on the running machine followed by a forty-minute workout on the pulse cycle. With a sigh, she turned back to Mrs Craig and casually studied her, her gaze travelling from the silvery fine hair pulled back in a bun to the straggly grey and silver eyebrows, the weathered cheek looking like crinkled polished leather, the small nimble fingers covered in beetroot juice. The woman had an aura of serenity as if she were truly content with what fate had given her. One day she, too, would have that serenity – once she had succeeded in becoming a Hollywood megastar.

'Is that bed comfortable enough fer you?' Mrs Craig asked.

'Yes, yes it is.' Peri smiled. 'Especially when I'm dropping with exhaustion!'

Mrs Craig chuckled. 'Aye – there's nae softer bed than when you've had a hard day's work.'

'Absolutely,' Peri murmured and sipped her tea, trying to think of something to say to the woman, but it was difficult since they had no common ground on which to converse. She replaced the teacup in its saucer and studied the surface of the wooden table, with its swirls and blemishes, its pale round rings made by hot pans, its dents and scratches. This was a very old table, she could tell, making her wonder who had sat here over the years; had they known happiness, sadness, or resignation to a dreary fate? Had little children sat around this table with crayons in their chubby hands, chatting eagerly to their mother who stood at the stove making their supper? Peri immediately blanked out the image and looked for something – anything – to do. The cutlery tray sat by her elbow and she took a small sharp knife from it, pushed her teacup away and picked up a beetroot, beginning to peel off the thick slippery skin.

'Here.' Mrs Craig dropped a piece of rag onto her lap. 'Keep this over yer troosers so they don't get stained.'

'Thanks.' Peri continued to peel the beetroot, watching her fingers and hands becoming covered in the thick, red juice. Somehow, it seemed strangely satisfying to get her beautifully manicured hands all messed up and gooey.

Mrs Craig rubbed her nose with the back of her hand. 'I

hear you'll be going up to Duggan Kirk Chapel when the rain clears.'

Peri nodded. 'Yeah, but I can't see the rain clearing.'

'You never know. At this time of the year the weather can do some strange things. Here.' Mrs Craig pushed a large white bowl towards her. 'And in the meantime, I'm going to show you the secret of making the finest beetroot relish in the world.'

Peri wanted to smile at Mrs Craig's grand announcement, but she replied with the words that the housekeeper would want to hear. 'I'm honoured. Thank you.'

This seemed to make Mrs Craig bustle with importance. 'What we've got to do now is tae finish peeling the beetroots, dice them up and put them in the bowl. Then we've got tae add some shredded cabbage and mustard powder. The secret ingredient for this is grated horseradish – that's the thing to give it bite. Here.' Mrs Craig gave Peri a lump of horseradish and a small grater.

Obediently, Peri began to follow the woman's instructions, grating the lump of horseradish into the bowl.

'When all the ingredients have cooked taegether for an hour, it goes into boiled jam jars and is pickled with vinegar.' Mrs Craig took some jam jars from the dresser behind her and put them on the table. 'It's a pity about all your lovely bottles getting broken,' she said. 'And all because of that cat.'

'But Hamish didn't know he was going to be thrown across the room, did he?'

'No – but he was standing at your door making such a racket. I've never heard the like. You'd have thought his tail had been cut off!'

Peri smiled. 'Oh, dear – and I never heard a thing.'

'We were all sitting down around the fire, saying, "Has she gone deef? Why doesn't she let him in and put him out of his misery?"'

Now Peri was laughing. 'I had my earphones in,' she gurgled. 'I couldn't hear any of it.'

Mrs Craig was laughing now. 'Well, Douglas threw his

book on the floor and marched out of the room, saying, "I'm no' listening tae that any longer." Then we heard him at your door shouting and shouting, and when there was no answer, me and Helmut got up thinking that maybe something had happened to you. It was when we got to the stairs we heard the crash of bottles and then . . .' Mrs Craig frowned, lowering her voice '. . . then we heard some words that a lassie shouldnae be saying!'

Peri bit her lip, her eyes dancing with the memory of it.

'Then we couldnae hear what was said, but when Douglas came doon the stairs looking sae red-faced, we didn't know *what* tae think!'

'Oh, dear,' Peri murmured guiltily. 'I was so horrid to him.'

'He shouldnae burst into a lady's room,' Mrs Craig said severely, chopping a beetroot in half. 'The great lump.'

Peri stopped and rested her wrists against the edge of the table, looking guiltily at Mrs Craig. 'I've been horrible to Douglas ever since I arrived, and yet he's been so kind to me. I feel awful.'

'Well, you've still got time to make it up tae him.'

'Yes. Definitely. I will.'

'He'll be going with you over to Duggan Kirk Chapel this afternoon, maybe you'll have a chance to have a quiet word with him then.'

Peri glanced towards the window and saw bright sunshine on the wall of the outhouse across the yard. 'It looks as if the rain's stopped.'

Mrs Craig followed her glance. 'Aye, it does. It's nice to see a bit of sunshine. The chapel is a bonny place when the sun shines, but at other times, it's no' so pleasant. It's certainly got some stories tae tell, mind – some good, some bad. It's been told that many years ago a clan chieftain from the Black Isles was journeying up through the mountains when he fell in love with a local girl. Well, he took her back wi' him and I cannae say if she were happy or sad, but a few years later she died in giving birth to his son. Now, as the story goes, she had made him vow on leaving her homeland that when she died she would be brought back and buried at Duggan Kirk Chapel, on the wester side where the snowdrops grow in spring, looking out towards the setting sun. Well, on her death the chieftain not only honoured his vow, but he also carried her himself across to the mainland, over the hills and glens, right up to the door of Duggan Kirk Chapel. And there he kissed her fer the very last time, before his long, long journey back tae his castle on the Black Isle.'

'Oh! That's so *sad!*' Peri exclaimed.

'Aye, tis a sad tale.'

'What was her name?'

'Mary Lomax.'

'But that's my name!' Peri cried.

Mrs Craig looked perplexed. 'Mary Lomax?'

'No, no. *Lomax*. That's my surname.'

'Och, I didnae ken. I've just known you as Peri. What a coincidence!'

'Isn't it?' Peri put down her knife and turned to Mrs Craig, eager to know more of the story, now that there was a connection with herself. 'Was she beautiful?'

'Most certainly – if a clan chieftain took her for his bride.'

'And he carried her body all the way home. Was it a long way?'

'Oh, aye!' Mrs Craig exclaimed, 'The Black Isle? It's more than . . .' Suddenly the telephone shrilled. 'Och, isn't that typical – me with my hands covered in beetroot juice. Douglas!' she shouted. 'Can you answer the telephone?' She looked back at Peri. 'I bet it's that agent of yours again. She'll be wanting to check in for an update.'

Mags was impatient. Every little thing that morning had proved difficult and now she sat with the phone to her ear, drumming her fingers on her desk, waiting. Why wasn't someone answering? She was just about to crash the receiver back in its cradle, when the ringing tone stopped.

'Hello. Douglas MacLeod speaking.'

It was that man again, the one with the slow sexy voice. 'Hello . . . Douglas? We spoke yesterday . . .'

'Oh, hello. Margaret-Anne, is it?'

He had remembered her name! 'You've remembered my name. How clever of you.' She could just melt at that voice! Suddenly the urgency of her call evaporated. 'Call me Mags, please. So – how are you?'

'I'm fine, thank you. And yerself?'

'Oh, stuck in this stuffy old office wishing I was out in the fresh Highland air.'

She heard that chuckle again . . . mmm . . . it made her spine tingle.

'It's certainly fresh,' he answered. 'And Peri's here to tell you just how fresh it is!'

Now she could hear Peri's voice in the background. 'I've got to wash my hands,' she was saying. 'Tell her to hang on.'

Douglas was back on the line. 'Can you please wait a while? Peri's washing her hands.'

'No rush.' How could she find out what he looked like? She would have to ask Peri. 'Have you been doing anything nice this morning?' she asked him sweetly.

'Yes and no. I beat Helmut at a game of chess earlier and now I've got to go out to the barn to replace some roof joists.'

'Oh.' So – the guy had muscles *and* intelligence!

'Here's Peri now. I'll hand you over. Cheerio for now.'

He was going. 'Goodbye, Douglas . . .'

Then Peri took over the phone. 'Mags. *Hi!*'

'You *have* to tell me what that man looks like!'

'Why?' Peri sounded puzzled.

'His voice, dear, his voice. It could melt butter. Is he still there?'

'No – he's just going out the door.'

'So tell me – is he handsome?'

'Well . . . um . . .' Peri hesitated. 'I . . . um . . .'

'Peri! Is he handsome or not? It's easy. This is not Mastermind!'

'Some women *might* think he's good-looking,' Peri said slowly, then added quickly, 'but he's *definitely* not my type.'

'So?' Mags replied impatiently. 'Is he short and fat, or tall, or pigeon-toed, or what?'

'He's tall. About six foot two. He's hefty but not fat . . . mostly muscle, I guess. He's got brownish red hair and his skin is tanned . . . weatherbeaten, sort of . . . rough. But his *eyes!*' Now she sounded enthusiastic. 'He's got beautiful blue eyes and they sparkle when he laughs and sometimes when the sun shines into them at a certain angle they seem . . . well . . .' Her voice slowed and came to a halt.

Mags waited for more but it didn't come. 'I don't know about you,' she said finally, 'but in my book that sounds like one handsome beefcake!'

'I don't know . . .' Peri sounded unsure. 'Anyway,' she said briskly, 'are you phoning to talk about *him* or me?'

'Sorry. Of course. It's his voice; it makes me go peculiar. Right.' With an effort Mags put the image of him out of her mind and concentrated on Peri. 'I've been phoning you. I've been so worried. Thank goodness for that housekeeper; she's been keeping me updated, otherwise I would have been thinking the worst. And Helmut has informed me that you were wonderful and that he's so pleased with you. Good girl! I knew you could do it!'

'Thanks,' Peri replied heavily.

Mags had heard the sarcasm, but chose to ignore it. 'I've asked Helmut to release a photo of you for *Hi!* and he said he would consider it.'

'I know.'

'Right. But don't you pester him. That's my job. You just remember to be nice to him and do as he tells you. On Wednesday I'll have a limo waiting to pick you up from the airport and take you straight to de Vere for a fitting. He's proved to be more than a little unhappy that you're not around this week. *And* – Carl Hansen has agreed to do your hair!' Mags paused and waited for Peri's exclamation of delight.

'Carl Hansen? Really? That's fantastic! How did you get him?'

Mags was pleased with herself. 'That's my little secret, but I'm glad it's made you happy.'

'Happy? I'm over the moon!'

Mags dropped her voice to a whisper. 'Please don't tell anyone – but he dropped Sophia Steinharden for you!'

'Really?'

'Keep it hush-hush, though.'

'Of course,' Peri promised, promptly making a mental list of all the people she would tell.

'This is a game of strategy, darling, quite similar to conducting a war. First you'll have the publicity of the Film Awards with your face on the front page of every newspaper, and then there will be the release of Helmut's photographs – hopefully one of them landing up on the cover of *Hi!* There will be one-on-ones for the American press which will automatically lead to your appearing on chat shows, first in this country and then in America. And once New York picks up on you, Hollywood's going to be reaching for its cheque book.' Mags knew she sounded good. 'And once—'

'Hang on a minute,' Peri exclaimed, 'back in a second.'

'What—?' But Peri had gone. Mags waited, straining to hear voices. Nothing. Why had Peri dashed off so suddenly? She waited. Then she heard the receiver being picked up.

'Mags? Sorry.' Peri sounded breathless. 'It was a rainbow. It was beautiful – like – amazing. It filled the whole sky!'

'Really?' Mags said coldly. 'How nice. But perhaps you would rather go and look at rainbows than have to listen to me telling you about the rest of your *life*.'

'Oh, no! No!' Peri exclaimed. 'I wouldn't have gone but it was Douglas – he called me out to see it.'

'Mmm.' Mags narrowed her eyes thoughtfully. Peri's voice sounded different, somehow . . . younger . . . lighter . . .

'Sorry. You were saying about New York picking up on me.'

'Right,' Mags said firmly, trying to remember what she had been about to say and annoyed that the interruption had spoilt the flow of her words. 'As soon as New York picks up on you,' she repeated firmly, 'Hollywood is going to sit up and take notice—'

'That's what I want,' Peri interrupted, 'I want to go to Hollywood. Oh, Mags, could it *ever* happen?'

Mags was pleased to hear the yearning in Peri's voice. The girl wanted it badly. 'Sure it will,' she answered soothingly. 'Together we are going to make it happen. And once we've got all our ammunition together, we're going to start an all-out bombardment! One big hype-fest!'

'Gosh! How exciting!'

'It certainly is. Well, I'll leave you to carry on. I hope I haven't disturbed you in the middle of a shoot.'

'Oh, no – it's been raining.'

'How grim. So what have you been doing?'

Peri paused. 'I'm . . . um . . . pickling beetroot.'

'*Pickling beetroot*?'

'Yeah. Mrs Craig has been teaching me from a secret recipe.'

'Oh.' Mags didn't know what else to say. It didn't sound as if there was any harm in it, though. 'That's nice. So it's raining?'

'Not now. It's just stopped.'

'Good. It would be such a shame if this assignment was ruined by the weather. And remember, Peri: it's vitally important that Helmut gets as many pictures of you as possible.'

'Okay.'

'So what's Helmut planned for this afternoon?'

'We're driving out to some chapel on the other side of the mountains to do a series of shots for a new book of his. Something to do with the romanticism of death – so I'm probably going to be working with a pile of gravestones for the rest of the day.'

'How morbid!'

'Absolutely. Listen, Mags, I've got to go. Helmut's calling. I think this is us getting ready to go . . .'

'Okay. Work hard, and phone me, eh?' Then Mags remembered. 'Oh, very quickly, there was something else I wanted to mention. Breast implants. Have you decided?'

'Not yet.'

'I think we should seriously consider it. Fashion is changing. The public is demanding curves, breasts. Shall I book you into the Porchester for next month?'

'I . . .' Peri hesitated. 'Let me think about it, eh?'

Mags sighed. She had hoped that Peri would simply agree to it. Now it looked as if it was going to be another battle of persuasion. 'Well, you've got to do it some time, so you might as well do it a.s.a.p.'

'Yeah. I suppose you're right. Let me just think on it . . . get used to the idea.'

'Okay. But, remember, you're going to have to make a few sacrifices before you hit Hollywood.'

'I know.' Peri paused and then spoke hurriedly. 'Okay. Book me in.'

'Good girl.' Mags was relieved. At least that was one thing she could cross off her list. 'I'll speak to you tomorrow. Have a nice day. *Ciao*.' She disconnected the line and immediately began to dial the Porchester Clinic. She would get the operation booked in for the Monday after the Film Awards – that would give Peri less time to change her mind. Annoyingly, the line was busy, so she replaced the receiver and waited, nibbling the end of her pencil.

'Here's the April issue of *Elle* – it's just arrived.' Tula came over and put the magazine on the desk, straightening up and folding her arms across the front of her acid-green linen jacket. 'How's she getting on?'

'Peri? She's fine, although she sounds a bit . . . peculiar.'

'Peculiar?'

'Yes. I can't explain it. Her voice . . . it sounds different.'

Mags shrugged, giving up the attempt to analyse it. 'Apparently, she's spent all morning pickling beetroot and running out to look at rainbows!'

'Sounds fun,' Tula said with heavy sarcasm. 'At least she's giving her Amex card a rest.'

Mags snorted. 'That's true!'

'So – did you find out if that guy's got ginger whiskers?'

'Ho, ho, ho!' Mags exclaimed triumphantly, sitting erect and banging the pencil on her desk. 'I certainly did. He's six foot two inches of rippling muscles – with brains – and Peri was practically writing poetry about his eyes!'

'Oh, no. She's not falling for him, is she?'

'No. No. She just likes his eyes; the rest of him obviously doesn't take her fancy.'

'That's lucky. Can you imagine the complications if she did fall for him?'

Mags shook her head vigorously. 'That would never happen. Unless, of course, he had a Ferrari and a beach house in the Hamptons – and somehow I don't think he has.' She picked up the pencil once more, scanning her daily list and promptly scoring a line through *Peri: Boob job*. 'After all that fuss, she's finally agreed to the boob job. Why does she always have to turn everything into such a battle? Let's hope she doesn't start a battle with this,' she added, picking up the neatly printed contract which had arrived that morning from her solicitors. 'I'm going to get her to sign on the dotted line on Wednesday – the second she steps off that plane.'

Peri sat in silence, thoughtfully staring at the road ahead. Thankfully, Douglas too had been silent since leaving the house, thus enabling her to think in peace. Again, she asked herself: should I go through with it? All the other girls are doing it, so why not me? She looked down at her chest, at the two small mounds protruding from her jumper; they could certainly do with being bigger and the operation was perfectly safe and there were no side-effects, although someone had said that it could result in problems with breast-feeding. Well, since she wasn't going to have babies, that wasn't an issue, was it? So why did she feel so unsure about it?

Suddenly, Douglas's cheery voice broke into her thoughts. 'It's turned into a fine day.'

'Yeah,' she murmured abstractedly. Up to that moment, she had been solely preoccupied with the telephone call, unaware of anything outside the car, but now she gazed out across the sparkling green meadows towards the soaring mountains. The sun shone in a blue sky and the grass along the verge glistened with raindrops, making the whole world seem fresh and clean. It was hard to imagine the lashing slate-coloured rain of only an hour ago.

'I'm truly sorry about what happened this morning,' he said. 'I insist on paying for the damage. Just tell me how much I owe you.'

'Don't worry about it. I can claim it back on expenses.'

'Are you sure?'

'Yeah.' She paused. 'I . . . um . . . I'm sorry for shouting at you like that. I just got a shock, that's all.'

'I bet you did – seeing supercat flying through the air!'

At the image of it, Peri smiled. 'He's had a traumatic day, hasn't he? First, I drop him on the floor and then you throw him across the room like a missile!' She chuckled. 'How do you make a cat wild? Leave him with Douglas and Peri for a couple of hours!'

Douglas guffawed. 'Anyway,' he said, 'enough of that cat. I've been wanting tae mention that I've had a couple of phone calls today, from my friends, asking aboot you. Everyone's been saying how beautiful you looked last night and asking who you were and if you were someone important.'

'Really?' Peri turned to him, warmed by his compliments. 'What did you say?'

'I pretended to be amazed that they hadn't heard of you. "What!" I said, "you don't know her? But that's *the* Peri Lomax. She's famous!" And as soon as I said that, they were stunned to silence, as if you were some awesome creature placed in their humble midst.' Douglas was smiling. 'Some folk are easily impressed, aren't they?'

'Yes,' Peri replied stiffly, annoyed by his comment and wanting to tell him that these people had every right to be impressed. After all, she had been the girl on every bit of advertising for Laguna cigars and she had appeared in countless television commericals and in *Vogue* and *Tatler* and *Marie Claire*. Of course, they should be impressed. She *was* famous! Once again, she stared at the grey asphalt road ahead. No, she wasn't famous, she admitted reluctantly. At the height of her success, she had sometimes been recognised in the back of a cab or walking into a wine bar, but it had always happened in London – nowhere else. No, it wasn't enough. To be truly famous, her name would have to spring easily onto people's lips, not just in London, but in Paris, Milan, New York . . . and even *here!* Yeah, she mused, that would be a measure of my success if the people in this *godforsaken* place recognised me. She glanced across at Douglas. He was humming a tune while concentrating on his driving, obviously happy with himself and his lot, with absolutely no conception of how awesomely famous she was going to be. Well, one day soon, he was going to be in for one big shock! Ha! The thought of it made her warm and tingly inside, but then, with the realisation of everything she would have to do to achieve it, she felt a growing impatience. She wanted it *now*. Not in three years' time, not in two, not in one, but *now*.

Douglas had started speaking again. 'Do you see up there?' he said, pointing a finger at the top of the windscreen. 'There's an eyrie up there.'

'What?' she asked dispiritedly.

'An eyrie,' he repeated. 'An eagle's nest.'

'Oh. Right.'

'I have to keep a close eye on the nest,' he explained. 'A golden eagle's egg can fetch a large sum of money on the world market.'

'Yeah.' Peri didn't want to discuss eagles and eggs, she wanted to be alone with her thoughts; but it seemed evident that she was not going to be given the chance.

'It would be great if you could come for the ceilidh. Then you'll see the hills covered in heather and gorse, see the crystal streams and feel the sweet soft breezes touching your cheek, just like a woman's caress.'

'Really?' Peri murmured. It was obvious that the guy was still trying to sell her the Kaylee idea.

'I can show you the roe deer,' Douglas continued. 'The fawns are born at the beginning of June and after hiding in the bracken for the first few days, they join the others. It's fun to watch them. I usually pitch up a tent for a couple of nights so that I can study them.' Douglas shifted down the gearstick as he turned the car up into a steep bend in the road. 'All through the night there's the sounds of squeaks and blabbering as the deer talk to each other, and come the dawn I peep out and watch them closeby. The fawns are just like lambs, bouncing up and down and chasing each other. Then they go back to mum for a quick suckle and then they're off again, racing up and down the hills. You'll have to come with me; you would really enjoy it. Have you ever slept in a tent before?'

Was this guy for *real?* Now was the time to get a few things straight with him. 'Listen, Douglas,' she said patiently, 'I want to thank you for your invitation, but there's no way – this lifetime – that I'm going to sleep in a tent, let alone sleep in a tent with the sole purpose of listening to the night-time chatter of a bunch of Bambis! I'm sorry. And also –' she carried on quickly as he attempted to interrupt her – 'I haven't made any promises about this Kaylee thing. I said I would if I could . . . but most probably I won't be able to.'

'Sure – okay,' he said casually. 'I won't try to persuade you any more. I'll give you my telephone number when you leave and then it will be up to you, if you decide to come back.'

'Thank you.' In the silence that followed, Peri gazed out

across the sunny meadows, suddenly experiencing an overwhelming desire to jump out of the car and run across the grass, to feel the breeze in her hair and the sun on her face. But she couldn't – not with Douglas watching, and of course there was Helmut following on behind. And knowing him, he would have the camera out in a second, ordering her to run around and to smile and to cavort as if it was all so unstaged and spontaneous. She turned to look out of the back window. There was the battered red hire car not far behind with Otto at the wheel and Helmut sitting beside him, his lips moving in unceasing chatter, making her glad that Douglas had persuaded her to travel with him instead.

'Are they still behind us?' Douglas asked.

'Unfortunately – yes.'

Douglas was quick to respond to the dreary note in her voice. 'It won't be so bad,' he said gently. 'And anyway, there's only about three hours of daylight left. That's if he's not intending to work in the dark!'

Peri shivered. 'God, I hope not.'

'So – do you know what you'll have to do?'

'Probably look very ill and sad and drape myself over a gravestone.'

'I bet this is all a bit different from what you're used to.'

'Absolutely. If I have to drape myself anywhere, it's usually over a poolside bar in some Caribbean retreat for multi-millionaires!'

Douglas nodded. 'Yep – I can just see you now. So, what are you doing up here?'

'Don't ask me,' she said heavily.

'This Helmut chap's got some funny ideas. Why's he making you look like some New Age traveller?'

'Because I'm meant to represent an Eco-warrior.'

'A what?'

'Someone who fights to protect the planet.'

'Oh, I see. Well, I wish there were a few more of you about. The planet could do with a bit of protection.'

'Mm,' Peri murmured, without interest. Protection of the planet had nothing to do with her.

'So – what's on the agenda when you get back to London?'

Peri considered his question. Should she tell him that she would be co-hosting the International Film Awards Ceremony this Saturday night? That she would be wearing a dress designed by Igor de Vere? That she would appear on the front cover of *Hi!* magazine? No. He hadn't believed her yesterday when she had told him that she was destined to become a megastar, so she wasn't going to tell him anything more. Let him find out for himself! 'Well, I've got to visit my hairstylist,' she said. 'And there's dresses to buy, parties to go to . . . men queueing in line to take me out.' Although the last statement was made in jest, she was puzzled to see that his smile was fading. Now he looked almost sad. But she didn't want him to look like that – she wanted him to be cheerful again, to look eager and interested. Well, she would *make* him cheerful. 'That job we did together last night? I'll send you a copy of the magazine as soon as it's published, and then all the girls round here will say, "Hey – what a hunk!"' She was pleased to see a small smile touch a corner of his lips. 'And hopefully they won't *all* have hairy armpits!' This startled a laugh out of him and she felt very clever; she had made him laugh. Suddenly an idea flashed thought her head: maybe she could do comedy?

'I hope that whatever happens, Peri, you will always be happy.'

The quiet sincerity in his voice caused her thoughts to tumble to a halt. She turned to him and studied his face: his kind blue eyes, his firm kind mouth, his thick unruly hair which had the habit of curling over his ears. Why did he speak like that? As if she *meant* something to him? She meant nothing to him. She was a stranger and he certainly wasn't going to get anything out of her – she had made that pretty obvious – so why all this *intensity?*

'So – you're going to be a megastar?' he said brightly.

Peri had heard the lightness in his tone, causing her to

wonder if perhaps she had imagined his intensity of a moment ago. 'Yeah. Sure thing.'

Douglas smiled. 'So, here I am sitting next to a budding megastar – it feels strange.'

She considered his words. 'I suppose it must do,' she replied. After hearing someone else voicing her dreams, she felt a sudden rush of joy. Yes, she was going to be a megastar! And Douglas was a real sweetie, she decided, and she would definitely arrange for copies of the magazines to be sent to him and, attached to them, would be a little handwritten note, signed *With love from Peri Lomax*. That would please him. He would probably go out and get it framed. With that decision made, she settled back in her seat and contentedly watched the world go by. In front of them the road narrowed, cutting through a wall of rock; this was the only bit of the journey that she could recognise from the previous evening. As they came out through the other side, she looked down, anticipating the sight of the town far below. Yes – there it was. It looked different from the previous night; then it had been a spangle of twinkling lights against the velvet blackness, now it had become a huddle of grey stone buildings with grey slated roofs, a church spire, and the ever-present mountains sweeping up from the valley floor. Why should people want to build a town here? she thought to herself. And how do they make a living?

Douglas braked gently as they took a steep bend in the road. 'Helmut's suggested we stop off at the Osprey on the way back for dinner,' he said. 'The food is excellent – better than you'd ever get in London.'

Peri wasn't going to argue the point. She felt benevolent, for once, at one with herself and content. 'Sounds great.'

'It'll give Mrs Craig a rest from cooking and a chance to put her curlers in and her feet up.'

'Yeah. That's nice – she deserves it.'

They drove in companionable silence until they reached the town. The wide, lonely street of the night before now bustled with people. There was the Osprey Hotel on the right, looking even more shabby and neglected in the daylight. On the corner of the pavement, a ginger-haired man with a wooden staff and a black dog caught sight of Douglas and smiled, touching the brim of his cap with a finger. Then he saw Peri and his mouth fell open in surprise. Further on, a pretty woman in a headscarf, surrounded by a cluster of little boys, also smiled and waved at Douglas, her eyes swiftly sliding a look at Peri, her curiosity obviously aroused by the beautiful girl in the seat beside him.

'There's going to be a few tongues wagging tonight,' Douglas murmured, saluting to an old woman who had just come out of the greengrocers. '*Och, that Douglas MacLeod,*' he said, suddenly mimicking a woman's high-pitched voice. '*Did ye see that lassie he was wi' today? Och, she was awfoo bonnie. Folk say she's up from London tae have her photograph taken.*' Douglas changed his voice to a deeper note: '*Och well, it will make him ken his manners, if nothing else.*'

Peri squealed with laughter. 'Okay!' she announced brightly, caught up in his mood. 'Next time we come down this road I'll give you a kiss in full view of everyone and then *that* will give everyone something to talk about.'

Douglas grinned. 'Okay, you've got a deal.'

It was obvious to Peri that he had spoken in jest, but it made her wonder what he really thought of her. Would he want to kiss her? Did he fancy her? She stared down at his big strong hand on the gearstick, at the fine golden hairs, aware of the power in that hand. His whole body had an aura of power, of being in control, of taking charge. What would he be like as a lover? Would he be rough and impatient, or tender and slow? What would that hand feel like against her soft skin? Suddenly she felt a tingling sensation vibrating from her clitoris and she jerked her eyes away from his hand and stared out of the window, trying to calm the tremors in her chest. Great! she thought disparagingly. This was a cheap scenario that was all too common: a beautiful rich girl fancying a bit of rough. Well, that wasn't going to happen to her because *she* had very high standards to maintain. As they drove through the town, she made a mental list of those men who would be eligible to be seen with her: any royalty, of course, earls, film stars . . . but not pop stars . . . not any more.

'We're nearly there,' Douglas said. They had left the town far behind and were now heading for the mountains beyond. Up to their left was a steep bank of tree roots, gnarled and twisted, bleached white by the wind and rain. Slowly, after skirting a massive boulder on the side of the road, they came round a sharp bend, and there high on a hill stood a tiny old church looking out across the valley, its back nestling close against the mountainside.

'There it is,' Douglas said. 'Duggan Kirk Chapel.'

Peri peered at it. 'It must have been a bit of a climb for people in the olden days to get up there.'

Douglas nodded. 'Aye – it must have been.'

They were travelling downhill, and for a moment the chapel went from sight but as they came out on to flat meadowland. It reappeared high above them, much closer, a rough track now visible winding its way up the hill towards it.

As they bumped along the track, Peri leant forward, peering up through the windscreen; there were a few stunted trees, their branches blown by time and set in a rigor mortis of arms stretching back towards the hillside; and behind the crumpled wall stood ancient gravestones, leaning heavily this way and that, overgrown and forgotten, surmounted by strange-looking crosses, each with a ring in the centre.

'They don't look much like English crosses.'

'That's because they're not; they're Scottish . . . Celtic.

'Oh.' Peri leant forward to get a better look. 'Is Mary Lomax's gravestone up there?'

'Mary Lomax? Oh, aye, Mary Lomax. So Mrs Craig has been telling you some of the old stories, has she?'

Peri turned to him. 'So, it's just a story?'

'No – I don't think so. It's more than likely to be true. Instead of recording events in writing, folk hereabouts tend to pass them on by word of mouth, from generation to generation. Something that happened a hundred years ago will still be talked about today and something that happens today will be talked about in a hundred years' time . . . that's if folk think it's interesting enough. It's possible that you, yerself, could go into local folklore, especially if you were tae kiss me in the middle o' the street!'

Peri smiled dreamily. 'I'm glad the story of Mary Lomax is true. It's so romantic and also, of course, my name's Lomax too.'

'That's right,' Douglas exclaimed. 'So it is! But I doubt very much if Mary Lomax would be a forebear of yours; there are a great many Lomaxes in Scotland . . . and England.'

'I know that,' Peri said quickly. 'I was just curious to know if her gravestone was still there.'

'I dinna ken. I've never thought tae look, but anyway there's no point; it would have been put there over a hundred years ago and the inscription would not have survived the elements. It could be there, mind; but we wouldn't be able to recognise it if it was.'

'Oh.' Peri was disappointed. It would have been wonderful to have found a link with the past, to fantasise, just for a moment, that she had found a relation.

'This is us.' Douglas came to a halt at the side of the track. 'We'll walk up from here. I don't think Helmut would appreciate having a rusty Land Rover in his photographs.'

As Peri opened her door, Douglas was there, ready to help her down.

'Thanks,' she said, putting out a hand and feeling his big strong hand enclosing her own, bearing the weight of her as she slithered to the ground. 'Not the most glamorous vehicle to get out off,' she said lightly, feeling strangely shy of him and not wanting to meet his eyes.

Suddenly his face came close to hers. Her heart stopped. Then he was whispering in her ear, speaking urgently. 'Don't look now! But we're being followed.'

Arrested by the urgency in his voice, she swung around in alarm, only to discover the little red hire car chugging along the road towards them. Helmut and Otto! In mock anger, she swung back to Douglas and slapped him across his arm, but did not look into his eyes. 'You beast – giving me such a fright!'

He was chuckling, pretending to ward her off with out-turned hands. 'Hey, leave me alone!'

Feeling her cheeks redden, she turned her back on him and looked towards the little red car winding up the hillside, willing it to go faster. Why did she suddenly feel nervous alone with this man? Thankfully, as the car drew up behind the Land Rover, Douglas walked towards it, away from her.

'What do you think, Peri?' It was Helmut, getting out of the car and looking over the roof at her. 'Isn't this magnificent?'

'Oh . . . yeah,' she agreed, dutifully scanning her surroundings before turning back to see that Douglas had taken the tripod and reflector from the back of the car and was carrying them towards her up the little track. She noticed how his big heavy chukka boots trod the ground with steady, powerful strides as if the ground belonged to him. Then she was looking into his eyes.

'Come on,' he said, drawing near. 'I'll take you up.'

As she went to follow him, Otto called out. 'Not just yet. I need to do Peri's face first.'

She walked down to Otto, who stood at the back of the car, laying out tubs and jars and coloured sticks along the floor of the boot. Patiently she waited and watched. She noticed his thin white delicate hands – city hands – and the way he fussed over a dust mark on a black cloak, beating it off with his hand, his brows knitted in concentration. What a waste of a life, Peri thought, having to spend your existence putting make-up on faces and worrying about stains and creases.

'I do not need to apply very much,' Otto began. 'Just dark shadows under the cheekbones and a little inside the eye socket and a dusting of white powder.'

Peri sat on the folding stool beside the table and tilted her face up towards him, feeling the colour stick smoothed gently over her skin, gazing idly at his pale thin nostrils, his colourless eyelashes, and then letting her gaze drift up to the sky, to a fluffy white cloud, to a big black bird gliding slowly in circles, around and around in the silent sky. A soft breeze rippled against her cheek, carrying a sweet herbal scent. It reminded her of something – but what? Oh yes, her Decleor face balm for tired skin. She could see it now, the white tube with gold lettering sitting on one of the glistening glass shelves above her bath. She had never before appreciated all those glass shelves lining the walls of her bathroom – just like the walls of a Parisian chemist's – all her beauty products laid out for quick access and easy identification. No, she had never appreciated those shelves – not until *now*, now that her cleansing milk, body sprays and deodorant had to share *one* tiny ledge with Douglas's shaving brush and shaving soap and his battered yellow toothbrush in a chipped mug. It was driving her demented not having space to spread out.

'Finished,' Otto said, giving a final sweep of the powder puff across her chin. 'Now we need to get this tunic over your head.' He lifted up a garment of dark grey wool and slipped it over her head, pulling the hem almost to the ground before tying a rope around her waist. 'If you would please remove your trousers and shoes,' Otto said, 'and put on these tights and boots.'

As soon as she had done this, Otto draped the cloak over her shoulders and held up a mirror for her inspection but she promptly swung away, not wanting to see herself – which she knew was unprofessional – but, at that moment, she didn't want to be thrown into a depression by the way she looked.

'Right. We're ready,' Otto declared, replacing the mirror in his bag. 'Let's go.'

She followed him up the track, delighted to discover a single clump of pure-white snowdrops in the grass; if only she'd had the time, she would have stopped and picked them. They reminded her of Douglas, and the way he had offered them to her on that first morning as a sign of apology and friendship. It was amusing to think, now, how much she had hated him.

Glancing up, she caught sight of him at the top of the track, sitting on the low stone wall, watching them. Had he realised how much she had hated him? Probably. She certainly hadn't made any effort to conceal her hostility. He hadn't deserved it, though. He was such a nice guy and yet she had been horrible to him. Why? Why had she been so antagonistic? She felt so ashamed of herself. Mags had been right to lecture her on her personality; changes were going to have to be made.

Douglas straightened up on their approach. 'Come on!' he boomed. 'You two are walking up that hill like a couple of geriatrics.'

'Geriatrics?' Otto enquired. 'What's that?'

'Old folk. Come on. Helmut's inside waiting.' He led the way up the narrow path between the gravestones, the sound of a bubbling brook coming from the other side of holly bush.

Peri noticed that the sunset had bathed the side of the church in a soft light, turning the old weathered stones to a rosy pink, the window of diamond-shaped glass glinting with a rainbow of colours. At the base of the wall, the ground sloped away, and there among the gravestones was a thick carpet of snowdrops, hundreds and hundreds of them. She had never seen anything so beautiful. She wanted to stop and walk among them but she knew that Helmut would be waiting for her, and so she had to carry on.

As they reached the chapel door, Douglas stood back to let them pass by, giving Peri a surreptitious wink. Now she was across the threshhold and into the chapel. The place was not at all gloomy, as she had expected, but warm and cheerful. Beams of sunshine streamed through the windows along one side, creating patches of bright yellow on the opposite wall and lighting up the silvery dust motes floating in the air. It was obvious that the interior had not suffered neglect; there was a glossy look about the old wooden pews and the air was filled with the smell of beeswax.

At the far end, Helmut had positioned the camera to the side of the altar and was just about to look into the viewfinder when he heard their footsteps. Now he turned to them. 'You look perfect, Peri. Excellent.' He smiled ruefully. 'But, unfortunately, the weather is not perfect; it is too sunny! But we will make the best of it. Now, Peri, if you could stand in the shadow over there . . . yes, in the corner . . . and look out of the window. I want you to look sad, thoughtful, imagine that you have lost someone dear to you.'

Peri got into position, putting her elbow on the window sill and cupping her chin in her hand, absent-mindedly staring out through the diamond-shaped window panes at the gravestones standing in the shadow of the chapel, and behind them the sheer-faced mountain rising up to catch the afternoon sun. She didn't have to bother trying to imagine losing someone dear to her; it was easy to look sad, much easier than looking happy. And Helmut seemed satisifed; he immediately started to shoot and, so far, he hadn't made any complaints. As she continued to stare out at the gravestones, she thought of Mary Lomax: could her gravestone still be out there? Had anyone ever thought of searching for it? Suddenly Douglas came into view, walking slowly, with his head bent and looking from side to side; then he stopped and knelt to the side of an overgrown stone slab and began to pull away the tangle of weeds and grass, as if searching. Searching! What was he searching for? Mary Lomax's grave? How exciting! Eagerly, she lifted her head out of her hand and peered closer through the window, watching him avidly.

'Peri!' It was Helmut. 'I want you to look sad – not as if you have just caught sight of a chocolate éclair!'

Having only caught the last few words, Peri was confused. 'Pardon?' she said, frowning at him.

Helmut sighed loudly. 'Tell me: what is it that has captivated your attention?'

Peri stared at him 'Umm . . . it's Douglas. He's . . . um . . . pulling the weeds off a slab . . .' Now Helmut looked confused; his puzzled expression made her want to laugh.

'We're looking for a gravestone,' she tried to explain, '. . . Mary Lomax's grave . . .'

'I'm sure that's very exciting,' he cut in sarcastically. 'But maybe you would be kind enough to work with me for a little while longer. Then when we have finished, you too will be completely free to join Douglas in scrabbling about for your ancestors.'

'But she's not. I don't want . . .' Peri stammered, trying to explain herself, 'It's nothing. It's not important. I'm sorry.'

As Helmut once again returned to the viewfinder, Peri quickly got back into position and glanced out of the window. She could tell instantly that Douglas had uncovered another slab but she had to be careful not to show interest and so averted her gaze from him. All of a sudden, she had an overwhelming urge to run out of the chapel. She didn't want to be standing here! She wanted to be outside, exploring. But she couldn't; she had to be obedient and stay put. It was like being a little girl again, watching all the other girls out on the grass playing with the new Wendy house, while she had to stay in for being rude to the warden. She had been resentful then and she was resentful now!

'No, no, no, no!' Helmut exploded, throwing his hands in the air. 'Now you look as if you want to hit somebody! Please,' he pleaded, 'try and look sad. You were perfect just a moment ago.'

His voice had been so unexpectedly loud that it made her tremble. 'I'm sorry.'

Helmut turned to Otto and spoke impatiently. 'Would you please ask Douglas to remove himself from Peri's view? He is obviously disturbing her concentration.' As Otto headed for the door, Helmut returned to the camera, and Peri, frightened to be shouted at again, did not dare look out of the window, but stared instead at a crack in the stone sill. They worked quietly for an hour before Helmut spoke again. 'Good. This scene is finished; now we can go outside.'

As Peri threaded her way through the benches towards the

door, she saw that the patches of sunshine on the wall had faded to a soft creamy colour, seeming to have moved up almost to the ceiling. There were no silvery dust motes gliding in the sunshine now; but dark shadows and an air of absolute stillness, making Peri feel that even if she were blindfolded, she would sense that the day was coming to an end.

On coming out of the chapel, she glanced down the path and saw that Douglas had resumed his place on the wall by the gate, and, with one knee drawn up in front of him, he was gazing out across the valley, into the sunset. What was he thinking? She wanted to go to him and ask, 'Did you find it? Is she here?' But she dared not. Quickly, she followed Helmut and Otto around to the other side of the chapel and Douglas was lost to view.

Helmut promptly set the tripod on a grassy mound, darting glances at the sky. 'The chiaroscuro is perfect,' he declared, 'but we will have to work fast.'

As he fussed about with the reflector, Peri looked around at the tumble of headstones and slabs buried beneath thorny brambles and weeds and realised that it would take time to uncover them all. Time that she did not possess. But it would have been nice to have found the gravestone and to imagine that she had discovered where her great-grandmother lay. Obeying instructions, she got into position, kneeling at the side of a grave, casually pushed the trailing ivy aside and strained to see the writing on the headstone. But it was just some woman . . .

Isobel McBain. Born 1883. Died 1931. Dearly loved by all her Family. 'Loved by all her family,' Peri whispered. Suddenly, a feeling of despair washed over her, overwhelming her with a sense of bereavement. *Family*, she thought bitterly, that is something I will never know. She tried to push off the feeling, but it remained, hanging about her like a grey shroud. This is stupid! she thought angrily. Why am I thinking like this, instead of thinking about next Saturday and how wonderful life is going to be? I'm going to be a megastar with servants and houses and perpetual sunshine, worshipped by the entire planet! But, oh no! I've got to have something to feel sad about, haven't I?

It's pathetic; I'm so desperate to find a sodding family that I'm ready to scrabble about on some mouldy old graves in sodding Scotland!

'It's looking good, Peri,' Helmut called out. 'Now put your hands together as if you are praying. Yes, that's correct.'

With hands pressed together in prayer, she glanced up over the hillside, up to the sky, and here her eyes came to rest, gazing longingly into the endless blue. 'Please God,' she whispered, feeling a terrible yearning rise up from within her. 'I want to be loved. *Please* let me be loved.'

'Fantastic!' Helmut exclaimed. 'That is just what I want.'

A part of Peri's brain registered that she should be happy with Helmut's praises, but she was locked in sadness, unable to feel anything but misery.

Helmut continued to work rapidly, instructing Otto to move the reflector ever more closer as the shadows lengthened, and now there was the sound of popping lightbulbs. Peri suddenly felt weary; her back ached from the strain of bending forward in this unnatural position, and she just wanted to finish and get out of this place. The air had become chilly and damp and she could feel the earth grow cold beneath her knees. When would they stop? Helmut carried on, instructing her to stand up, lean against the wall, then kneel down again. Automatically she moved from position to position, trying desperately to think pleasurable thoughts. What day is it today? Sunday. Three more days to go and then I'll be heading home. There will be mail waiting: party invitations and bills . . . lots of bills . . . don't think of them . . . think of . . . Saffron! She will be watching me on TV on Saturday and feeling positively demented! She'll—

'That's it. Finished.' Helmut straightened up and wearily rubbed the palms of his hands up and down his face, his youthful golden tan suddenly looking a little grey. Gratefully, Peri got up slowly and massaged her back. She waited until the men had dismantled the equipment and then followed them, keeping close and snatching nervous glances back over her shoulder; with the gathering dusk, this corner of the churchyard had become dark and eerie, so it was a surprise to her, on coming round to the front of the building, to be met by the creamy light of sunset, the sky a turquoise blue and covered with fluffy islands of pink and purple.

'I wonder where Douglas has gone?' Helmut said, reaching the path through the gravestones.

Otto had walked on ahead to the gate. 'He's down in the Land Rover.'

Halfway along the path, Peri suddenly stopped. What had caught her attention? That cross. A Celtic cross, weathered and pitted with time, snapped apart, the top part embedded upside-down in the ground. In its entirety it would be bigger than the rest, much bigger – a cross built for someone of importance. A cross built for a chieftain's wife. The cross and its stump stood among the thick carpet of snowdrops, facing west, facing the setting sun. *This was it.* She had found it. Douglas had been searching in the wrong place. It was here. To think that he and Mary Lomax had been sitting side by side, together, looking out across the valley at the setting sun.

'Are you okay, Peri?' It was Douglas calling to her from below.

She tore her gaze from the cross and carried on walking. 'Yeah. Fine.' She let the gate swing back behind her as she walked down towards him. She would not mention the grave; she wanted to forget it, forget this place and the misery it had evoked. Now she just wanted to get to the hotel and get drunk.

'So the ghoulies and ghosties didn't get you then?' he said, grinning as he came towards her.

She didn't meet his eyes but shook her head instead. 'No.' He was expecting her to smile but she couldn't. Only a short time ago, she had been laughing with him. Now she wanted to cry.

'Did everything go okay?' he asked, a note of concern in his voice.

It was Helmut who answered. 'It was perfect,' he exclaimed

delightedly, stowing the reflector into the boot of the car. 'The light, the mood, Peri – everything was perfect.' Otto stood by the car, waiting to help her change, and once he had removed her make-up, she headed over to the Land Rover.

Douglas had waited by the passenger door until Peri had finished and now he held out his hand to help her up into her seat. 'Christ! Your hands are cold!' he exclaimed.

'Every *inch* of me is cold,' she informed him, letting him put the sleeping bag over her lap. Although she had a companion, she felt strangely alone, isolated, and the warmth in his voice could not reach her. She no longer felt that he was a friend.

'You'll soon be in the warm,' he said and closed her door. She heard an engine start and looked behind to see Helmut's car reversing down the track. Then Douglas was in beside her, banging the door. 'A glass of Tobermory whisky will soon have your veins on fire.'

'I hate whisky,' she said peevishly. She could hear the childish tone in her voice but she couldn't help herself. She wanted to retaliate against this feeling of misery – lash out against the pain and everyone around her.

'Okay, we'll get you something else.' As he began to reverse the Land Rover, he swung around on the seat, arching the crook of his arm over the back of the seat for support and looking down at the track behind them. 'So I was disturbing your concentration, eh?'

'Pardon?' She didn't know what he was talking about.

'Back there. Otto came out and told me to keep out of sight because I was disturbing your concentration.' He slid his gaze towards her and winked mischievously. 'Couldn't keep your eyes off me, eh?'

Misery sparked into anger. *What?* How dared he imply that she fancied him! 'Yeah, that's right,' she drawled in heavy sarcasm. 'Boy! Was I having the hots for you! I had to stop myself from running out of the church and *throwing* myself into your arms.'

There was silence as he threw her a thoughtful sidelong glance, as if considering what she had said.

He thinks I mean it! she thought angrily. 'You don't *honestly* think I mean it, do you?' she said with incredulity.

He answered quickly. 'No, of course not.'

'*Good*.' She wasn't in the mood for this stupid conversation. She turned and stared miserably out of her window, presuming the matter closed.

But the matter wasn't closed. 'Well, maybe I don't *want* you throwing yourself into my arms!' he retorted.

Peri gave him a steady, weary look. The guy was obviously defending his male pride. 'Well, *that's* handy, isn't it?' she said sharply, 'because there's no way – this lifetime – that I'm going to be throwing myself into *your* arms. I'd rather throw myself into the arms of a *baboon*.'

He had reversed the car onto a piece of flat ground and now he stopped and gave her a brief hard glance. 'I see,' he said coldly, thrusting the gear into first. 'Well, I can only thank you for your kindness in sharing that piece of information with me.' The sarcasm in his voice had matched her own. As he pushed down hard on the accelerator, the tyres spun briefly on loose scree before making a purchase and carrying them up onto the road.

They travelled along in hostile silence. A part of her was glad that she had hurt him but another part felt confused. Now she felt anger at herself but she was quick to deflect it; this is not *my* fault, she thought, it's *his* fault – he goads me into it. He doesn't appear to realise who I am! He seems to think I'm some old *buddy*! How dare he think that I could possibly fancy him – even in jest. He still hasn't got it into his thick skull *who I am!* And he's got no right reading the labels on my beauty products – it's got nothing to do with him – it's private! And if he were a gentleman, he would remove all his things from the bathroom shelf and let me have it all to myself; and also, he shouldn't let me suffer this awkward silence; he should say something, anything, instead of being too obstinate to speak to me. Anyway, why should I care if he's decided to throw himself into a mood?

She sat rigid, scowling out of her window. They drove slowly up the winding road, around the boulder and past the bank of tree roots until they reached the summit. There before them was the sky, a vast dome of silken turquoise, luminescently pure, but strangely giving no light to the shadowed world below. Peri had never seen so much sky! It was beautiful. And there was a star! And another! Suddenly, their petty quarrel paled into insignificance. She wanted to speak to Douglas, to share it with him, but, on turning towards him, she saw the hard glint in his eyes and quickly changed her mind. He definitely didn't look in the mood to talk about the scenery. Well, that was *his* problem – so she swung back into her seat and folded her arms, determined to ignore his silence and enjoy the view. As she gazed out at the twilight world before her, she felt a sense of tranquility slowly settling upon her, soothing her troubled heart. Life suddenly didn't seem so bleak. She breathed deeply. All this beauty seemed to be theirs alone, a moment's gift before blackness of night wiped it away.

And yet they were squandering this gift, too busy squabbling to really appreciate it.

Was that the town below? Yes. The buildings seemed to be huddling together, indistinct in the gathering gloom as they slowly merged into the encroaching blackness. Then, one by one, spots of light appeared at the houses until, all at once, in a glittering flourish, the streetlights came on, cutting a dazzling line through the centre of the town. Now she *had* to say something. 'It's like Vegas!' she exclaimed.

'Pardon?' Douglas said in a cool voice.

'The lights,' she repeated. 'They're a bit o.t.t., aren't they?

'I don't understand what you're saying.'

'They're o.t.t. – "over the top". Haven't you heard that expression before?'

'No.'

Goodness! he was making this hard work. Why did he have

to be like this? Just because she told him that she didn't want to throw herself into his arms! Maybe she shouldn't have said that 'baboon' bit.

In silence they drove through the town and in silence they pulled up in front of the Osprey, and in silence he helped her down from the Land Rover, the sleeping bag trailing behind onto the pavement. Since he made no move to put it back inside, she had to do it herself. Then he banged the door shut. She had expected him to storm off into the hotel leaving her behind, but instead he paused and waited for her.

'Look. I'm sorry,' she said impatiently.

He looked down at her steadily. 'No, you're not.'

She opened her mouth to speak and then closed it again; in the brightness from the streetlights, she could clearly see the hurt and anger in his his eyes. Now he was *really* trying to make her feel guilty. 'I'm sorry,' she insisted, raising her voice. 'What more can I say?'

'Nothing.' He stood rigid, unyielding, looking down at her with cold dignity, his lips pressed together in a hard line.

'Jesus,' she murmured, glancing away. What a pain! She swung back to look up at him again, trying to think of words that would soften him, and in that instant the absurdity of his expression suddenly struck her. There he stood, stiff and dignified, his tight face showing plainly that he had been gravely offended, and obviously determined to make a big deal out of the whole thing. Treacherous laughter bubbled up inside her. He looked so stuffy! With an effort, she tried to keep the laughter out of her voice.

'How about I *show* you that I didn't mean what I said?' She lifted up her arms towards him, suddenly feeling devilish. '*Look, Douglas!* I'm going to *throw* myself into your arms!'

He took a step back, warding her off with the palm of a hand. 'Don't bother.'

'What!' In astonishment, she dropped her arms to her sides. Then she narrowed her eyes speculatively, thinking: *he doesn't mean what he says, of course, he just needs more coaxing*. Smiling again, she took a step towards him, saying teasingly, 'Don't be silly.' Swiftly, she put her hands up against his shoulders, but just as swiftly he stepped back so that her hands slid down, away from his chest.

'No,' he said grimly. 'I don't want you to.'

Now she was laughing outright. He was being *so* pompous – behaving as if it was the end of the world or something! 'Don't be a fart-head,' she chortled, knowing that at any moment he would relent. 'Please,' she pleaded in a little-girl voice, 'I *want* to throw myself into your arms.' At that, she leapt forward and threw herself up against him, ready to clasp her hands tightly around the back of his kneck.

But he moved swiftly, his hands coming up and grasping her wrists, pulling them away. 'It's too late, Peri.'

Christ! It was as if he really meant it! In stunned amazement, she watched him turn towards the entrance.

'It's cold,' he said. 'I'm going in.'

She couldn't believe it! He had rejected her and now he was simply walking away. And after all the effort she had made trying to be nice to him! How dare he! Anger and humiliation swelled up in her chest but commonsense took control. Of course he wanted her to throw herself into his arms – it was obvious – otherwise he wouldn't have reacted the way he had. Perhaps it hadn't helped, though, that she had laughed at him . . .

Now he stood in the hotel entrance porch holding the door open for her and pointedly keeping his gaze fixed on something inside the building. Right, Scottie! she thought determinedly; you might think this is the end of the matter – but it's not! No one rejects Peri Lomax. She marched along the pavement and up to the door, muttering as she brushed passed him, 'I *know* you want me to throw myself into your arms.' She didn't hear his answer and she didn't see his expression, but she didn't care: one way or another, she was going to throw herself into his arms that night – whether he liked it or not! She marched on through the hallway and into the bar, letting the door swing back in his face. At a brisk glance she saw the place was empty, apart from

Otto sitting over by the fire and Helmut leaning up against the bar, talking to the barman.

'Just in time,' Helmut called out cheerfully 'What would you two like to drink?'

Peri was the first to answer: 'A glass of white wine, please.'

Helmut swept his arm towards Otto. 'There's a bottle of white wine on the table, Peri – please help yourself.' He turned to Douglas and smiled. 'Let me guess? A double Singleton?'

Douglas grinned. 'That would be great. Thanks.'

Peri noted with smouldering fury that his bad mood did not extend to others. She threaded her way through the tables and chairs until she reached Otto, and there she stopped and gave him a cursory nod before picking up the bottle of wine and sloshing it into a glass. Then she banged the bottle down on the table and picked up the glass and drank it down in one go. When she had finished, she put the glass on the table and sat down, facing Otto across the table. 'God, it's fucking cold!'

Otto gave her a quizzical look. 'You seem upset?'

'Do I?'

'Is there a problem?'

'Yeah, actually there is!' She picked up the bottle and began to fill her glass once more.

'Can I can do anything to help?'

'Yeah. All you've got to do is to get a man called Mr Spock to walk through that door and tell him to beam me back to civilisation – *now!*'

Otto looked puzzled. 'Who?'

'Nobody.' She lifted the glass to her lips, sipping it steadily as she turned her gaze to the flames. What a nerve that man had! Rejecting *her*! Well, she would show *him*. By the end of the evening she would find an excuse to throw herself at him, and do it in such a way that he wouldn't be able to push her off. Confronted with her sexual come-on, he would relent. Ha! By the time she was finished, he was going to be panting for her.

'Here is the menu.' Otto began waving a big sheet of

cardboard in front of her. 'We've been waiting for you and Douglas to arrive before ordering.'

'What? Oh . . . yeah.' She put her glass on the table and slipped her arms out of her coat, draping it over the back of her chair before taking the menu from him. Now she was hungry.

'When you're finished with it, pass it back to the bar for Helmut and Douglas.'

'Okay.'

'I'm having the trout,' Otto informed her. 'Cameron tells me it was freshly caught this morning.'

'Cameron?'

Otto nudged his chin towards the bar. 'The owner.'

As Peri glanced over her shoulder towards the bar, her gaze alighted on Douglas who was still wearing his coat. At the sight of that coat an idea began to materialise. It was a great idea – an idea that filled her with malicious glee. Without a second thought, she jumped up and carried the menu across to the bar, placing it on the counter between the two men. 'Here's the menu.' Then she stopped and looked up at Douglas. 'Oh, Douglas,' she exclaimed. 'You've still got your coat on. You must be *boiling*. Come on – let me take it off and hang it up for you.' With that, she put her hands up to his lapels but then stopped abruptly. 'Oh, dear, there's a thread come loose on the back of your collar – let me break it off for you.' She stood on tiptoe and put her arms up and around his neck, pretending to be busy with the thread, and at the same time bringing her mouth close to his ear. '*There!*' she hissed. 'I told you I'd *throw* myself into your arms!' Grinning triumphantly, she tilted her head back to see what response she was getting, and immediately snorted with laughter. He was staring fixedly at a point beyond her head with an expression of grim tolerance, a frown-line etched deep between his eyebrows. Ha! She wanted to shout with laughter.

Then, with a sigh, he patiently settled his gaze on hers; and she was ready and waiting with a jaunty grin. But something happened. In the moment his eyes looked into hers, her heart gave a sudden lurch. Now it was pounding, leaving her breathless, confused. What was happening to her? She tore her gaze from his, frantically looking anywhere, anywhere but into those eyes. Hot blood filled her neck, moving up and over her face. She was blushing. Now she felt the sheet of cardboard slip into her hands and automatically she looked down at it, staring vacantly at the writing. What was going on? A finger appeared, pointing to a word on the cardboard, and as if in a trance her eyes travelled up the finger, up the arm and up to the face; it was Helmut, speaking to her, his lips moving in slow motion, his words coming to her from a great distance.

'Have you decided what you want?' he was saying.

Flustered, she looked down at the writing again, desperately trying to concentrate but conscious of her thoughts darting and swirling in her head, making it almost impossible to hold them still. *Baked Trout with Parsley Butter.* What was happening to her? *Venison in Red Wine Sauce.* Why were her cheeks burning? *Roast Pheasant with Chestnut Stuffing.* Was everyone staring?

'Well?' Helmut was waiting for her.

She looked up at him and then swiftly looked back at the menu. *Baked Trout with Parsley Butter.* Christ! what was happening? Even her hands were trembling. It was as if . . . as if . . . she had fallen in love! Oh, God, no! Not with *him!* Not *here!*

Helmut spoke again. 'Peri, the man is waiting.'

She nodded vigorously. 'Roast pheasant, please . . . no, no, I mean the baked trout.' She shoved the menu towards Helmut and turned away, heading for the table. She had to think. Jesus! it was so hot in here – suffocating! She got to her chair and sat down, gripping her hands on the edge of the table to steady herself.

Otto began to pour wine into her glass. 'What did you choose?'

'The pheasant . . . no . . . no . . . the trout . . . I think.' She shook her head, wanting to clear her brain of these jumbled thoughts; but through everything, the vision of his eyes kept coming sharply into focus and just as sharply she pushed it away. It couldn't happen like this! Not like this! *Please! No!*

'Are you sure you're okay?' Otto said, peering closely.

'Yes, yes,' she answered, nodding firmly. She would talk to Otto, that's what she would do, and then everything in her brain would settle down and then everything would go back to normal. 'Gosh, it's hot. Are you hot?' She stared at him intently, determined to concentrate on him and him alone.

Otto leant forward, his brow furrowed in concern. 'Are you sure you're okay?'

At the sound of his tender concern, Peri wanted to burst into tears. She felt so vulnerable and weak and scared. 'I'm just so hot,' she explained, involuntarily glancing over her shoulder towards the bar. At the sight of Douglas, her heart thumped even faster. She had to get out of here! Abruptly she stood up. 'I'm going to the loo.'

Once inside the ladies' lavatory, she flung herself back against the tiled wall and pressed her hand to her heart, taking a deep breath to fill her lungs, pausing for a moment and exhaling slowly. Again and again, she repeated this, until the pounding eased and she could breathe more steadily. Now she was able to think clearly. She was going to be honest with herself and to rationalise what was going on in her head. Right! Had she fallen in love? No! Definitely not. It was purely sexual attraction – nothing more. But why now? For no reason? And with *him?* In her mind's eye, she saw his lips, strong but tender; how would they feel against her own? And how would it feel to have his big, strong hands exploring her body and feel his hard cock pushed up inside her? As if electrocuted, she jerked upright, and began to pace the floor, feeling dizzy and breathless and hot . . . so hot! She went into a cubicle and sat down and did a pee, thinking, thinking. She would go for a walk. Get some air. She wiped herself with a ball of toilet tissue then stood up, feeling the moistness in the crotch of her panties as she pulled them up against her body. Coming out of the cubicle, she caught sight of her face reflected in the mirror above the sink, her eyes staring back, big and luminous and scared, her cheeks blazing red. She approached the sink and gripped the edge of it, leaning forward to look deeply into her eyes. 'Peri, please – *stop it!*' she pleaded. Unbidden, the image of his hand on the gearstick came into her mind; she could almost feel it, rough and dry against her soft naked breast, evoking a soft, tingling sensation to run lightly down her spine and over her buttocks. She spun round, pushing the thought of it from her brain, and headed for the door. She had to get out of here. Get some air.

Otto was still sitting where she had left him. 'I'm going for a walk,' she said, scooping up her coat. 'To get some fresh air.'

He looked bewildered. 'Fresh air?'

'Yeah.' She turned and made for the exit, not allowing herself to look towards the bar. Out on the pavement, she shrugged into her coat and turned up the collar. The air was icy against her cheek but this was what she needed – something sharp and cold to clear her brain. With her shoulders hunched and her arms folded tightly against her ribs, she started to walk. Right. She was going to be honest with herself. Why had this happened? Was it the wine? The circumstances? Just another worry she had created for herself? After all, she always had to have something to worry about – it was a way of protecting herself, she reasoned, a way of keeping herself prepared for the worst. She knew from long experience that the minute she relaxed and allowed herself to be happy, something bad would creep up and pounce on her. So – was this another worry? Was it? She didn't know.

'Oh, God!' Peri muttered. 'This is crazy!' How could someone like her have such desire for someone like him? Everything had been so simple. He was just a guy who was helping out, friendly, kind, nothing more. Until tonight. Until the moment she grinned up into his face and he looked down at her with a look of weary patience. Something had sparked inside her, leaving her with an all-consuming desire to feel his lips pressing down on hers, to feel his stubble against her cheek . . . to smell him . . . to feel his hands exploring her body, feel his hot urgent breath on her neck. Oh, God! She walked faster and faster. Now she was running, running hard from these treacherous thoughts. But, oh! how she wanted him. Just for a second. Just to feel his lips. Nothing more.

Suddenly she stopped. This was the final lamp post and beyond lay only blackness. She had come to the edge of the town. She would have to go back. Slowly but firmly, she turned and retraced her steps. Whatever happened, he must never know her feelings. She must stay away from him, not look at him, ignore him. There were only three more days, then she would be gone . . . three more days . . . three more days . . . three more days . . . she would repeat it over and over and over in her head, as if each word was a brick and every brick was building up a wall against her treacherous desires.

As she re-entered the bar, she kept her eyes fixed firmly on Otto, aware that there were more people in the room. Otto still had that worried look on his face as he watched her approach.

'Are you okay?' he asked.

She saw that the table had been set for dinner. 'Oh, much better,' she answered briskly, sitting down and slipping off her coat. Not knowing what else to say, she picked up her glass of wine and began to sip it, staring with sudden interest at the shield above the mantelpiece. Then she heard Helmut's voice.

'Where am I sitting? Here? Beside the lovely Peri?' He pulled back a chair and sat down beside her. 'Where have you been?'

She knew that Douglas was taking the seat on the opposite side of the table to Helmut. 'I went for a walk,' she said simply, keeping her eyes firmly on the salt cellar.

'A walk?' Helmut sounded surprised.

She nodded. 'Yes.' Thankfully, they were interrupted by the barman who began putting plates of food on the table.

'*Wunderbar*!' Helmut exclaimed. 'I believe we have truly earned our dinner tonight.'

As she gazed down at the food in front of her, she found that, for some strange reason, she had lost the edge to her hunger; but there was nothing else for her to do but to pick up her knife and fork and eat. It was laughable to think – now – how she had envisaged this assignment. At this precise moment, she should be radiating charm and bonhomie, shouldn't she? She should be laughing uproariously at Helmut's anecdotes, feeling beautiful and confident, instead of sitting here like a trembling schoolgirl, too nervous to open her mouth, too shy to take her eyes off her baked trout.

Suddenly a voice boomed out from the head of the table, '*Faich germah*, Douglas!' Startled, Peri looked up. There, standing by Douglas's arm, was a little old man with a green woollen hat on his head and a pipe in his hand. Now he prodded his pipe into Douglas's arm and chuckled, 'So you've got the lassies throwin' themselves at ye, eh?' He grinned at Douglas and then, to Peri's horror, he was grinning at her. 'I saw you two oot there,' he nudged his head towards the window, 'when I wae givin' Angus his walk. Well, it had me and him pondering, I can tell ye!' He drew closer to Douglas and whispered loudly, 'I hope you two made up in the end.' With a good-natured grin at Douglas and a conspiratorial wink at Peri, he turned and shuffled away, a little white dog close at his heels.

Peri felt sick. She swung back to fix her gaze on her baked trout and try to think through what the man must have seen. He would have seen her throwing herself at Douglas, *that's* what he would have seen!

Helmut was obviously curious. 'What was that all about?'

There was a stomach-sliding pause before Douglas answered. 'I don't know what he's talking about – he must have got us confused with some other folk.'

'Well he might have got *you* confused,' Helmut said. 'But he couldn't possibly get Peri confused with anybody else.'

Douglas cleared his throat. 'Well . . .'

This was too much for Peri. She took a deep breath and spoke quickly. 'I know what happened. It must have been when Douglas and I arrived and we were arguing about Scottish cuisine – remember, Douglas?' Now she was looking at him, at his blue, blue eyes, feeling as if her bones were melting. God – how she wanted him!

He held her gaze. 'Yes, you're right. I remember now.'

Peri felt the blush on her cheeks and tore her gaze from his.

Helmut murmured dubiously but – thankfully – he carried on with his meal. So, too, did Otto and Douglas. Reluctantly, Peri loaded her fork with food, forcing herself to go through the motions of eating, feeling the food turn to sawdust in her mouth. Her throat had become so dry that she could barely swallow. She had to get back to the house, end this nightmare, now! But she couldn't go with Douglas; she couldn't trust herself and the mood she was in. It would have to be with Otto. But how could she arrange it without anyone suspecting?

Then she got her chance. Towards the end of the meal, Otto got up and went over to the bar to buy some drinks. Immediately she stood up, saying she needed another napkin and made straight for Otto. 'Otto,' she hissed as she came to stand beside him. 'Listen! I have to go back to the house and I want *you* to take me.'

'But Douglas will . . .'

'No! I don't want Douglas to take me. I want *you* to take me.'

He was looking suspiciously at her through narrowed eyes. 'Why?'

Christ! She wanted to stamp her foot in fury! 'Because Douglas and I have had a disagreement and he was rude to me and I don't like him any more.'

'Just don't speak to him – that's all.'

'Listen! Are you going to take me or not?'

'No,' Otto retorted, but seeing her expression added quickly, 'I can't. Helmut will expect me to drive him – and he will not want to leave for a long time still. He's arranged to see someone about buying a kilt.'

'Douglas can take him back later! They're so buddy-buddy anyway! I'm surprised they're not kissing each other!'

Otto was looking at her closely. 'What's going on, Peri?'

'Nothing.' She put a hand on his arm. 'Please, Otto, please.'

'Okay. Okay. I'll take you back . . . *if* it's okay with Helmut.'

'Thank you, Otto. I will never forget this.' She returned to the table and sat down, relieved that soon she would be safely snuggled up in bed, safe in a dreamless sleep . . . the sleep of sweet oblivion that had always been her refuge through bad times.

Otto returned, putting a glass of whisky down on the table in front of Helmut. 'Peri would like me to take her back to the house,' he said simply.

'What? Now?' Helmut turned on her.

'Yes. I'm not feeling very well.'

'What a pity. Is there anything that I can do for you?'

'No. No, thank you.'

'Well, let's get you back.' He looked over at Douglas. 'I'm sorry about this, Douglas – but would you be good enough to take Peri back.'

'*No!*' Peri almost screamed the word. From around the table, startled eyes stared at her. Forcing calm, she carried on, 'It's okay – Otto will take me. I don't want to spoil Douglas's evening.'

'I need Otto to stay,' Helmut explained. 'I've arranged for someone to come in with a selection of kilts and I will need Otto's advice on choosing the right one; but I'm sure Douglas will be happy to drive you.'

With her eyes fixed firmly on her plate, she heard Douglas say, 'I'm ready when you are, Peri.'

Without looking at Douglas, she stood up and gathered her coat into her arms, resigned to her fate. 'Thank you for dinner,' she said to Helmut and turned for the door. All was lost! She was going to be alone with Douglas! She prayed that he would still be angry with her, that he would refuse to speak. If he was nice to her . . . if he touched her, or even looked at her . . . heaven knew what would happen!

She could sense all eyes staring at them as they made their way through the tables. What were these people thinking? Were they thinking that Douglas was her date? Oh God! she thought in horror, suddenly remembering the little man with the green woolly hat and the grinning face. Had he been going round telling everyone what had happened between her and Douglas out on the pavement? That she had repeatedly flung herself at him? How awful! God – how glad she was that she would never have to set foot in this place ever again!

Douglas went ahead, bidding farewell to those around them, before opening the door for her, but she kept her gaze fixed firmly on the carpet, only murmuring 'thank you' as she passed by, but conscious of a tingly sensation at being so near to him. She would not talk to him, she decided firmly, nor look at him, and as soon as she was in the Land Rover she would pretend to go to sleep; then as soon as they arrived back at the house, she would simply say goodnight and go straight to her room. It would be simple.

Out on the pavement, she slipped into her coat and folded her arms against the icy cold, heading for the Land Rover and thankful that Douglas did not seem to want to talk. In silence, he opened the passenger door and helped her up, putting the sleeping bag over her lap and closing the door. As he walked around the front of the bonnet, she saw him stop and look thoughtfully up at the black sky. Then he was in beside her. 'I think it's going to snow,' he said and turned on the ignition.

This shocked her into speaking. 'Snow?'

'Aye. I may be wrong but I don't think so.'

'But it can't snow! Otto telephoned the Met Office this morning – I heard him – and they didn't say anything about *snow*!'

'They've been known to get it wrong,' he said derisively, looking into the rear-view mirror before drawing away from the kerb. 'I'll have a word with Helmut. It might be a good idea to have your bags packed tonight.'

'Tonight?'

'Yes. It might simply be a snow flurry or it might turn into a blizzard – it's best to be prepared. And if there's any sign that it'll turn into a blizzard you'll have to leave first thing in the morning.' Now they were driving out of the brightly lit town, heading for the blackness beyond. 'But there's no need to panic,' he added.

Panic? What a *joke!* She was ready to whoop for joy! Just think: this time tomorrow she could be walking barefoot across her softly carpeted bedroom, wearing only a silk kimono, going into the bathroom and feeling the warmth of the under-floor heating against the soles of her feet, switching on the Jacuzzi and sinking into the hot bubbles. Then she would order a Thai takeaway from Sami Tang's and watch a romantic video and forget him, and forget his dog, and forget the Osprey, and forget everything that had happened as if it had just been a bad dream. But then . . . but then . . . this would be her last night with him . . . wouldn't it . . . ?

'How you feeling?' Douglas asked, pushing the gearstick down into second gear as they climbed the steep, winding road.

He was talking gently to her now. She didn't want him to talk gently. She didn't want him to talk at all. 'Fine,' she answered. 'I mean . . . a little bit ill.'

'We'll soon be home.' He paused for a moment before continuing: 'I know how you're feeling,' he said quietly, 'and I think we should just forget what happened between us tonight . . . don't you?'

Peri shot a look at him, thinking wildly. *Forget what happened between us. I know how you're feeling.* Oh no! Did he realise that she had fallen in love with him? 'What do you mean?' she asked cautiously.

'What do you think I mean?'

She twisted her hands nervously, staring at him. 'I don't know.'

He sighed patiently. 'I mean: when *you* put me in a category lower than an ape and when *I* rejected you out on the street – that's what I mean.'

'Oh – I see!' she exclaimed, her voice high with relief. 'Of course! I'm so sorry that I was rude to you; it was the cold and I was tired and I didn't feel very well.' She chattered through the string of excuses, relieved beyond measure that he had not, after all, discovered her feelings for him.

'That's okay,' he said. 'Friends again?'

'Yes, of course – definitely . . .' She was heading onto dangerous ground. 'Yeah. Why not? Um . . . do you mind if I have a nap?'

'Sure – go ahead. And if you're asleep when we get home I'll just carry you in.'

'*No!*' The word exploded from her lips. 'But thank you,' she added, forcing herself to sound casual. 'I'll be able to walk in by myself.'

'Okay. Here – take my jumper.' He pulled a jumper from the back of his seat and put it on her lap. 'Use it as a pillow.'

'Thank you.' She balled it up and wedged it between her head and the window, just as she had done the previous night, but, unlike last night, she did not feel sleepy at all but wide awake and jittery. There was the same smell to his jumper but now that smell had a different meaning to her; it was his smell, and at the thought of it she felt a surge of desire. Maybe there would be no harm in letting him kiss her. Just once. Then she would know what it would feel like and be satisfied. Suddenly, a thought hit her: but maybe he wouldn't want to kiss her? Maybe his pride wouldn't allow him to? Maybe she would never know the feel of his lips? She had presumed he fancied her – but maybe he didn't? No – that was impossible – unless he was gay – and he definitely wasn't gay. *No, no, no*, she told herself firmly. *Stop it!* She was crazy even to think of kissing him. He was a nobody! And if she did kiss him, she would regret it, because the minute she returned to London, the realisation of what she had done would hit her and she would cringe with the embarrassment of it for the rest of her life. No. She had not fallen in love; it was purely sexual . . . a perverse attraction . . . an excuse to have something else to worry about. One day she would fall in love properly and it would be exactly how she had always imagined it would be – with someone with sleek black hair and smooth olive skin, a jetsetter who knew everyone, who owned a Ferrari and houses in Antibes, Rome, New York, someone who would lavish expensive gifts upon her. Of couse, she wouldn't want to marry him, but he would be the man she would be photographed with, the man that every woman wanted. In fact, he would be the complete opposite to Douglas.

God! Just imagine what Saffron would think if she ever found out that Peri Lomax had fallen for a Scottish . . . a Scottish . . . a Scottish what? She had no idea what he was. Well, whatever he was, it would be embarrassing! No – she wouldn't kiss him. She would be pleasant to him, and polite, but that would be all. And if he mentioned the Kaylee idea again, she would tell him firmly, but kindly, no. Definitely no.

The asphalt road rolled towards them, illuminated by the pale yellow glow from the headlights. It was strange to think that she was here with this man, miles from anywhere and alone in this blackness. He could do anything to her, if he wanted to, and she wouldn't be able to stop him. She slid a glance towards him and saw in the dim light that his face was set in grim concentration. What was he thinking? Perhaps he was thinking: *God! I want to rip her panties off and fuck her.* Or perhaps he was thinking: *God! what a spoilt brat – I'll be glad to see the back of her.'*

What a pity! she thought sadly. If only they had met in London; and if only he had been wealthy – a man of importance – then none of this would have happened the way it had. Instead, she would have been nice to him from the very beginning and this would have been their first date. Right now, they would be driving back from a film première or a party, and he would be wearing a satin-lapelled tuxedo and she would be wearing a brief flimsy cocktail dress with stiletto-heeled shoes and stockings and a Mirabella suspender belt . . . and right at this moment he would be putting his big rough hand on her knee, moving it slowly up, up, under her dress with the confidence of ownership, while at the same time casually driving his red Ferrari with his right hand, not letting up on speed, even when turning into Hyde Park Corner. Then on reaching Buckingham Palace Road, he would accelerate hard, the force of the world's most powerful car engine pushing her back into her seat and by the time they reached her apartment, the sound of the engine would have dropped to a lion's purr and his fingertip would have slipped underneath the elastic of her panty leg and she would be ready for him . . .

'Wake up, Peri,' Douglas whispered, swinging the steering wheel and driving off the road and down a bumpy track. 'We're nearly there.'

She lifted her head and yawned, pretending to come awake. Down in the icy blackness shone a solitary light, probably coming from the kitchen. The tiny glow looked somehow vulnerable, almost as if it were threatened by the sinister blackness around it; and it made her strangely sad to think that the reality of this situation was a million miles from her fantasy. There was no Hyde Park Corner, no exciting lights of a London night, but utter blackness and an evening spent in a tatty old bar with peeling paint. And here was Douglas, sitting beside her in his crumpled coat smelling of woodsmoke and earth, while she wore woolly tights and socks and boots, her face probably still looking as if it had come from a coffin fitting. Instead of the roar of a Ferrari, there was the clatter and banging of an old Land Rover; and no chance that Douglas would ever put his fingers into her panties.

'This is us.' Douglas swung in through the gate and came to a halt in the yard. The house was in darkness except for the light at the kitchen window. 'It looks as if Mrs Craig may have gone to her bed,' he said, switching off the ignition. 'We'll have to go in quietly.' He got out and came round to her door and opened it, holding out his hand to help her. The minute her hand made contact with his, she felt her heart begin to flutter and her knees tremble. When she was safely on the ground, he released her hand, and in that moment, she experienced a thud of disappointment.

Now she followed him across the yard and up to the front door. Should she linger a while or should she go straight to bed? She must go straight to bed, she told herself firmly. But this could be her last chance to know what it would be like to be kissed by him. Should she . . . ? Oh, God! What should she do?

Douglas was opening the door. She had just seconds in which to decide. Suddenly, Bruce jumped out at them, wagging his tail furiously, overwhelmed with joy at seeing his master. At first, Peri had recoiled in alarm, mistakenly thinking it was some strange thing jumping out at her; so it was with great relief that she realised it was only Bruce. Admittedly, she was still a little cautious of him, but at the same time she was beginning to get used to him padding around the place. Douglas must have seen her alarm because he immediately knelt down and gripped the dog firmly by the collar, restraining it. 'Okay, boy, okay. Sit. Calm down.' He waited until the dog was sitting and then turned to look up at Peri. 'I'm sorry he scared you. But, honestly, he wouldn't hurt a fly. Come spring when the orphaned animals are brought in, he'll be like a surrogate mum to them all.'

As she gazed down into his blue, blue eyes, she felt herself grow soft, as if she could melt through the stone floor.

'Why don't we try and overcome your fear?' he suggested. 'I'll hold Bruce by the collar and you can touch his ear. That will be a start.'

At that moment she felt that she would do anything he asked of her. She transferred her gaze to the dog, who sat with his tail swishing the floor, looking up at her with bright eager eyes and a lolling tongue. In a trance, she stretched a hand towards the furry head, slowly, slowly, getting closer, when – suddenly – the dog's head jerked and a long, slimy tongue slurped across her fingers. 'Euch!' she cried, jerking back her hand, and holding it to her chest as if it had been bitten. 'Douglas, I can't do it,' she wailed, snapping out of her trance. 'Don't ask me, *please.*'

Douglas spoke gently to Bruce. 'Good boy, go to your bed.' Shamefully, the dog slunk away to his basket in the corner, delicately stepping onto the cushion before collapsing with a sigh. Douglas straightened up and turned to her. 'I'm sorry, Peri,' he said. 'I shouldn't have suggested it.' Suddenly he smiled and the hard lines on his face softened and his blue eyes sparkled mischievously. 'Just think,' he exclaimed. 'You'll probably be gone in the morning, and then you won't have to worry about dogs and snow and buzzards . . . and a Neanderthal like me.'

She gazed up at him. He seemed to be encouraging her to smile and she tried to, but suddenly it was as if she didn't know how to. Instead, she could only continue to gaze up at him, mesmerised, feeling her world contract within to these four walls, encircling her and this man in a soft golden orb. One kiss. That was all she needed. Just one kiss. He was sensing her mood – she could tell – the smile on his face was slowly fading and his eyes were growing dark, penetrating, laying bare his desire for her. He wanted her!

She tilted up her chin, willing him on. *Please!* she wanted to beg. *Please!*

He was coming towards her, his face getting closer, closer, and then, softly, he was pressing his lips down on hers. At the touch of them, a delicious warmth spread through her veins until she felt her limbs would dissolve, the smell of him filling her head, overpowering. His arms folded around her, effortlessly pulling her up against his body and now she could sense his urgency. Of course, in just a second, she would break free of him and apologise. In just one second . . .

She could feel his lips carressing her neck, sending hot shivers tingling finger-light up her spine. Now a big hard hand was inside her coat, moving across her hips, over her buttocks, possessing her. She gasped for breath, overwhelmed by a desperate craving for him. She wanted to feel his naked body pressing down on hers; she wanted to feel his cock pushing up into her; she wanted . . .

A door banged. Voices out in the yard. Helmut! In the same instant they broke apart and seconds later the door opened.

Peri had swung round to face the sink, her heart pounding. Had they been seen? God, how embarrassing! The kettle. She grabbed it, stuck it under the tap and turned on the water.

'Hello.' It was Otto.

'Are you making coffee?' Helmut asked.

Peri kept her back to them. 'Yes.' Her cheeks blazed and her hand trembled as she put the kettle on the stove. This was unreal, confusing, like being sharply awoken from a deep, deep sleep.

'We decided to come back,' Helmut said. 'Just after you left, the kilt man phoned to say he couldn't make it, and then for some reason everyone in the place started singing. I think my brain is still buzzing from the noise of it!'

'That sometimes happens,' Douglas said. 'I should have warned you.'

Peri could hear chairs being scraped back across the stone floor. They were sitting down. She had to escape.

'I don't want to panic anyone,' Douglas said casually, 'but I reckon we're going to have snow.'

As he was speaking, Peri was fumbling with the knobs on the stove, trying to work out how to light it. Bloody thing! It made her want to cry. Why wasn't this bloody thing working!! Then Douglas was beside her, striking a match and turning a knob, setting the gas alight.

'No, no,' Otto was saying, 'it won't snow. I phoned the London weather station this morning and they didn't say it would snow.'

'They sometimes get it wrong,' Douglas answered, putting the kettle over the flame. 'The weather up here in the mountains is always unpredictable, especially when you're sitting in an armchair in London.'

'A flurry of snow would be perfect,' Helmut said cheerfully. 'Especially for our final shot.'

'It might be more than a flurry,' Douglas said. 'I think you should have your bags packed tonight – just in case.'

With her back firmly turned to the others, Peri laid out four mugs and began to spoon coffee into them.

'Fair enough,' Helmut agreed. 'We shall pack our bags tonight and make a decision in the morning. But for now we shall have coffee and then I would like you all to join me in a glass of schnapps.'

Peri dropped the teaspoon into a mug and headed for the door. 'If you'll excuse me, I think I will go to bed. See you in the morning. Goodnight.' She went straight up to her room and began to pack, throwing handfuls of clothes into her case with a grim urgency. Her body cried out for him but her brain was now beginning to take control. Why did she do it? He was a nobody – a country yokel! She should feel humiliated at allowing him to kiss her. Well, hopefully it would snow tomorrow and then she would be gone and that would be the end. Oh, but how she ached for him!

As she lay in the darkness, she could hear their voices muffled below. So that's how it happens, she thought miserably; like something out of a cheap romantic novel: pounding heart, trembling, breathlessness, overwhelming desire. But why couldn't it have happened on Saturday night, at the Awards Ceremony, with a stinkingly rich movie mogul, and not in some dingy bar with a Scottish . . . with a Scottish . . . ? What the hell *was* he? She turned over and gathered her pillow to her cheek, praying for sleep, but remaining wide awake and staring hard into the blackness.

Was it the wind that had woken her or the sound of a door banging out in the yard? She snuggled deeper under the eiderdown and slowly drifted back to sleep.

Now there were voices – urgent voices. Suddenly the room was filled with light and someone was shaking her by the shoulder. 'Peri! Get dressed. Quickly!' It was Otto.

'Please – no,' she whimpered, burrowing her head deeper

into her pillow. 'It's the middle of the night. I don't want to work.'

'This is not work. This is an emergency. We have to leave.' He shook her again. 'There's a blizzard. We're going to be snowed in if we don't go *now*!'

The words seared her brain. Immediately she was up and scrabbling for her clothes. 'I don't want to be snowed in,' she wailed, but Otto had gone.

Her mind raced as she began pulling on pants and trousers. *Snowed in:* what did it mean? Would she be trapped here? Yes, of course; but for how long? What if she missed the Awards? God, no! Don't even think it! Panting hard, she dragged the thermal vest over her head, followed by two sweaters and then she threw herself down on the edge of the bed to slip on socks and a boot. Where was the other boot? 'Fuck it!' she breathed, looking under the bed. She couldn't be snowed in! This was horrible. *There* was the boot! With trembling hands, she pulled it on and flung herself into her coat. Next, she took her vanity case into the bathroom and swiftly but carefully began filling it with her few remaining bottles of oils and creams.

'Hurry up!' It was Douglas, shouting up from the foot of the stairs.

'I'm coming!' She rushed back into the bedroom and grabbed the handle of her suitcase, thankful that Douglas had told her to pack it; then she threw a cursory glance around the room for anything forgotten. But it didn't matter, she realised; whatever was left behind could be sent on to her. The most important thing was that she got out. With her vanity case in one hand and the suitcase in the other, she lumbered along the corridor, down the stairs and into the kitchen.

Everyone was there. Mrs Craig was coming towards her with a cup of tea, her head covered in pink plastic rollers. 'You'd better get that down you,' she said and tried to smile, but the fear in her eyes belied the smile on her face.

'Thanks.' Peri put down her vanity case and took the cup, lifting it, trembling, to her lips.

Helmut and Otto had their coats on, gazing anxiously up at Douglas, who stood by the front door issuing instructions to them. With his lower face covered in a scarf and a black woollen hat tight against his head, he looked exactly the same as when she had first laid eyes on him. 'We'll take both vehicles,' he was saying, 'and I'll lead the way. Hit your horn twice if you run into trouble.' He pulled on black leather gloves, muttering to himself, 'If only Ian had returned my snow chains.' With his hand on the latch, he turned to them. It was as if he had become a stranger. No more the laughing eyes and the jaunty eyebrows; now his brows were gathered in a fierce frown and his eyes had become as hard as flint. 'You will see poles on either side of the road,' he said. 'Keep between them. Understood?'

Helmut and Otto nodded rapidly.

Then he saw her. 'Okay, Peri?' Their eyes met for a split second. The hardness in his eyes seemed to soften in that moment and then he was looking back at Helmut. 'We've got to get you over the Pass,' he said, 'and down off the mountains. I just hope we're not too late. Ready?' He opened the door and immediately the distant hum of the storm became an almighty scream as an icy wind swirled around the kitchen. '*Let's go!*'

'Good luck,' Mrs Craig called out, keeping in step with them as they hurried to the door, her feeble hands fluttering towards them as if wanting to hold them back.

Even though her heart was thudding, Peri was able to muster up a brief smile for her. 'Thanks for everything, Mrs Craig,' she said hurriedly, picking up her vanity case. 'I'll phone you as soon as I get back to London.'

In an instant, the old woman was up on tiptoe, gathering Peri's face in her small dry hands and pulling it down towards her. 'You mind yerself – do ye hear?' she said sternly and kissed Peri roughly on the cheek. Just as quickly she released her.

'I'll try.' With tears pricking her eyes, Peri swung away, and headed for the door, her vanity case in one hand, the bulging suitcase in the other. Now she was out in the yard, twisting her face from the shards of snow slashing at her cheek, staggering against the icy blast. Where was the car? She couldn't see anything but flashes of white against the black sky. Panic lay coiled up like a snake in the pit of her stomach, ready to leap up. This shouldn't be happening. *'It's not fair!'* she wanted to scream. *'Not fair! Not fair, not fair, not fair!'*

A dark bulky shape loomed out of the blizzard towards her and then she felt her suitcases being taken out of her hands. Now she was at the car. Her hand scrabbled for the door handle and found it. But she could barely open it against the force of the gale. 'Help me!' she screamed. Someone pushed in beside her and suddenly the door was open. She threw herself into the back seat and the door slammed shut. In the merciful stillness, she peeled her wind-whipped hair from her face, conscious of the ringing in her ears. Helmut was already at the wheel, starting the engine and chattering urgently in German to Otto who was getting in beside him. Helmut pointed to the blanket of snow on the windscreen and they both looked at it, watching the windscreen wipers uselessly pushing against it. Suddenly a big arm swept across the glass and the snow fell away.

Moments later, from out of the blackness, two orange lights appeared in front of them, flashing urgently, on and off, on and off, and Peri realised instantly that they would be the hazard lights from the back of the Land Rover. Helmut released the clutch. They were moving. Peri looked back towards the house with the shape of Mrs Craig standing in the doorway, and for a moment she was tempted to jump out and run back to its safety and warmth. But she couldn't. She had to get to London. Her whole future was waiting for her. This must be Monday, she thought rapidly. Then there's Tuesday, Wednesday. Three more days before she had to be in London, to be standing in de Vere's studio having her final fitting. Three more days! But what if they got stuck on the road? What if they couldn't make it to the airport? God! *Why* were they going so slowly? 'Can't we go faster?' she demanded, clutching the back of Helmut's seat. They were practically crawling along.

'No, Peri, we can't!' Helmut snapped, his eyes focused on the flashing lights up ahead.

She gazed through the windscreen, watching with horrified fascination the millions of white spears coming at them from out of the blackness. 'But we shan't be able to take off in this!'

'I know!' Helmut replied sharply. 'But we have to get out of the mountains – down to a main road. If we get stuck up here, it could be weeks or months before we can get out.'

'But that's impossible!' she cried.

'No, it's not,' Otto insisted. 'I have a friend who got snowed in on the Fernpass last year. It was three weeks before we saw him again.'

'*Oh, no!*' she cried. This was a nightmare – a ghastly nightmare. This couldn't be happening – not to *her*. 'I mustn't get stuck,' Peri wailed, hearing her voice rising hysterically, 'I've *got* to get back to London – I've just *got* to!'

'None of us want to get stuck,' Helmut shouted. 'So please be quiet and allow me to concentrate.'

Peri fell silent. She could feel the panic stirring in the pit of her stomach. But what if they did get to a main road? What good would that do? They would still be trapped, and the plane wouldn't be able to take off – not with snow on the runway. But they would have snowploughs in Scotland, wouldn't they? She balanced on a knife-edge of suspense as she asked, 'Do they have snowploughs up here?'

'Not up *here*!' Helmut replied, exasperated. 'The snowploughs will be down on the main roads – that's why we have to get down there.'

'Oh.' She wished that Helmut wasn't being so snappy with her. 'So that means they'll use snowploughs to clear the runway?'

'Yes!'

Peri lapsed into silence, calculating. As soon as they got to the main road, they would have to wait for the blizzard to ease up . . . sometime in the morning, probably. Then they could follow a snowplough to the airport, so that would mean they would probably take off sometime in the late afternoon . . . So about teatime she could be sitting on the plane, winging her way back to London . . .

But first they had to get down to the main road. This was agonising! The car seemed to be winding up and up, forever up. Why weren't they going *down?* She sensed they were up very high. Exposed. The gale roared louder, hurling itself against the car as if desperate to push it over the edge. No one spoke. At one point the hazard lights ahead disappeared, and Peri could feel her heart thudding, knowing that without Douglas she would disintegrate into hysteria. When the lights reappeared, she felt faint with relief.

She couldn't sit back in her seat – she was too tense. She had to cling to the back of Helmut's seat, her nails digging deep into the plastic, willing with every fibre of her being that they would keep moving forward. Every inch, every yard meant that they were one inch, one yard, closer to the airport. She was prepared to go slowly now, not caring how many hours it took, just as long as they got there. An idea flashed through her brain. It would make great news coverage, she realised, swiftly trying to imagine how the headlines would read: *Peri Lomax, English actress, flees Scottish blizzard to host the International Film Awards.* It wouldn't matter that she wasn't a real actress – yet – but it would start to get people used to the idea. She would telephone Mags as soon as she got to the airport. Of course, it would be too late for today's edition, but it could go in for Tuesday's. Her thoughts turned bitterly to Mags, sleeping safely in her king-sized bed wrapped up in a satin duvet, completely unaware of what was happening to her 'darling' Peri at this moment. She would never, ever, be able to forgive Mags for this.

Caught up in these thoughts, Peri gazed blankly at the hazard lights of the Land Rover up ahead. Suddenly she saw the brake lights flash red. Then there was a blast of a horn. Once! Twice! Immediately, Helmut squeezed the brake pedal and the car glided for a moment before coming to a halt. Quickly, he wound down his window.

'Why are we stopping?' Peri yelled.

'I don't know,' Helmut shouted.

Silently, they waited. Then Douglas's face appeared at the window, his eyebrows thick with snow. Peri knew, before he spoke, what he was going to say.

'We're not going to make it,' he shouted above the roar of the gale. 'This is our last chance to turn around. If we go any further, there will be no turning back.'

'I can't go back!' Peri screamed.

Douglas looked at her sadly. 'I'm sorry, Peri, but if we get stuck out in this, we will die.'

'But we're nearly there!'

He shook his head regretfully. 'No, we're not.'

'*Please*, Douglas,' she begged, 'let's keep going. I *know* we will make it.'

He shook his head once more and drew away from the window, disappearing into the blizzard.

She had to get away! She *had* to! He didn't understand. She would go to him and *make* him understand. Swiftly, she pulled back the door handle and tried to push the door open but it would hardly move against the force of the wind. Desperately she shoved her shoulder against it, opening it far enough to be able to squeeze out; then it banged shut behind her and she was left huddled in a crouching position against the wheel, facing the full force of the storm. *Jesus!* She couldn't see a fucking thing! Arrows of icy snow slashed the blackness, hitting her in the eyes and making her blink rapidly. Instinctively she held up a hand to shield her eyes but it was useless; the snow was coming at her from all directions. Oh God – where was he? Where was the Land Rover? Look for the hazard lights! She pushed herself off from the side of the car and peered into the storm. Yes – the lights were still there! All she had to do was to get from the car to the Land Rover. Right! It was now or never! Bending double, with her whole body leaning into the wind, she staggered through the snow towards the Land Rover, keeping her head tucked into her chest, her hands blindly groping the blackness. She must be there by now! Pausing, she lifted a hand to shield her eyes and squinted ahead. No! No! The Land Rover was moving away! 'DOUGLAS!' she screamed, but the word was whipped from her mouth and swallowed up in the howling gale.

The flashing lights were disappearing! Gone! Now, a steady glow of soft light swept across the blackness, making the spears of snow look brilliantly white. Headlights! Douglas was turning round! He was coming back down the road. She dived across the beam of headlights. The Land Rover stopped. Sobbing with relief, she frantically felt for the door handle, and then suddenly the door swung open and she scrambled up into the passenger seat and slammed the door shut.

Douglas was staring at her in astonishment. 'What . . . ?'

'Please, Douglas, please,' she begged, wiping the melting snow from her eyes.

'No!' He thundered and released the clutch pedal.

'You can fuck me!'

'What?'

She nodded eagerly, confirming her offer. 'If you get me out of here – I will let you fuck me. I promise.' She was bewildered to see a flicker of pain move across his eyes.

'Calm down, Peri,' he said sternly. 'You don't know what you're saying.'

'Yes, I do! Oh, Douglas, I have to get away. It's vital!'

The urgency in her voice caught his attention and he put his foot gently on the brake and turned to her.

This was her last chance to persuade him. 'I *have* to be at the Film Awards ceremony on Saturday evening,' she explained hurriedly. 'If I'm not there, the person I hate most in the world will take my place.' She could tell by his expression that this wasn't enough to persuade him. 'Igor de Vere has created a ballgown especially for me . . .' she paused so that he could absorb the importance of this 'and . . .' She stopped speaking.

He was looking at her with incredulity, as if she were crazy. This stupid idiot was not even *trying* to understand! God, how she wanted to slap that stupid look off his stupid face. *'Don't you understand?'*

'Listen, Peri,' Douglas answered in a low angry voice. 'All I know is that if we don't go back – *now* – we will *die!*'

'I hate you!' she screamed.

They were moving again. 'I'm truly sorry that we have to turn back. But don't give up hope. You may still get to your Film Awards ceremony. It may still be possible.'

'Liar!'

'Please believe me,' he said earnestly. 'If we continue, we are going to be blown off the top of Randolph's Pass or die in some ditch. Isn't it better to miss this ceremony thing than to die in a ditch?'

'No!'

'Don't be soft!' he snapped. 'And what about the others, eh? Perhaps they don't want to die tonight!'

'Well, they can go back to the house while we can carry on . . .' she tried lamely. '. . . And . . .'

'No, Peri, I can't do that. When you are with me, I am responsible for your safety. I wish it could have been different – I really do.' He began to console her, speaking gently, but she ignored him. 'You never know,' he added, 'if the blizzard stops within the next hour or two, and if the weather warms, you might be out on Saturday . . . it's possible.'

'Saturday!' she screamed. 'Saturday is no good to me! I've got my final fitting with de Vere on Friday!'

'Okay, okay,' he said soothingly. 'We will see what the blizzard does. It might stop any minute and then you'll be fine. No problem.'

Peri continued to ignore him. He was a liar! It was all lies, lies, lies! Why had she let him kiss her? She must have been out of her mind. He was only some half-witted yokel who must have thought he was on to a good thing. How humiliating! God – and she had offered her body to him as well! She sat rigid in her seat, clenching her teeth and hating him.

It seemed like only minutes and yet they were coming back into the yard. She wanted to sob with bitter frustration. Now she would never, ever, leave this horrible, horrible place. She would be buried alive in this cold dreary house, reduced to having to live with this man day after day, with his flea-bitten dog staring at her.

Suddenly, miraculously, from out of nowhere, she had an idea – a brilliant, stunning idea, a marvellous idea! Why hadn't *he* thought of it? It was *so* obvious! As soon as they came to a halt, she shoved her shoulder against the door and squeezed out, feeling her boots sink into the snow. The blizzard raged on, but now she wasn't angry or frightened; instead she felt an overwhelming sense of triumph. She staggered across the yard and into the kitchen, beaming a smile at Mrs Craig who stood waiting with Bruce just inside the door.

'What's happening?' the woman asked, obviously bewildered by Peri's radiant face.

'I know how I'm going to get out of here,' Peri declared triumphantly, standing in the middle of the kitchen.

Mrs Craig looked puzzled. 'How?'

'I'll tell you in a second.' Peri looked towards the door, waiting for Douglas. Then he appeared, holding two suitcases and stamping snow off his boots and onto the mat, speaking words of welcome to Bruce.

'I know how I'm going to get out of here,' Peri gloated.

Douglas stopped and looked at her. 'How?'

'Mountain Rescue!' she said simply. 'We'll phone them and then they can come with their helicopter and rescue me.'

Douglas looked at her wearily and swung the suitcases up against the wall.

It was as if she hadn't spoken. 'Why not?' she demanded angrily. 'That's what they're there for: to rescue people. And I want to be rescued.'

'But you only call them in a real emergency,' Mrs Craig explained. 'And this is not a real emergency.'

'But it is!' Peri wailed. Now Helmut and Otto were coming through the door, stamping their feet on the door mat.

'It's not, dear. A real emergency is when a wee bairn contracts meningitis, or when a lassie goes into premature labour and she's got tae get tae a hospital before she and her baby die.'

'Mrs Craig is correct,' interjected Otto. 'It is the same in Germany.'

Peri stood with folded arms, staring at the floor, refusing to be fobbed off.

Mrs Craig paused and then continued again. 'There could be someone – right now – trapped in the snow and dying from hypothermia.'

'But I don't mind sharing the helicopter,' Peri conceded.

'For heaven's sake, Peri!' Douglas exploded. 'Stop thinking about yerself and try and imagine what's happening oot there!' He waved a hand towards the door, accidentally clipping the side of Otto's head.

Peri saw Mrs Craig hold out a hesitant hand towards Douglas, as if warding off his anger, but he steamed on . . .

'There's babies and children – countless folk who will be needing that helicopter.' The anger in his voice began to subside. 'Listen, Peri.' He came towards her and held her by her arms. 'We've only got two helicopters to cover the north of Scotland. Only two . . .'

Peri refused to look at him, hating his slimy voice, hating the way he was making her appear like an hysterical child.

'Anyway,' he sighed wearily and continued in a subdued tone, 'the helicopter cannae take off in these conditions, so there's no point in thinking about it now. Let's go back to bed and take stock of the situation in the morning. You never know, the blizzard might stop just as quickly as it started.'

She looked up at him eagerly. 'And then will you call for a helicopter?'

'Oh, Peri! When this blizzard stops, that helicopter is not going to be able to cope with all the emergencies coming in. You don't want to take the place of someone who desperately needs an airlift, do you? Someone who would die if not rushed to a hospital in time.'

Peri gazed down at his boots, her mouth pressed together in a mutinous line, feeling the last rays of hope slipping away.

'And how would I explain it to the rescue team after they've risked their necks getting here?' Douglas said impatiently. '*Please, can you take this woman to the nearest airport urgently, because she's got a ceremony tae go to?*'

'But it's not just a ceremony, it's . . .' Oh, what was the use! Tears of anger and bitter frustration welled up inside her and she shoved his arms away. 'I *hate* you. You just want to keep me here. But let me tell you: I *hate* this place and – *yes* – I would rather die in a ditch than stay *here* with *you!*' She swung around and rushed to the door, glimpsing the look of horror on Mrs Craig's face as she passed by. Now she was pounding up the stairs and along the corridor.

Once in her room, she banged the door shut, kicked off her boots, and, still wearing her coat, she threw herself down on the bed and pulled the eiderdown up to her chin. She hated him more than anyone else in the world! She hated Mags. She hated Helmut. Why had she agreed to do this job? She must have been out of her mind. She had known that something would go wrong – she had just felt it. Now there would be no Film Awards. No Igor de Vere ballgown. No paparazzi excited and eager to take her photograph. No flirting with movie moguls and dancing with film stars. There would be no hushed whispers: *Look! That's the new Helmut Reuther girl! Isn't she beautiful! She had to escape a terrifying blizzard to get here tonight . . .*

The glittering dream slowly faded as she foresaw the true outcome of this terrible disaster: Saffron, sleek and expensive in de Vere's dress, smiling her silly smile while sashaying onto the stage, taking the microphone and speaking in her slimy voice and looking at the cameras with supreme confidence.

The bitch! There was a tightness in Peri's throat now, and her chest felt hot and churning. She wanted desperately to cry but she didn't know how to . . . not any more. Once upon a time it had come easily, but the long and lonely years had hardened her to it, teaching her that she must never be defeated by life, teaching her that she must never cry. Now, at last, she lay defeated, exhausted, resigned to the fact that no matter how hard she tried to find happiness, it would always be snatched away. Why? Why *her*? Something or somebody up there hated her. But why?

'Peri?' It was Mrs Craig, tapping at the door. 'I've got your bags here. Shall I bring them in?'

'No.'

'Okay, dear. I'll leave them just outside the door. Would you like a cup of tea?'

'No.'

'Okay, then. You just give me a call if you need me.'

Peri yearned to call out, to have Mrs Craig come in and put her arms around her and talk soothingly, to make it all better. But even she couldn't make it better . . . nobody could. Now, she listened to the woman's footsteps receding down the corridor, leaving behind an empty silence, and a terrible loneliness. 'No one cares,' Peri whispered. 'They pretend to; but they don't. Mrs Craig pretends to care; but *she* doesn't. Douglas pretends to care; but *he* doesn't. Mags pretends to; but *she* doesn't.

Peri lay with her head on the pillow, gazing at the crack of light beneath the bedroom door but her mind's eye looked back across the years, seeking out a memory of someone who cared . . . a scrap of love . . . a moment of being wanted . . . something . . .

The pretty lady with the daisy earrings had come and taken her away, smiling and saying that Peri would be her special little girl. But then she had returned Peri back to the home, saying that she was going to be too ill to look after a little girl. But Peri had known it was a lie.

Mr and Mrs Tidy had returned her, too, saying that their

dog wasn't happy at having to share the house with a little girl. But this time she hadn't cared. She hated them and she hated their dog. Mrs Tidy had tried to take her teddy away saying that it was ready for the dustbin but she had pleaded with her and eventually the woman had capitulated. But when she got back from school later that day the teddy was gone. There were bits of it in the back yard, chewed-up bits as if a dog had attacked it. She had felt grief and fury all mixed up and she'd cried and screamed, blindly kicking the dog, distraught that the only link with her mother had gone forever.

And then there were Bob and Judy. They smiled at her and gave her toys and talked to her a lot but she couldn't trust them, knowing that at any minute they would want to get rid of her. Which of course they did. They said she was too naughty and they couldn't do anything with her, which at least was the truth.

She was always returned at night, when the others girls were asleep. The suitcase would click open, her nightie would be taken out and given to her and then she would climb into bed. The door would close, the footsteps would walk away and she would be left to gaze at the crack of light beneath the bedroom door . . .

. . . just as she was doing now.

Peri rolled onto her back and stared up into the blackness, feeling a terrible ache in her heart. How could she take away this pain? The pain of a lifetime's loneliness . . . a lifetime of never knowing love. But she didn't feel the pain as long as she kept moving, kept running, kept hoping, kept dreaming – never looking back. Now, suddenly, all hope was gone and she was trapped and unable to run, unable to stop the long-buried memories flooding back, wave upon wave of them, pushing and shoving as if filling the very room. Tired and defeated, she let them come, and, for the first time in twenty-four years, she felt a tear trickle down her cheek. Then she knew that, in the long black hours to come, she would finally cry the tears of that lonely little girl.

Chapter Six

It was 8 a.m. precisely. Mags yawned as she walked into the sitting room, throwing a cursory glance through the picture window at the Thames far below. Once she had been thrilled by this view but not any longer. It was like most things in life: you just got used to them. Straightening the collar of her towelling robe, she sat down at the breakfast table and scanned her eyes across it, noting the shiny cutlery, the starched white napkin, the rose in the vase, the glass of orange juice, the pile of mail to her right, the pile of newspapers to her left. Good. Maria was learning. But where was the remote control? Mags sighed dispiritedly, but she refused to get up and look for it. Maria would have tidied it away – again! Mags was rapidly coming to the conclusion that a Filipino maid was a false economy. A maid was intended to be a labour-saving device – like a dishwasher – but not if she kept tidying things away in the wrong places. Mags had spent half an hour the previous night looking for the tea strainer; and the night before that – when she had guests – she had to practically tear the place apart looking for the corkscrew. It seemed to be happening all the time! Mags couldn't bear to count the wasted hours just *looking* for things.

There was a rattle of crockery as the kitchen door opened. 'Good morning, madam.' Maria came towards the table, carrying a tray.

'Good morning, Maria,' Mags replied primly, watching the

boiled egg and the plate of toast being put down in front of her. 'Would you remember – always – to put the remote control on the breakfast table in the mornings?'

'Yes. I am sorry.' Maria crossed over to the television and brought back the remote control and put it on the table beside the pile of mail.

Mags was satisfied now. She was all set for a pleasant, leisurely breakfast. 'That's all. Thank you.' The girl turned promptly and went back into the kitchen.

With the napkin across her lap, Mags picked up her knife and sliced off the top of her egg. The yolk was hard! Again! This was too much! Christ, what did she have to do to get a soft boiled egg? *Beg?* 'Maria,' she called wearily, putting down her knife.

Maria came out of the kitchen and stopped. Mags studied her for a moment, noting the brown pock-marked skin, the nervous smile showing pearly white teeth, the piggy brown eyes staring in apprehension. 'I thought you told me you could cook,' she said at last.

'I can, madam, I can,' Maria protested.

'Well, how come you can't cook a soft boiled egg, eh? Don't you have soft boiled eggs in the Phillipines?'

'Yes, madam, of course.'

'Well, perhaps I should go to the Philipines for my soft boiled egg because it doesn't look as if I'm going to get one *here*.'

The girl smiled nervously but didn't speak. Mags pushed her plate away, annoyed that her lovely breakfast had been spoilt by this inept creature. 'All you have to do is to put an egg into boiling salted water for four minutes. That's all. I am not asking you to split the atom. Please, try again.'

The girl took the plate and hurried back into the kitchen.

Mags sighed and turned back to the table, picking a letter from the pile of mail. She recognised the lilac manila with an American postmark, her name and address scrawled across it in purple ink. Rupert Murray, faggot designer from Paradise Beach. She flipped it over, slicing a knife along the top edge and taking out a lilac-coloured letter. What did he want *now?* As she began to read, she casually picked up the remote control and aimed it at the television, clicking it on. Then she turned back to the letter and read: *Hi! Mags. How you doing?* . . . Suddenly an urgent voice caught her attention. It was coming from the television screen. '. . . had winds of up to forty miles an hour.' It was a news reporter, holding a microphone in his gloved hand, the fleece-lined collar of his coat turned up against the flakes of snow floating gently about his head. Behind him was an upturned car stuck in a ditch of snow and beyond that lay fields and mountains of snow. The man was speaking urgently, his breath coming out in puffs of steam. 'There is chaos on the roads and all train and air services have been cancelled. The Met Office gave a statement an hour ago saying that this has been a freak blizzard blowing down from the Arctic and they are unable to state at this time whether the blizzard will return. Meanwhile, the people of the Highlands can only wait and pray. This is Sam McCullen speaking . . .' Mags stared at the screen, stunned. The Highlands? Peri? *No!*

The telephone shrilled and she swung round and snatched it up. 'Margaret-Anne Stanwyck.'

'Mags!' It was Tula, speaking in a rush. 'Have you seen the news?'

'I can't believe it! It's too terrible!'

'I know. Poor Peri. How are we going to get her out of there?'

Mags's brain raced. 'I'll phone her now – that's if the lines haven't been blown down. Then we'll re-group. Wait by the phone.' She banged down the receiver and looked around for her bag. Where the hell was it? There! She scooped it up and took out her Filofax, skimming through the pages until she found the telephone number and then, carefully, she dialled. There was a ringing tone. Good. She waited, conscious now of her rapid breathing.

The slow soft voice of a Scottish woman answered. 'Hello, Cadha Mor Lodge.'

'Mrs Craig? This is Mags. What's happening?'

'Och, dear, we've had the most dreadful blizzard.' The woman suddenly spoke in a rush, as if relieved to be talking to someone. 'It came from nowhere. We just weren't expecting it. Douglas tried tae get everyone across the Pass but it was too dangerous and they had tae come back.'

'So? Are you snowed in?'

'Aye, I'm afraid so.'

'Oh, no! This is terrible. I've got to get Peri out of there. Let me speak to her. No. No. Let me speak to Douglas first.'

'Douglas is away oot mending the rabbit hut. Do you want me tae go oot and get him?'

'No. Just get Peri.'

'Och, I'm not wanting to wake her. She's had a terrible, terrible time. She was out wi' the others, trying to get through the blizzard and when she came back she went wild, saying she had to get back tae London. She got herself in such a terrible state.'

Mags could well believe it. 'What about Mr Reuther? Is he still sleeping?'

'Oh, aye.'

'Okay – don't wake him. But you've got to get Douglas to phone me – *pronto*. I want to know how bad the situation is up there. Tell him that Peri's got to be back in London by Saturday morning – the latest! – and ask him what her chances are.'

'Oh.' The woman's exclamation fell flat and heavy.

'What? Don't you think she's going to make it?'

'She might. She might.' It was as if the woman was trying to convince herself.

Mags needed answers. 'Do you have any idea whether this blizzard might start up again?'

'Och, I couldn't tell you. But I hope not. If we have any more snow like last night, it'll be weeks before we can get out of here.'

'Weeks?'

'Aye.'

'What's happening now. Is it still snowing?'

'No. It seems tae have stopped.'

'Right. I'll phone the Met Office, find out if the blizzard is going to return. You tell Douglas to find out when the roads will be clear. Presumably you've got snowploughs up there?'

'Not up here in the mountains – no.'

'What?' This was impossible. Peri wasn't going to make it. 'So there's no chance of Peri getting out of there before Saturday, is there?' Mags's tone was almost accusatory.

'There might be a chance. It all depends if the sun stays out tae thaw the snow. It's probably too early tae tell at the moment, but it looks as if it might be a sunny day today. That's a start, anyway, so I don't think you should give up hope – not just yet.'

'Okay. Okay. I'll hang fire until I get the info from the Met. You've got my number. Tell Douglas to give me a buzz.'

'Right. I'll go and do that now.'

'Thanks.' Mags pressed her finger firmly on the cut-off button and then dialled Tula's number. There was an immediate answer. 'Hi. Tula. It looks like no-go. She's snowed in. No snowploughs. We're going to be bloody lucky to get her back before Saturday morning; and if the blizzard comes back, we ain't going to be seeing Peri again for a very long time.'

'How awful!'

'Yeah, isn't it! The Awards committee are going to bust a gut! Put Saffron on standby. It looks as if she's going to have to replace Peri. I'll know within the hour. Stay by the phone. *Ciao.*' Mags banged down the receiver and swung round to pick up the remote control. She got Ceefax. *Weather. Today: bright and sunny. Tuesday: bright and sunny.* Promising, but it wasn't enough. She would phone the Met Office. She dialled directory enquiries and got the number, immediately dialling it. Engaged. Damn.

She dialled Sally Walker at the *Times* newsdesk. 'Sally, do me a great favour, will you? This blizzard in Scotland – is it going to come back? I've got one of my girls stranded up in the

Highlands and I've got to have her here in London for Saturday a.m. What are her chances?' Sally would phone back within five minutes. Good. She put the receiver down, keeping her hand on it and thinking: was there anything else she could do? No. Not yet.

'I hope this will be okay for you.' It was Maria, timidly placing a boiled egg in front of her.

'Not now!' Mags exploded, thrusting the plate away. 'Can't you see I'm busy?' The phone was ringing. 'Just get me a coffee,' she said quickly, picking up the receiver. 'A strong one. Hello?'

'Mags?' It was Douglas speaking. 'I received yer message. Last night's blizzard seems tae have been a freak incident. At the moment, there's a high pressure coming in from the south-west bringing warm air and if the sun stays out for the next couple o' days, there will be rapid thawing. Even so, the mountain roads will still remain impassable by car, so we will all have tae squeeze into my Land Rover for the journey. I've also arranged tae have snowchains waiting for us at the halfway point – *they* will get us through. With all these factors in our favour, I estimate that Peri will arrive at Inverness airport, mid afternoon, Friday.'

'So, there'll be no more snow?'

'Not for the next few days – no.'

Mags exhaled with relief. 'Thank God for that.' Then she thought: how does he know? 'How do you know all this?' she asked.

'Intuition.'

'Intuition?' Mags didn't like the sound of that. She wasn't going to make a vital decision on someone's *intuition*. 'Well – thanks for the information. Tell Peri and Helmut to call me when they wake.'

'Okay. You'll be booking their seats for Friday, then?'

'Yeah – definitely. I'll catch you later. *Ciao*.' Mags put down the phone. She intended to books seats for Friday *and* Saturday – just in case. The phone rang and she was straight there. 'Sally?'

'Hallo, Mags. Good news. The blizzard has been swept north. No more snow. There's high pressure coming in from the south-west which will create rapid thawing across the Highland region. Your girl should be booking herself on a flight for Friday afternoon.'

'Thanks, Sally. I owe you.' As Mags replaced the receiver, she realised that this information was the same as Douglas's. She shrugged and dialled Tula's number. 'Everyone's telling me that Peri's going to make it but I've got a bad feeling about this one. In any case, book three seats on flights leaving Inverness airport on Friday evening and Saturday morning – just to be on the safe side. Phone Helmut's office, speak to his secretary. Keep Saffron on standby. Get the script across to her. Get her to meet Igor de Vere and explain the situation. Contact Bruce Weller on the Awards Committee. Meanwhile I'll shoot into the office and start phoning the media. We've got to be prepared if anything goes wrong.'

'Do you think Peri's going to make it in time?'

'She might. Just. But even if she does, she's not going to have much time to prepare herself. Can you believe it?! The most important gig of her life and she's going to be lucky to have time to put on lipstick.'

'Oh, I know. She must be going wild!'

'Not at the moment, she's not, because she's still sleeping. But I'll tell you something: I'm mighty glad that I'm not going to be around when she wakes up! Boy – can you imagine it? She's going to be throwing chairs through the window. Anyway, I'll catch you later. Okay? *Ciao.*' Mags put the phone down and sat thinking. Everything pointed to the fact that Peri would make it, after all. But would it be a catastrophe if she didn't?

Yes, unfortunately it would. The mere fact that Helmut Reuther had chosen Peri Lomax had sparked off a chain reaction and now the world was ready and waiting for her: chat-show hosts, magazine editors, TV advertising, the tabloid press, cable. The media circus was pointing a finger at Peri because Peri was in fashion and everyone had to have what was fashionable, hadn't they? Mags sighed. Why couldn't it have been Saffron? Saffron with the dimpled smile and charming personality, not Peri with her black moods and childish tantrums. 'Well, it's not my decision to make,' she said aloud, picking up her glass of orange juice and slugging it back. Then she shovelled her mail into her handbag and stood up. This was Peri's time – the world was waiting – and Margaret-Anne Stanwyck would, of course, be creaming twenty-five per cent off the top.

Slowly, Peri opened her swollen eyelids. A sliver of bright light shone through the gap in the curtains. Daylight. Everything was silent. What time was it? How long had she slept? Did it matter? Did anything matter any more? She would be trapped here for weeks and weeks, so why bother with time? Why bother to get up? But she needed a pee. Wearily, she swung her feet to the floor and trudged across the room, noticing her bags stacked against the wall, just inside the door. Had Douglas brought them in? Had he been shocked by her vicious attack? Shocked that she had offered her body to him in exchange for escape? She knew that she should feel shame and frustration and anger but at that moment she didn't feel any of these things. Instead, she felt at peace with herself, her mind strangely clear and uncluttered by emotion.

She checked the corridor was clear before tiptoeing across and into the bathroom, locking the door behind her. There was the familiar smell of carbolic soap, and there, perched on the edge of the shelf, stood Douglas's shaving brush with the usual blob of foam left on the bristles. What was he doing now? Would he greet her with stony silence? Would he ignore her? She was too tired to care. It was hard to believe that only the night before she had been overwhelmed by such passion; but now she could not imagine ever experiencing such emotion again . . . and, frankly, she didn't care.

She pulled down her trousers and hitched up her coat and sat on the toilet, thoughtfully studying the cracks in the linoleum floor, the exposed pipes along the skirting board, the thin grey towel hanging limply over the edge of the bath. She, too, had lived liked this. Once. In another life. A life she had hated. A life she had tried so hard to leave behind. She flushed the toilet and walked to the door, not bothering to look at herself in the mirror.

Back in her room she switched on the fan heater and got into bed, pulling the eiderdown up to her chin and curling into a ball, wanting only to sink back into that deep and dreamless sleep. She was tired, so tired.

In those bleak hours before dawn, she had finally confronted the shame and anguish of a lifetime of loneliness. It was as if she had come to an abrupt standstill, turned and squarely faced the demons of her childhood. Forgotten images had flashed one after another into her mind, painful images that had stabbed at her heart. Then, slowly, the pain had turned to hate – molten hate – making her weep with fury. She had thumped the pillow in bitter frustration, knowing that she was powerless to retaliate against the life that she had been given. Ruthlessly, she had forced herself to remember all the fear and humiliation, seeking out the buried memories and dragging them out into the light, seeing herself as the little girl who had cried out for the warmth of loving arms and for the tender smile on a loving face, the little girl who had waited, waited . . . until, finally, she had given up waiting, finally resigning herself to the fact that she would never know the comfort of a mother's arms, never have a daddy to lift her up onto his shoulders and give her a ride . . . never have someone to *truly* care for her. Her childhood had gone. And she had been cheated of it.

Peri sighed and turned on her back to gaze up at the ceiling. Although a touch of sadness still lingered, she did not feel anger; instead, she felt remarkably unburdened. The tears and anger of the night had proved to be cathartic. She knew that she would never be able to erase her memories, but at least she could now handle them as an adult and not as a child. She may still have feelings of shame but now she would be able to understand them and know that it had not been her fault. She would no longer blame herself.

Suddenly, there was the sound of scratching – just outside her door – followed by a pitiful miaowing. Peri turned quickly. Hamish! Hamish had come to see her. She swung out of bed and crossed the room to open the door for him. He purred loudly when he saw her, leaping into her arms as she bent to pick him up. 'Hello, sweetie,' she whispered, feeling his fluffy head brushing against her cheek. 'Have you come to say hello?' As she got back into bed, Hamish began pawing the collar of her coat and rubbing his soft chin against her face. 'I really wish I could keep you,' she whispered. 'I would look after you much better than Douglas.'

From the corridor came the sound of crockery rattling on a tray, followed by the gentle tap-tapping on her door. 'Peri?' Mrs Craig popped her head around the open door. 'Can I come in?'

'Sure,' Peri replied casually. Although pleased to see Mrs Craig, she felt awkward, embarrassed by her violent outburst during the night. Aware that her face must look ravaged by tears, she bent her head over Hamish and hoped that Mrs Craig wouldn't notice.

'I've brought you a nice cup of tea,' Mrs Craig said, coming into the room and putting the tray on the bedside cabinet. 'Oh dear!' she exclaimed suddenly. 'You've got your coat on. You must be freezing.'

'No – I'm fine. I just forgot to take it off.'

'Och. Last night must've been just terrible for you. But there's been good news this morning.' Mrs Craig's voice brightened as she bustled towards the window. 'Douglas has been out since early keeping an eye on the weather. Now he says that the blizzard has gone and there's warm air coming in from the south-west and he told me to tell you that there's no reason why you shouldn't be back in London for Friday night. Isn't that good news?'

'Yes.' Peri was surprised by the tone in her voice. Why

wasn't she overjoyed? Why wasn't she skipping around the room? This was wonderful news, wasn't it? So why did she feel untouched by it?

With her hands on the curtains, Mrs Craig swept them open, allowing the sunshine to fill the room. 'Now isn't that a bonny sight? And to think that . . .' She had turned and was now staring at Peri in horror. 'Oh lassie, lassie, you've been crying!' She came and sat on the edge of the bed, taking Peri's hand in her own. 'What is it, dear? Tell me.'

Peri looked down at the woman's hands and shrugged. 'I was just being silly – feeling sorry for myself.'

'Well, I can understand that. You've had a terrible time.' Mrs Craig squeezed Peri's hand and smiled. 'But everything will be okay. Now you'll be able tae get tae your film ceremony after all. Douglas told me that you've got a special ballgown waiting for you, too. Oh, aye, and Mags telephoned twice this morning, and said she's going to book your seats on the aeroplane leaving on Friday night. She says that she's been frantic wi' worry and you've got tae give her a buzz, as soon as you're fit.'

Peri nodded. She didn't want to phone Mags. She didn't want to be sucked back into the turmoil of ambition. She just wanted to remain in this vacuum, where nothing could touch her . . .

Mrs Craig frowned at Hamish. 'Look at that animal!' she said with mock severity. 'I hope he's not making a nuisance of himself!'

'No, no, he's fine,' Peri protested and gazed down at Hamish who lay like a contented baby in her arms. 'He's my teddy bear.'

'Och, he certainly wasnae like that before you came; it's probably because he'd never been pampered before. But look at him now! He's certainly making up for it. What a sapsy!' Hamish had wriggled and now lay with his back paws around his ears, cradled in Peri's arms and looking like an indistinguisable bundle of striped fur. 'You should hear what Douglas has tae say,' Mrs Craig continued. 'Only yesterday, he was complaining,

"This cat's bowffin! Who's been pouring perfume on him? He's no' going to be scaring rats wi' that smell – he's going to be confusing them!"'

Peri bit her lip, wanting to laugh but feeling guilty. 'Oh, Mrs Craig – that's my fault!'

'What? You've been pouring perfume on him?'

'No. Not exactly. He just seems to be around when I'm spraying myself with perfume, you see.'

'Och, I ken. The mystery's solved – although Douglas suspected you had something to do wi' it, since it was your perfume he was smelling.'

Peri smiled to herself, imagining Douglas's suspicions and how his face must have looked. As she glanced up, she saw Mrs Craig beaming with delight, making her realise that the woman had been trying to cheer her up all along; and for that, she was grateful. 'You've been so kind to me,' Peri said quietly, looking at her steadily. 'I shall never forget you.'

'Och, don't be daft,' Mrs Craig interjected, blushing. 'I just wish that you'd had a happier visit. But you'll soon be away home. Will your mother be there for you?'

Peri lowered her eyes once more, about to give the usual answer: *No, she's on holiday*. How many times had she said that? But for the first time in her life, she heard herself admit the truth. 'I don't have a mother,' she said, and glanced up to see Mrs Craig's reaction.

Mrs Craig looked shocked. 'No mother?'

'No. She left me with my aunty when I was four, and I never saw her again.'

Mrs Craig seemed to pounce on this. 'But you've got an *aunty*, though.'

Peri was reluctant to disappoint her. 'I haven't got her either. She remarried a Canadian and went back to live with him, so the simplest thing for her to do was to put me in a children's home. I think she thought that my mother would one day come and get me.'

'But . . . she didn't . . . ?' Mrs Craig's words trailed off.

Peri shrugged and opened her eyes brightly, trying to make light of it. 'Nope.'

'Och, that is so, so sad. The stupid woman. Why did she do such a thing?'

'Who? My mother or my aunt?'

'Yer mother!'

'I don't know. I never found out. It was all hush-hush. And since *she* wasn't going to come looking for *me*, then I wasn't going to go looking for *her*.'

Mrs Craig gazed at her sadly. 'Life can be so cruel, eh? I had always wanted children. So did my husband Alec. A little girl of our very own. But it was not to be.' She sighed and gazed at the wall beyond Peri's head, as if staring to a far horizon. 'You without a mother,' she whispered, 'and me without a little girl.' For a moment her words hung in the air between them.

Peri gazed down at the wrinkled liver-marked hands of the old woman, knowing exactly what she was thinking. Yes, life could be cruel.

It was Mrs Craig who broke the silence, speaking briskly as she patted Peri's hand. 'The only way to make up for all that lost love is for you tae have your own wee bairns.'

'Bairns?'

'Children. They will give you the love that you have never known.'

Peri began to shake her head, causing Mrs Craig to speak firmly. 'Yes, they will. A child will always love its mother – no matter what. You will never know true love until you hold your very own baby in yer arms. I know this, even though I have never had a baby for myself.'

Peri saw the gentle kindness in the old woman's eyes and felt a moment's sadness for her, sensing how she must have yearned for a child all those years ago. 'Yes, you're probably right,' she agreed, saying the words that the woman would want to hear.

Mrs Craig squeezed her hand and looked at her intently. 'And Peri, I want you to know that, whatever happens, I will be here for you. If you need to share an unhappiness or worry, you only have tae telephone to me. Do you promise?'

Peri nodded, trying to smile but feeling the tears prick her eyes. 'Yes.'

'Well, that's settled. And when you've had your first baby, I want you tae come straight back here and say, "Mrs Craig, you were right!"' She patted Peri's hand once more and stood up. 'Now, I've got tae go and take a fruit cake out of the oven. Would you like me to cut a slice for ye?'

'Yes, please.'

She winked. 'With a bit o' butter on it?'

Peri smiled and nodded.

'Good girl.' Mrs Craig smiled and bustled towards the door.

'Oh, Mrs Craig?' Peri said and waited for her to turn. 'Please don't tell Douglas.' Nervously, she circled her finger around and around Hamish's ear. 'I don't really want him to know.' She smiled, shrugging it off. 'He would probably end up adopting me – you know – like all the rest of his animals.'

Mrs Craig nodded. 'I won't speak a word of it. I promise.' She turned for the door once more, closing it softly behind her.

Peri heard her footsteps heading off down the corridor. 'Mrs Craig?' she called out, suddenly remembering, but it was too late – the woman was out of earshot. Peri had wanted to ask about Douglas. Was he angry? Did he despise her? She dreaded the thought of having to face him again. 'He probably thinks I'm completely neurotic,' she whispered, looking down at Hamish. 'What do you think?' Two hazel-coloured eyes gazed up at her in adoration. 'Oh, sweetie, I wish I could take you back to London with me.'

. . . London. The Film Awards. Now she would be able to go. A flame of her old excitement flickered into life but just as quickly it died. She was too tired. Too weary. Too ugly. Although the turmoil of the night had washed her brain clear, it seemed also to have washed away her aggressive thrust to succeed. Images of the Film Awards now floated away in a cloud of mist and she was not perturbed to realise that she was unable to picture clearly her face on the cover of *Hi!* No. She would not go to the Film Awards. There would be other jobs. If the media wanted her so badly, they would just have to wait.

Dreamily, she gazed out at the bright snow-covered world; from the top of the window hung an icicle, sparkling in the sunshine, and at its point hung a pearl of water, quivering for a moment before dropping below. Suddenly, from out of nowhere, Bruce came bounding into view and began leaping into the air, churning up the snow and rolling around in it until his fur was caked with chunks of white. He looked as if he'd gone crazy, biting and snapping at the clouds of snow falling about his head. Then he began to chase his tail, around and around and around. As Peri watched she felt a smile spread across her face. Suddenly she, too, wanted to be out there, frolicking crazily in the snow, running free, throwing handfuls of the glistening white powder up into the blue sky and feeling it fall softly on her face, to bound up through the snow until she reached the highest point and there she would stop and shout out across this Christmas-cake world, *I don't give a damn!*

From somewhere near at hand, a whistle blew. Abruptly the dog stopped, panting heavily, his long pink tongue hanging down from his mouth. It was as if he were taking a moment to catch his breath before leaping up and bounding away, out of sight.

'What the hell!' Peri muttered, throwing back the covers. 'I'm going out.' She would get well away from the house, she decided, out of sight, and then she would throw herself into the snow and mess it all up, just like Bruce had done! She left Hamish on the crumpled bed and quickly got ready, pulling on her boots and brushing out her hair, resisting the urge to look at herself in the dressing-table mirror. It was difficult, though, very difficult; it was as if a powerful force seemed to be pulling her eyes towards it. Then she looked. 'Oh, fuck!' she whispered, bending forward across the dressing table to inspect the red and puffy skin, pulling up an eyelid to look with morbid fascination at a bleary, bloodshot eye. 'I'm wrecked!' She had never looked so awful. 'Well, it's just too bad,' she muttered, heading for the door. 'I just don't care!' She knew she should immediately phone Mags, but she wasn't going to. She didn't want to get caught up in all the hassles and worries of the real world; she just wanted to remain in this state of limbo, not thinking about yesterday nor thinking about tomorrow. She was going for a romp in the snow – and that was all that mattered.

Her pace quickened as she hurried along the corridor. Halfway down the stairs, she stopped and stared. A brown baby rabbit had come out of the kitchen and was now making for the sitting room. How peculiar. It seemed to know exactly where it was going. Where had it come from? Treading softly, she began to follow it, noticing how it limped and how it kept stopping to lick its back leg. There was something wrong with it. Hurrying forward, she picked it up and held it gently but firmly, as it began to wriggle in protest. Immediately she saw the problem: there was a splinter of wood embedded in the thigh of its leg. She would have to get help. No, she decided, she wouldn't get help; there was no reason why she couldn't solve the problem herself. She had a pair of tweezers, and they would be more finely tuned than any to be found in this house. She carried the rabbit back to her room, took the tweezers from her vanity case and sat on the bed, holding the struggling little creature firmly on her knee. Swiftly, she grasped the splinter with the tweezers and pulled sharply. It came straight out, leaving only a droplet of blood. 'There,' she whispered. 'That's better, isn't it?' She waited to see if a whole lot of blood spurted out and when it didn't, she realised there was nothing more she need do. 'Let's get you back, eh?' She was curious to find out where it had been heading, and so she returned it to the spot from which she had taken it.

At first it didn't move but, instead, licked the blood on its leg. Then it continued on its way heading for the sitting room.

As it went through the door, she leant forward and peeked into the room and saw it nuzzling against Bruce, who was stretched out in front of the fire, his coat glistening with melting snow, his tail thumping the floor in lazy welcome.

'Oh, how sweet,' Peri whispered, tiptoeing in. She couldn't resist picking up the rabbit once more. It was a baby. She took it over to the sofa and sat down with it on her lap. 'Aren't you the cutest thing,' she crooned, stroking its ears. 'How on earth did you get in here? Where's your mummy?'

Suddenly, a glossy-black nose appeared by her knee. It was Bruce. He sat quite still, staring at the rabbit with sad dejected eyes. Even his ears looked dejected. 'So you want to be stroked too, do you?' she said kindly. But as she put out a hand to touch him, she was suddenly overcome with a strange anxiety, and she hastily withdrew it. She couldn't do it! She wanted to – but she couldn't. 'I'm sorry, Bruce. I'm sorry.' For a moment his big sad eyes rolled up to look at her through his fringe and then he turned and padded back to the hearth rug where he heaved a sigh and lay down, resting his muzzle on his paws and staring at the carpet.

Jesus! He was making her feel guilty and horrid. 'I can't help it,' she told him. 'It's nothing to do with you.' But still he refused to look at her, so she got up and dumped the rabbit back beside him. 'It's not my fault,' she told him and marched out of the room. Why did he have to look like that? And why did he have to make her feel so rotten? 'For Christ's sake,' she said to herself, 'why are you getting so uptight? It's only a bloody dog!'

Frowning, she headed back down the corridor, passing two more rabbits as they hopped towards the sitting room. 'This is like a bloody zoo!' she muttered, angry at herself.

She had reached the kitchen door and now slowed to a halt, resting her shoulder against the doorframe, savouring the tranquility inside the room washed over her. Mrs Craig stood at the sink humming softly while peeling potatoes and on the kitchen table stood wire racks covered in hot, golden scones.

The floor was littered with newspaper and there was the smell of roasting meat, and from the radio in the corner came the sound of a soft Scottish voice lazily intoning the shipping forecast. This is a real home, Peri thought, not just an elegant showcase where you ate and slept, but a place of contentment, enfolding its warmth like a mother's arms, making you feel safe from the world outside.

'Peri!' Mrs Craig exclaimed, turning away from the sink and wiping her hands in her apron. 'I didn't know you were up. How are you feeling?'

'Fine, thank you.'

'That's good.' Mrs Craig lit the stove and put the kettle on the flame. 'You'll have tae excuse all the newspaper but we've got the rabbits in the house at the moment.'

'Yes, I know. I've just done a bit of surgery on one of them.'

Mrs Craig looked perplexed.

'It had a splinter,' Peri explained, 'which I took out with my tweezers.'

'Well done. Is it okay now?'

Peri nodded.

'Good. The splinter more than likely came from one of the hutches. They were badly damaged in the storm last night and Douglas is out there now mending them. That's why we've got to have the rabbits in the house.' She took a flask from a cupboard and set it on the table. 'But I don't know why I bother with newspaper in here because as soon as Bruce is in the house, they're off after him. They've all been orphaned, you see, and since Bruce has always been there for them, they think he's their mother!'

'Oh.' Peri felt even more guilty. The dog had actually mothered all these baby rabbits and yet *she* couldn't even bring herself to touch him! She was a horrible coward!

'Would you take some coffee up for Douglas?' Mrs Craig asked, spooning coffee powder into the flask.

'Um . . . well.' Peri folded her arms against her body and

stared down at the floor, shuffling a sheet of newspaper with the toe of her boot. 'Actually, I don't really want to face him . . . you know . . . after last night.'

'Och! He understands. It was all so terrifying for you and—' She stopped and cocked her head, as if listening to something; then Bruce padded through, wagging his tail at the front door. There was the sound of the latch clicking, and in the next instant Douglas stood on the threshhold, his great bulk filling the doorway. He saw her immediately and grinned. 'Hi, Peri. How're you feeling?'

As his blue eyes looked steadily into hers, she felt a strange fluttering in the pit of her stomach. 'Yeah, great.' She glanced away, feeling strangely shy. 'I . . . um . . . I want to apologise for last night,' she stammered. 'I . . .'

'No, no,' he answered, stamping the snow from his boots and onto the mat. 'I'm the one who should apologise. I was foolish enough to drink half a bottle of schnapps last night – otherwise I would have heard the storm sooner.'

'Oh, no!' Mrs Craig remonstrated. 'Don't blame yerself. I didna hear it myself – and I'm a light sleeper.' She picked up the kettle and began to pour boiling water into the flask. 'It was a freak blizzard, for sure. I've never seen the like.'

'Aye.' Douglas knelt down to ruffle Bruce's ear and smile up at Peri. 'Has Mrs Craig told you the good news?'

Peri nodded.

'This fine weather will hold long enough for us tae leave on Friday morning, and I've arranged with my friend Ian tae meet us at Randolph's Pass with my snowchains.'

Peri gazed at his lips, bemused to think that they had kissed her the night before, that the mere touch of his hands had sent her into a paroxym of sexual desire. Would she ever be capable of feeling such passion again?

'Mags phoned just five minutes ago,' Mrs Craig said, pouring milk into the flask. 'She's managed to book seats on the Friday afternoon flight; and she says for you not to worry about your dress fitting. You can do it all on Saturday morning.'

'So, you're going to be back in time for the Film Awards ceremony,' Douglas said, giving Bruce a final pat before standing up. 'I was having a chat with Mags this morning and she was telling me all about it. Sounds grand. I bet you're excited.'

Peri nodded. With his words, she expected to feel excitement but there was nothing. Her relentless drive for fame had simply evaporated.

Douglas approached the table and cast his eyes over the scones. 'Helmut told me to tell you that you've got to take things easy this morning. Relax and unwind, he said, and he'll see you when he gets back.'

'Where's he gone?'

'They've been out most of the morning scouting out a location. Helmut was saying something about doing a shoot this afternoon.'

'Oh, no!' Peri wailed. 'I don't want to. I'm too tired. I look a wreck.'

'I can understand how you must be feeling,' Douglas said gently. 'It doesn't seem fair, especially as he's still got two full days yet tae take the rest of his photos. You need time tae recover!'

Peri sighed dispiritedly. How could she explain to him that she no longer had a desire to be photographed, neither today nor tomorrow? 'I'm just so exhausted.'

'Don't you worry,' he said firmly. 'I've got an idea. Why don't we simply avoid him?'

Peri stared at him blankly, her brain too numb to work out what he was saying.

'You don't want to work, do you?' he repeated.

She shook her head. 'No.'

'Right. So we'll just have tae make sure he doesnae find you.'

Mrs Craig came round the side of the table. 'What are you saying, Douglas? That the lassie should *hide?*'

'Aye.'

'Oh, no, Douglas, you cannae suggest that.'

'Why not?' he retorted and looked straight at Peri.

Peri recognised the sparkle in his eyes and the way his right eyebrow slanted up at a jaunty angle, the same silly expression that usually made her want to smile – but not now. He was being absurd. Ridiculous.

'So, Peri, what's yer answer?' He was challenging her.

Suddenly she felt a thrill of devilment but just as suddenly it went. 'I don't know.' Why was everything so complicated? Why couldn't she just be left alone?

'Helmut will be back any minute. So, you've got tae decide. Do you want tae come wi' me, or not?'

Mrs Craig started to wipe her hands in her apron. 'Oh, Douglas, you cannae just take the lassie off like this! It's wrong of you.'

Douglas was still staring at Peri. 'Come with me, Peri.'

She bit her lip, thinking. She didn't want to stay and have to work. She gazed at Douglas, not knowing what to do. She could sense that he was willing her on, and strangely, she could feel herself being pulled towards him. Taking a deep breath, she nodded. 'Yes,' she said firmly. 'I want to come with you.'

Douglas grinned. 'Ready when you are.'

Mrs Craig solemnly shook her head: 'Well you'd better think up a good excuse before ye get back, Douglas MacLeod.' She turned to Peri. 'And what aboot your agent – you still havnae phoned her.'

'Oh, she'll be out of the office right now,' Peri lied. 'I'll phone later.'

The woman sighed. 'Okay.' She handed a rucksack to Douglas. 'Here's a flask of coffee and some sandwiches.' She opened up a drawer and took out a scarf and a woolly hat and gave them to Peri. 'I bet you're getting weary of having to be bundled up like an eskimo, eh?' Then she paused and tilted her head to one side. 'I've just had an idea,' she exclaimed. 'Why don't we have a party? Tonight? What do you think Peri? Then we can put on our party frocks fer a change?'

Douglas nodded slowly as if considering it. 'Yes. That's a good idea.'

Peri wound the scarf around her kneck. She didn't really care if they had a party or not, but Mrs Craig seemed so excited about it, that she didn't have the heart to disappoint her. 'Great!' she replied, sounding enthusiastic.

'We'll have party games,' Mrs Craig continued eagerly. 'And I'll make some sausage rolls and fairy cakes. Good – well, that's settled, then.' She flapped her hands towards them. 'You two had better run along before the others get back. Go on. And – here – you can take some tattie scones to eat on yer way.'

With a scone in each hand, Peri felt herself being hustled towards the door. A moment later, she and Douglas and Bruce were out on the doorstep with the door closed firmly behind them. Suddenly, she felt shy and nervous, not knowing what to say to Douglas. Perhaps this wasn't such a good idea. Maybe she should go back inside.

Douglas made the first move. 'Come on,' he said, striding off across the yard with Bruce bounding along beside him. 'We'll head up to the aviary. We'll be safe there; Helmut and Otto have gone in the opposite direction.'

But Peri's feet wouldn't take her off the doorstep.

Realising that Peri was not with him, he turned and looked back enquiringly. 'Don't you want to come?'

As her eyes gazed into his, she felt her head nodding.

He waved her towards him, speaking with mock impatience. 'Well, *come on*, woman!'

A strange lightness spread up through her body and then she was off the doorstep and going to him, her boots scrunching and squeaking in the sparkling snow. The sun shone brightly in a crisp blue sky and there was an utter stillness all around, as if the snow had smothered every little sound. This was like a beautiful gift that had been presented to them. A glorious day; and it was all theirs. As she bit into her scone, there was a shower of crumbs down the front of her sheepskin coat but she didn't care. She didn't care about anything. For today she would live for today, not for tomorrow, not for yesterday, but for today!

'I thought you were on a diet,' he said with mock severity, but she just answered with a shrug of her shoulders.

'Helmut and Otto have gone over to Cairn Elrig Falls,' he chatted, walking along beside her. 'It's a beautiful waterfall, way out in the mountains, and I would have so liked to have taken you there myself.'

Vaguely, she could recall something Otto had said. 'A waterfall?'

'Aye – that's right. Did Helmut mention it to you?'

'No – but Otto said something about it – when he picked me up from the airport.' She paused in thought. 'Just think! That was only four days ago. It seems like years.'

'Does it?'

She heard the regret in his voice. She didn't want to deal with emotions right now – not hers, not his. She'd had a night of emotional upheaval and now she just wanted to feel numb. 'Of course it seems like years!' she said with forced cheerfulness, sweeping away this encroaching intimacy. 'What with everything that's happened to me! I should imagine a month spent with survival troops in Antarctica would go a hell of a lot faster than these last few days!'

Douglas laughed. His laughter had become a familiar sound to her, a sound that could make her glow inside, could make her feel witty and clever.

But, now . . . now she didn't glow inside. Now the sound of his laughter suddenly made her want to put her head on his big chest and to feel his big arms coming round her shoulders, to comfort her, to give her the strength to go on . . .

Douglas reached the gate before her. 'I haven't had time to shovel the snow away,' he said, 'so we'll have to climb over. Do you want me to help you?'

'No, thank you.' She didn't want his help. She didn't want him to touch her and risk igniting his ardour. It was all over. There was no more passion left inside her. Silently, she put her foot on the first rung and swung her leg over, jumping down into the snow on the other side.

He did the same and landed beside her, staring out across the snow. 'It's hard tae imagine that storm last night, isn't it?'

'Mm.' Suddenly, she had an image of herself scrambling up into the Land Rover, pleading with him to continue their escape, telling him that he could fuck her. It all seemed so dream-like now, so unreal. She should feel humiliation, but she didn't.

'Are you feeling a wee bit happier?' he asked.

'What do you mean?'

'Mrs Craig told me that you'd been crying.'

Peri gazed down at her boots. 'I'm okay. I was just feeling sorry for myself – that's all.'

'You'll soon be home. Four more days.'

She nodded. *Soon be home*. Why didn't she *feel* something? She should be feeling overwhelming relief, joy – *something* – but she felt nothing.

'Will you come back and see me?' he asked quietly.

She couldn't look at him. 'No, Douglas, I don't think so.'

There was silence. Somehow she knew that he understood. They walked on, side by side, the crunch of their boots in the snow the only sound to disturb the stillness, and the memory of their kiss hovering in the air between them.

'Well, you just remember tae take some of Mrs Craig's beetroot home with you,' he said sternly, breaking the silence. 'She's got jars and jars of the stuff all lined up. I don't know how she thinks you're going to carry it home, mind, especially as we'll all have tae squash into the Land Rover for the journey!'

She knew that he was pretending this cheerfulness, playing a game of easy nonchalance. 'Pickled beetroot!' she exclaimed, gladly joining in his game. 'Yuk! I've never eaten pickled beetroot in my life and I'm not going to start now! What if the media ever found out?'

Douglas laughed but, for the first time his laughter did not ring true.

He would forget her one day, Peri decided. He would realise that this had only been a silly infatuation. He would find another woman. Get married. Have children. Forget her. And what would *she* do? Maybe move to Hampstead and get a cat and buy a flower shop. It would be safe and easy; no more highs, no more lows, no more rejections.

She followed Douglas through a gap in the hedge and out through the other side and now she stopped and gazed at the world before her. The sparkling snow seemed to stretch on to eternity, shimmering in the sunshine as if millions of diamonds had been scattered across it. 'This is beautiful,' she whispered, taking lungfuls of pure, crisp air. 'Like something out of a Bambi video.'

'A bit different from London, eh?'

Peri nodded thoughtfully. London. Grey slush in the gutters and the constant hum of traffic, familiar and comforting. Sweet-scented dress shops and slick shiny wine bars with friends in designer outfits holding glasses of champagne and chattering. It would be cold in London. Not as cold as here, but it would still be cold, cold enough to wear her new full-length mink coat. And, of course, if she *had* been going to the Film Awards she would have had to have worn it . . . Peri gazed down at the shiny, silvery river far, far below. Now Saffron would get the job. She mustn't think about that because it would only make her feel anger, and she didn't want to feel anger.

Douglas was telling her something about bird migration. 'I'm sorry,' she said. 'What did you say?'

'I was just saying that, in a couple of weeks, the Greenshank will be returning to these mountains to build their nests. It's a—'

As Douglas continued speaking, Peri nodded, trying to concentrate on his words, but finding it more and more difficult as an image of Saffron grew bigger and bigger, until it seemed as if it would burst her brain. Saffron would win *again!* It was impossible not to think of that collagen-implanted Barbie doll taking her place on stage, oozing fake sexuality like pus oozing out of a yellow-head, flaunting herself in front of the cameras. And after the Awards ceremony? What would she say? *Oh, Peri, darling, whatever happened to you? I told everyone that you'd got stuck up a mountain and everyone was so sorry for you. And guess what? Roberto Rossini's offered me the lead in his next film. I know I shouldn't gloat, darling* . . . For a moment, Peri glided out of her thoughts to catch Douglas's words . . .

'The babies are covered in a soft down,' he was saying, 'and they look like tiny balls of cotton wool.'

'Really?' Peri made no attempt to listen to him now. She was consumed with fury. *Saffron!* God, how she wanted to scratch that bitch's eyes out! She hated her. *Loathed* her! No – she couldn't let Saffron take all the glory . . . she just *couldn't!* Peri tried to clear her brain, to think calmly. Apart from this total lack of enthusiasm, she also looked a wreck. How much time would she have before the Awards? Friday night and all day Saturday. Enough time for a lengthy massage, two whole hours with Eduardo and at least three hours with her beautician. Would that be enough to repair the damage? And, of course, once she was dressed in Igor de Vere's ballgown and loaded down with diamonds, she would feel much more enthusiastic. And if none of that worked, a thorough pep talk from Mags would certainly fire her up. Yes – she *would* go to the Film Awards.

Saffron was not going to take it from her!

Abstractedly, Peri kicked up the snow with the toe of her boot. Last night's grief was behind her now – gone – she mustn't allow it to drag her down and destroy her. She had worked too long and too hard. She deserved happiness. She'd had more than her fair share of misery and pain, but – *no more!*

A memory flashed into her brain. It had been her first assignment. Trinidad. She and the girls had been working on the beach all afternoon. The girls had accepted her so easily and the photographer was delighted with her. Everything was perfect. With the work finished, she and the other girls had splashed in the sea, laughing, and then they ran back up onto the beach to take glasses of ice-cold calypso cocktails from a silver tray. At that moment Peri had known that all the misery was behind her: she was starting a new and wonderful life, a life that she had only dreamt of. She had watched as a barbecue was set up and then the girls had volunteered to gather driftwood, and almost immediately she had discovered a big log. As she picked it up, a splinter of wood tore up under her fingernail and lodged itself firmly into her flesh, sending waves of pain up through her hand. She couldn't believe it! Why had this happened to *her?* She stared at it angrily, determined that it would not spoil her happiness for one second! Casually, she enquired if anyone had tweezers with them. No one had. So, calmly, she picked up a sharp knife from the table and walked behind a rock, and there she slipped the tip of the knife under the edge of her fingernail and gouged out the splinter. She refused to feel the pain, refused to be bothered by the blood and simply sucked her finger and wrapped it in a headband. When she returned to the barbecue, she slipped the knife back onto the table and carried on with the fun as if nothing had happened.

Well, the same was going to happen *now*. She would carry on as if nothing had happened, and refuse to let the pain of her childhood cloud her judgement. Yes, she thought decisively; I *will* go to the Film Awards and I *will* be more beautiful and more confident than I have ever been in my life.

This is just the beginning!

The old familiar feelings of hope and excitement bubbled up inside her. She had to phone Mags! Now! Tell her that everything was going to be okay. Oh, but it was impossible to phone now because she would risk bumping into Helmut; but she would, as soon as she got back to the house. She floated free from these thoughts to hear Douglas talking to her.

'I wish you could see this place in spring,' he was saying.

'What? Oh, yes . . . yes . . . so do I.' She would be on the Friday afternoon flight – so she would tell Mags to book Cynthia for a two-hour massage.

'You would?'

'What?'

'You would like to see this place in spring?'

She nodded absent-mindedly. 'Sure.'

'I want you to know that you can come here any time you like.'

'Thank you.' The diamonds! Had Mags got it sorted out with Cartier?

'I hope you will.'

The sadness in his voice pierced the thoughts that were darting and tumbling in her brain. She didn't want this complication – not now. She was getting everything sorted out in her head, fitting it all neatly back together. She was going back into battle, travelling light and lean, with no room for emotional baggage.

He stopped and turned to her but she carried on walking. She sensed what was about to happen. Swiftly, his hands caught her sleeves and pulled her round to face him but she looked steadfastly at his boots, refusing to meet his eyes.

'Peri?' he said softly. 'Tell me: will you miss me?'

She remained silent, not daring to look at him. The touch of his hands on her arms gave her a rush of desire, a yearning for more of him, but swiftly she steeled herself against these feelings. He could never be a part of her life, just as she could never be a part of his. Once she was gone from here, she would simply forget him.

She had to.

'Peri?' His voice was gentle. It was the voice that he used for his animals.

Slowly she raised her chin until her eyes came up to meet his own. And, there, in those blue, blue eyes, she saw love – a lifetime of love. In that brief second, her soul cried out in grief, knowing all that she would lose.

'Will we ever meet again?' he asked softly.

She lowered her eyes before shaking her head.

Silently, he gathered her up in his big arms and gently pressed her to him. She made no effort to resist, and laid her head against his chest. Didn't he realise that once she had left this place, she would have to continue on a precisely charted course, and would never allow herself to think of him again? Although, maybe, just maybe, in the years to come, some little thing might jog her memory – perhaps the smell of carbolic soap or hot buttered scones, the sight of a falcon soaring and snow sparkling in the sunshine . . . or the sound of silly laughter . . . Hot tears pricked her eyes and she pushed away from him, swinging round to walk on up the hill. 'Let's not talk about it now. We've only got a few more days – let's just enjoy them.' She quickened her pace, wanting to run and run and leave this aching sadness behind. Only a moment ago, she had been so happy, so fired up, but now the only thing she could feel was this pain in her heart. 'I'll race you to the top,' she yelled, forcing the sound of gaiety into her voice, forcing herself to run from the pain.

Bruce began to bark as she started off up the hill, blundering through the snow in her heavy boots, puffing and panting. Then Douglas was overtaking her. When he reached the top, he fell against the wall of the aviary and shouted down at her. 'Come on! For heaven's sake! I'm not having *you* on my team!'

She was grateful to him for resuming their game of pretence, grateful to him for letting her go. 'Oh, fuck off!' she teased, slowing down to cover the last few yards. This had been a fleeting, bitter-sweet romance, she realised, a perfect memory that she would fold in white linen and put in her bottom drawer, to keep forever.

'Right,' Douglas exclaimed, jerking his thumb towards the aviary wall and dropping the rucksack onto the bench beside him. 'This is your last chance to fly a peregrine falcon. In you go.'

'Oh, no, Douglas.'

'Oh, yes.'

Her dismay was half-hearted. This was a good idea, she

thought, as she followed him in. Flying Kirsty would stop her thinking. Would stop Douglas speaking the words that she didn't want to hear. Would help them forget . . . if even for a short while.

Kirsty watched them enter, her bright yellow eyes alert, expectant. Slowly, she stretched out a wing and then folded it neatly back against her body.

'Hello, Kirsty,' Douglas said. 'I've brought your friend to see you.'

Peri stroked the bird's head. 'You want to fly – don't you?' she whispered, 'I can tell.' She took the leather glove from Douglas and put it on, remembering that first time and how they had argued. It seemed so long ago now . . .

'Once she's on your glove put this over her head,' Douglas said, taking the tiny leather hood from a nail on the wall. 'It will make her feel more secure as you're walking about.'

'Okay.' Peri laid her gloved hand against the perch, and without hesitation Kirsty hopped onto it. 'Aren't you a clever girl?' Peri exclaimed warmly, knowing that – even if she had to do this a thousand times – this feeling of pride and awe would never diminish.

On the way out, Douglas pointed to a red plastic bin in the corner. 'That's where I keep her food. Mostly rats and chicks donated by our local farmer.'

Peri grimaced. 'Dead?'

'Yes,' he said casually, taking a leather strap from a plastic bag. 'I've already made up her dinner. Here.'

Peri gingerly took the leather strap, staring suspiciously at the messy lump at the end of the rope. It looked like bits of fur, congealed blood and little bones.

'It's called a lure,' he explained. 'You saw me swinging it around my head yesterday.' He opened the door and smiled proudly at Peri as she walked by.

'This is unreal,' she muttered, shaking her head. 'Here I am, holding a raptor in one hand and a lump of dead rat in the other. My friends aren't going to believe it.'

'Yes, they will.' Douglas took a small black camera out of his pocket. 'Now you'll have proof.'

'No!' Peri shook her head vehemently. 'I look hideous. I'm not even wearing make-up.'

'Oh, Peri. For heaven's sake! Is that all you think about? How you look?'

She stared at him, puzzled by his accusation. 'Well – yes – of course.'

Douglas looked taken aback by this simple statement but said no more.

'Of course I've got to think about how I look,' Peri continued, walking along beside him. 'It's my living.'

'I understand that, but you're not working now, are you?'

'No,' she said slowly. 'I guess not.'

'Well, let me take a photo. Tae keep as a memento.'

'Okay,' she said quickly. 'But don't you let the media get their hands on it.'

Douglas had taken the camera out of its cheap, plastic case. 'I swear it.'

As he put the camera to his eye, she turned three-quarters, lifted her chin and gazed coolly from the corners of her eyes. This was her look. Her trademark.

'Oh, Peri!' he wailed, lowering the camera. 'You're posing! I want you to look natural.'

'But that's my best angle,' she retorted.

'I don't care. I just want you to look natural.'

She noticed that his jaw was set in a stubborn line and it made her want to laugh; she could readily identify with that feeling, a feeling she knew so well. 'I've got to pose,' she explained patiently, 'otherwise I won't look my best.'

'Well, I'm not taking the photo,' he declared, beginning to put the camera back in its case.

Now she felt devilish. 'Okay. Okay,' she said quickly. 'How about *this?*' She half closed her eyes and lifted her chin towards him, running her tongue slowly and sensually over her lips.

Despite his mood, he burst out laughing.

As a final gesture, she put a hand on her hip and wiggled sexily.

Immediately, he had the camera out of his case, but before he could take the picture, she had changed expression. Now she was pushing up her nose with one finger and squinting her eyes in an ugly grimace.

'Oh, Peri!' he said in disappointment, lowering the camera once again.

'Tough cookies,' she said, shrugging and walking off. She grinned to herself, glancing back over her shoulder at him. There was a 'click' sound before she realised that she was looking straight into the lens of his camera. 'You bastard!' she exclaimed.

He was grinning triumphantly. '*There*. That's what I wanted: a natural look. Wasn't too difficult, was it?'

'I'm not playing with you any more!' she said in a mock childish voice, turning her back on him and walking on ahead.

'Do you know that there are some African tribes who are terrified of being photographed? They believe it will take away their souls.'

Peri slowed to let him catch up. 'I'm the opposite. As long as I look good, I'm happy to be photographed for *hours*.' She did not add that, from the very first moment that she had stood before a camera, she had felt a wonderful sensation of power and confidence. For the first time in her life she had felt what it was like to be wanted, admired, cosseted. No – the camera could never take away her soul.

Now, they had come to the high post at the edge of the hill where Kirsty had perched the previous day, and Douglas stopped. 'You can take the hood off.'

Peri gently removed the hood and transferred Kirsty onto the perch. 'Good girl,' she whispered, feeling at that moment that her chest would burst with pride.

'Right. Follow me.' Douglas set off across the snow. 'We've to put a good distance between us and her.'

In the middle of the flat ground, he stopped. 'Now, all

you have to do is circle the lure in the air – like this.' He stood behind her and held her wrist, raising it high to swing the rope over their heads. 'Kee, kee, kee,' he cried.

Maybe it was the feel of his body against hers or the strength of his hand on her wrist, but for a moment her attention slipped. Then, suddenly, there was a flash of brown and white and the sound of beating wings. It was Kirsty, her talons outstretched, poised to lock onto the mangled lump that whirled above their heads.

'Now!' Douglas yelled, jerking Peri's wrist and sending the rope spinning out of its orbit, snatching the food from Kirsty's grasp. Kirsty flew on, her talons empty, soaring into the sky, higher and higher, slowly veering around in an arc before coming to land on the perch once more.

'Right, Peri – you're on your own.' He started to walk away. 'Give her a couple of practice runs before you let her have the food.'

Helplessly, Peri looked to his receding back, wanting to shout, *Don't leave me! I can't do it! Come back*!

Now she was alone. She stared at the bird and the bird stared back. 'Oh, Christ!' She could feel the muscles in her stomach knotting tight and she had a sudden desperate need to do a wee. Whatever was going to happen would happen in the next two seconds.

Without taking her eyes off the bird, she began to swing the rope above her head, around and around. 'Kee, kee, kee,' she yelled.

It was coming at her. Like a fucking missile. Wings spread out, huge yellow talons hooked forward, ready . . .

Peri jerked the rope but she had left it too late. *Thump!* Kirsty's talons hit the lump of flesh and the rope was torn from Peri's hands.

The bird flew on, gliding inches above the snow before coming to rest on a flat rock, and there it crouched over the mangled flesh and began shredding the flesh with its vicious yellow beak.

Peri felt faint. Her knees began to tremble and a burning slash throbbed across her palm.

'That was quite good,' Douglas shouted. 'But you should have jerked the rope a bit sooner.'

She couldn't speak, but put a hand to her chest to calm her pounding heart.

'Wait until she's finished before calling her,' Douglas instructed. 'Then you can take her back inside. We'll try again tomorrow.'

Peri nodded, gazing at the bird with morbid fascination and a rising euphoria, realising that here she was, standing alone at the top of a mountain, completely in charge of a wild and savage creature. Above her head, heavy dark clouds sailed across the sky and a cold wind tossed her hair about her cheeks. This was like being in an action movie. She glanced back over her shoulder to see that Douglas was watching her thoughtfully. She shot him a quick cheeky smile before turning her attention to Kirsty once more.

After a little while, Douglas shouted again. 'Get ready.'

Kirsty gulped down the last lump of flesh and looked round as if waiting for a call of command, and immediately Peri held out her arm. 'Kee, kee, kee,' she cried and the bird came to her, sailing slowly on outstretched wings and landing with a gentle flutter on the glove. 'Good girl, Kirsty, good girl.' Peri wanted to have another go, to get it right. She knew she could do it. 'Can I try again?' she called out.

'No,' he shook his head as he walked towards her. 'Kirsty's intake of food has got to be precisely monitored. Now that she's eaten, she won't be dependent on us and will probably fly away. But she will be getting all the exercise she needs next week because that's when I'm going to be releasing her.'

'Oh.' She gazed at Kirsty, feeling deep sadness, knowing that she would not be here to see it.

'Let's get her back inside. We'll fly her again tomorrow.'

'Okay.' With her left hand, Peri took the little hood out of her pocket and held it up ready. 'Right, Kirsty, I'm just going to put this on you.' As the bird turned its head, Peri could see the flecks of bright gold in its eyes, and on the tip of its beak there was a streak of blood. Gently, she slipped the hood over its head and started towards the aviary. 'Good girl, Kirsty. Good girl. I'll come back and see you tomorrow. Okay? We'll get it right then.'

Once inside the aviary, she settled Kirsty on the perch, said a few more words and then came out, closing the door firmly behind her. Douglas was coming up the hill towards her and she grinned and threw her arms wide, dancing little steps. 'I did it!' she cried triumphantly. 'I did it!'

Douglas grinned. 'You're a natural.'

'Do you think so?' she asked excitedly. 'Did you see her coming towards me? Gosh! I stopped *breathing!*'

He chuckled and hung the lure on a nail in the door. 'Well, after all that, I reckon you deserve a crab-paste sandwich.' He picked up the rucksack from the bench and sat down with it.

'Gosh! Food! I'm starved.'

Side by side, they sat on the bench with their backs against the wooden wall, facing the sun.

'Oh, Douglas, that was so exciting. Thank you so much. I shall never, ever forget it. Really!' She turned to him, smiling her gratitude but she was unable to see his face because he had suddenly bent forward over the rucksack and was now busy taking out the flask and sandwiches. 'My heart is still pounding,' she continued, resting her head back against the wall of the aviary and gazing contentedly out across the mountains. She took the proferred sandwich and bit into it. 'I've been thinking,' she mumbled, pausing to swallow. 'You know you said that you needed money for your conservation work? Well, have you thought about getting sponsors, companies who will support you in return for getting free advertising and tax deductions?'

'How does that work?'

'I don't know, but I could get Mags to find out for you. And you could also use your land for film locations.'

He was looking at her closely, his eyes bright with interest.

'And I was also thinking that these advertising agencies that use wild animals for commercials, should actually pay for their appearances – like they do for a model or actor – except the fee would have to go into a wildlife fund. Maybe agencies do it already, but I don't think so.'

'Hey.' Douglas exclaimed. 'You've got some good ideas there.' He nodded slowly, looking out to the horizon thoughtfully. Then he turned to her abruptly. 'How would you like to become my partner?'

She tried to smile but quickly glanced away, not wanting him to see the sadness in her eyes.

'I mean it.'

Her smile trembled and she forced herself to look at him. 'I . . . I . . . I'm—'

He put his hand briefly on her knee. 'It's okay. I know this sort of thing is not up your street, but if you ever change your mind, you know where tae find me.'

Why did she feel so sad? Her emotions had returned and she hated them. She wanted to stay free of emotion. Not to care. 'Know where to find you?' she declared, trying to force herself to be cheerful. 'I know I'm in Scotland but that's about it! I would *never* find you in a million years!'

He smiled, throwing a chunk of bread into the snow for Bruce and thoughtfully watching him.

Unobserved, she was able to gaze at Douglas, at the straight line of his nose, the curve of a nostril, the tiny scar just below his eyebrow, the curl of hair around his ear, the blueness of his eyes beneath dark lashes. Fervently, she imprinted these images into her brain, knowing that this memory of him would have to last her her lifetime.

As he turned his head, she quickly looked away.

'You're not going to find a bonnier sight than this, are you?' he said.

She shook her head. 'No, I'm not. It's truly beautiful.' She had been trying to ignore the urge for a pee but now, sitting on this cold bench, she knew she would not be able to wait for much longer. 'Actually, Douglas,' she said, looking behind her. 'Is there is a loo around here?'

'Och, no. Just go behind the shed.'

'What? Do it in the snow?'

'Aye.'

'No. I'll wait.'

'Don't be daft. There's nobody aboot. People have been having their wee-wees in the snow for thousands of years. You won't be the first.'

She hesitated. She was on top of a mountain, for God's sake. What if someone saw her? But, suddenly, she was bursting.

'Och, go on.'

She put her mug of coffee down and got up, feeling silly and embarrassed. But she had no choice. She went around to the back of the aviary and stopped, carefully looking across the mountains and valleys, but there didn't seem to be anybody about. Hastily, she pulled down her trousers and squatted, hitching her coat up around her waist, her eyes scanning the hills around her. There was a sizzling sound as her wee hit the snow and when she was finished, she pulled up her trousers and looked down at the yellow hole in the snow. Embarrassed, she kicked the snow over it to cover all traces and then returned to Douglas, expecting to hear some silly comment, but, instead he continued to eat his sandwich whilst gazing out over the hills.

'Everything okay?' he said casually.

She sat down beside him. 'Yes. Thanks.'

'Do you want another sandwich?' he asked.

She was glad that he wasn't about to make one of his silly jokes at her expense. 'Yes, please.' She took another sandwich and sipped her coffee, and there they sat in companionable silence, eating their picnic. After a time, Peri realised that it was pleasant to sit in silence like this, and not have to feel that she should be making conversation. This was one thing she had learnt from him: it was not necessary to fill the silence with chatter; sometimes just being with someone was enough. It was she herself who eventually broke the silence. 'This is like another world,' she murmured, then paused, thinking. 'Do you realise something?' she said slowly. 'Our lives are so totally different that we might as well be living on different planets.'

Douglas looked down at his boots. 'Aye, I know.'

She had heard the note of regret in his voice, as if he had been well aware of the fact. Yes, she thought, we inhabit totally different worlds; so different, in fact, that it would be impossible for either of us to inhabit the other's. 'Have *you* ever lived in London?' she asked, wanting to change the course of their conversation.

'Only for a couple of months at a time.'

'When you were in the SAS?'

He glanced at her briefly before turning to look out over the hills. 'That was a long time ago.' He was looking at her again. 'I thought you didn't want to exchange life histories?'

'Right,' she nodded. 'Of course . . . yeah.' She kept on nodding. 'That's right.' Why did she feel this ache inside? She took a bite of her sandwich and looked away, gazing out to a line of tall fir trees along the horizon, their dark branches heavy with garlands of bright snow. Of course he was right; why exchange life histories? There was no point. But she would have liked to have known something about him . . . before it was too late. She swallowed her mouthful of sandwich; it felt like a lump of cardboard stuck in her throat.

Douglas put his mug beside him on the bench. 'In a couple of weeks, these huts will be full of animals; orphaned deer, snared foxes, owls, baby stoats. I get so busy that I don't know what I'm doing! I end up giving fox food to the deer and rabbit food to the stoats!'

Peri put a bright smile on her face. It came easy. Just another pose. Douglas stretched forward to ruffle the dog's ears and as he did so, she studied his big square hands, remembering the night before and how those hands had explored her breasts and her buttocks, holding her in a vice-like grip. There could be no escape from the strength of those hands. A quiver of desire shot through her but swiftly she smothered it and looked away. 'Don't *think* about it!' her brain screamed. 'Just don't *think* about it!' She felt her eyes move down to gaze at his hands once more. But what if she just touched his hand? Just for a second? Nothing sexual. Just to feel the warmth of his skin? Her gaze travelled to his ear, to the dusting of freckles along the top. She would never forget his ears, and the way his hair curled around them. She would never forget the perfect flare of his nostrils and his kind, firm mouth, and how it had pressed down on her lips. Once more, she looked down at his hand. What if she touched it . . . ?

Abruptly, Douglas threw the dregs of his coffee into the snow. 'It will be safe to head back now.'

'What?'

'It's too late for Helmut to think about working now,' he explained. 'The sun's going down.'

She followed his gaze to the horizon. 'Oh.' In the same instant, an icy breeze touched her cheek, and suddenly she realised that there was no longer any warmth from the sun. The row of great fir trees along the horizon had turned black, casting long purple shadows across the snow, their garlands of pretty white now dull and grey.

Douglas stood up and swung the rucksack over his shoulder. 'Ready?'

'Um – yeah.' The moment had gone. Another second later – and what would have happened? She stood up. 'I just want to say goodbye to Kirsty,' she said, walking towards the aviary door. 'You go on and I'll catch you up.'

'Okay. But don't forget, we're coming back tomorrow.'

'Yeah – I know.' As Peri reached the aviary, the falcon was busy preening herself and didn't look up. 'Goodbye, Kirsty,' she whispered, feeling the warm tears fill her eyes. She would never see Kirsty again. Out across the pearly sky floated ribbons of pink and yellow clouds. She would never come here again because she would never again take the chance of being left alone with Douglas. From that moment on, all this would become a memory, a conversation piece, an after-dinner anecdote along with the after-dinner mints.

Yes, she loved Douglas – that much she knew – but she didn't trust her love. The feeling was alien to her; she couldn't judge whether it would be ever-lasting or simply transient. It may not even be love; it could be lust. But, if it was love, was it strong enough to last a lifetime? Strong enough to survive harsh winters and isolation? No – she could not believe that it was.

'That would make a great photo,' Douglas shouted up to her. 'You looking out at the sunset like that. Just perfect for the cover of the Highlands Holiday brochure.'

Peri brushed the tear from her cheek and turned to him, twisting her face into a grimace. 'Who in their right minds would want to come *here* for their holidays?'

'Hey, just you watch it!'

'I can just see it now,' she said, fanning out her fingers in front of her face. *'Come to the Highlands and experience the thrill of frostbite. Forget your diet! Eat clootie dumpling and see those hips EXPLODE!'*

Douglas threw his head back and laughed, the way he always laughed. Peri felt that stab of pain to her heart. She wished he hadn't done that. Just seeing him like that, it made her yearn . . . for him . . . for how it could have been. She put the smile firmly back on her face and walked towards him. As she drew level, he turned and side by side they walked down through the snow towards the house.

'This is a lovely time of day, isn't it?' he remarked.

'Yes.'

Silence.

She didn't want to feel this ache in her heart. She *had* to remember that soon she would look back and realise that all of this was just a fleeting romance. Nothing more. Maybe this was true love. She didn't know. All she knew was that it could never work between them. It would be wiser to part *now* with sweet memories, memories that she would always be able to conjure up at will. Perfect memories. And for the rest of her life she would be able to walk with him in her daydreams, talk to him and laugh with him. In her daydreams . . . where nothing could ever go wrong . . .

She gathered her coat collar tightly around her neck and stared down at her boots as she walked. Three more days and she would be drinking champagne, dancing with film stars and mingling with her own kind of people, swirling gracefully across the dance floor, her diamonds glittering in the light from the chandeliers. Meanwhile, on the edge of the dance floor, American film producers would be watching, ready to grab her, to ask for her agent's number. At the thought of it, she suddenly shivered with excitement. She was going to become a *star!* She wanted to talk to Douglas about it, to share it with him, to explain why they could never be together, but she couldn't; she must not even hint at her feelings for him. He must never know.

He walked beside her, his hands in his pockets and a thoughtful look on his face. She could sense his sadness. But she didn't want him to be sad because it was making *her* sad. There was nothing to be sad about, really. She would become a star and then – maybe – she would come back and visit him . . . some time . . . when she wasn't too busy . . .

She refused to think about it. 'Shall we play musical chairs tonight?' she said quickly, slipping her arm through his, wanting to coax him out of his sadness. 'What party games do you like?'

He shrugged. 'I don't know any.'

'You *must!*' Peri exclaimed, looking up at him in mock horror. Although he was smiling, there was still that sadness in his eyes.

'Well, I can always get my bagpipes out,' he offered seriously, 'and play a tune.'

'Oh, no!' Peri wailed. 'Not *bagpipes*!' She shouted so loudly that Bruce, who had been padding along up in front, spun round in alarm, his ears cocked.

Douglas burst out into genuine laughter. 'And what's wrong with them?' he demanded.

'Because they give me an earache!'

'Och – you don't know what you're talking about. I bet you've never heard them.'

'I have.'

'I bet you haven't. And, anyway, you cannae stop me playing them.'

She pushed away from him. 'Well – I won't *listen*!'

'You'll have no choice.'

'Yes, I will.'

'No, you won't.'

'Yes, I will – I'll stick my fingers in my ears.'

'That's not going to do any good because I'm going tae be standing right behind you.'

'Horrid beast!' She bent forward and scooped up a handful of snow, pressing it firmly into a ball. 'Do you know what I do to big hairy men who make me listen to their bagpipes?'

He saw what was coming, but too late. As he spun away, the snowball smacked him on the back of the neck. He roared and dropped to one knee, sweeping up handfuls of snow. 'Right – you've had it!'

Now she was in trouble. Desperately she searched for cover . . . the water barrel. But too late – just as she reached it, she felt a massive thud between her shoulder-blades, the impact nearly throwing her forward into the snow. Quickly she scuttled behind the barrel and began to make hard, round balls of ammunition.

Bruce had been barking excitedly at their game but, now, suddenly, he was growling. Puzzled, she peeped over the top of the barrel and saw that the dog was clinging by his teeth to the hem of Douglas's trouser leg, tugging and growling. 'Get off, you stupid mutt,' Douglas shouted, shaking his leg to break free. But Bruce hung on, tugging sharply, evidently over-excited by all the fun and laughter.

'For God's sake – let go!' Douglas shouted. But this only made Bruce more excited. As Douglas kicked out, Bruce tugged, lifting his master's boot clear off the ground. Now

Douglas stood on one leg, spinning his arms as he tried to keep his balance. 'Get off!'

Peri gurgled with laughter, delighted by the look of sheer panic on Douglas's face, and knowing what was about to happen.

'Get off!' Douglas shouted again. But it was hopeless. He swung his arms like a windmill and crashed backwards into the snow.

Peri didn't hesitate. With a snowball in each hand she bounded across to Douglas and leapt onto his chest. 'Snow is absolutely wonderful for the complexion,' she announced and dropped the snowballs onto his face.

'Aargh!' he gurgled, choking on a mouthful of snow and laughter.

Immediately she was up and ready to run, but quick as a flash he grabbed her ankle and she fell forward into the snow. He turned her over, and now he was above her, pinning back her arms and grinning, his eyes sparkling blue against the ruddy flush of his cheeks. 'And do you know what I do to beautiful ladies who won't listen to my bagpipes?'

She tried to wriggle free but it was impossible. Hopelessly overpowered, she lay still, looking up at him. What would he do to her? Would he kiss her? She could almost feel his warm lips on hers.

He was gazing into her eyes now, his face alive with laughter, and then slowly, very slowly, like a cloud floating across the sun, the laughter went from his face and a sad yearning touched his eyes. Then all at once he was up on his feet, holding out a hand to help her up. 'We'd better get back,' he said. 'It's getting late.'

She put her hand in his and felt herself being effortlessly pulled to her feet. Her brain spun. What had happened? He was going to kiss her, wasn't he? So why didn't he? To mask her confusion she made a show of brushing the snow from her coat while bitter disappointment lay heavy on her chest.

'Okay?' he asked.

She nodded without looking at him, and then, in silence, they carried on their journey down through the snow towards the house.

She wished for all the world that he had kissed her and yet, for all the world, she was glad that he hadn't. That one kiss could have led to the biggest mistake of their lives.

Ahead of them Bruce frolicked in the snow, pausing with legs akimbo to look back at them as if eagerly waiting to carry on with the game – not knowing that it was over.

Peri dialled the numbers and waited. The kitchen was empty, the house silent. Mrs Craig had gone through to the sitting room, closing the door behind her to give Peri privacy. Helmut and Otto were upstairs getting ready for the party and Douglas . . . ? After rounding up the rabbits, he had put them in a cardboard box and gone back out into the snow, taking them with him. That was ages ago and he still hadn't returned.

The ringing stopped and a voice answered. 'Hallo, Mags speaking.'

'Mags. Hi. It's Peri.'

'Peri! Where have you been? Why haven't you phoned? I've been so worried! I . . .'

Peri remained silent, letting her agent's anger wash over, knowing that she should have phoned that morning. Why had she acted so unprofessionally? 'I'm sorry,' Peri managed to fit in as her agent drew breath.

'Well, you should be. I . . .'

The tirade continued and she was glad; this was what she needed – to be brought up sharp, to be jolted back to reality, to be put back in place.

'So where have you been for the last four hours?' Mags stopped and waited.

'I've been busy.'

'Busy? You certainly haven't been working for Helmut because he told me that he couldn't even *find* you! So what's there to be *busy* about? Eh? Pickling more beetroot, perhaps?' she said heavily.

'I didn't know Helmut wanted to shoot today,' Peri lied. 'So I just went for a walk with Douglas.'

Silence. Then Mags began again, in a low and ominous voice. 'You went for a walk with Douglas?'

'He's just a friend,' Peri said quickly, defending herself. 'I thought it would be nice to get some fresh air; and his falcon had to be fed, so I volunteered to do it. That's all.'

'*You* volunteered to feed his falcon?' Mags sounded incredulous.

'Yes.'

'Mm,' Mags murmured. 'just so long as you don't fall for this guy.' Hearing the truth spoken aloud, Peri denied it in a violent exclamation. 'Oh, God, no!'

This seemed to satisfy Mags. 'Good.' She continued more briskly, the incident forgotten. 'Now I've been keeping a close monitor on the weather up there and so far it looks as if its going to behave itself. Thank goodness! Oh, boy! – did I get a shock when I saw breakfast telly this morning! It was headline news! And talking about headline news: I've been very clever and contacted practically *every* editorial news team in the world, outlining exactly what's been happening to you. I don't see why we can't get worldwide coverage on this. So remember, when you're interviewed, tell them the sort of blurb they'll want to hear: that you were terrified, that you drove through the blizzard and just managed to escape certain death – that sort of thing.'

'But I *was* terrified!' Peri protested. 'And I *did* drive through the blizzard and escape certain death!'

'Great! That's great! You tell them that!'

Peri sighed. This woman wasn't about to dish out any sympathy, was she?

As if realising this, Mags changed tack. 'I'm not sounding very sympathetic, am I, darling? But for your sake I want to create something positive out of a negative. Was I wrong?'

Peri shook her head. 'No. No.'

'I really have been worried about you, you know.'

'Have you?' All of a sudden, Peri was conscious of the syrupy note in her agent's voice. Had she always sounded like that?

'Was it simply awful?' Mags continued.

'Yes – it was.' Suddenly, she had a vision of Douglas bending over her, his blue eyes staring into her, his lips so close . . . 'Oh, Mags,' she burst out. 'I just want to come home. I want this all to end.'

'I know, darling, I know; but it won't be long now. Three more days to go.'

'Yeah.' Three more days to go, Peri thought. Not long. Three more days and she would be opening the door of her apartment, picking up an armful of party invitations and walking barefoot across a luxurious carpet, going into the bathroom and turning on the Jacuzzi. Three more days . . . then she would never see Douglas again . . .

'Guess what?' Mags's voice had brightened. 'Because you've been such a brave girl, I have sent a crate of Bollinger to your apartment. That will cheer you up, won't it? And I've had a rather handsome producer from CBS asking all about you and suggesting he take you out to dinner, to get to know you better!'

'Great,' Peri said dutifully, but her voice sounded flat.

'I'm coming in the limo to pick you up from the airport. Friday. That way, I can brief you. I'll be missing a dinner party – but that's not important. What's important is *you!* There will be a crowd of reporters waiting when you arrive – so look good. You'll have a brief round-table discussion with them and a couple of soundbites for TV. I've personally rescheduled Tina for nine a.m. Saturday and Carl Hansen for one. Final rehearsal at three p.m. Time will be tight. Will you need a full manicure?'

Peri glanced at her nails. 'Gosh!' she exclaimed. They were in a terrible state. Two of them were cracked and she hadn't even noticed!

'Oh, dear, I do hope you've been looking after yourself.'

'Of course I have.' For a moment, Peri was tempted to

tell the truth: *Actually, Mags, my face hasn't seen a molecule of liposome hydration in two whole days. I haven't flossed. I haven't waxed. My eyebrows are positively shaggy and my beauty products have been smashed to smithereens!*

'Good,' Mags said, satisfied. 'Now the most important thing in the *whole world* right now is your final fitting, so I'm taking you straight to de Vere's as soon as we fight our way through the barrage of press. Okay?'

'Yeah.' Peri watched Hamish pad towards her along the sideboard and when he reached her, he brushed his whiskers against her cheek and purred a greeting. 'Mags?' Peri enquired, stroking Hamish's ear. 'There was something I wanted to ask you: who would you have chosen to replace me?'

'Oh, darling, let's not talk about it. I could never, never replace you.'

'But if I hadn't been able to get back, you would have had to replace me. I just want to know who you would've chosen.'

'Well . . . Saffron, of course.'

'Does she know what's been happening?'

'Yes. I've had to have her on standby. I didn't want to, of course, but I had no choice.'

'And does she know that I'm going to make it after all?'

'Yes, I told her earlier.'

'Was she upset?'

'Of course, dear! Wouldn't you be?'

'Poor Saffron,' Peri said, trying to sound sincere. 'Poor, poor Saffron.'

Peri tugged the cream-coloured cashmere dress over her head and smoothed it down over her body. Saffron! she thought triumphantly. Well, Saffron had lost the chance of a lifetime! Presumably she would have been hovering by the telephone all day, waiting and waiting, and then she would have got the call: *Sorry, darling, but you won't be needed, after all.* How would Saffron be feeling now? Pig-sick! Ha!

Hamish sat on the dressing table and watched with his

usual interest as Peri began to apply her make-up. 'Saffron will disappear into nothingness,' Peri told him. 'Maybe she will do a couple of coffee commercials and then she'll be gone . . . *forgotten!* And I will be the winner!' She picked up the eyeliner pencil, expertly tracing a line of black kohl along the edge of her lashes, extending it out beyond the corner of her eye. Once again she could feel that steady all-consuming drive for fame. The conversation with Mags had worked wonders, thrilling her with the talk of limos and reporters and rehearsals. It was quite amazing, she thought, but the instant she had replaced the receiver, it was as if her life had come sharply back into focus. It was hard to believe that only that morning she had been prepared to give it all up, even consider the idea that she could spend the rest of her life with Douglas. During these last few days she had simply lost direction, that was all, and her feelings for Douglas had simply been an aberration. Yes, she liked him. He was a great guy and she would miss him terribly. But her feelings for him could never be as strong as her feelings for greatness. How could she imagine that a momentary feeling of love could possibly wipe away a lifetime's craving for stardom?

'You're back on course, sweetie,' she whispered to herself. 'Nothing will stop you now.' As she gazed at her sparkling green eyes in her exquisitely beautiful face, she felt that familiar surge of joy, that overwhelming pleasure in just looking at herself.

Finished, she pulled herself away from the mirror and stood up, taking a glass bottle from her vanity case. Holding the bottle at shoulder height she sprayed a cloud of Elysium into the air and then she gathered Hamish up into her arms and walked through the cloud of perfume and out of the door.

The music of an Abba record came from below and she followed the sound of it down the stairs and into the sitting room. They were all there, chattering and drinking in the candlelight. Douglas stood talking with Helmut by the window, an open book in his hand, pointing to something on a page; then he saw her and stopped and stared, looking at her with unconcealed admiration. He was wearing a white shirt and tie and kilt. He looked so strong, so handsome, his face brown against the whiteness of his shirt. She smiled briefly and turned away, grimly determined to ignore the tingling feeling in the pit of her stomach.

'Och, Peri, you look wonderful.' It was Mrs Craig coming towards her with a glass in her hand. 'Here you are,' she said, giving the glass to Peri. 'A glass of champagne, courtesy of Mr Reuther. I've just been telling Otto here that I haven't had a glass of champagne since nineteen fifty-five!'

Peri put Hamish on the floor and took the glass. 'Thanks. That's great.'

'You look lovely,' Mrs Craig exclaimed. 'Just like a film star.'

'Do you think so?' Peri opened her mouth, ready to confide in her that – in actual fact – she would be a film star within the year; but before she could speak, Otto came up and said something to Mrs Craig and then they began to talk about pastries. Peri stayed with them and pretended to be interested, reluctant to drift away in case she ended up alone with Douglas. She glanced at him and saw that he was still talking to Helmut; suddenly he was looking at her and she looked away sharply, pretending to be interested in her surroundings. She mustn't look at him. She would talk to Mrs Craig, she decided. But instead she gazed around the room. It looked good, she thought with pride. Earlier, she had helped Mrs Craig to get the room ready for the party; decorating the curtains with silver Christmas tinsel and hunting for candlesticks and empty bottles into which they jammed as many candles as they could find. It had been her idea to turn off all the overhead lights but keep the anglepoise lamp aimed at the ceiling. They had loaded the table with sausage rolls on paper doilies, crusty sandwiches and crisps and cakes. On the mantelpiece, she had placed twigs of holly amongst the photographs. The photographs that she had ignored when she had first arrived. Then, she hadn't been interested, but now . . .

Well, it was too late.

'I bet you're looking forward to getting back to London,' Mrs Craig said suddenly, turning to her.

Peri was startled. 'Oh – yes.' Otto had gone over to the table, leaving her alone with Mrs Craig.

'I hope – one day – that you will come back and see us.'

'I would like that.'

'Good,' Mrs Craig beamed at her. 'I've noticed that you and Douglas get on sae well together. I think he's going tae miss you.'

Had Mrs Craig seen them return that afternoon, covered in snow? 'It's a pity you don't have a television,' Peri said, wanting to change the conversation, 'because you could see me televised on Saturday night – live – from London.'

'Do you mean that Film Awards ceremony?'

Peri nodded. 'Yes.'

'You'll be on television! I didnae know. How exciting! Will you be on the wireless too?'

Peri shrugged. 'I don't know.' Suddenly it occurred to her that, no matter how famous she got, Douglas and Mrs Craig would probably never know about it. 'You should get a television,' she suggested. 'I couldn't live without mine.'

'Douglas did have one but he gave it away. He never watched it. And I've never been keen on it myself – it always sends me to sleep. But tell me: is Howard Keel still alive?'

Peri stared at her. Who was Howard Keel? 'Um . . . I don't actually know.'

'He was my idol. I've kept every record he's sung.'

'That's nice.' How melancholic, Peri thought, visualising Douglas and Mrs Craig sitting here night after night listening to the same old records. 'How long have you been living with Douglas?'

Mrs Craig looked surprised. 'I don't live wi' Douglas. I live down in Mairloch wi' my husband. I've only stayed on to help oot during yer visit.'

'Oh!'

'Normally, I just come in once a week tae clean up.'

'So, Douglas lives here *alone?*'

'Aye – that's right.'

Peri fell silent, thinking. So, Douglas lives here by himself. *Alone.* She could picture him sitting on that sofa night after night, staring into the flames . . . alone, with only his faithful dog to keep him company.

'We must get an early night tonight, Peri.' It was Otto, returning with his plate of food. 'We do the last shoot tomorrow.'

Mrs Craig turned to him. 'Will that be up at Cairn Elrig Falls?'

'Hopefully – yes,' Otto replied.

Peri nodded abstractedly, absorbed in the lonely picture of Douglas and his dog. He would have all those empty hours and months and years to sit by that fire, remembering her. Was that a good thing, or not?

'Time for a dance,' Mrs Craig shouted and went over to the record player and turned up the volume.

Oh, no! Peri thought. I hope she doesn't expect *me* to dance. Suddenly, from out of the shadows, Douglas came walking straight towards her. 'Otto,' she exclaimed, grabbing his sleeve. 'Dance with me.' He seemed flustered, but obediently he went with her into the middle of the room and stopped alongside Mrs Craig, who had already begun dancing with Helmut.

As Peri started to dance she could sense Douglas looking at her. What was he thinking? Was he, too, taking a final imprint of her image? Would he sit, night after night, remembering this moment? With a terrible bitterness, she realised that fate had brought them together and it would be fate that would keep them apart. It would have been better if they had never met. Two people who could never survive in the other's world. Peri shuffled her feet as the Abba record played on, scratched and shrill.

At the end of the record, Otto sidled away, leaving her

suddenly alone and exposed. Quickly she grabbed Helmut and continued to dance with him. She mustn't be left alone with Douglas. She mustn't! Record after record, she held on to Helmut insisting he dance with her until finally he begged to be released.

'Peri?' It was Mrs Craig, her cheeks flushed and her grey wispy hair curled damply against her forehead. 'Why don't you dance with Douglas?'

'I've got a better idea,' Peri cried quickly. 'Party games! Let's have party games.'

'That's right.' Mrs Craig clapped her hands. 'A party's no' a party without party games. Now . . .' she swayed drunkenly and frowned at the carpet as if thinking hard '. . . hide and seek,' she cried at last. 'Hide and seek!'

'I know the hide and seek game,' Helmut announced, stepping forward. 'I shall seek – you will all hide, please. Now I will count to the number thirty.' He turned to face the curtain. 'Ready? One, two, three, four . . .'

All this had happened so quickly that everyone hovered, not knowing what to do or where to go. Then Douglas was gone, then Otto, then Mrs Craig. Peri was now caught up in the excitement and ran out of the room and into the hall.

'. . . fifteen, sixteen, seventeen . . .'

Where could she hide? Then she remembered the understairs cupboard at the back of the house. Quickly she raced along the corridor, turned the corner, down some steps into total darkness. Her hand felt for the door handle and found it. She yanked it open and flung herself in, expecting to fall forward into a soft wall of coats and scarves, but instead she hit a body, a hard body.

'Peri?' It was Douglas's voice.

'Oh, I'm sorry. I . . . I didn't know.'

'I'll go and hide somewhere else,' he whispered, but it was too late.

'. . . twenty-nine, *thirty!*' Helmut yelled. 'I'm coming!'

Peri quickly closed the door behind her. Now they were

enclosed in total blackness, their bodies pressed together inside the narrow cupboard, with only the sound of Douglas's rapid breathing to disturb the silence.

Peri could feel her whole body tingling. Why didn't she jump out of the cupboard? Why was she letting herself be pressed against him like this? This was crazy! She tried to inch backwards but, as she was standing on a pile of boots, it made it difficult for her to move. Suddenly her foot slipped, buckling under her. Immediately Douglas grabbed her by the arms, holding her steady. The instant his big strong hands caught her, she felt a spark of desire flame up from between her legs, hot and liquid, spreading out over her belly. Now she too was breathing rapidly, acutely sensitive to the tingling in her nipples as her breasts touched his chest. She tried to think, tried to get a grip on herself, but it was so hot and there was no air and she couldn't breathe.

Far, far away in the distance she could hear voices. There was Helmut's shout of surprise, followed by Mrs Craig's laughter. Now there were heavy footsteps coming down the corridor, closer and closer, towards the cupboard. Instinctively, Douglas tightened his grip on her arms and, not realising his strength, was unaware that he was hurting her.

She had to grit her teeth against the pain, unable to speak. The footsteps had stopped, just around the corner. Silence. Then the footsteps started again, heading back down the corridor, becoming fainter and fainter. Helmut had not discovered them.

Slowly, Douglas released his grip. 'Do you want me to leave?' he asked quietly.

'I . . . um . . . well.' No – she didn't want him to leave; she wanted him to rip off her knickers, spread her legs and fuck her. 'Yes – I think you should.'

As he squeezed past her, she could feel his penis, hard inside his trousers, brush against her hip. 'Douglas?' she whispered, and then suddenly she didn't know what she wanted to say.

'Yes?' he asked. 'What is it?'

'Douglas?' She lifted her face to his, feeling his hot breath on her eyelashes. She just wanted to feel the touch of his lips. If only for a moment. 'Kiss me.'

In the blackness, his lips found hers. At the touch of them, she felt her bones grow soft. His kiss was tender, yearning, but she could sense his passion mounting and now his kiss was hard, crushing down with a desperate urgency, his arms coming round her, pulling her up hard against his body, his lips moving down along her neck and up over her cheek to her ear. 'Peri,' he whispered. 'I shall come to your room tonight. Be ready for me.' Now he was squeezing past her. 'You stay here,' he ordered softly. Then the door opened and closed and he was gone.

Peri fell back against the coats, staring up into the blackness as her legs trembled beneath her, her body electrified with desire. 'No, Peri, no!' The words screamed in her brain. This was all wrong! Desperately, she tried to blank out her feelings but they would not go away. She had to know how his hands would feel on her soft skin, to feel naked beneath him. Just once. Only once.

She didn't know how long she remained in the cupboard. When Helmut found her, he was grinning and chattering in German. She got up and followed him into the sitting room, blinking against the light. It was like a dream: the laughing faces looking at her, the clinking of glasses and the rosy glow from the fire. She was aware that Douglas was sitting in an armchair by the fire, stroking Bruce, but she didn't look at him. She was trembling and confused. 'Mrs Craig,' she said, putting a hand on the woman's arm. 'I . . . I think I'll go to bed. I'm feeling rather tired.'

'Of course, dear, of course. Well done for winning the hide and seek. For a moment there, I thought we'd *never* find you!' Mrs Craig smiled. 'I switched on your electric blanket earlier so you should be nice and warm.'

'Thank you.' Peri had her hand on the door handle as she looked back into the room. 'Goodnight, everyone,' she said, and then, as if her eyes were being drawn by magnets, she was looking at Douglas. He was staring at her thoughtfully, his eyes dark, his mouth grim.

As soon as she was out in the corridor she ran, taking the stairs two at a time, and, once in her room, she closed the door firmly behind her, feeling her whole body tremble. She mustn't let this happen! She must stop him. She looked for a key in the door but there wasn't one. She could drag the dressing table over and barricade herself in. No! She tried to calm herself – to think rationally. This was stupid. She would simply say to him, 'Sorry, Douglas, I don't think this is such a good idea. We're getting ourselves in too deep and we will only regret it.' Yes! That's exactly what she would say.

She undressed quickly, put on her nightdress, clicked off the electric blanket and jumped into the warm bed. 'I shall simply tell him to go away,' she whispered.

She lay rigid, staring up at the shadows on the moonlit ceiling, feeling a pulse throbbing steadily in her neck. What would he be like? He would be big, she knew. Would he hurt her? She could feel a spurt of hot juice from between the lips of her vulva, feel them engorged and ready.

Suddenly there was the sound of Mrs Craig's voice . . . she was calling out *goodnight* to the others, followed by her footsteps on the stairs and then her bedroom door closing. Peri listened, straining her ears to every sound below. There were more voices. Helmut and Otto were saying goodnight, and there followed the sound of more footsteps mounting the stairs. The bathroom door opened, the toilet flushed, the bathroom door closed. Again, the bathroom door opened, the toilet flushed and the bathroom door closed. Now there was silence.

What was he doing? Peri was ready to scream with the suspense of waiting.

She would let him kiss her, that would be all, she thought calmly. Suddenly, there was the sound of the creaking floor-board outside her door. It was *him!* As if electrocuted, she jerked upright and gathered the bedclothes to her throat. In the light from the moon, she could see the door handle turning and the door opening. He was in the room! For a moment he stood with his back against the door, his face deep in shadow, his naked torso a ghostly white in the light from the moon. He came closer, his face moving into the eerie white light and she could see that his mouth was set in a hard line. There was a flash of white as the towel slipped from his waist and onto the floor.

Now she was trembling uncontrollably. 'Douglas,' she whispered, ready to plead with him. She wanted to tell him to stop just for a minute, to talk about it.

He sat on the edge of the bed, and softly his hands cupped her shoulders, gently beginning to push her backwards; but she resisted this by remaining rigidly upright. Feeling her resistance, he stopped. 'Hey,' he whispered, 'it's all right. We don't have to do this if you don't want to.' There in the dim light, his eyes were soft and tender, gazing into hers. 'Is this the little vixen who bullies me?'

The sound of his voice slowly relaxed her and now she was smiling.

'You're such a fierce wee thing. That's the reason why I fell in love with you, you know. You almost had me terrified!'

She chuckled and then suddenly, without warning, the need for him hit her like a punch to her stomach. She wanted him. Oh, God, how she wanted him. 'Kiss me, Douglas,' she whispered pleadingly. 'Kiss me.'

Slowly his lips came down on hers, pressing her back onto the bed. 'It will be all right, Peri,' he whispered. 'I won't hurt you.'

His hard, rough hand moved slowly down over her shoulder and arm, leaving a trail of quivering nerve-ends. Impatiently he shoved the bedclothes away, and, taking the hem of her nightie, pulled it up over her head, exposing her, naked, beneath him. For a moment he stared down at her body and then he began to stroke her, down over her breasts, her waist, her hips, her thighs.

Fuck me! she wanted to scream. *Fuck me!* His hand was so slow, so painfully slow. She would arouse him, she thought desperately, quicken his desire. She stroked her hand over the hairs on his chest, across the muscles of his shoulders and down across his stomach. Suddenly, she felt his penis knock against her hand as if coming forward to meet her. As she folded her fingers around it, he gasped. It was big and hard, pulsating under her touch, and, knowing that at any second this would be inside her, she moaned, her buttocks squirming in anticipation.

His hand was pushing her thighs apart now, moving over her vulva, his fingers exploring, probing, rolling her clitoris. 'I love you, Peri,' he whispered.

'Oh, Douglas!' She had to have him – *now!*

'Do you love me, Peri?'

'Oh, Douglas – yes, I do.'

In answer he kissed her on her nipple, rolling his tongue around it.

It was unbearable. 'Fuck me!' she pleaded, 'fuck me! *Please.*'

She heard the sharp intake of his breath, felt his arm, hard against her back, lift her up and move her over, positioning her. He spread her legs and, kneeling between them, cupped his hands under her buttocks and tilted her towards him, exposing her vulva. Now she could feel the head of his penis against the lips of her vulva and then he was inside her, pushing, pushing, pushing against her tightness, opening her up. Now she was completely filled by him and she moaned and clutched the sheet, wriggling her hips, desperate to feel him thrust, in and out, in and out . . .

But his penis remained still, filling every inch of her. 'No,' he ordered, and held her hips in a vice-like grip, preventing her from moving.

She tried to jerk her hips forward, but she couldn't. Helplessly, she could only toss her head on the pillow and whimper, subjugated into submissiveness as his penis throbbed deep within her.

'Shh,' he ordered. 'Do you like that?'

'Yes,' she breathed. Why didn't he move inside her? Why didn't he release her from this torture?

'You feel so good,' he murmured.

She opened her eyes and stared desperately into his. 'Please, Douglas, please,' she begged. It was as if she were looking into the hard cold eyes of a stranger. Slowly, his penis began to move out of her, and then slowly it pushed back in, slowly, firmly; and with each stroke she whimpered. She wanted to move her hips wildly, to swing them forward to meet his penis, but his grip tightened, hurting her.

'Keep still,' he ordered.

She could do nothing but accept the force of his penis, thumping in and out, in and out, and with each thump came a growing intensity, exquisite at first, but getting fiercer and fiercer, sharper and sharper, pushing her higher and higher and higher. She gasped. Now she was on the edge. Hovering. Hovering . . . Suddenly her clitoris exploded, arching her back, sending shockwaves of fire streaming through her veins, up through her stomach, down along her thighs, wave upon wave upon wave. Her voice cried out as her body shuddered. Then she lay still. Softly, the waves became ripples . . . ripples of warm, soft honey and her clitoris throbbed.

She heard his breath come quickly, as if he were gasping for air. His penis was brutal now, pounding into her as if out of control, his fingers digging into the flesh of her bottom. Then he sobbed and, for a moment, his body shuddered and stiffened and then he released his grip on her. 'Jesus!' he breathed and knelt for a moment longer before falling beside her onto the bed.

After a moment, his arm came about her. 'Are you okay?' he asked softly.

Peri sighed. It was as if she were cocooned in a bundle of cotton wool. Even her toes felt glorious. 'Mmm,' she replied dreamily, yawning.

She felt his kiss on her nose, felt him fold her to him, nestling her cheek against his chest . . . felt the bedclothes falling across her body . . . felt a dreamy sleep carry her down. How long after, she couldn't tell, but there was the touch of his lips on her temple and the rustle of bedclothes and he was gone.

Chapter Seven

Peri felt glorious, absolutely glorious. She paused for breath after the steep climb and lifted her face to the sun, filling her lungs with the crisp mountain air. The sky was all around her, the colour of forget-me-nots, soft and silky, vast and empty; while up ahead the water sparkled gold, bubbling and tumbling down through the snow-covered rocks. This was going to be the most perfectly wonderful day of her whole life.

That morning they had set off in the Land Rover, but after only a short distance, they had to abandon it in the snow and continue on foot. Surprisingly, she hadn't cared. The sun shone, she'd had a wonderful fuck the night before, her hopes and dreams were alive once more, and her face had the reassuring feel of make-up; although her false eyelashes felt strangely uncomfortable. But she didn't care about that either. She was going to be a Russian princess. Once again, Douglas would see her in her natural state, see how truly beautiful she was. Douglas. Her eyes scanned the hillside. There he was, way ahead of them, with Bruce zig-zagging across the pathway, sniffing the ground. Although burdened with an enormous rucksack, Douglas seemed to move effortlessly up the mountain path and now he disappeared from view, leaving Helmut and Otto to trudge on, their backs bowed with the weight of bags and cameras and tripods. Peri followed behind empty-handed, humming softly and feeling so elated that she could have skipped from hillock to hillock like a goat. With every movement she felt the delicious pain between her legs and the throbbing of bruised skin across her hips. It had been a wonderful fuck, and, like a scene in a video, she played it over and over in her head.

She had finally made the decision. She couldn't just walk out of his life and never see him again. No. She would definitely come back and see him. In May, perhaps, but only for the weekend because she wouldn't have the time to stay longer. Then she would come again in the summer and the autumn. This would become their very own place of enchantment: fresh mountain air, invigorating walks and glorious love-making. He couldn't come to London because he would look odd and out of place, and that would make him unhappy. No. His place was here, up in the mountains waiting for her, and, tonight, when everyone had gone to bed, she would tiptoe into his room and do such wildly erotic things to him that he would never, ever, be able to forget her.

'Come on, Peri!'

At the sound of his voice she looked up, feeling her tummy flip over at the sight of him. He was stood high on a snow-covered boulder grinning down at her, with Bruce standing beside him, wagging his tail happily, his tongue lolling from his mouth.

'I'm definitely not having you in *my* team,' he shouted.

'Good!' she retorted. Oh, how she wanted to feel his lips on her, feel his big strong hands caress her fine soft skin. The hours of waiting seemed to stretch endlessly towards the night.

Douglas knelt down on the edge of the boulder with his hand outstretched. 'Pass up the bags first,' he shouted to Helmut and Otto below. When he had taken their bags, he helped them up the steep incline and then turned to Peri. Without hesitation, he grabbed her by the wrists and pulled her up and onto her feet as if she had been a small child.

'Cairn Elrig Falls,' he declared, sweeping out an arm in introduction.

For some time she had been conscious of a distant hum, but now, standing at the foot of this huge waterfall, she could feel the impact of its thundering roar, feel the icy mist brush her cheek. The water fell like a sheet of amber glass, crashing into foam and bubbles into the pool below. It was hypnotising . . . and strangely scary.

'Okay, Peri.' Helmut leant forward to make himself heard. 'I shall set up the cameras here while you go over there.' He pointed a finger at the opposite bank.

Peri's gaze followed his finger. *'What?'* He had to be joking!

'It's okay,' Douglas assured her. 'I'm coming with you. There's stepping stones along the top and I shall be holding your hand.'

Although his words relaxed her a little, she couldn't help but gaze nervously at the crashing water.

Otto stepped in front of her. 'Let me finish you off,' he said, producing a stick of lip-gloss and spreading it over her lips. 'That's it – you can go.'

Douglas took her hand and began to lead her away. 'I'll come back for the bags,' he said over his shoulder. Suddenly, he paused and waggled a finger at Bruce who was trotting alongside. 'You *stay!*' he said sternly and the dog stopped and stared up at him with big haunted eyes. 'No!' Douglas added. 'You stay.'

Peri was surprised that an animal could put so much expression into its eyes, and for a moment she felt sorry for it; but Douglas was pulling her on and obediently she followed.

She didn't need him to hold her hand – they skirted the edge of the waterfall easily, climbing the stones as if it were a staircase – but it was lovely to feel his warm strong hand holding hers. She couldn't wait to tell him of her decision; he was going to be so delighted.

'This is it,' Douglas announced, pulling her up to stand beside him.

They had reached the top and now they could see further up the mountainside, up to where a network of tiny rivulets came together, feeding into one big foaming river, and that river rushed and tumbled as if in frantic haste to throw itself off the edge of the cliff, but as it poured over it fell smooth and glossy – like maple syrup. And there, set back from the curve of the water was a line of huge stone slabs leading to the far side.

'Keep your eyes on where you're putting your feet,' Douglas ordered, his grip tightening as he put his boot on the first stone. 'Okay?'

'Yes,' she answered, glad now that he was holding her hand. With her heart thumping, she followed him out across the water, obediently keeping her eyes from the churning foam far below, but terribly aware of the powerful current rushing between the stepping stones beneath her feet. For a split second she imagined what it would feel like to lose her balance – to fall into the black pool below – and she shivered.

'Nearly there!' Douglas shouted. Then he was on the other side, swinging her onto a flat rock beside him. 'The water's pretty powerful today,' he said. 'It's because the snow is melting. Come summer it's like a garden fountain; it can lull you to sleep.'

She smiled up at him, knowing that this was the right moment to tell him, but, suddenly, he had turned and was heading back across the water. 'I won't be a second,' he shouted.

She watched him jump from stone to stone, sure-footed and fearless, and then he was on the other side. Her gaze followed him for a moment, noting how his hair gleamed almost red in the sun, then slowly, as if drawn by magnets, her eyes began to stare down at the churning water below. Around the edge of the pool the water was shallow, a clear amber colour, but in the centre it was black, so black that it was impossible to see its depth.

With an effort she pulled her gaze away and looked out across the snow-covered landscape. This was like standing on top of the world. She could see so much: the stream tumbling down the mountainside along the path by which they had come, a line of yellow posts dotted in the snow where the road should have been, and the patches of dark forests beyond. She could see everything except the house.

'Here we go!' It was Douglas. He jumped off a stepping stone and onto the bank beside her, holding two big bags. 'This is your gear. Helmut wants you to lie back on that white rock down there. Use your own judgement, he says, but don't stand up.'

'Okay.' Peri unzipped the first bag and took out a long white fur coat patterned with brown markings. 'Could you hold this for me, please?'

Douglas took it and frowned. 'This is not real, is it?'

'No, no,' Peri shook her head. 'But it looks real, doesn't it?' She began to unwind the tartan scarf from her neck. 'Department stores have stopped selling proper furs,' she explained, 'so the fashion houses have had to start making fakes instead.'

'About bloody time!' he said fiercely. 'How can these women wear fur coats knowing that, because of them, hundreds of rare and beautiful creatures have been slaughtered?'

Peri shook her head and looked suitably indignant. 'It's just terrible,' she agreed, and for a second she felt a twinge of guilt. She herself owned a beautiful beaver jacket, a full-length mink coat, and, with her next pay cheque, she was going to buy a silver-fox fur cape. But why should she feel guilty? *She* hadn't killed them, had she? And by the expression on Douglas's face it was lucky she hadn't thought to bring them all with her! But he was right, though. She hadn't thought it through before, but it was true: because of her vanity, rare and beautiful animals had been slaughtered. Well, she would never buy another fur coat in her life! Swiftly, she replaced her wellingtons with a pair of suede boots, then took a cardboard box out of the second bag and opened it. 'This isn't real either,' she said, lifting out a slim silver tiara and fixing it onto the top of her head with the wired grips. When she had finished, she gathered her coat lapels to her chin, flung her head back and arched a haughty eyebrow. 'I'm meant to look like a Russian princess – what do you think?'

Douglas put his head to one side and considered her. 'You look fantastic,' he declared. 'The most beautiful woman in the world.'

She thrilled to the words. 'You are a sweetie.' As she stared up into his eyes, she saw his smile fade and his mouth become grim, an expression she had come to know so well.

'I want to kiss you,' he said, moving closer.

'Well, you can't because you'll ruin my lipstick.' She tried to make light of it, but, as she stared up into his blue eyes, she could feel her breath quicken and the desire for him spreading up from between her legs. She yearned to feel his lips on hers and to hell with her lipstick! To hell with the others!

'I want to thank you for last night,' he said, his face only inches from hers. 'I—'

'Peri! *Peri!*' Helmut stood on the far bank, waving and shouting for her attention. Peri snapped to attention. What was she doing? This wasn't the time for romance. 'Okay, okay,' she shouted back and hurriedly climbed down over the rocks. They would have plenty of time that night for kissing, she thought happily, as she reached the smooth white rock by the water's edge.

Helmut bobbed up and down behind the camera a couple of times and then he gave the thumbs-up and shooting began.

Peri lay stretched out on the flat rock with her elbow resting on a small boulder beside her, pouting seductively at the camera and holding the collar of her coat up against her cheek. The sun shone and the water sparkled and she knew she looked beautiful. This was her life, she thought, her reason for living: to be the centre of attention with all eyes focused on her and her alone; to be worshipped, with the camera as the instrument of that worship.

Remembering their photo session in the bar, she wondered how they would look in the photographs together. What would the other girls say when they saw the photo spread? Would they ask who he was? Probably. Well, she would simply explain to them that he had been a local man who had been sitting in the bar; they need never know about her visits to him. It would be her secret. No one would ever see them together . . . except for Mrs Craig and a herd of animals.

A thought struck her. Mrs Craig . . . ? But Mrs Craig didn't live at the house, did she? So who would look after them? Who would cook and turn on the electric blanket, and who would do the washing-up?

And the animals? In May! She was going to come back in May. Would Douglas be too busy with his animals to spend time on her? Would he expect *her* to help him? No! She was adamant about one thing: *She* wasn't going to come all the way up here to be nursemaid to a herd of sick animals. *No!* She would have to make this absolutely clear to him before they came to any agreement. He would have to hire help, that was all. And she would have to make sure that the hired help didn't discover who she was and then sell the story to the media. Whoever it was would have to sign a confidentiality agreement. Then they would have to ask Mrs Craig to do the cooking for them, so that she and Douglas would be free to roam the hills, to make love in some sunny glen.

Pleasantly, her thoughts drifted to London, with images of the Awards Ceremony and the dress and the Cartier diamonds glittering around her throat. Then her thoughts switched to the image of her and Douglas sitting side by side in the Land Rover, driving over the snow-covered hills, down to the airport. Having to say farewell as if they were strangers. How romantic. Like something out of *Dr Zhivago*. She would be sad but beautiful, whispering to him that she would come and see him soon and to wait for her. And then, one day, when someone was writing her biography, they would find out about this love affair and . . .

'Good!' Helmut's face popped up from behind the camera and he grinned, giving her the thumbs-up sign. Next, he held up a flask and pointed to it.

Gosh! The time had just flown! 'Coffee break,' Peri announced cheerfully, holding out a hand so that Douglas could pull her up.

He took her hand but instead of pulling her up, he sat down beside her. 'Forget the coffee break,' he said. 'Let's stay here – we've got so little time left to be alone.'

'Okay,' she agreed brightly, turning to him, thankful that she wouldn't have to go across the waterfall again so soon, and knowing that this would be the right time to tell him of her decision.

'Peri?' Now he was looking steadily into her eyes. 'Will you marry me?'

'*What?*' She stared at him in astonishment. Of course she hadn't meant to sound so shocked but it was so unexpected. 'I . . . I . . .' Maybe it was one of his silly jokes. 'You're joking?' She half-smiled, ready to share the joke, but then she saw the pain in his eyes as he turned away.

'No,' he said, beginning to rise. 'I wasn't joking.'

Oh God! What was happening? 'Sit down – please – sit down,' she begged. 'It's a shock – that's all. Let's discuss it.'

She waited until he was once again sitting beside her. 'Now, Douglas,' she said earnestly, turning to him. 'I do like you – really . . .'

'*Like* me?' Douglas looked astounded. 'You *like* me?'

She could not meet his eyes. 'Well . . . yes.'

'After all that has happened between us, you can simply say you "like" me? What about last night?'

Glancing up, she saw the pain in his eyes. Quickly, she looked down at her hands. She didn't want to see his pain, but he was trying to make her feel guilty, trying to force her to say that she loved him. Suddenly she couldn't breathe, overwhelmed with panic and fear. He was getting too close, wanting too much. He was forcing her into unknown alien territory and it was terrifying.

'What about last night?' he repeated.

He was forcing her into a corner. She felt trapped. 'I . . .

I . . .' She threw back her head and glared at him, attacking to defend herself. 'What about last night? We fucked – okay? But that doesn't mean we have to get *married!*' Why was she speaking like this? Now he was looking at her as if she'd suddenly sprouted horns! Something in her cried to see the look in his eyes but she couldn't stop herself. 'You've got no right to look at me like that!' she yelled. 'You're not going to make me feel guilty. You can't honestly expect to marry someone like *me!*' She didn't mean to say it like that – but it was true, wasn't it? Oh, God, what was happening?

He turned slowly and gazed out to the horizon, shaking his head as if shaking off the dizziness from a heavy blow. When he spoke his voice was low and angry. 'Don't say any more. I have heard enough.'

She heard the sneer in his voice. But he was meant to love her! Suddenly she felt overwhelming fury. Everything was spoilt. 'You've spoilt everything!' she shouted, jumping to her feet.

He, too, rose slowly to his feet and stared down at her with hard cold eyes. 'Have I?'

'Yes, you have. This is all so . . . so . . .'

'What?'

The air crackled between them. '. . . humiliating!' she said at last, staring up at him in defiance.

'Jesus!' The word was spoken on a long breath. 'I must've been crazy to think that I wanted tae marry *you!*' He shook his his head. 'Phew! That was a narrow escape!'

'You're prehistoric!' she snapped. 'Just because we fucked – you think we should get married. And just because I say no – you get nasty!'

'*What?* I'm no' getting nasty – I'm just bloody *relieved.*' He turned away and clambered up to the next rock, making it obvious that the conversation was over.

Peri wanted to grab him, to stop him going. Make him understand. 'Well – for your information,' she shouted, catching up with him, 'I *had* decided to come and see you again. In fact, I was going to come to see you *twice* a year!'

He turned suddenly and looked at her coldly. 'What for?' he asked. 'To have a fuck with no complications? Then you wouldn't have tae feel love, would you? Oh, no. That would be too abhorrent for you, wouldn't it?'

The truth of his words hit her like a thunderbolt and she could only stare, open-mouthed. How did he know?

His eyes flashed. '*So I'm right!*'

She hated him, hated him, hated him. 'Drop dead!' she snarled, pushing past him to get up onto the next rock for her wellingtons. She wasn't going to hang around *here!* 'Did you honestly think that I would marry someone like *you?*' She sat down on the plastic bag and pulled off her suede boots. 'You might as well have asked me if I wanted to be buried alive!' She thrust her feet into her wellingtons and stood up. 'Are you too stupid to realise that I am the most beautiful woman in the world? That the richest men on planet Earth would cut off a limb so that they could have me? That . . .'

'Oh, shut up, for God's sake.' Douglas sounded more irritated than angry now. 'You're just a spoilt rich kid, pampered your whole life by parents who should have . . .'

His words thudded into her chest. '*Parents?*' She laughed harshly, staring at him through narrowed eyes. '*You know fuck all!*' With her brain spinning with anger and confusion, she hitched up her coat and swung away, planting her boot firmly onto the first stepping stone. She wasn't going to hang around here listening to this shit.

'Hey! Wait!' Douglas bounded up onto the rock behind her. 'Be careful!'

She was nearly halfway across now. She didn't need *his* fucking help and she would tell him so! She swung round to shout at him, 'I don't need your f—' Suddenly her foot slipped and for a split second she wavered, desperately trying to throw her weight backwards. Then she was falling forward . . . falling . . . falling. *No!* her brain screamed. *No! No! No!*

She hit the surface and went straight under, her sodden coat dragging her down, down into the icy blackness, the freezing water knocking the air from her lungs, thumping a massive blow at her heart. She had to have air. She had to get the coat off and get to the surface. She had to get out, she *had* to! Icy water filled her mouth, her throat. She was dying . . . dying . . . Images flashed through her brain. A woman's sad face staring through railings. White skin, black hair. The ball bouncing towards her across the playground . . . catching the ball and looking back . . . but the face had gone . . .

Hot bitter liquid gushed up into her mouth, making her choke and cough, spluttering the liquid out onto the snow. She opened her eyes, vaguely curious to see the snow right in front of her face. What was happening? A man was shouting behind her. 'For God's sake, Helmut – help me get her clothes off!' She closed her eyes again and slipped back into that dreamless sleep.

Now she was blind! No. It was something being dragged up over her head. Two long white legs appeared before her, stretched out in the snow with a black and white dog licking the toes. The man was shouting in her ear. 'Helmut! Hurry! Or she'll die!' She closed her eyes again, content to slip away once more.

When she opened her eyes again, she was hanging upside-down, the ground bobbing about beneath her head, her long black hair swishing from side to side. She was hanging over someone's shoulder and her head kept bouncing against a squelchy-wet jacket. Who was it? Where were they going? It was all so difficult. Now there was a muttering voice. It was a man's voice. A really nice Scottish voice. 'You idiot,' he was saying softly. 'What the hell's wrong with you?' Who was he talking to? She was drifting away again, slowly, dreamily.

Suddenly, something sharp pricked her toe. There was more pricking, as if from hundreds of needles, moving over her toes and feet. Her jaw started jerking in quick spasms but she couldn't stop it, she couldn't control it. There was the sound of her teeth clashing and she was terrified. What was happening to her?

'You're okay, Peri.' It was the man's voice again, speaking gently, reassuring her. 'You're in shock but you'll be fine. I promise. We're nearly home.'

Home? What home? She didn't have a home. Although she was unable to answer, the voice had soothed her and she knew that she would be all right.

Peri drifted into consciousness as if floating up through a veil of gauze. She could hear murmuring voices and a crackling fire and above her head the ceiling glowed orange. She was in the sitting room, on the sofa, swaddled in eiderdowns, feeling a strange quivering sensation in her limbs.

'I canna believe it!' It was Mrs Craig's voice, hushed but indignant. '*He* – of all people – knows about survival. So why did he tramp all the way back here in freezing wet clothes? Didn't either of you offer him yours?'

'I couldn't.' Helmut was speaking. 'I'd already given mine for Peri.'

'He didn't ask me.' It was Otto sounding scared. 'He was in such a hurry. He nearly knocked me over. I . . . I didn't know what to do.'

'Will he be okay?' It was Helmut's voice.

'I don't know, I don't know.' Mrs Craig sounded agitated.

Douglas! Peri tried to lift herself up but she was too weak. 'Where's Douglas? I have to see him.'

Helmut bent over her holding a glass to her lips. 'Try and drink this.'

'Don't give her that!' Mrs Craig exclaimed. 'You never give alcohol to someone with hypothermia.'

'Oh.' Helmut stepped back, letting Mrs Craig bustle forward.

'How're you feeling, dear?' she asked kindly.

'Where's Douglas?'

'Don't worry about him. You just think about yerself.'

'But I have to speak to him.'

'Whist now. Have you still got the shivers?'

'Yes – my body can't stop trembling.'

'That's a good sign,' Mrs Craig told her, taking something out of her apron pocket and shaking it. 'I just want to put this thermometer under your tongue a minute.'

'But—' With the thermometer in her mouth, Peri was unable to say more. Helmut and Otto looked on apprehensively. The house was so silent. Where was Douglas? Why wasn't he here with her, looking worried like everybody else?

Mrs Craig removed the thermometer and studied it in the light from the table lamp. 'You're going to be fine, Peri,' she announced. 'All you need now is plenty of rest.'

'Please – can I speak to Douglas?'

'Aye, a wee bit later. I'm just going to give you this hot soup and then we'll carry you up to yer bed.'

By the time Peri had eaten, she was exhausted, and as they gently put her into bed she could feel herself rapidly falling into a deep sleep, all thoughts of Douglas slipping away.

She opened her eyes and looked around the room. Where was she? This was not her apartment. So – where was she? The memories hit her suddenly, and in disjointed flashbacks she saw herself falling through the air, drowning in icy blackness, the coat pulling her down like a malignant force, the sheer terror of knowing that she was about to die. Douglas bending forward with love in his eyes. *Peri, will you marry me?* Pain in his eyes. Anger. 'Oh, Douglas,' she whispered. 'What have I done? I'm so, so sorry.'

A heavy feeling, like a lump of stone, settled on her chest. Why? Why had she spoken to him like that? Why had she been so cruel and vicious? Had it been fear? Fear that she would be seduced by his love and that all her plans and dreams would be destroyed? Yes, this was partly true, but an inner voice told her that there had been a greater fear, fear of acknowledging her love and knowing that it would only be thrown back in her face. It had happened throughout her childhood; innocently, naively she had been willing to give love but each time it had been ground in the dirt. She had long ago discovered that it was better not to love than to give love and have it destroyed. She would go to him, explain about her childhood and then he would understand and she would be forgiven. Everything would go back to how it had been.

Swiftly she pushed herself up, ready to get out of bed, but she had to stop, overwhelmed by the dizziness swirling in her head, squinting her eyes against the sparks of silver dancing before her face. After a few minutes her head began to clear and she stood up and padded slowly towards the door, aware now that she was wearing someone else's clothes, baggy trousers and a purple jumper. Who did they belong to?

As she descended the stairs, she clung to the banister hoping that Douglas would see her like this and rush to her aid, putting his big strong arms about her and carrying her into the sitting room and placing her gently on the sofa.

But he did not come.

There was the sound of a cough. In the kitchen. It sounded like Otto. She veered towards the kitchen and stopped at the door, leaning against the door frame for support. On the other side of the kitchen, Mrs Craig stood with her back to the room, holding the telephone to her ear and gazing silently out of the window. Why didn't she rush over, clucking and fussing? And what about Helmut and Otto? They just sat there, staring at Mrs Craig with such intensity that they didn't seem to realise that Peri had come into the room. But where was Douglas?

'Where's Douglas?' she asked, her voice carrying clearly across the silence.

'Peri!' Helmut exclaimed. Immediately he and Otto rushed over and helped her to a chair. 'You should be resting.'

'I have to see Douglas.'

There was silence – a strange and awkward silence. Otto sat down and shuffled in his seat while Helmut studied his fingernails. And still Mrs Craig stood there, holding the phone to her ear and staring out of the window. Why didn't they speak? Something was wrong – she could sense it. 'What's the matter?' she asked slowly, staring from one to another, alert now to every sound and movement.

Helmut looked at her apologetically. 'Douglas is very ill.'

The sudden surge of fear made her voice sharp. 'What do you mean?' she demanded.

'Douglas is suffering from hypothermia.'

'So? I've got hypothermia and I'm all right.'

Helmut shook his head sadly. 'This is bad. Very bad. He does not respond to anything that we do for him.'

Peri clutched the edge of the table and stared at the floor. This was all her fault! 'This is not my fault,' she muttered to herself. 'It's *his* fault.'

'Does it matter whose fault it is?' Helmut said wearily.

She spun round to face him. 'When's the doctor arriving?'

Helmut shook his head miserably. 'He will not be arriving. He will not be able to get through the snow. We are trying to contact him now, to get his instructions.'

Peri felt as if the air had been punched from her lungs. No doctor! This couldn't be happening! Her brain whirled. But Douglas was okay – he had carried her through the snow, hadn't he? He was strong. Like an ox. Cold water couldn't hurt him! Could it?

'Thank you, Lena.' It was Mrs Craig speaking. She replaced the receiver and for a moment bowed her head over it. Then she turned to them looking grey and very old. 'The doctor still hasnae been contacted. His wife says that all we can do for Douglas is tae keep him warm and bide by the telephone.'

'This is *ridiculous!*' Peri exclaimed, jumping up, but immediately a wave of dizziness filled her head and she clung to the table, preventing herself from falling forward onto the floor. 'This is not happening,' she whispered, putting a hand over her eyes.

'Oh, lassie,' Mrs Craig said quietly, coming over and putting an arm about her shoulders. 'Dinnae fret yerself.'

Peri waited until the dizziness had subsided and then straightened up and marched out of the kitchen and up the stairs. She fell silent as she opened his door. His room was in shadow, the curtains firmly closed against the sunlight, and over on the bed was the silhouette of a mountain of coats and blankets. She went straight towards it, but as she reached it she tripped over Bruce. 'Fuck!' she exclaimed.

Bruce quickly jumped out of the way and turned to look up at her with big sad eyes – almost as if he were questioning her, accusing her.

'And why are *you* looking so pathetic?' she hissed. 'He's not going to bloody *die*, for God's sake!' Gently, she bent over the bed and softly peeled back the covers. 'Oh!' she gasped. This was not Douglas. This was the face of a stranger, all white and bloated and blotchy. 'Douglas,' she whispered. 'Oh, Douglas.' Tenderly, she stroked the hair back from his forehead, and as she did so she felt the cold flesh beneath her fingertips. 'Douglas,' she pleaded desperately. 'I'm sorry – so sorry. Please forgive me.'

His eyelashes flickered and then he was looking up at her but she could see what an effort it was for him. She put a bright smile on her face even though she wanted to weep. 'You should have let me drown. I deserved it!'

The corners of his mouth turned up. He was trying to smile! He was getting better! She had made him better! 'Everything will be okay,' she said in a rush. 'I will look after you. I will . . .'

His eyes were closing . . . closing. Closed. He was gone from her! 'Douglas!' she shouted, thrusting her hands under his shoulders and trying to shake him awake. *'Douglas!'* she pleaded, her tears blinding her vision. She put her hand to his lips and felt the hot tickle of air against her skin. Yes – he was breathing – but *only just!*

She straightened up. 'Right!' she announced grimly, wiping her eyes with the heels of her hands. She could feel the panic stirring, ready to send her spiralling out of control. She had to keep a grip. 'Okay!' she said grimly, 'Right!' She took a deep breath and tried to think. What could she do? There must be something? But what? Then she knew with a calm certainty that there was only one thing she could do . . .

Swiftly, she turned and ran from the room, bumping into Mrs Craig who was coming up the stairs.

'Oh, lassie, I heard you shouting.'

'I'm going to phone mountain rescue,' Peri said briskly. 'What's their number?'

Mrs Craig followed her into the kitchen. 'Well . . . you cannae telephone direct. You've got to telephone the emergency services first.'

Peri had the telephone in her hand. 'What? 999?'

'Yes. The police. Ask for the police.'

Peri dialled and listened to the ringing tone. Then she put her hand over the receiver and spoke quickly to Mrs Craig. 'He's unconscious.'

The woman pressed a hand to her mouth, her eyes wide in horror. 'Oh, lassie, lassie!'

Peri heard a click on the line. 'Which service?' asked a woman's calm, unhurried voice.

'Mountain Rescue.' Peri replied.

'I'll put you through to the police station,' said the voice.

Peri waited, hearing her breath come fast and shallow.

There was a click. 'Cairngorm police,' said a gruff Scottish voice.

'Can you please send a rescue helicopter, *immediately*,' Peri demanded.

'Hold on. Hold on. You'll have tae give me the details first.'

'We have a man here who is suffering from hypothermia and has become unconscious.' Peri was aware of the brisk, neutral tone in her voice, as if she were unconnected to what was happening. 'He looks as if he's going to die.'

'Where are you?'

Peri's mind went blank. Where was she? She had no idea! Quickly she turned to Mrs Craig. 'Where are we?'

'Cadha Mor,' Mrs Craig answered. 'The Ranger's house.'

Peri repeated this into the telephone. 'Cadha Mor,' she said quickly. 'The Ranger's house.'

'Och, I know,' said the man's voice. 'Douglas MacLeod's place.'

'Yes – that's right. It's Douglas who's ill.'

'Douglas? With hypothermia?' The man sounded incredulous. 'But that's imposs—' He stopped short. 'Well, never mind that now. I'll get on to Kinloss right away. I'd better tell you that there's only one helicopter in service and it's out on missions right now but I'll try ma best. I'll call you straight back.'

'Don't you want our phone number?'

'No, lassie. I know it already.'

'Right. I'll wait by the phone.' The line went dead, and now there was nothing else she could do but wait. As she replaced the receiver into its cradle she realised that her hand was trembling but she held on, clutching it tight, her only lifeline to hope. 'The helicopter is out on its missions but they're going to try their best,' she said, without turning round. She couldn't bear to face the others and see the fear in their eyes.

'I've got tae go up tae Douglas,' Mrs Craig exclaimed. There was the scrape of a chair followed by rapid footsteps across the floor and up the stairs.

Peri continued to stare at the telephone. Her whole being willed it to ring, willed the man to say that a helicopter was on its way, willed Douglas to live. What if he . . . ? No! No! She couldn't think about it!

The minutes ticked away. Suddenly the telephone shrilled, startling her, and she yanked up the receiver, feeling her heart pounding. 'Hello?'

The man spoke urgently. 'I've just heard: the blizzard's about tae strike again. The helicopter's had to be recalled back to base, but—'

'No! *No*!' Peri wailed.

'Listen!' the man ordered. 'But it's flying back – right over the top of you – so it can stop to make a pick-up. But it's no' going to be hanging about.'

Relief overwhelmed her and she squeezed her eyes shut in silent gratitude, feeling a surge of hot tears.

'The pilot has got your map reference,' the man was saying, 'but he needs a big flat area to land on. Do you know the high ground up where Douglas keeps his birds?'

'Yes, yes, I do.'

'Good. Mark out an area, about thirty feet in diameter, using flares or torches, or anything brightly coloured, so that he can get a fix. Okay?'

'Yes, yes.'

'Don't move Douglas, but have his suitcase ready at the pick-up point.'

Peri suddenly had an idea. 'Is there room for four passengers? And luggage?'

'There could be. I'll radio through and find out.'

Peri replaced the receiver and spun round to face Helmut and Otto. 'Get your bags packed. Quick! The blizzard's coming back. Tell Mrs Craig to pack a suitcase for herself and Douglas – but don't mention the blizzard; it will only frighten her.'

Chairs scraped back as they dived for the door. 'Make sure to get space for the camera equipment,' Helmut called back.

'Yeah. Yeah.' She turned back to the telephone and gazed at it. Now she was alone. Waiting. What could she use to mark out the landing site? Suddenly the telephone shrilled and she grabbed it. 'Yes?'

'You're in luck. The helicopter hasnae completed its missions so there'll be plenty of room for people. But don't bother wi' suitcases – you havnae got the time. The blizzard is going tae hit within the hour and it's going tae be a bad one.'

'Right!'

'Get that landing area marked now. You're going tae have tae move fast.'

'Right!' Peri slammed down the receiver, feeling a surge of fear and adrenaline fizzing through her veins. 'Mrs Craig,' she shouted, bounding up the stairs. 'Have you got flares and torches. Quick!' She banged on Helmut's door as she rushed past, calling out to him. 'We've got twenty minutes!'

She dashed into her bedroom, pulled out the drawers to the dressing table and grabbed handfuls of clothes, throwing them into her suitcase. The man had told her not to pack but it would only take a few seconds, wouldn't it? She kept her pink negligee, her lemon-yellow kimono and an orange scarf separate, stuffing them into a carrier bag. Should she change out of these clothes and put on some of her own? No. There was no time for that. Swiftly, she carried her vanity case into the bathroom and swept the bottles off the shelf and into the case, her mind registering, for a split second, the irony of having done all this before. Then she was carrying her cases along the hall and down the stairs.

Mrs Craig was in the kitchen, rummaging around in drawers. 'I know Douglas has got flares,' she muttered. 'But I don't know where he keeps them.' She turned with two big torches in her hands. 'Will these be enough?'

Peri dropped both cases on the floor and began shrugging into her coat. 'They'll have to be.' She took the torches and cradled them in one arm, and with the other hand she picked up her suitcase, suddenly spotting her vanity case sitting alongside. She looked at the torches in her arms and then back at her vanity case on the floor. She couldn't carry both. Well, she would have to come back for her vanity case, she decided, turning for the door. 'Come on!' she shouted. 'We've got to hurry.'

As she spoke, Helmut and Otto staggered into the kitchen with their bags, puffing and panting. 'Hurry up!' she yelled from the doorway. Immediately they followed, streaming out of the house and across the yard, lumbering with heavy suitcases and shoulder-bags up the hill towards the sheds.

With her head bowed Peri marched on ahead, following the line of footprints in the snow, the footprints made by her and Douglas the day before; and there, over to the right, lay a patch of trampled snow where they had rolled, laughing . . . No! She mustn't think about that now. She quickly averted her eyes and looked straight ahead. It was then that she noticed a bird wheeling low above the aviary. Had Kirsty escaped? No. It was another bird. What was it doing? As she approached, it flew off and she thought no more about it.

She had reached the top of the hill and promptly dropped the suitcases into the snow, feeling as if her left arm had been pulled from its socket. Far behind her, Mrs Craig staggered through the snow, looking suddenly small and frail, and Peri had to stop herself from going to help her. There wasn't time. Swiftly, she began to survey the ground before her.

'I'm going back for the rest of the equipment,' Otto said, dropping his suitcase and letting this shoulder-bags and tripod fall from his arms.

'No!' Peri ordered. 'Stay here. We've got to get the helicopter landed first.' She pulled the carrier bag off her wrist and opened it, taking out the pink negligee and handing it to Helmut. 'Go and stand over by that bush and wave this as soon as you see the helicopter. 'Here!' She gave Otto the orange scarf and a torch. 'We've got to mark out the landing area. Go over there to that rock and put the torch into the snow.' Peri spread out her lemon-yellow kimono and then wedged the remaining torch into the snow.

As Helmut and Otto scattered across the hillside, Peri realised that there was something missing – Bruce. It seemed odd not to see him bounding about, wagging his tail, but of course he would still be sitting beside Douglas's bed.

Oh, Douglas! Please don't die!

Peri glanced at her watch; twenty-five minutes had gone by. The helicopter should have been here by now. Had they missed it? Had it come and gone? She was suddenly filled with sickening fear. They shouldn't have wasted time packing their cases. Oh, God! Desperately, her eyes scanned the purple clouds, straining to hear an engine but all was quiet. A vacuum of silence. It was as if the whole world waited with them, hushed and still. Oh, God! *Hurry up!*

'Mrs Craig?' Helmut called over. 'Is the hospital near to the airport?'

'Yes,' she replied. 'It's only a fifteen-minute drive.'

'Would it be okay that we go straight to the airport from the hospital? Will you be able to look after Douglas on your own?'

'Oh, yes, I'll be fine. Don't worry.'

Peri had only been half-listening and now looked at Helmut. 'What did you say?'

'When we arrive at the hospital, we can take a taxi straight to the airport. I am sure we will manage to get seats on the next flight.'

Peri shook her head and looked back up at the sky. 'I'm not going with you. I'm staying with Douglas.'

'But the Film Awards!' Helmut exclaimed. 'You will miss them. I thought it was important to you?'

She shrugged.

'Don't worry about Douglas,' Mrs Craig added. 'I will be there to look after him. You go to your Film Awards. It would be what he would want.'

Peri wished that everyone would shut up so that she could listen for the helicopter.

'Peri!' It was Helmut again. 'Think of all the people you will disappoint. Your agent. All the viewers, the organisers. Who will they get to replace you at such short notice?'

'Saffron Bayley,' she replied heavily. 'That's who.'

'Saffron Bayley?' Helmut repeated. 'Do I know that name?' He turned to Otto for the answer.

'You were going to use her for this assignment,' Otto explained. 'Before you met Peri.'

Peri ignored this. Her conflict with Saffron seemed petty now. It was no longer of importance.

'Oh yes,' Helmut exclaimed. 'I remember now.' Sadly he shook his head at Peri. 'She is no substitute for you,' he said. 'She does not have your beauty or charm. You will disappoint many people, and it would be a grave mistake for you to miss this opportunity.'

'Mr Reuther is right,' Mrs Craig interjected. 'Go to your Film Awards and as soon as it's finished, you can come back up here. Douglas would want you to go.'

Peri shook her head. For a moment, her eyes swept across the horizon, coming to settle upon the aviary. There was Kirsty, sitting motionless, looking like a cardboard cut-out in the fading light, patiently waiting for Douglas to come with her dinner. Maybe she *should* go the Film Awards? Perhaps it would be a good thing. It would give her a chance to step back from Douglas and to rationalise her feelings for him, to decide once and for all whether she truly wanted to spend the rest of her life with him. 'Are you sure I should go?' she asked Mrs Craig.

'Of course, dear. Douglas would want you to. *I* want you to go.' She smiled. 'I want to be able to tell my friends that I know somebody who's been on television!'

Peri smiled. 'Okay. I will go. But I will be straight back.'

'That is good,' Helmut declared. 'I hope—' He stopped and listened.

Peri heard it. The sound of an engine! It was definitely the sound of an engine; and it was getting *louder.* Frantically her eyes searched the sky. A flashing light! 'There it is!' she screamed, jabbing the air with her finger.

They began to wave wildly, screaming up at the tiny flashing dot in the sky, Otto shaking the orange scarf above his head, Helmut swinging the pink negligee in a wide arc back and forth, and shouting in German.

As if pulled by a magnet, it came straight at them, growing bigger and bigger and bigger until it was thundering above their heads, the rotor blades swirling and whipping up puffs of snow as it slowly began to descend. It was a huge yellow helicopter, its ear-splitting roar filling the sky.

Peri saw the face of a little boy framed in the back window, staring down at her with big frightened eyes, and then the door slid back and two airmen in green fatigues jumped down and ran, with their backs bowed, out from underneath the blades. The first one was a giant of a man with a red beard and the second one was only slightly smaller and he carried a bag and a pole.

'Follow me!' Peri shouted, beckoning with her hand. As they approached, she turned and ran down the hill, leading them towards the house. Just before the gate, they came abreast of her. 'Where is he?' shouted the bearded man.

'In that house. Down there,' she yelled, pointing. 'The first bedroom at the top of the stairs.'

'Right.' The two airmen vaulted the gate and sped onwards leaving her behind.

Otto rushed passed her and flopped against the gate, panting. 'There's still the cartridge cases and reflector to come. Can you help me?'

'I'll try, but I've still got my vanity case to get. Come on. We have to hurry.' She swung herself up and over the gate, aware now that the roar of the helicopter engine had dropped to a gentle patient whine.

Within minutes they had reached the house. Otto stopped in the kitchen and began to hitch the strap of a canvas bag over shoulder. 'I just want to check on Douglas,' Peri said, rushing passed. 'Don't wait for me – just put on the table what you want me to carry.' She rushed into Douglas's bedroom and stopped, taking in the scene at one glance.

Douglas lay motionless on the bed, wrapped in a blanket of silver foil, one arm stretched out, uncovered. The bearded airman sat on the edge of the bed, pushing a needle into Douglas's arm. 'We've got an SAS man here,' he said, withdrawing the needle.

'How do you know?' asked his colleague, swiftly unrolling a stretcher across the floor.

'He's got his blood group tattooed on his arm,' answered the bearded man, standing up.

'So how come he's got himself into this state?'

'I don't . . .'

'*Because he saved my life!*'

The two men swung round and stared at her. It was the

bearded man who spoke. 'Are you the English lassie who phoned?'

She nodded.

'You got us here just in time,' he said, pulling down Douglas's sleeve. 'And there's a controlled warming unit ready and waiting for him at Raigmore.'

'Will he be okay?'

'Aye. Don't you worry. But we'll have tae move fast because the blizzard is heading this way. You'd better go on ahead of us.'

'Okay.' She hesitated a moment, watching as Douglas was lifted up onto the stretcher and the belts buckled across his chest. It seemed wrong, somehow, that such a strong and powerful man should be lying there helpless. Then they were carrying him towards the door. She tried to see his face but it was covered over and the two men were moving quickly now, along the corridor, down the stairs, through the kitchen and out of the house.

Peri grabbed the reflector from the kitchen table as she rushed past. The two airmen were way up ahead now, out of the yard and through the gap in the hedge, moving fast, with Bruce running alongside. She saw them reach the gate and stop, swiftly transferring the stretcher from one side to the other. This delay gave Peri time to catch up. Soon, she too had reached the gate, throwing the reflector over and into the snow before climbing over and picking it up once more. Bloody reflector! Why the hell did she volunteer to bring it! Fuck it! She flung it away and carried on. She tried to keep up with the men, but inexorably she slipped further and further behind. Her legs felt so weak – so very, very weak.

'Aahh!' she cried and stopped, doubled over with the pain in her ribs. Up on the hill, the airmen were overtaking Otto, as they made straight for the black hole in the side of the helicopter. Suddenly, she remembered! Her vanity case! She had left her vanity case in the kitchen. She twisted round to take a look at the house. It was too late. If she went back for it now, the helicopter would leave her behind. She couldn't take that risk. Suddenly, a mighty roar filled the sky. It was the helicopter. It was starting up. Now the rotor blades were swishing slowly through the air, beginning to move faster and faster.

She saw Mrs Craig waving frantically from the helicopter doorway, hastily stepping aside as the first airman swung himself up, pulling the stretcher on board. The second airman also swung himself up, closely followed by Bruce and Otto. Now, suddenly, there was nobody left on the ground. No bags. Nothing. She was alone. She was going to be abandoned! Gasping for air, she struggled on, every breath tearing a pain through her chest. She had to keep going. She was nearly there! Please, God, please! *Don't let them leave me.*

The bearded airman appeared in the doorway, took one look at her and jumped down, running towards her. Suddenly she was swept off her feet and carried onwards. 'I thought you were going to leave me,' she sobbed, but her words could not be heard above the roar of the engine.

As the man swung her up to his waiting colleague, she caught a glimpse of Kirsty, still waiting patiently for her dinner. *Kirsty's dinner!* Who was going to feed her? And Hamish! And all the other animals? Who was going to look after them? But there was nobody left! She felt hands pulling her on board. Mrs Craig was putting an arm about her now, steering her towards a seat, but she swung free and gripped the old lady by the arms. 'The animals!' she cried. 'They're going to die!'

'Dinna fret,' Mrs Craig said, standing on tiptoe to shout in her ear. 'I'll get Ian McBride tae come up tomorrow.'

'No! No!' Peri spun on her heels and saw the ladder being pulled aboard, the door sliding shut. They were leaving! 'The blizzard!' she screamed. 'The blizzard is coming!' Mrs Craig looked confused. Everyone around her looked confused. Why didn't someone understand? Frantically, she stared at Douglas who lay unconscious, an intravenous drip now being attached to his arm. Oh, Douglas! What do I do? There was no hope of anyone getting through to those animals now. They were going to die. *And it was all her fault!* Kirsty would never again fly free. And Hamish! *Oh, God!* If they all died, it would break Douglas's heart.

With his hand on the door lever, the bearded airman paused and stared at her thoughtfully, the look of confusion suddenly clearing as a spark of comprehension lit his eyes. He understood! But the helicopter was lifting off. It was in the air! Quickly, she stepped up to him, pointed a finger at her chest then pointed towards the door. He nodded. As he pulled back the door, she felt a cautionary hand on her arm but she shrugged it off and hurled herself out, dropping five feet into the snow. There, she remained crouched low, shielding her eyes against the biting, swirling snow, looking up. From the open doorway Bruce appeared, held out from within two great hands; then suddenly he was released, falling into the snow below and the great steel door finally slid shut.

The helicopter was ten feet off the ground now, twenty feet, rising higher and higher. She could see Helmut's face framed in a window, staring down at her with a look of sheer horror, his fingers splayed across the glass. It made her want to laugh. He looked as if he was going to burst a blood vessel!

The helicopter banked away, heading out across the valley, growing smaller and smaller and smaller, its thundering roar gradually becoming a gentle *flut-flut*, its canary yellow metal fading into the purple clouds. Then silence. Absolute silence. The flashing light was the last thing she saw before it, too, vanished, leaving behind a vast and empty void. And into that void surged fear and utter isolation. She was alone. Completely alone. '*Oh, no!*' she whispered. *'What have I done?'*

Even though the helicopter had disappeared, she continued to gaze up to where it had been. It had gone, taking away the man that she loved. Leaving her behind! Alone! The whole world had finally left her. A whimpering sound startled her and she glanced down. It was Bruce. He was sitting in the snow staring up at the sky. *Bruce!* She wasn't alone. She had Bruce! Thank God! She bent forward, feeling a rush of relief, and spoke gently to him. 'Douglas is going to be okay now. He's safe.' Then she realised that the animal couldn't understand what was happening; all he knew was that the one person in the world who loved him had gone. She felt a surge of sympathy knowing how he must feel. 'I'm going to be looking after you – won't that be nice? And I'll give you a biscuit,' she added brightly, hoping that it would cheer him up. 'In fact, you can have all the biscuits!'

Bruce turned his head to look up at her with big sad eyes, his ears flat to his head, and she knew by his expression that he was feeling rejected. She patted her thigh as she started to walk off. 'Come on, Brucie – we've got work to do and we haven't got much time.' Reluctantly he got up, taking one final look up at the sky, exactly at the spot where the helicopter had vanished, before following her. 'We'll feed Kirsty first – I know where her food is. What about the rabbits? They eat carrots, don't they? And the pine marten – what does that eat? Heavens! I'll just have to give it a mixture: carrots, biscuits and dead mice. Then it can choose for itself.' As she headed towards the aviary, she scooped up her lemon-yellow kimono and orange scarf. The pink negligee was gone. 'Helmut's probably got it stuffed in his pocket,' she told Bruce as he trotted along beside her. 'That will give those airmen something to think about!'

On the far horizon, storm clouds had gathered, black and menacing. The blizzard was on its way. It was strange – but she could almost smell it coming. 'How about me giving you a bath, eh? I've got some wonderful hair conditioner,' she chatted, trying to block out her growing anxiety. 'Eduardo's liposebum almond oil therapy for split ends – you'll love it!' She glanced down to see the dog looking up at her, as if listening to every word she was saying. 'Maybe we could give your eyebrows a trim, too. What do you think?' As she opened the aviary door, she paused and leaned against the door frame, overcome by a yearning to lie down and sleep – just there against the pile of straw. Just for a few minutes . . .

Chapter Eight

One by one, Mags spread the prints out around her, and when she had finished she straightened up and thoughtfully tapped a finger against her lips. Peri was everywhere: on the sofa, on the armchairs, propped up against the television cabinet, laid out in a semi-circle on the carpet. There was Peri in sepia holding a falcon, Peri in monochrome praying at a gravestone, Peri in brilliant colour smiling through a spray of sparkling water.

Peri so alive . . .

'It's guilt!' Mags exclaimed, putting her hands on her hips. 'I only asked for one negative and look what he's sent me!'

Suddenly the doorbell buzzed. She glanced up. That would be the florist, she decided, and waited for Maria to answer the video entryphone. Abstractedly, she watched Maria hurry through to the hallway and then she turned, glancing momentarily at Peri's suitcase by the sofa, before gazing out through the rain-streaked window, out to the spikes of the Millennium dome, across to the bargeboats huddled on the river. Far below, a car horn hooted angrily and from the kitchen came the smell of French onion soup. Everything was normal.

It was hard to imagine what could be happening to Peri right now . . . If she were still alive . . .

She sighed heavily. This whole business was astounding! Infuriating! And there was no way she was going to accept the story that everyone was telling her to believe! No way!

She heard the front door open and looked up, surprised to see Tula in the hallway. 'Any news?'

Tula shook her head as she peeled off her gloves. 'No. The lines are still down.'

'I can believe it!' Mags muttered. 'It's been *four days*!'

'Gosh!' Tula exclaimed, coming into the room and gazing at the photographs. 'When did these come?'

'Ten minutes ago.'

'But there are so many of them!'

'It's guilt,' Mags replied heavily. 'He thinks a room full of photographs is going to make up for killing my best girl!'

'Mags! You can't say that!'

'Maybe I can't say it to the press but I can say it to you. It was his idea to send her to Scotland. Scotland! In March! She must have been freezing!' Mags pointed a finger at the photograph propped up against the television. 'Look at that!'

Tula bit her lip thoughtfully as she approached it. There was Peri, high on a mountain, hair streaming back in the wind, swirling storm clouds beyond; she looked cold. Cold and resentful. 'How grim,' she murmured.

'Too right!'

'But look at that waterfall picture,' Tula exclaimed, pointing. 'She looks *so* different. Really happy. I never knew she could look like that.'

'But it didn't last long, did it?'

The ominous note in Mags's voice made Tula look up sharply. Their eyes met and held. 'Of course,' Tula whispered slowly. 'This would've been the last photo taken of her.'

Mags nodded solemnly. As they stood in silence, she sensed that Tula was also trying to visualise the events of that fateful afternoon. Douglas had saved Peri from drowning – that much they knew – but he had not been able to stop her from jumping out of the helicopter. Once again, Mags assessed the information that she had been given and still she came up with the same question: why didn't she phone me as soon as she returned to the house? I would have been the first person she would have contacted. She had almost an hour before the telephone lines were blown down by the storm. Why didn't she call? Mags gazed out of the window, thinking hard. It didn't make sense. Words hovered on her lips, the same words she had repeated over and over since Wednesday. 'I still think she was pushed!'

'Why do you keep saying that?' Tula said irritably. 'Everyone saw what happened. Peri jumped of her own accord. Why can't you accept that?'

Mags turned on her. 'Think about it! Think about what we've been told. There was a godawful blizzard coming and Peri knew it; Helmut said that he actually saw her crawling through the snow, she was that desperate to get on the helicopter.'

Tula nodded her agreement.

'Then she's safely aboard, knowing that she will be taken to safety, knowing that soon she will be on a flight home. Then, presto! she changes her mind and decides to feed the animals!'

Tula interjected: 'They were about to be stranded. They would have starved otherwise.'

'So – *you* are telling *me* that Peri risked her neck to feed some *animals*?'

Tula nodded. 'That seems to be the story.'

Mags couldn't believe that Tula could be so stupid. It took her breath away. 'Are we talking about Peri Lomax here?' she asked with incredulity, 'or Jane of the jungle?'

Tula didn't reply.

Exasperated that Tula wasn't even trying to work it out, Mags banged her fingertips against her forehead and answered her own question. 'We're talking about Peri Lomax, right? The girl who wouldn't work with Helmut Reuther because he might've – just *might've* – used a dog? The girl who refused the Givenchy promotion because she would have had to stand by a horse – not do a rodeo, not even *sit* on it – but *stand* by it? And the Galapagos Islands? Remember? Sanctuary to a billion iguanas? And what happened? She saw an iguana and told the guide to shoot it. Now I'm being told to believe that she's jumped out of a helicopter in mid-air, knowing that she's about to be stranded in a mountainous blizzard – and just because she wants to feed the animals!'

'Yeah,' Tula admitted, thoughtfully. 'I can see your point.'

Mags ground her teeth in frustration. Peri was no longer just another model. Peri was hot property – red hot! – and Mags could not afford to lose her. Not now . . .

'Don't worry,' Tula murmured. 'She'll be all right. There's plenty of food and heating in the house.'

'But what if she didn't reach the house? Eh?' Mags frowned. 'Why didn't someone phone her, for God's sake, then we would've known.'

Tula shrugged. 'As Mrs Craig said, she was too busy looking after Douglas to make the call immediately; and Helmut was too frantic trying to get on a flight. Then by the time they did phone, the lines were down.'

'Mm,' Mags murmured thoughtfully. If Peri was dead, these photographs could still be used. It would make a sensational story; the media would love it. Unfortunately, the profits would be finite. But – if Peri *did* survive, it would be just a matter of coaxing her back to London, offering the usual words of motherly affection, and then simply watching the money roll in . . .

'Shouldn't you be getting ready for the Awards?' Tula remarked.

Mags looked at her blankly before remembering. 'And shouldn't you be taking Saffron to the hairstylist?'

'I have already. She's there now – but I had to leave. You've got to listen to her to believe it. She keeps chattering on about Peri, saying what a tragedy it is, but it's obvious that she can't keep the smile off her face. It's sick!'

'No, it's not,' Mags retorted. 'It's healthy competition. That's what this business is all about. Survival.' As she turned to brush past Tula, she noticed her mobile phone tucked in the corner of her handbag. Mobile phone! she thought suddenly, fear gripping her chest. 'Oh, God!' she moaned, putting her hands to her mouth. 'She's dead!'

'What?'

'Peri's mobile! She always carries it with her. Okay – the telephone lines are down but she could still use her mobile, couldn't she?'

Tula stared, her eyes wide with fear.

Mags could hardly breathe. 'So why hasn't she used it?' This was becoming a nightmare! 'Damn it!' she exploded. 'If I don't get an answer in the next three hours, my evening is going to be totally *ruined!*'

Chapter Nine

Douglas sat on the bed and tied his shoelaces. Then he stood up and shrugged on his jacket, eyeing the door through which he would go, anticipating the barrage of female voices raised in protest – but no one was going to stop him. First, he must wait for Mrs Craig and the cash that she would bring him.

Impatiently, he turned to the window once more. Using the flat of his hand, he shaded his eyes from the glare of the sun and levelled his gaze at the range of mountains to the south-east. She was out there. Alone. The thought of it was driving him crazy. If only he could talk to her, but it would be another twelve hours before the telephone lines were finally connected. Twelve hours . . .

His eyes scanned the vast snowscape stretched out before him, a picture of tranquility sparkling under a summer-blue sky, showing little evidence of the horrors which had created it. But he well knew what Peri must have endured in those first forty-eight hours: shrieking gale-force winds battering the house as if the devil himself wanted to get in; the crash of a roof tile torn from the rafters, the crack of a tree branch, and, throughout it all, the snow mounting higher and higher, suffocating the world in an icy grip until, finally, all means of escape had been irrevocably cut.

Once again, he shifted his gaze to the south-east. He had calculated her position using the angle of the sun and the time of day. If this were a map before him he would be able to draw a straight line from him to her. But this was not a map. This was a treacherous no-man's-land of ten-foot snowdrifts, of snow-covered gulleys ready to suck a search party down in seconds. Landing a helicopter was impossible; hovering low above the ground was suicide; the rotors recirculating loose snow would make visibility nil, effectively wiping out any visual reference the pilot would have had, and, unbalanced, the helicopter would hit the deck. It was suicide. And RAF pilots were not trained in suicide.

No one could help her. No one except him . . .

Frustrated with inactivity, he could only stare down at his big scarred hands on the window sill. Hands that lay useless. But his brain was active, calculating, planning, assimilating Peri's situation and, once again, mentally ticking off a checklist of those things that would keep her alive.

Heating? Ready supply of firewood and kindling in kitchen. Back-up supply in yard.

Cooking? Gas cylinder replaced ten days ago. With moderate use it would last fourteen days.

Lighting? It was difficult to gauge the amount of petrol remaining in the generator. If the electricity was used sparingly, it could last until Monday.

Monday . . .

But what if he was wrong? At the thought of it, Douglas instinctively balled his hands into fists. A reflex action in the face of anger. In his mind's eye he could see the petrol cans lined up in the shed, row upon row, enough fuel to last six months. And the shed stood alongside the generator, within arm's reach. So simple. So very simple . . .

He thumped a fist against the sill. Why hadn't he told her how the generator worked? But how was he to know how vital that information would become? For a split second he had a vision of her sad green eyes looking up at him but immediately he shook it away, forcing himself to keep on track, forcing himself to review the checklist:

Food? Adequate provisions in fridge, freezer and larder.

This had been one of the first questions he had put to Mrs Craig on regaining consciousness. She had answered rapidly, her eyes wide in apprehension, her fingers unbuttoning and buttoning her cardigan. 'Potatoes,' she had said. 'Plenty of potatoes, parsnips, four or five carrots, leeks . . .'

'Fresh fruit?' he had asked, trying to keep his voice soft, but – even to his own ears – the words sounded harsh as if spoken in interrogation.

'Cooking apples,' she had replied. 'And two bananas.'

'Tins?'

'Plenty: peaches, salmon, peas, sweetcorn, custard, corned beef . . .'

'Dried food?'

'Rice. Smash. Macaroni. Porridge oats.'

'Fridge?'

'Bacon. Sausages and milk. There's only one egg but the hens are still laying.'

He had nodded. 'Freezer?'

'One loaf, two shoulders of lamb and three legs of pork.'

'Matches?'

'There's one carton left in the cupboard.'

He had calculated this. 'Six boxes?'

Mrs Craig had nodded. 'Aye.'

With that information gathered, he had rolled his head back onto the pillow, exhausted, and stared hard at the ceiling. Mrs Craig had stood silently beside him and from the corner of his eye he had noticed her fingers still working in agitation but he could not bring himself to comfort her or forgive. In his mind he had asked himself the question that, only moments ago, he had asked her: *Is Peri all right?* But Mrs Craig had been unable to tell him.

Douglas sighed and gazed out to the horizon, unseeing. Why hadn't Mrs Craig made the call earlier? The minute they'd arrived at the hospital? Why had she left it so late? But he could understand that she must have been too concerned with him to think of phoning Peri immediately. Then almost one hour after arriving at the hospital she had made the call, but by then the telephone line was down. Assuming that Helmut would have been in contact, she had phoned him, eventually discovering that he, too, had left it too late to speak to Peri.

Douglas ran a hand back through his hair and gazed down at the car park, hardly aware of the crying seagulls flying low above the cars. No one could tell him if Peri had reached the house safely . . .

Christ! this was driving him crazy!

He swung round and looked at the door. Still no sign of Mrs Craig. Wearily, he sank down into an armchair. Across the coffee table lay the Saturday papers. Saturday! Almost four days he had been in this place doing nothing, while Peri had been out there – alone. Unprotected. The thought of it made him want to hurl the table across the room. But it had been her decision to stay, to look after his animals. Why? Was it guilt? Was it love? Again he saw her beautiful green eyes looking up at him, and it made him want to put his head in his hands and sob.

Last night he had had a dream: he had been walking the hills. It was springtime and he could feel the warm fragrant breezes brushing against his cheek. He was heading home with Bruce and as he came through a gap in the hedge, he was shocked to see that while he was gone everything had been buried in snow. Then he saw a snow-covered body lying face-down, black hair spread about like an ink stain on the snow. He knelt quickly and tried to turn the body over, but as hard as he tried he could not turn it over to see the face.

Douglas put his elbows on his knees and his head in his hands, staring down at the carpet. She would be okay, he told himself. Why wouldn't she be okay? There's plenty of food and warmth in the house. But what if she hadn't reached the house? She might have been weak, too weak to reach it . . .

This was all his fault. He should never have got into the state that he had. He shook his head with incredulity. He had become a textbook case of extreme hypothermia. Everything he had learnt had been ignored. But there had been only one thing in his mind and that was to ensure Peri's survival. After dragging her from the water, he had forced Helmut to strip, and, refusing their help, had carried Peri over his shoulder, tabbing at a swift even pace over high ground and stumbling through trenches of snow on the low ground, concentrating only on moving forward while calculating the wind-chill factor and the distance. No problems. But within ten minutes he had realised the one mistake that he had made. His wet clothes had frozen to his flesh, spreading ice through his body; his limbs trembled and his hands shook so badly that he could hardly keep a grip on Peri's trousers. This was the onset of hypothermia, the first stage. The shivering became extreme, every muscle in his body working into a spasm. But shivering was good, shivering meant that his body was still working correctly. Then the shivering had stopped, and somewhere in his befuddled brain he knew that his core temperature had finally dropped to below 37C: his body had finally lost the ability to reheat itself.

By then he had been within sight of the house, and, still refusing help from the other men, had stumbled on down the hill, knowing that Peri was his responsibility and that only he could get her to safety. Then – suddenly – as if wafted in on a breeze he was standing in the kitchen, watching Mrs Craig come towards him. Peri was taken from his arms, taken away from him. 'Put her into a warm bath,' he had said, his words slurred and thick, but the door had closed behind them. Then he must have fallen forward because in the next second he saw the kitchen table coming up to meet him.

'You should be in bed!'

Startled, Douglas glanced at the tray of food being set before him and then looked up into the smiling face of the pretty blonde nurse.

'You're an awful patient,' she exclaimed teasingly, stepping back and rubbing the palms of her hands down over her hips. 'Don't you want me tae make you better?'

Disturbed from his reverie, he could only stare for a moment, trying to gather his thoughts. 'Aye,' he said softly. 'You've done a grand job. Thank you.'

'It's been my pleasure.' Her voice was husky as she bent low towards him. 'Perhaps I'll let you take me out for a drink.'

He tried to smile, not wanting to hurt her feelings. 'Och, I'm afraid I've got a lassie waiting at home fer me.' He saw the disappointment in her eyes as she straightened up.

'Aye. Well. You know where I am, if you change yer mind.' She frowned suddenly. 'You're not cold, are you?'

'What?'

She tilted her chin towards him. 'You've got yer coat on. I hope you're not thinking of taking a stroll.'

He shook his head. No, he was not thinking of taking a stroll. Instead, he would be strapping a loaded bergen onto his back, and, with a pair of skis, would be winching himself down from a helicopter to the summit of three thousand feet.

The pretty nurse waggled her finger at him. 'You eat that dinner, mind, and I'll be back with your chocolate sponge in a wee while.'

He watched her walk away. Why couldn't I fall in love with someone like her, he thought; someone with a willing smile and soft eyes holding the promise of an easy life? Why did I have to fall in love with someone like Peri? In his mind's eye he could see her now, standing in the ruined cottage on the hill. Their very first meeting. He had been stunned by her fury, confused, unsure; and yet if she had been an enemy soldier with a raised rifle butt poised to smash his skull, he would have known immediately how to react. But, as it was, he had been confronted by a vicious green-eyed female, spitting words like venom and he'd had no idea what to do.

He grinned at the thought of it. She would be a great one to take into battle!

Merely looking into Peri's eyes was a challenge. It lit a spark in him, an urge to meet that challenge. Just being with her gave him a thrill of excitement.

Was that love? Well, yes, partly. But then there was that

constant desire to look at her, look at every tiny detail of her, the way her lips moved, the way her long thin neck could hold the weight of all that long black hair piled up on top, the way her eyes sort of slid a look towards you. And then there were all the colours in her eyes which he still hadn't been able to identify yet . . .

'Oh, Peri,' he moaned. 'Oh, Peri.'

He remembered the look on her face when he had asked her to marry him. Christ! Even now it made him want to curl up with the shame of it. She had acted as though the idea was incredible to her, as though they had never laughed together nor made love together. When he had questioned her, she had become furious – but now with hindsight he questioned her fury. It had been too violent, too violent from someone who was denouncing a casual fling. It was as if he had touched something deep inside her, something that she feared.

Abruptly, it brought to mind an incident which had happened many years before, when he'd been a boy of ten. He had discovered a scarred and terrified cat hiding at the back of some packing crates. Although the animal had hissed a warning at him, he had ignored this, knowing that it was frightened and in need of food and comfort. But as he put out a hand, the cat scratched it viciously, drawing blood. Angry and upset, he had abandoned it. Only in later years had he realised that the animal must have been so badly treated it was unable to take help or comfort.

Why had he remembered that incident? What had made him think of it?

Suddenly he was confused, remembering how Peri had kissed him. Did she love him? Or didn't she? For Christ's sake! He had seen love in her eyes. She wasn't going to tell him that she didn't love him.

He had seen it.

Impatiently, he raised his eyes to the clock and as he did so he saw Mrs Craig coming towards him. Quickly, he stood up and went towards her.

'Here ye go,' she said, handing him a wad of money. 'Forty pounds.'

'That's great.' He took it and put it into the pocket of his jacket. 'I'd better be off.'

'Are you sure you're well enough tae go?'

'Aye.'

'So what have you planned?'

'I'm heading to the base at Lossiemouth – I've left the telephone number on top of my suitcase – and on the way I'll pick up dried milk, matches and fresh provisions. Then it will just be a matter of biding my time.'

'Is there a chance that you will be flying out today?'

'I've no idea. I can only wait until there's a mission going in the right direction.' He saw the anguish in her eyes and hastily added, 'but I'm sure it'll be today.'

'Oh, I hope so.'

He squeezed her arm. 'Don't you fret. I just want you to keep phoning the house. Okay?'

She nodded miserably.

'Och – I nearly forgot: Helmut phoned while you were out and I told him you would contact him if there was any news.' He zipped up his jacket. 'It's strange that Peri's family hasnae tried to contact her. You'd have thought that someone from back home would have phoned her by now.'

'Well, no, you see – oh dear!' Mrs Craig put a hand to her mouth. 'I shouldnae be telling you this. I promised Peri . . .'

He frowned. 'What is it?'

'Oh, Douglas, she hasnae got a family, nor a home. She was brought up in an orphanage.'

He stared at her. Suddenly it was as if all the pieces in a jigsaw puzzle slotted together. Now he understood. Oh Peri! But he didn't have time to think about it now. 'I've got to go,' he said and bent down to kiss Mrs Craig on the cheek. 'I'll see you soon.'

Then he turned and headed for the door.

Chapter Ten

Cluck. Cluck. Cluck.

Shit! Peri's eyes snapped open and she stared grimly at the chicken walking across the hearth rug. As it reached the fireplace, it clucked contently and began to scratch among the twigs and matchsticks, pecking with its small pointed beak and flicking a matchstick over its shoulder.

She hated this chicken.

Every morning at the crack of dawn it had woken her with its stupid clucking; it had even tried to perch on her head! Now she wished that she'd left it out in the storm. Bloody thing. If only she knew how to pluck it, she would do so gladly and shove it in the oven.

But the oven wasn't working, was it?

And neither was the fan heater, nor the lights . . .

As the dread of a new day settled upon her, she pulled the eiderdown up over her ears and miserably gazed at a matchstick spinning through the air. Everything had gone so terribly wrong.

In her naivety, she had assumed that the supply of gas and electricity would be limitless, just as it was in London. Blithely, she had kept the house lit up like a Christmas tree in an effort to deter intruders; and, for warmth, she had kept the gas stove burning night and day. It was only when the gas ran out that she discovered the gas cylinder under the sink. Then, when the lights went out, she remembered the muddy handbook on electricity generators which had been lying on the bureau.

But it was too late.

There would be no more heat, no more light, and soon there would be no more food. Of course, the shelves in the larder were packed with tinned food, but unless she found the tin opener, they would be useless. It was ironic to think that she had stayed behind to feed the animals and yet – in the end – she wouldn't even be able to feed herself.

At first, there had been plenty to eat: bacon, eggs, sausages, one egg, raw vegetables and bread. Finally – without the tin opener or the cooker – they'd had to live off tinned sardines and corned beef, but soon that too would be gone. All that would remain would be jars and jars and jars of pickled beetroot . . .

At least Kirsty and the pine marten would survive for another week, she calculated, thankful that she had left them so much food. And today she would carry on digging the trench, making a pathway through the snow in order to reach them.

But she didn't want to get off the sofa just yet; she was warm and cosy, submerged under a mound of soft eiderdowns and fully dressed in trousers, woolly mittens, jacket, jumper and balaclava hat. I must look like a tramp in a dosshouse, she thought dispiritedly, gazing around the room. The carpet was peppered with tiny black balls of rabbit poo, the grate was littered with firewood and over on the pile of blankets lay the animals fast asleep. At that moment, one of the rabbits stretched to its fullest length before contentedly curling back into a tight ball. None of the animals felt her anxiety, she realised; they merely assumed that she would look after them – feed them. But what would happen when she couldn't feed them any longer?

'Oh, Douglas!' she whispered. 'I need you.'

She yearned to hear his voice, to see his smile, to feel his big strong arms around her. Was he lying in a hospital bed right now thinking of her? Had he forgiven her for treating him so cruelly? She was desperate to see him, desperate to explain. She remembered the way he had sneered at her and it made her feel sick. Had she destroyed his love? No – he must still love her, otherwise he would not have dived into the water to rescue her. Maybe it had nothing to do with love, maybe . . . She blanked out these thoughts, knowing that she would simply give up if she believed that he no longer loved her.

Through the gap in the curtain she saw that sunshine was now breaking through the cloudy dawn. Another sunny day. Another day closer to rescue, another day closer to seeing him again. But how long would it be? Why didn't the snow fucking *melt*, for God's sake! As long as it stayed like this, he could not reach her. Why didn't the phone ring? *Why* had she packed her mobile phone in her suitcase?

Where was her suitcase now? Probably at Mags's apartment. How was she reacting? Was she worried? Angry? Saffron would be triumphant, of course, for tonight she would be walking on stage to co-host the International Film Awards. The image of it did not disturb Peri; in fact, it made her wonder why she had been so manic about it in the first place. That life was finished. She never wanted to go back. Instead she would spend the rest of her life up in the mountains with Douglas. But maybe he wouldn't want her after all. Maybe – with time to think – he had decided that she would not be right for him, that she would simply be a waste of space, unfit to help him in his life's work.

And he would probably be right, she thought miserably, staring at the pile of logs in the cold grate. She couldn't even light a fire! She remembered how she had thrown the stick across the room, shouting: *Prehistoric man could light a fire – why can't I?* She had tried putting twigs on top, then underneath, then poking them in from the sides, until in the end she was practically crocheting the bloody things! A can of petrol would have done the trick, she thought ruefully. But even if she found some, she didn't have a match left with which to light it.

She sighed. How she longed to have a bath, but the hot water had been used up by the second day. At the time, there had been nothing else to do but to soak in hot fragrant bubbles while trying not to think of the screaming wind howling around the house. For a change of clean clothes, she had rummaged in all the bedroom drawers, soon discovering that there was no alternative but to put on Douglas's things. After that, she had considered ways to keep herself occupied and had promptly put Bruce in the bath, laughing at his mournful and bedraggled face staring up at her. 'But you're going to look wonderful!' she had exclaimed, coating him in conditioning cream. She had dried him in front of the fan heater until he exploded into a puffball of fragrant fur, and then she had set to work with the scissors.

She gazed at him now as he lay asleep beside the rabbits. In her anxiety to keep herself occupied, she had trimmed and trimmed until he looked as if he'd been attacked by a lawnmower. Christ! What was Douglas going to say? She had mutilated his dog!

In one way, she was glad that that Douglas would not walk in and see her in this state, but in another way, she yearned to hear his voice calling her name, yearned to hear him say, 'Peri, would you like a bacon and egg sandwich? With brown sauce? And a cup of tea?' She groaned at the thought of it. She was so hungry.

She mustn't think about it. She had to keep busy.

Determinedly she swung her legs off the sofa, put on her boots and stood up, moving softly in order not to wake the animals. She wanted to prolong the moment when they came to her, pleading hunger with their eyes.

Passing the mantelpiece, she paused and gazed at the photographs, singling out Douglas's laughing face and brushing a tender finger across the glass. Oh! how she wanted to see him, to tell him the truth, to fling herself into his arms and tell him how much she loved him and how much she wanted to be his wife. But what if he didn't want to marry her?

She marched out of the room. Well, she would just have to prove to him that she would be a perfect wife, not just a waste of space. Somehow, she would keep his animals alive. She would dig a trench from the house right up to the door of Kirsty's aviary. She would keep the house tidy. She would have another look for the tin opener and a box of matches. She would be in control!

In the kitchen, she lifted the telephone to her ear, grimly accepting that it had still not been fixed. She could do without it! She banged it down, threw the curtains wide, grabbed the two plastic basins and opened the front door to challenge a new day. Blinking against the bright sun, she stepped out and looked around the yard. Nothing had changed. There was still the enormous snowdrift up against the outhouse while the broken-down car in the corner was still a mound of white. She surveyed the trench before her. Yesterday, she had been proud of it, but now she realised that she'd hardly made any progress whatsoever.

'Right!' she muttered, stepping into the trench. As soon as she reached the far end, she carried on from where she had left off the previous day, scooping up bowls of snow and throwing them out on either side, glad that she had something to occupy herself, something that kept her out of the cold dark house. Glancing down, she saw Bruce close behind, looking up at her with bright eyes, his tail wagging. 'You think this is a game, don't you?' she said, scratching his head. 'Oh, Bruce, I wish it were.'

She carried on digging, the sun hot on her cheek, and impatiently she pulled of her balaclava and jacket and threw them onto the snow. The sun was high in the sky when she finally reached the gate, and swiftly she clambered up onto the top rung, and from there up onto the wall. Standing straight, she gazed out at the wilderness of sparkling snow. It could have been such a wonderful day . . . Blanking out this thought, she began to walk along the top of the wall, holding out her arms for balance. At the far end, she stopped and looked across the vast expanse of snow that lay between her and the aviary. 'Oh no!' she moaned. 'It'll take weeks to dig through that!' Without a snowplough or thirty men, she just wouldn't do it in time. Kirsty and the pine marten would starve long before that.

But she was damn well going to try!

Suddenly, she noticed a bird circling above the aviary. Had Kirsty escaped? No. It was another bird. Was it the same bird she had seen the other day? What was it doing? Probably just interested in the mound of food lying on the aviary floor. But why was it still hanging about? It was not important, she decided, and put it from her mind.

She had to keep going.

Cautiously, she edged down from the wall, feeling her boots sink deeper and deeper into the snow until she felt the icy wetness around her hips. She would not be able to walk through this; she would have to keep digging. She set to work once more, but after a short while she stopped, too hungry and thirsty to continue; her trousers were wet through and she knew she would have to go back to the house.

When Bruce saw her returning across the wall, he trotted along the trench to the gate and waited. 'Hiya, Brucie. Do you want some dinner?' she said. 'Come on then.' As she walked through the trench towards the house, she saw the rabbits sitting on the doorsep in the sunshine. 'God! I feel like Snow White,' she muttered, stopping to stroke them. 'Mustn't get our paws wet, must we?' She stepped over them and into the kitchen. First, she would change her trousers and then she would open the last two tins of corned beef. She would also have to remember to put on her sunglasses before going back outside.

In Douglas's room, she paused for a moment and gazed at his bed. 'Oh, Douglas,' she whispered. 'I'm so sorry, so sorry.' With a heavy heart, she turned to his drawers and took out a pair of trousers and a jumper and changed into them, tucking the jumper into the trousers and tying her belt tightly around her waist. As she rolled the trouser legs up around her ankles, she noticed a book lying on the floor. This would have been the book that he had been reading. She picked it up and began to leaf through the pages. It was all about birds. Wasn't it strange to think that she had fallen in love with a bird watcher. An anorak! Suddenly, her attention was caught. She went back a page and looked at a photograph of a peregrine in flight. The text beside it read: Peregrine falcons mate in March and early April. To attract the female, the male makes a distinct mating call . . . Slowly, Peri lowered the book and gazed into space. What had Douglas said? 'One day soon I will release her. She needs to go and find a mate.'

Peri threw down the book and bolted for the door. Of course! That bird flying above the aviary was not interested in food. It was a male peregrine and it wanted to mate with Kirsty. She ran through the kitchen, leapt over the rabbits and hurried along the trench. But what if it was too late? How long had it been waiting? Four days? What if it had given up trying and had flown away, never to return? She climbed up the gate and onto the wall, swiftly walking along its length until she came to the end. Here, she stopped and looked. Yes! There it was! She watched as it circled above the aviary making a screeching noise. 'Oh my God, oh my God! He fancies Kirsty but she's locked inside and I can't open the door.' Helplessly, she stared across the vast expanse of snow, desperately wanting to run across it.

But it was impossible to get across. Or was it? An idea was beginning to form. Would it work? Swiftly she returned to the house, jumping over the rabbits on the doorstep once more before scrabbling among the pile of newspapers on the floor. Then she found what she was looking for: squares of thick cardboard. She grabbed the scissors and a ball of string from the drawer, put them in her pocket and returned back across the yard, up the gate, along the wall until she reached the end. Sitting down, she punched holes in each corner of the cardboard with the scissors, cut up lengths of string and threaded them through the hole and the cardboard to the soles of her boots. Snowshoes! She had snowshoes! Just as she was about to take her first step, the telephone started to ring. She swung round to look back at the house. The phone! It was working! She hesitated. She should go back and answer it? But what if she did? What if, in those few minutes, Kirsty's mate flew away? No – she would not answer it. Obviously it was working and so she would be able to phone out as soon as she got back to the house – after she had freed Kirsty.

Right! With that decision made, she turned back once more and took her first step. Her boot sank into the snow, but it was only a couple of inches. She was going to do it! She took another step and another. She was walking on snow! She glanced up at the aviary. How long would it take? The telephone started to ring again but she ignored it. She wanted to walk faster but she couldn't risk sinking into a snowdrift.

Now she was almost halfway there! She could see Kirsty clearly, flapping wildly and screeching. She sounded desperate. 'Hang on, hang on,' Peri muttered, quickening her steps.

As she approached, she saw that the snow had driven up against the wooden wall of the aviary, leaving the other side almost clear. Thank goodness she wouldn't have to fight her way through a snowdrift to open the door. With her bare hands, she swept the snow aside. Oh no! The male bird was flying away. She had frightened it off. She watched for a moment before realising that it had only flown out of the risk of danger. Kirsty's screeching had become frantic.

'I'm coming, I'm coming.' As she opened the door, she saw that all the dead animals were gone from the floor while Kirsty sat on her perch looking bloated. 'Oh, Kirsty!' she wailed. 'You've eaten everything. Bloody hell, you're not going to be able to take off!' Impatiently, she lifted the glove from the nail, put it on and placed her arm against the perch. Kirsty immediately hopped onto it, flapping her wings. 'Okay, Kirsty,' Peri whispered as she stepped back through the open doorway. 'Be a good girl and try not to give him a hard time.' And with that, she thrust her arm up high and, at the same time, she felt the weight of Kirsty push down as she took to the sky. Kirsty knew exactly where she was going. She flew straight towards the male bird and suddenly they twirled around one another as if falling like bundles of feathers to the earth. It looked as if they were fighting. 'Oh, fuck!' Peri cried. 'He's going to kill her!' The second she said it, she knew she was wrong. He wasn't trying to kill her, he was playing with her.

Gradually they flew further and further away, becoming two dark specks in the sky. 'Good luck, Kirsty,' Peri whispered, her vision suddenly blurred with tears. She wiped them away with the back of her hand and took one last look before the birds faded from view.

With the excitement over, Peri slumped down on the bench and gazed out at the world below her. This was such a beautiful place. Would she die up here? What would happen if help did not get through to her in time? Would she starve? Would the animals starve? Would she end up sharing the last pickled beetroot between them?

For a moment, she could visualise all the tins stacked in the larder, tins of peaches, sweetcorn, ham, cream, tuna fish . . . Tins that she could not open. Or could she? What about the axe? She could use the axe to smash them apart! Yes! Eagerly, she stood up and turned to go. Of course it would make a bit of a mess on the kitchen floor but that didn't matter. She was going to have a huge bowl of tinned peaches and cream then tuna fish mixed with butter beans and . . .

She heard a sound. An unusual but strangely familiar sound. She stopped and listened. It was getting louder. *Flut, flut, flut.* It was the sound of a helicopter engine! She spun around and searched the sky. There it was! And it was coming straight at her. Frantically she waved, tripping slightly as she hurried out onto the hillside. Was it coming for her? She would refuse to be rescued – she had to stay here with Douglas's animals – but at least she could tell the pilot to bring food. But how would the helicopter land in all this snow? Surely, it would sink.

As she looked, she saw that the helicopter was hovering high above the hilltop and from the doorway a figure appeared, descending on a cable. Who was it? Suddenly her heart began to thump in her chest. Could it be Douglas? From this distance, it was difficult to tell. The man wore skis. He was landing on the snow. He seemed to be unhooking the cable from his belt. As it swung free, he turned, thrust up his goggles and grinned.

It was him! It was him!

'Douglas!' she screamed. 'Douglas!' She wanted to run to him but with the cardboard tied to her boots she could only plod slowly. Now he was coming towards her, gliding effortlessly on skis, his white teeth flashing against brown skin. Then, suddenly, he was standing before her, staring at her as if he could not believe what he was seeing. 'Peri,' he whispered.

The way he was staring made her feel embarrassed and she looked away, suddenly shy and nervous. Now she didn't know what to say. She had planned for this moment: to throw herself into his arms and tell him how much she loved him. But now? Now she couldn't find a word in her head.

'How are you?' he asked gently.

She shrugged casually and glanced about. 'Yeah, fine, fine.' She looked down and began to fidget, sliding the cardboard sole on her boot backwards and forwards across the surface of the snow.

'You're wearing ma troosers!' he thundered.

This unexpected accusation made her look up, startled, but he was grinning. Picking up on his mood, she put her hands on her hips and wiggled. 'Sexy *or what?'*

He chuckled. 'Sexy. Definitely sexy!'

She laughed. 'Liar! Well, *you* look like the man from the Milk Tray ad.' At his puzzled expression, she shook her head and smiled, realising that he didn't know what she was talking about. 'It doesn't matter.'

He was looking at her boots. 'I like your snowshoes. That's a good idea.'

As she followed his gaze, she saw the leather glove on her hand. 'Oh, Douglas,' she said hurriedly, remembering what she had done. 'I hope it was all right, but I've just released Kirsty. There was a male peregrine and it kept flying around waiting for her and so I let her go. Was that okay?'

He smiled. 'Aye. That it was.' He looked up to the sky. 'So she's away now, is she?'

She too looked to the sky. 'Yes. She seemed desperate.'

'I'm glad.' He turned to her once more and gently took her hand in his. 'I hope they will be happy,' he said softly.

'I hope so, too,' she whispered, gazing up into his blue, blue eyes. There had been so much that needed to be said but now she knew she didn't have to say a word.

'Come on, Peri,' he said softly, 'let's go home.'